THE LOST STORY

· THE ·

LOST STORY

A NOVEL

MEG SHAFFER

BALLANTINE BOOKS

NEW YORK

Copyright © 2024 by 8th Circle LLC

Published in the United States by Ballantine Books, an imprint of Random House, a division of Penguin Random House LLC, New York.

BALLANTINE BOOKS & colophon are registered trademarks of Penguin Random House LLC.

ISBN 9780593598870

Printed in the United States of America

Crow art by jan stopka/Adobe Stock
Star art by Happy-Lucky/Adobe Stock
Map by Andrew Shaffer

To my sister

And to everyone still searching for their Shanandoah . . .

Some day you will be old enough to start reading fairy
tales again.

—C. S. LEWIS

THE LOST STORY

· ✳ ·

PROLOGUE

ONCE UPON A TIME in West Virginia, two boys went missing.

They'd been missing since May, vanished during an end-of-school field trip to Red Crow State Forest.

They were gone long enough that people had stopped referring to them as "missing," which implied a temporary state of being, and now simply called them "lost." You looked for missing children. You mourned lost ones.

By that November, the boys' missing posters on the signboard at Red Crow had faded and wrinkled behind the protective plexiglass. When Maggie and Tom noticed the posters while looking for the trail map, they remembered that they'd forgotten all about the lost boys. Because that's how it worked. First you were missing. Then you were lost.

Then you were forgotten.

Maggie hadn't paid much attention to the story even when it was fresh news. That morning, standing at the signboard while Tom retied his boots, she really looked at the two boys for the first time. One was a blond who seemed incapable of smiling, the other a redhead wearing a shit-eating grin. The class clown and his quiet sidekick, she assumed.

Ralph Stanley Howell, d.o.b. 6/15/92, 5'4, 118 lbs. Caucasian. Blond hair. Blue eyes.

Jeremy Andrew Cox, d.o.b. 5/28/92, 5'6, 129 lbs. Caucasian. Red hair. Hazel eyes.

"They never found those boys?" Tom asked.

"Nope. Probably never will." Maggie was a nurse, and because she'd seen the worst, she knew to assume the worst. If the boys went missing in the Crow, odds were they'd died the first or second night. If they weren't missing but kidnapped as some had theorized . . . they probably wished they were dead. She didn't say that part out loud to Tom. It was only their fourth date, and she didn't want to spoil the mood.

Holding hands, Maggie and Tom strolled the main trail to a scenic overlook. Below and before them lay the still autumn-lovely woods. Trees upon trees upon trees rising and falling in endless waves, an ocean of forest, and two boys drowned in it.

Before leaving the scenic overlook, Tom took pictures with his digital camera. It was the last day he would have that camera. The police would take it from him, and he'd never get it back.

Two hours and a bucket of sweat later, they reached the Goblin Falls, a small waterfall in a hidden ravine deep in the woods where the air always smelled like moss and cold rain, and the rock formations looked like little men with strangely twisted faces. Maggie squatted next to one of the goblins and made a face while Tom took her picture.

"Nice." He laughed.

"Was I hideous enough?" she asked as she stood up.

"Disgusting."

As he helped her down, a few stones at the top of the ravine skittered over the falls, hitting the water behind her with a sudden slap. Maggie jumped at the sound.

"Damn," Tom said, holding her tight as he looked up and around. "You all right?"

"Yeah. Fine. Can I see the pictures?"

He gave her the camera, and she clicked through the photos. The first was a close-up of her and the rock goblin. The second was a wider shot of the falls. And the third was . . .

Maggie narrowed her eyes at the display screen.

"What?" Tom asked.

She showed him the picture on the camera's display screen. The falls behind her. The rocky cliff rising ten feet above her. And something else.

The shadow of a man.

They scanned the cliff again but saw nothing. The Goblin Falls were off-trail, but people knew about them and hiked to them all the time. Just another hiker. That was all.

Still, when Tom said they should head back, Maggie said she was ready. She put her jacket back on, then her backpack. She bent to pick up her water bottle, and that's when she saw them coming down the hill.

She stood up at once and froze in place, hand up to warn Tom not to speak or move.

"What's wrong?" he whispered. She pointed.

Under her breath, Maggie said, "It's them."

And it was them, the lost boys.

One boy stood upright, mostly. The other boy was slung over his shoulders in a fireman's carry. They were shirtless, wearing pants six inches too short but no socks or shoes. Bare feet in the forest in November?

The standing boy struggled under the weight of the other boy. Sweat-damp red hair hung across his face. The boy on his shoulders had blond hair that hung loose and long.

Tom started forward, but Maggie grabbed his arm to stop him. Why? She didn't know. Instinct. Fear. The uncanny feeling that they'd crossed the border into a story they didn't belong in . . .

The one with the red hair met her eyes. Serious eyes. Older-than-his-years eyes. Carefully, he made his way down the narrow game trail, then walked right past them as if they weren't there, carrying the other boy to the bank of the falls. He went down on one knee and gently eased the other boy onto the soft earth in the lone patch of sunlight.

When Tom opened his mouth, Maggie shook her head. The boy with red hair had an animal's quiet readiness about him. One wrong word, and he might bolt like a deer, take flight like an eagle, vanish like a ghost.

The eyes of the other boy were open, but he was clearly confused, dazed. Head injury?

They stood a few feet away from the boys, watching them warily.

"Can you get a signal on your cell?" she whispered.

He opened his flip phone, then shook his head no.

The blond one on the ground let out a groan. Before she could stop him, Tom rushed to them, knelt, and reached out toward the boy on the ground.

It happened so fast, fast as a cobra striking. The red-haired boy struck out with his arm and caught Tom by the wrist.

Tom froze. Maggie gasped. Her heart hammered in her chest so hard she thought she might faint. She ran to Tom's side.

"Jeremy." She said it sharply, trying to break the spell.

Because it was Jeremy, of course. Jeremy Cox, whose name or face she would never forget again. And if he was Jeremy, the other boy was Ralph Howell.

Jeremy looked at her.

"It's all right, Jeremy," she said. "I'm a nurse."

He still had Tom's wrist trapped like a vise.

"You," he said to her, stern as a four-star general. "Not him."

She nodded. Jeremy released Tom's wrist.

"Run for help," she told Tom. "Right now. Go!"

He didn't argue. He seemed relieved to get away from this moment that asked more of him than he had to give.

In her backpack, Maggie kept a small first aid kit, a flashlight, and her stethoscope. She checked Ralph's pupils, breathing, heart rate, and temperature. All good. All strong.

"Help me roll him," she said. They rolled Ralph onto his side so she could check his back for injuries. Damp leaves stuck to his skin. She peeled them off one by one, revealing long, narrow scars. Deep animal scratches? A run-in with barbed wire?

She touched the scars. They were older wounds, long healed. Gently, she laid him onto his back again.

"Where did you go?" she asked Jeremy.

He looked at the boy on the ground, then at her, and his one-word answer was frightening enough that she asked him nothing more.

"Far."

Then Jeremy, who had been so eerily calm until that moment, silently wept. Relief? Happiness? No. He and Ralph had just been found. Why did he cry like something unbearably precious had been lost?

Then the EMTs arrived and pushed Maggie out of the story.

She watched from a distance as the first responders did their work. Jeremy, who had stopped crying by then, refused a stretcher, so he walked out of the forest at Ralph's side. Maggie and Tom followed them silently, like the final members of a religious procession.

By the time they reached the parking lot, the cavalry had arrived. A dozen cop cars. A dozen fire trucks. Four ambulances for two boys. Everyone wanted to see this show.

Maggie watched silently, Tom at her side, as EMTs loaded Ralph Howell into the ambulance, Jeremy climbing in behind him.

Tom said, "He almost snapped my wrist. How does a kid lost in the woods for six months get that strong?" He rubbed his wrist and eyed Jeremy, who should have been a skeleton, but instead, he and Ralph looked muscular and well fed, not the boys in their missing photos but young men now.

Maggie didn't answer. She was still reeling, trying to make sense of her last moments in the woods alone with the boys. Before the EMTs and forest rangers arrived, Maggie sat in silence and listened as Jeremy spoke under his breath to Ralph in a language she had never heard before and never would again. His words were like the sound of dry leaves rustling and skittering on the breeze through an autumn wood. And whatever he said, she knew that if she understood the words, she would understand one of the deep secrets of the world, a secret the world needed to keep.

When he stopped speaking, a red bird landed on a branch above their heads. Cardinal red but not a cardinal. A red crow, though there was no such thing as red crows, even in Red Crow.

She looked at Jeremy. He raised his finger to his lips.

Surely she'd imagined it. She'd been swept up in the moment, half-crazed with adrenaline. No red crows. No magic words. A good story, yes, but not a fairy tale. They didn't have fairy tales in West Virginia. They were lucky to have a Target.

Then again, why not here? Why did France and Germany and all those places get to have fairy tales but not West Virginia? Wild West Virginia. Wonderful West Virginia. Beautiful and dangerous and dark and strange West Virginia. Why didn't they get to have magic here, where the hills rolled like ocean waves and the morning mist was as thick as the silence of a family keeping secrets? If fairies were in the world, they couldn't find a better place than the Crow to tell their tales . . .

Maggie never saw the boys again after that day. It wasn't her story, and neither is this one, but she never forgot the moment when the universe allowed her to brush her fingertips along the spider-lace edges of a true-blue fairy tale.

Boys vanishing into the woods, then magically reappearing after everyone thought they were dead . . . if that's not a fairy-tale ending, what is?

It actually wasn't a fairy-tale ending.

It was, in fact, only the beginning.

A Recipe for a Fairy Tale

HELLO. THIS IS YOUR STORYTELLER. You may already be wondering why I'm intruding onto the story like this, which is a fair question. But this is a fairy tale and fairy tales play by their own rules. I wanted you to be aware of these rules so we could all, pun intended, be on the same page. First, what is a fairy tale? A wise and kind teacher I once knew worked up her own recipe. It went something like this . . .

Mrs. Adler's Recipe for a Fairy Tale

For any fairy tale worth its salt, you will need most, if not all, of the following ingredients . . .

- *One princess in some sort of trouble and/or distress.*
- *One magician. If a magician is unavailable, you may substitute a wizard and/or wise woman. Basically, anyone with magic powers who knows more than they're willing to tell.*
- *One hero, the more unlikely, the better.*
- *One to three villains worth fighting (and don't skimp on the evil deeds).*
- *A member of a royal family disguised as a nobody.*
- *A pinch of unusual animals.*

Place all ingredients into a world that is not our own, mix well, and let it rise.

You'll know you've created a good fairy tale if your story ends happily ever after for the heroes and badly for the villains.

You may have noticed "The Storyteller" isn't listed in the recipe, but I am there, I promise you. We'll play Rumpelstiltskin's game, and I'll let you guess my name.

Oh, for this story, you should also know about the rule of three. In fairy tales, things are always coming in threes—three bears, three wishes, three clicks of your heels to get back home.

And fairy tales also begin with "Once upon a time . . ." and end with "They all lived happily ever after."

And of course, fairy tales are fiction. Always.

Well, except for this one.

CHAPTER ONE

OUR STORY NOW BEGINS

THE DRIVE FROM Emilie Wendell's house in Milton, Ohio, to Bernheim Forest outside Louisville took a good two and a half hours. She'd wanted to make it in two hours and fifteen minutes, but accident traffic caused a bottleneck on I-65 south. She prayed the taping would be delayed. These things never started on time, right?

For weeks, she'd been internet-stalking Jeremy Cox, hoping and praying he'd somehow end up near her house. Then finally, that morning, she'd woken up to a Google alert in her email. A documentary TV show called *Whereabouts Unknown* would be doing a taping at Bernheim that day—special guest, the famed missing persons investigator Jeremy Cox. She'd thrown on yesterday's clothes—red leggings, a T-shirt, and a hoodie—stuffed her feet into her boots, and ran out of the house.

Two and a half hours of frantic driving was a small price to pay for the chance to meet with Jeremy Cox in person. As soon as she arrived, she parked, grabbed her backpack, and then jogged down the path to the visitor's center.

The day was October 10, and the weather was cloudy and cold. Cold for Kentucky anyway. Even so, she was sweating by the time she reached the outdoor stage. She found two park employees putting chairs back into stacks. A flyer printed on neon orange paper advertised Jeremy Cox's safety talk. It seemed to be over already.

"Did I miss the show?" she asked one of the employees, embarrassed by her breathless voice. "I'm supposed to meet with Jeremy Cox," she added, so it wouldn't sound like she was some creepy fangirl but someone who had an appointment.

An older woman pointed down a trail. "The talk's over, but they're doing the taping near the pond by Little Nis."

"Right, Little Nis." Emilie thanked the woman and ran down the trail.

She found the pond and walked around the bend until she spotted the first of the Forest Giants. She'd read about the famous art installation but wasn't prepared for the sheer size of them. Twenty feet tall or more. Impressive in photos but jaw-dropping in person. There were three of them, she knew, a family of enormous trolls. This was Little Nis, the son. Somewhere in the park was his pregnant mother troll and his sister.

Emilie and her mom had planned to see them, but they'd never made the time. And then, of course, there was no more time to make.

She pushed thoughts of her mom out of her head. Emilie had never been great at focusing, but today, she would do it. She had to.

And there he was. Jeremy Cox. He stood on a footbridge with his back to the pond. He looked just like all his pictures online. He had rust-red hair, a perfectly groomed beard, and was dressed like a hip young rock climber. Gray fitted long-sleeved T-shirt. Canvas cargo pants, the kind made for climbing. Brown hiking boots, well worn, she noted. A TV crew of three surrounded Jeremy while a woman with a pitch-perfect NPR voice asked him questions he'd probably been asked a billion times before.

INTERVIEWER: So, Jeremy, why only girls? You have this incredible skill, but only use it to help find missing girls.

JEREMY: Girls and women.

INTERVIEWER: Right. But why just them? No boys at all?

JEREMY: Women get lost differently than men, who get lost differently than small children, who get lost differently than the elderly. A lot of psychology goes into it. It makes sense to specialize.

INTERVIEWER: In ten years, you've found fifty missing women and girls and recovered fourteen bodies. That's an astounding level of success for one person. And all over the world too.

Emilie listened while the woman ticked off some of the countries where Jeremy had tracked and found missing people. A toddler who'd wandered off the family farm in Brazil. The girlfriend of a billionaire who'd disappeared on vacation in St. Barts. A French hiker with a broken leg trapped in a ravine in Greece.

Even in countries he'd never stepped foot in before, in harsh climates, in unforgiving landscapes, Jeremy Cox had an uncanny knack for finding the lost, dead or alive.

INTERVIEWER: Do you always find your man? I mean, your woman? Your girl?

JEREMY: Not always.

INTERVIEWER: No?

JEREMY: There's still one out there I'm looking for.

INTERVIEWER: But only one? Unbelievable. What's your secret?

JEREMY: There's no magic to it. I've been on the other end of a search party. Most people in search-and-rescue haven't. I know what it's like to be lost. And I'm very, very lucky.

INTERVIEWER: Let's say I'm lost in a wooded area like this. What should I do to aid in my own rescue?

JEREMY: Even in thick forest terrain, someone lost can travel about two miles per hour. In two hours, that's a four-mile radius, making for a possible search area of over fifty square miles. That's why we tell people to stay put and let someone find them. Unfortunately, studies have shown about sixty-five percent of lost people in that situation don't stay put.

INTERVIEWER: Why is that?

JEREMY: Denial.

INTERVIEWER: Denial?

As if sensing Emilie's stare, Jeremy glanced at her. They were only twenty feet apart, close enough that she knew he was looking at her, searching her face. His brow furrowed as if he was trying to place her, but then he turned back to the woman interviewing him.

JEREMY: Nobody wants to admit they're lost.

The interviewer laughed. She turned to the director.

"That's good," she said, sounding like a completely different, almost normal person. "Good line to end on."

"Are we finished?" Jeremy asked. He had the slightest hint of an English accent.

"One more," she said, then turned her NPR voice back on.

INTERVIEWER: If Ralph Howell were lost out there again, would you make an exception to your "girls only" rule and try to find him?

Emilie watched as Jeremy Cox's jaw set and his eyes turned to granite. They would get an answer from the Forest Giants before getting one out of him.

"You were right," Jeremy said, glancing her way again. "That was a good line to end on."

While the camera guy was getting some footage of Little Nis and the surrounding woods, the woman interviewing Jeremy took him aside and whispered something. An apology, maybe? Was the topic of Ralph Howell forbidden or something?

Whatever they were talking about, it was over in minutes. An assistant even younger than Emilie helped Jeremy remove his mic pack from his shirt and jacket.

Jeremy shook a few hands, waved a quick goodbye to the crew, and started down the trail back toward the visitor's center.

Emilie jogged after him.

"Hello?" she said as she caught up to him.

"Hey," he said and kept walking, but he slowed down a beat, which she appreciated.

"I'm not with the show." Her breath was short and fast, but she pasted on a smile and pretended she wasn't about to pass out from overstimulation. "My name's Emilie. You're Jeremy Cox, right?"

"Usually," he said. "What's up?"

"Can I talk to you for a second? I won't bring up Ralph Howell, swear."

He glanced at her, the ghost of a smile on his lips. His eyes were alive now, not glazed over like they'd seemed during the interview.

Jeremy shrugged. "Thanks. He's a private person. I ask people to leave him alone. They just can't."

Nodding, she said, "Right, right. Stevie and Lindsey all over again."

He looked at her. "Who?"

She'd jogged in front of him and then stopped, which forced him to stop. She unzipped her hoodie to reveal her T-shirt underneath—a vintage Fleetwood Mac concert shirt, the one with the penguins and the baseball sleeves.

"Stevie Nicks. Lindsey Buckingham. Everybody wants to get the band back together."

"Nice shirt," he said. He had hazel eyes, like a summer forest—evergreen trees, rich earth, golden sunlight—and they lit up when he smiled or even almost smiled. She had a feeling there was a very different Jeremy Cox underneath the stone-faced TV persona.

"Thanks. Stevie Nicks is my lady and savior."

His eyebrows slightly lifted. "She's a little before your time, isn't she?"

"Stevie Nicks transcends space and time," she said. "Was that weird? I talk too much when I'm nervous. Or just in general. Can you say something weird so I'll feel less awkward?"

"I've had impure thoughts about Ann Wilson," he offered. She snorted a laugh. She'd been right. The true Jeremy Cox had peeked out from behind the façade, and she already liked the guy.

"Ann Wilson from *Heart*? No, that's not weird. Awesome, but not weird."

"I tried," he said, and though he sounded apologetic, she could tell he was trying not to laugh at her.

"Anyway, thanks for letting me talk to you. I promise I won't take up much of your time, Mr. Cox."

"Call me Jeremy. You said you're Emilie?"

She nodded. "Yeah. I'm down from Ohio. We used to be neighbors. I mean Ohio and West Virginia, not, like, you and me personally."

"Are you going to tell me who's missing, or do you want me to guess?" The question was abrupt, but she didn't mind. She wanted to get this over with too.

"My half sister. Kidnapped."

"Recently?"

"Twenty years ago. If it means anything to you, she was from West Virginia too."

Clearly, it did mean something to him. "Anything for a fellow Mountaineer. Let's find somewhere to talk."

They decided to walk and talk along the trail that led to the other Forest Giants. It was an easy trail, and she was finally able to catch her breath.

"You ever been here before?" she asked Jeremy.

"Never," he said. "Bit small for people to get lost in. You can hear the highway."

Had he been in search-and-rescue so long that he judged forests not by their beauty but by how easy or hard it was to get lost in them?

"I almost came here this summer," she said, pausing to study Little Elena, the daughter of the giant troll family. The figure sat on the ground, playing with a large stone like a toy race car. "Mom and I had this thing we did. Whenever someone died, we'd go into the woods. The first time, this sweet outdoor cat I'd been feeding got hit by a car. We buried him in the backyard, but I couldn't stand to go back inside the house and act like everything was normal, you know? So Mom took me to a state park, and we walked. We walked until we were too tired to feel sad." She started walking again, Jeremy right at her side. "Mom died in June. She'd wanted to see the giants, so I thought about coming here, but I couldn't. Guess I'm doing it now."

"It's called 'searching behavior,'" he said. "People who lose someone will find themselves walking for miles or driving for hours . . . Lots of theories on why. I think it's guilt. Misplaced usually. We think we should have been able to stop it, but we can't. Even after they're gone, your body keeps trying to do something to help even though you can't."

His eyes scanned the woods around them as if searching for someone missing. Whoever they were, he didn't find them and set off walking again. After a few minutes, they reached the last forest giant, Mama Loumari, who leaned back against a tree, her hand resting on her pregnant belly.

"So, tell me about your sister," he said. "You said she was kidnapped twenty years ago? How old were you?"

"I was three when it happened. But I just learned about it. Technically she's missing, presumed dead. Never found the body. You need to write this down?" She unzipped her backpack and removed the file she'd brought.

"No," he said. "How do they know she's dead if they've never found a body?"

"The police say she is. Legally she is. And her kidnapper's body was found two days later, and my sister never came home, so . . ."

"How did the kidnapper die? Any chance she killed him?"

"It's pretty gross. They assume he slipped and fell down a hill while fleeing the scene."

"How is that gross?"

"When they found his body, birds had pecked out his eyes."

"Gruesome," Jeremy said, sounding almost impressed or maybe pleased. "Over here."

He lightly tapped her arm, indicating she should follow him to a picnic table. She sat on the bench, and he sat across from her, the file folder from her backpack between them.

When she'd first started digging into her half sister's disappearance, she'd found a profile of Jeremy in *Esquire* magazine. "The Patron Saint of Lost Girls," the article was called—the unbelievable true story of a former missing boy who found missing girls. In one photo, Jeremy posed on a reservation road with two Lakota teenagers. He stood with his arms crossed, his black T-shirt showing off his biceps for the cameras. The girls looked small beside him but lovely, proud, and defiant. They'd been abducted by white men from a nearby pipeline worker camp. Tribal police had no luck finding them. State police wouldn't bother looking, saying they'd likely run away from home. The family had called Jeremy. Thirty-eight hours later, he found them locked in the back room of a trailer. As the article stated, they were only two of the dozens of women and girls he'd rescued over the years.

And if he wouldn't help her, no one else could.

"All right, what's her name?" Jeremy asked.

"Shannon. Shannon Katherine Yates. But the first thing you should probably know," Emilie said, though it was the last thing she wanted to tell him, "is that . . . I sort of never met her."

"All right. You have my attention."

It began with her mother dying of breast cancer in June. It had always been only the two of them, and they'd liked it like that. Emilie always knew she was adopted. That was never a secret, but her mother had asked her to stay away from DNA and ancestry websites, which Emilie never questioned, but maybe she should have. Emilie loved her mom, and her mom loved her. When her mother said, "Maybe don't do that," Emilie wouldn't do it.

So, no looking up relatives on Ancestry or 23andMe. Until her mother died, and she was so lonely she went fishing for family.

"Sorry about your mother," he said.

"Thanks." She would've said more, but she was trying to get through all this without crying. "Um . . . anyway, so I did one of those DNA tests—"

"Bad idea?"

"Well . . . I learned pretty fast why Mom warned me off those sites."

Emilie had always known the truth about her birth parents. Nobody knew who her father was, and her biological mother suffered from alcohol and drug addiction before her death in a car accident years ago. Sometimes Emilie had wondered about her birth family, but she'd never felt any particular connection to them. Not until her sister.

"So you had your DNA tested and found a half sister?" Jeremy asked.

"The only hits on my DNA were two distant cousins and someone listed as 'Unknown/Close Relation.' But there was no info, no one to contact. I was about to give up on the whole thing when I got a private message from a West Virginia homicide detective. He asked me to call his number. I thought it might be a scam, but no—real detective working on cold cases. That 'Unknown/Close Relation' was my half sister. He said they wanted to get all my info in case her body was ever found. They could use my DNA to identify her. I didn't even know I had a half sister. The day I found out about her was the day I found out she'd been kidnapped and murdered." Emilie ran her fingers through her hair. "I spit in a tube to get my DNA on that site. They got hers from the blood in the trunk of his car, where she'd cut up her hands trying to escape."

"Wow," Jeremy said. She was perversely proud of herself for having a story that made the guy with an almost mystical ability to find missing people say *Wow*.

"Right? I found some old newspaper clippings and stuff about her kidnapping." She pointed at the file. "Age thirteen, kidnapped by a known sex offender on a Friday after getting off the school bus. By Monday, they'd found his body in the woods. Never found hers." She took a breath. "My mom's buried near my house. I walk there every single day. I want to bury Shannon there too. Have a real funeral or something? Even if no one shows up but me, she deserves that."

Emilie already had the tombstone engraving planned—*Shannon Katherine Yates. She deserved a better world than this one.*

"Why is this so important to you? Because if the answer is that you think finding her body will help you deal with your mother's death . . . I promise you, you'll be wasting your time and money."

"I have plenty of money to waste," she said. "Seriously, I don't blame you for thinking that. Mom died, and within a week, I'm looking for relatives? And maybe that was true when I started, but . . ." She took a long breath. "But when that cop got me on the phone, the first thing he said was 'I need to talk to you about your sister.' It's stupid, I know, but there was this split second when I was so happy. I had a sister? Nobody had ever used that word with me before. The first time I felt anything other than completely alone since Mom died. Well, except for Fritz."

"Fritz?"

"My pet rat. Named after Stevie Nicks's first band. You didn't need to know that. Sorry."

"Look, Emilie—"

"Please, please, please don't say no. Mom left me a lot of money, so I can pay you a lot. And I can help. It's not like I have a job."

"I wasn't going to say no. But the forest can be a beautiful resting place," he said. "And after twenty years, you need to understand there might not be much left of her body to find."

She appreciated that he wasn't trying to get his hands on her money, wasn't trying to give her false hope. That made her trust him even more.

"I used to work as a vet tech before Mom got sick, and I quit to take care of her. One day, this guy came in with his daughter's pet fancy rat. He said he was fighting his new cage-mates, so he wanted to euthanize him. We refused to do it. That evening I took the trash out like usual. He'd thrown the rat away in the dumpster. I mean, at least he hadn't killed him. But still, you don't throw living things away like that, like trash. And if somebody does, the least you can do is go and find them, right? I wouldn't leave a rat in a dumpster, and I'm supposed to leave my thirteen-year-old sister's body in the woods? Would you?"

He didn't answer at first but then nodded slowly.

"All right. Let me see what you have."

"Oh my God, thank you," she said as she pushed the file across the table to him. He reached for it and started to open it. "I should tell you something before you open the file, though. My sister went missing in the Red Crow State Forest."

He looked up at her.

"In the Crow?"

"Yeah, five years before you and Ralph Howell went—"

"Sorry. I can't help you."

"What? Why?"

"You can guess," he said and stood up.

"Look, I'm sure you're pretty traumatized and everything but—"

"I have a flight to catch tonight. Wish I could help, but I can't." He started to walk away.

"Wait," she said and got up so fast she nearly tripped over the picnic bench. She opened the file on top and thrust a photo envelope into his hand. "That's her picture. Just look her in the eyes and tell her you don't care what happened to her. All I ask. Take it."

He took the envelope and carefully slid it into his jacket pocket.

"Go home. Let your sister rest in peace," Jeremy said. He started to leave again.

She called out after him. "If that was Ralph Howell's body in Red Crow, would you walk away?"

He stopped, but only for a second before doing just that.

CHAPTER TWO

MUSIC WAS MAGIC for Emilie, especially the music of Stevie Nicks. For as long as she could remember, Stevie's crushed-velvet voice could calm her racing mind even on the roughest days. And since her mother died, there had been a lot of those. But today, it wasn't working. The music blasted through her earbuds, but her mind spun like a top that never slowed, never stopped.

Finally, Emilie got up, dressed, and walked a few blocks to the old Jesuit Spiritual Center. The property wasn't huge, but it had a nice view of the river, and almost nobody went there except a few weeks a year when they hosted retreats.

Today, Emilie had crisp October weather and the place to herself. With "Nightbird" playing in her ears, she walked the center's labyrinth. Like a record skipping, a broken lyric echoed in her mind—*walk away, walk away, walk away* . . .

The police had already tried to find her sister, failed, and given up. Jeremy was her only hope, her last hope, and he had said no and walked away.

She reached the labyrinth's center, then turned on her heel and started to walk it back to the beginning.

The labyrinth wasn't very big or fancy, only a painted stone circle. At first glance, it appeared as if there were a hundred lines, dozens of paths, twisting and turning and doubling back over and again. But no, there was only one line, one path. Order hidden inside the chaos. That's why Emilie liked it. Usually. Because though it looked impossibly complex, she always found her way through it.

But she wasn't going to find her way this time.

Walk away . . . walk away . . . walk away . . .

Why did she care so much? She'd never met her sister, who'd been dead for two decades. Why go to all the trouble?

She knew why. Because the whole thing was like a fairy tale or something. Two sisters who never met raised by two different families, each not knowing the other exists. And one lives in luxury with a loving mother and everything she could ever want handed to her on a silver platter . . .

And the other sister gets kidnapped by a known sex offender on the way home from school.

Why was Emilie the lucky one? Why was she the princess, not the pauper?

They'd found her sister's blood in the man's car. She'd dented the trunk from the inside with her frantic kicking. And she'd lost that fight. Who would fight for Shannon now?

Walk away . . .

But walking away wasn't an option. The least Emilie could do was give her sister a place to rest. The least she could do was not leave her in the woods.

"Help me, Shannon," Emilie prayed softly under her breath as she rounded a turn in the labyrinth, her hot pink Vans looking ridiculously out of place against the solemn old stone beneath her feet. "I'll keep trying, but if you can send a little help from beyond, I'll take it because I can't find you alone."

With a sigh, she stepped out of the labyrinth and looked up.

Jeremy Cox stood a few feet away on the hillside.

"Jesus." She popped out her earbuds and stared at him, wild-eyed.

"Wrong guy," he said. "But I think I saw him over there." He pointed to a white marble statue of Jesus by the maintenance shed.

"Not funny," she said. "You said you had a flight."

"I lied."

"Oh great. Thought you were some big hero."

"I am, apparently. I'm also an asshole. They're not mutually exclusive."

She stared at him, trying to decide if she was glad to see him, terrified, or both.

"What are you doing here? You scared the shit out of me."

"If you hadn't been blasting music directly into your ear canals, you might have heard me calling your name."

Yes, definitely could be a bit of an asshole.

"My birth mother took drugs when she was pregnant with me. It made me very fussy as a baby, and only music calmed me down enough to sleep. Stevie Nicks—probably because she's literally the fairy queen of rock—works better than any other music." She paused for a breath. "Sorry, I didn't need to tell you that, but the doctors said the drugs probably wired my brain a little differently. To quote my seventh-grade teacher verbatim—'Emilie has trouble self-censoring.'"

"I find that refreshing actually." He glanced around at the center grounds. "Are you Catholic?"

"I'm nothing. What are you?"

"I'm everything," he said.

"This is a bizarre conversation. I'm extremely freaked out."

Understatement. Her heart pounded. She'd never expected to see him again, and suddenly here he was? But under all her fear was hope. He wouldn't have driven all the way to tiny Milton, Ohio, just to say hi, right?

"Sorry." He shrugged. "But it's only going to get worse before it gets better."

"Will it get better?"

"Yes, if you can answer a couple questions for me."

"Um . . . okay?"

"Why didn't you want to be found?" he asked.

"What?"

"I know it sounds like an existential question, but I'm being literal. Were you scared of someone finding you?"

Not often in her life, maybe twice, had Emilie been speechless. This made three.

"How did you know?"

"So I'm right. You didn't want to be found?"

"I'm adopted. And the adoption was legal, except nobody ever knew who my biological father was, so he never signed off on it. Mom was always a little worried he'd show up out of nowhere and try to contest the adoption. She never told me that, but when I was four or five I overheard her talking to a friend about it. I prayed a lot as a kid that nobody would ever find me."

"Then your mother died and you started feeling lost?"

"Very lost. Yeah. Who wouldn't?" She took a step toward him.

He took a long breath, then looked up to the sky as if he'd finally understood some deep mystery the universe had been keeping from him.

"How did you know?" she asked. "I mean, that I didn't want to be found?"

He ignored the question and instead pointed at the stone platform, spinning his finger to indicate the painted twisting lines. "What is this?"

"A labyrinth?" she said. "You've never seen one?"

"Where's David Bowie?"

"Ha ha." She was freaking out and he was making film references. "A labyrinth is a spiritual journey in miniature. They took the concept of a 'pilgrimage to the Holy Land' and shrunk it." With both hands, she mimed shrinking the world down to a size walkable in ten minutes. "That's a labyrinth."

"Thank you, Princess."

She stared at him. "Why did you call me Princess?"

"Why does it bother you?"

"I didn't say it did." It did, in fact, but she hadn't said it bothered her, so technically, she wasn't lying.

She waited for more of an explanation but didn't get one. Jeremy moved to the start of the labyrinth and began to walk it.

"What are you doing?" she asked.

"Going on a spiritual pilgrimage in miniature. More questions. Ready?"

"Ask away."

"What would you say if I said your sister had been abducted by aliens?"

"You think my sister was abducted by aliens?"

"I don't think that at all. But if I did think that, and I told you she'd been abducted by aliens . . . what would you say?"

"I would say . . . 'Goodbye, Jeremy? Thanks but no thanks.'"

"Fair. Very fair. Next question. Do you believe in Heaven or Hell? Other planes of existence? Other realities? Anything like that?"

"I . . . I don't know." She turned as he turned, following his slow, winding progress. "Maybe? I have trouble believing this is all there is."

"Good start. What about miracles? Resurrections, et cetera?"

"Not really, no."

"Why not? Skeptic or cynic?" The path made almost a complete circle before doubling back. Jeremy nearly stepped off the line but gracefully caught himself at the last moment, pivoted, then carried on.

"Both. My mom was Catholic. Mostly in name only, but she did go to mass sometimes. When she was diagnosed, Father John gave her a St. Agatha medal. She's the patron saint of breast cancer patients. Mom loved it, wore it, and prayed to St. Agatha. Then she died. And the medal's lost now, which sucks. A lot. She wanted to be buried wearing it, but I couldn't find it. Ask me how good that made me feel." She stopped for another breath. "Anyway, Mom was the best mom ever. Hands down. No contest. And she died horribly of a horrible disease with that medal around her neck that was supposed to help heal her. Wouldn't you be a skeptic or a cynic too?"

He stopped about two feet from her, still not at the center but getting closer.

"Try asking St. Anthony for help finding your medal. One saint to another."

"Which one's he? I forgot."

"Patron saint of lost people and objects."

"Is that the medal you're wearing?"

She'd immediately noticed the saint medal hanging around his neck, just like her mother's she'd lost somewhere.

"No, this is St. Hubert. Patron saint of hunters." He held that medal out for her to see. A man knelt in front of a deer.

"Because you hunt people?"

"It's not mine," he said.

He tucked the chain back under his shirt, then swiftly finished the labyrinth path.

When he reached the center, she said, "Welcome to the promised land."

He pulled the photo she'd shoved into his hands yesterday out of his jacket pocket and held it up to her.

"This is your sister? Your sister who was kidnapped and supposedly murdered twenty years ago?"

"Yeah, why? Wait, what do you mean 'supposedly'?" Emilie waited for the punch line to the joke, and when it came, it just felt like a punch.

"Because she wasn't murdered in the woods."

"How do you know?"

"Because . . . when we were lost in the woods, we saw her."

Cry Wolf

YOUR STORYTELLER HERE AGAIN. Eventually, you're going to start wondering why Jeremy doesn't come out and tell Emilie everything he knows. Remember that old fable, "The Boy Who Cried Wolf"? Two strikes and that kid was out. Now only imagine what would've happened to "The Boy Who Cried Werewolf."

CHAPTER THREE

EMILIE WANTED HER MOM. She'd thought she understood what grieving was—crying herself to sleep at night, barely eating one day, bingeing the next, hugging the couch pillows and trying to find the scent of her mother's perfume—Joy from Jean Patou—lingering in the fabric. But she'd never felt it like this before, this fierce animal need for her mother that went deeper than pain or tears. Her sister might be alive? This was the best news she'd ever heard, and whenever anything good happened, she would tell her mother first. She didn't know what to do with all this hope and despair fighting inside her heart.

So she did nothing but bend over and breathe through her hands while Jeremy drove his car, a gray Subaru Outback, to her house. She sat up when they pulled in front of the white two-story house she'd grown up in, a hundred-year-old Queen Anne with a picture-perfect front porch, stained-glass panel in the front door, and backyard sloping down to the Little Miami River, where her mother had taught her to skip rocks.

"Pretty house," Jeremy said as he parked at the curb.

"I know. I hate it." She didn't get out. She was never in a hurry to go back into her empty house.

"Do you?"

"I didn't," she said. "Until I found out I had a sister who grew up in a

West Virginia trailer park. That makes me sound like a snob. I'm not. I just wish she had it as easy as I did."

"It's not your fault you got dealt a better hand."

She stared at the house that had once been a haven. She'd never wanted to leave home. Her friends all wanted to go to California for college or Florida or Texas or England or anywhere but Ohio. If her mother had lived, Emilie could have stayed in this house forever without feeling like she was missing a thing. Now, it was only a fancy storage shed for her memories. But if she had a sister and her sister needed a home . . .

"Is she living alone in the woods? Like those off-the-grid people?"

"Out," he said.

She got out of the car and led him to the front door. Was she actually letting a strange man—frankly, a *very* strange man—into her house? Not something she would usually do, even in Milton. Bad idea? Maybe, but it was worth it if there was any chance her sister was out there somewhere, and he could find her. Find her sister like he found—

She stopped with her key in the front door and turned around. Jeremy waited with his back to a porch column.

"How did you find me?" she asked. "I didn't tell you my address, right?"

He looked at her, and his eyebrow arched so high it nearly scraped his hairline.

"Oh, right. That's what you do."

"It's what I do."

"I'm a little terrified of you, but I'm going to let you in my house anyway. If you do kill me, make it gentle. Nitrous-oxide me or something first."

"We can stay on the porch if you want."

"No, no. I'm going to trust you."

"Here, let me help." He held up his hand to shush her, then closed his eyes. Mesmerized, she watched as his lips moved as if saying a silent prayer. How long it lasted, she didn't know, but long enough for a cool autumn breeze to sweep down the street and send orange and gold leaves skittering across her lawn.

"Jeremy?"

"Your mother's St. Agatha medal is under the bed where she died."

"What?"

He met her eyes. "Go and check."

"I checked under the bed."

"Go and check again. It could be trapped under the mattress or something. I'll wait here. You can lock the door behind you. It won't hurt my feelings."

"You're being very weird."

"I realize that, but also, I'm right."

What did she have to lose? Emilie opened the door and went into the house. Without even hitting the lights, she walked straight to her mother's old home office, which had become her bedroom when they'd brought the hospital bed in for her. The mattress was bare, and the whole room reeked of Lysol and Clorox bleach.

She had checked the bed for the missing St. Agatha medal. She remembered digging through the covers for it after her mother's body had been taken to the funeral home.

Once again, she pushed her hands down into the gaps between the sides of the bed and the mattress. Nothing. She really, really wanted that necklace to be there. Because if he could miraculously find her mom's necklace, maybe he could find her sister.

Nothing on the rug. Nothing under the rug.

And then . . . and then . . .

Cold afternoon sunlight streamed into the room. Under the bed, something glinted.

Emilie lay on her stomach and flipped onto her back like a mechanic about to perform an oil change.

There it was. Just as Jeremy had said, the silver chain of her mother's necklace had gotten caught in a slat.

She held it in her palm, her whole body shivering. Could he have planted it? She'd told no one but him it was missing, and even then, only about ten minutes ago. No, the house was locked up tight.

She walked out to the porch and held up the necklace.

"How?"

"Lucky guess," he said. Jeremy held out his hand, and she gave him the necklace. He spun his finger. She turned and let him clasp it around her neck. "But let's just say . . . I'm luckier than most people."

"Nobody's that lucky," she said.

"Do you trust me now?"

Having her mother's necklace back felt like having her mother's blessing.

"Starting to," she said. "You can come in. Want some coffee?"

"More than life itself."

SHE LEFT HIM IN the living room and went into the kitchen. While the coffee percolated, she returned to the living room and found Jeremy taking off his jacket while staring through the bars of the enormous four-level rat cage filled with toys, mazes, and even a little rat castle.

"This cage would rent for two thousand a month in Brooklyn," he said as he tossed his jacket onto the back of the armchair.

"It is not a cage. It is Fritz's sanctuary."

"You think the rats that live in sewers resent the one-percenter rats that live in castles?"

"At the vet clinic, we always said, 'You can't save them all, but today we will save one.' Kept you going on the rough days."

He nodded. "Good point. Excellent point."

She opened the little door. Fritz, white with gray spots, ran out to her hand and scrambled up her sleeve to sit on her shoulder. "You aren't afraid of rats, are you?"

"Only the two-legged kind." He held out his hand to pet Fritz, but her rat took it as an invitation and crawled into Jeremy's palm. "Hello, Fritz," he said, his tone dry as the Sahara Desert.

She watched him intently, making sure he wouldn't accidentally hurt Fritz, but Jeremy did a good job, holding him with one hand close to his chest and petting him with the other. She didn't trust people who didn't like her rat, and so far, Jeremy Cox was passing the Fritz test.

"He likes you," Emilie said.

"How can you tell?"

Half a hoodie string landed on the floor. She hoped it wasn't an expensive hoodie.

"He just chewed through your hoodie string instead of your finger. I go through two charger cords a week."

"What's all this?" He nodded toward the piles of books on the fireplace mantel. *Do You Dare?—A Manual for Finding Your Courage. Braver Every Day. The Personal Power Handbook. How the Lamb Became a Lion . . .*

"Oh, um, I need to get some of that stuff back to the library. With Mom gone, I guess, you know, I've just been trying to find myself."

Holding Fritz nose-first like a pointer, he made a show of counting the books. Seven in total.

"Find yourself? How many of you are there?"

She glared at him. "I felt kind of bad about bringing up Ralph Howell yesterday after I swore I wouldn't. I don't feel bad anymore."

"You shouldn't."

"Good. Now give me my rat back."

"Goodbye, Fritz," he said and relinquished him, she noticed, a little reluctantly. "I need to see everything you have on Shannon."

"It's all in the dining room. I'll get the coffee."

Emilie went into the kitchen and took two large white mugs from the cabinet. As she was adding cream and sugar to hers, she heard piano music. Live piano music.

They had an old upright piano, but Emilie rarely thought about it. Her mother had treated it like a second mantel, perfect for flower vases and picture frames. But Jeremy had opened the fallboard and was playing a few stray notes of some piece she didn't recognize. It sounded like a spring storm to her—willows swaying in the wind, clouds racing across the sky, the waking earth eagerly drinking the dark gray rain . . .

His fingers paused on the keys, and he looked up at her as she stood in the doorway staring.

"Your piano is out of tune."

"Neither of us played. It was Grandma's. You're good."

"I'm crap compared to Mum. She was a classically trained pianist," he said. "Concert level. Music professor at WVU. I never had to clean my room or do the dishes. All she ever asked of me was to get good grades and practice piano one hour a day."

"Single mother?"

"Exactly."

"Same."

She gave him his mug, and they clinked them together in tribute to the women who'd spoiled them rotten.

"So . . . you find missing girls *and* play piano *and* you can guess where missing necklaces are . . . and . . . anything else I should know about? Olympic gymnast, maybe? Sew your own clothes? Parkour?"

"I ride horses. I can sword-fight. Fairly good at archery."

"Sword fighting. Okay. You are unreal."

"I had a strange upbringing," he said.

"Apparently."

"Shannon's file?"

"Right, right." Still dazed, she went to the sideboard and opened the front doors to where she'd stored her sister's file and a large bankers box. She brought it all to the table and set it out.

He went for the folder she'd cobbled together from the copies of her sister's police file and news articles she'd gotten through the library. The detective she'd spoken to had even sent her copies of photographs of her sister.

Jeremy ignored the police reports but arrayed the photographs in front of him on the table.

"I wish I looked like her." Emilie leaned over his shoulder. "We have the same mother, but she got the cool nose."

She pointed at a photograph of Shannon Yates and another girl holding small trophies while standing before a red curtain.

"Seventh-grade honor roll," she said. "She'd made straight As on every report card. They gave her a trophy. I never got straight As. Mom didn't care about grades."

"You do look a little like her," he said. "I didn't realize how much until—" Whatever he was going to say, he stopped before he said it.

"What's she like? Can you tell me that?"

"If I start talking about your sister, I'll never stop." He put the photograph down and picked up another one—her sister dressed for a school play. She was some sort of autumn queen in a red gown and a crown of antlers. "So you're her sister."

"Baby sister, I guess. I had gotten so used to thinking of her as my baby sister. Forever thirteen? But she's ten years older than I am. If she's alive, I mean. She'd be thirty-three."

Emilie took the lid off the bankers box. "The detective put me in touch with a school friend of my sister's. She'd kept a bunch of Shannon's old things. You know, hoping she'd come back someday. When I told her I was her sister, she sent me everything she had."

Jeremy began removing items from the box. He was careful with them and respectful, but she noticed his hands were shaking.

"Jeremy?"

"I'm fine," he said.

She doubted that but didn't argue as he laid out all her sister's things on the table. The box contained all the stuff in it you'd expect from a dreamy thirteen-year-old girl. Fantasy novels—*The Last Unicorn*, *The Hobbit*, *Dragonsbane*, *The Clockwork Raven*. A plastic toy horse, black with gray and white painted spots, and a flowing mane. A single polished moonstone in a velvet bag, something she might have bought in a museum gift shop. Old VHS tapes with garage sale stickers on them—*The Princess Bride. Matilda. Mulan. Robin Hood: Prince of Thieves. The Never-Ending Story . . .*

Fritz crawled out of her hood, down her arm, and trotted over to the piles of books and things. He tried to climb onto the horse toy but only managed to knock it over.

"Kind of breaks your heart a little," Emilie said as she gently stroked Fritz. "Her sad little treasure chest. A rock. A toy. Some old fifty-cent VHS tapes from garage sales. Library discards falling apart."

She ran her fingers over the ratty spines of her sister's Chronicles of Narnia books held together with old rubber bands. She knew it was a seven-book series, but Emilie counted only six. A notecard tucked inside one book read, *Discard, missing book.* Her sister had gotten the series for free because one book got lost. Meanwhile, Emilie had owned the entire series in beautiful hardcovers, and she never even read them. Her mother had eventually given them away to a neighbor's son.

"One's missing."

Jeremy gave the books a quick, almost cursory glance and said, "*The Silver Chair.*"

She laughed. "You know them all?"

"C. S. Lewis wrote those books in Oxford. I was born in Oxford. My parents met while students at Oxford. I lived in Oxford. I went to Oxford. So yeah, I know them all," he said as if annoyed that she even questioned his deep ancestral knowledge of Narnia. "What's this?"

He opened a folded sheet of poster board covered with pictures Shannon had cut out of magazines. A page of fairies and elves. A page of tigers and wildcats. Doors without walls, freestanding in strange deserts. Giants. Goblins. Queens and princesses and knights and archers and girls with swords. Valkyries. Lost boys. Smoke-colored foxes. Dragon boats on rainbow rivers.

On the top of the page, it read in a girl's looping print, WHERE I WILL BE IN TEN YEARS.

"Guidance counselor project, I think. He wrote on the back that she was supposed to do a collage of what she wanted to be doing for a job in ten years," Emilie said. "Not make up a fairy world to live in. He gave her a B− for not understanding the assignment. Jerk."

It appeared she'd tried to do it the "right" way and had quickly given up on that. In the bottom corner of the page was a pencil drawing of a teeny tiny girl sitting at a desk. Wouldn't anyone rather be a queen than have a desk job?

"She understood the assignment," Jeremy said, more to himself than her. He ran his fingers across the magazine pictures—the strange mossy forests, the fairy circles, the mythic animals—almost tenderly, like they were family photos and not some kid's old homework.

"Check this out." Emilie pulled out a sheet of paper. "She did get an A on this one in English class."

The Nobody Queen

BY SHANNON K. YATES

Once upon a time, in a world unseen.
A nobody girl became the queen
Of a land of magic so wild and airy
Full of giants and tigers, ghosts and fairies
Wizards and wolves, battles and glories
Told in unicorn songs and old crow stories.
Fierce girls with swords and princes and knights
Went on brave quests, turned wrongs into rights.
They searched for a princess. At last, she was found.
The loneliest princess, lost and then crowned.
So that's the whole truth and most of the lore
Of the nobody queen, nobody no more.

"Straight As," Emilie said. "Writing poetry. Won awards. Was in the school play. Who knows what she could've done with her life, what she could've been? Then one day a monster picks her at random, and the whole story of her life is just . . . lost. Forever."

Jeremy didn't seem to be listening. He read the poem again, looked at the pictures on the collage, tore through the box looking for more.

"Is there anything else?"

"They never found her backpack, so that's it. You okay?"

He set the box down again.

"Sorry. Having a mild mental breakdown. Ignore me."

Suddenly, Jeremy sat up straight and ran his hands through his hair, slicking it back. He breathed through his fingers, eyes red like he was trying not to cry.

"Jeremy?"

His head fell back and he laughed. He laughed like he'd won the lottery, or better, like he'd won the heart of his true love. Or even better than that, he laughed like the doctor had said they'd made a mistake, and he would live a good long life after all. She'd never heard a more beautiful laugh.

In a flash, so fast she gasped, he grabbed her hand, looked up, and met her eyes.

"Thank you," he said. He wasn't laughing anymore.

"For what?"

"For finding me," he said.

"Okay, you're scaring me again."

"Good."

"Good. What does that even mean?"

"I mean, there's no bringing her here. We go to her."

"So she is alive? Can you tell me that much?"

"Yes. I believe so. And I tend to be right about these things."

Emilie sat back in her chair. "She's alive. She's really alive."

He nodded.

"In the woods? Is that where she is? Red Crow State Forest?" she asked.

"That's where we'll find her."

"Okay . . . okay . . ." She stood up and paced around the dining room table. "I can, um . . . I can handle this. I think. Maybe . . ."

"You can."

She needed to hear that. "What now?"

"I need to go home," Jeremy said.

"Home? Oxford?"

"Home. West Virginia. Rafe. We can't find her without Rafe."

"Rafe? Who's Rafe?"

"*Ralph* Howell." He said the name "Ralph" like it caused him physical pain.

"You call him Rafe?"

"Old joke. Posh Brits pronounce it like Rafe."

"Okay, so does *Rafe* know where Shannon's hiding?"

"First, she's not hiding. And no, Rafe doesn't know where she is. He doesn't remember anything about when we were missing."

Emilie raised her voice in exasperation. "Then how precisely is he going to help us?"

"Because he's Rafe, and that's what he does." Jeremy was already up and walking to the front door. She trailed behind him. "I need to go and—"

"Okay. Let's go get Rafe and find my sister."

He leaned back against the doorway, arms crossed over his chest.

"Not that simple. I'm not his favorite person. Safe to say he hates me a little. Admittedly, I can't fault his reasoning, though I do argue with the conclusion he's drawn."

"I'll talk to him then."

"No, absolutely not." He shook his head no, no, no. "Rafe is not safe for human consumption."

"I want to meet him, not eat him. If he hates you, maybe I'd have better luck talking to him. Think about it."

He jabbed his thumb toward the stack of library books on the mantel. "Your courage books are working, Princess. You should renew them."

She narrowed her eyes at him.

"Look, things are very complicated and delicate between Rafe and me. Let me handle him."

"I'm just trying to find my sister. I don't need you to protect me—"

"I'm not trying to protect you. I'm trying to protect *him*."

"Jeremy, she's *my* sister."

Finally, that got through to him.

"All right," he said. "I'll talk to him alone first. If I can't get through to him, you can try."

She exhaled heavily. "Thank you."

"Fair warning. Things are about to get very weird."

Emilie scoffed. "About to?"

The Holy Grail

TIME TO MEET our hero. Well, meet him again, I mean. The last time we saw Rafe, he was fifteen and mostly unconscious. He probably didn't make much of an impression. But he is our hero and per the recipe, a bit of an unlikely one.

Regarding heroes, a famous professor named Joseph Campbell, who studied the world's fairy tales and folktales, once wrote, *The journey of the hero is about the courage to seek the depths; the image of creative rebirth; the eternal cycle of change within us; the uncanny discovery that the seeker is the mystery which the seeker seeks to know.*

In other words, a hero on a quest for the Holy Grail isn't looking for the Holy Grail. The hero is trying to find himself, and the only way he can find his true self is by going on a journey, being tried and tested until he knows if he is a hero in name only or a hero in truth.

And that's why the world has Holy Grails—not because the world needs Holy Grails but because the world needs heroes.

Oh, and Jeremy was right. Things are about to get weird. Ready?

* ✳ *

CHAPTER FOUR

HALF AN HOUR BEFORE sunrise on Starcross Hill, Rafe was already in the woods, hunting.

The sky was only beginning to turn from black to pink, but he knew these woods by heart and didn't need much light to make his way up the hill. Intruders were in the forest, and it was them he hunted.

The shortest route up the hill was also the steepest, so steep it was like climbing a wall in some places. In the cool dawn damp, Rafe sweat through his gray T-shirt. He paused to rest under a spruce tree and catch his breath.

In a nearby rhododendron, a robin woke and started a song. Rafe spotted him on a low branch. He had a bright red breast and one oddball white feather in his wing. Rafe always paid attention to birds. It was the birds who'd warned him about the intruders. Rafe had gone on his usual hike yesterday, climbing to the Queen's Tower Rock, where he could survey all of Starcross Hill. He made the trek daily, and the animals had long ago accepted him as part of the landscape. He could sit in the shade by the silver creek that wound down his hill. Deer would stand five feet away from him to drink, barely blinking at his presence. Coyotes jogged past him on the game trails. Birds kept singing when he passed under their branches.

Except yesterday, the birds had been suspiciously silent. High on

Queen's Tower Rock, he'd peered through his binoculars and spotted tire tracks on the neighbor's logging road. Poachers. And they were back again.

When his breathing eased, he started off again. The robin's song suddenly changed into a loud whinny. Rafe froze, then heard a soft rustle of leaves. His eyes, now accustomed to the low light, spotted a fat black rat snake, nearly six feet long, darting across the trail, disappearing under leaves. He'd almost stepped on it.

He glanced at the robin and whispered, "Thanks, buddy." Then he hiked on, telling himself "further up and further in," which was something Jeremy used to say when they were hiking, though he didn't remember what he'd gotten it from.

The first tendrils of bloodred sunlight were streaking over the summit as Rafe reached the western boundary of Starcross Hill. A shiny black Dodge Ram, so new it still bore dealer plates, sat parked at a bend in the logging road, only twenty feet from one of the hundred NO TRESPASSING—PRIVATE PROPERTY signs. The driver of the truck was nowhere to be seen. Inside the truck bed, he found a few boxes of ammunition. Bear load.

Rafe pulled an arrow from his quiver, tempted to slash the tires. But then he had a better idea.

Three sets of footprints disappeared into the woods. Rafe followed them until he didn't need the prints anymore to find his way. The stench led him to the poachers' bait pit—stale donuts and fish guts. He stayed in the shadows, but even thirty feet away, he nearly vomited from the smell of rotting meat.

He made a wide circle, scanning the woods until he spotted two hunting blinds behind a fallen oak, the trunk green and furry with moss. Three men in camo, head to toe, stood outside the blinds, loading their rifles. They entered the blinds. Black rifle barrels glinted in the first light of morning.

Quietly as he could, Rafe eased two smoke bombs from his pocket. As he crept closer to the blinds, a black bear lumbered toward the bait pit. Two cubs trotted at her side, each about eight months old.

With a flick of a cigarette lighter, Rafe lit the fuses on the smoke bombs. He tossed one in each blind, then ran.

A shot rang out, but the bullet went wide of the mark, hitting a limestone boulder, sending powder flying and the bears roaring and racing into the woods. The three poachers tore from the blinds, coughing and gagging. Tears streamed down their faces.

"What the hell?" one screamed, then again. Another poacher tripped and fell into the blind, tearing it down. The third man dropped his rifle on a rock, and it fired. The chaos was going to get one of them killed. Rafe stepped out of the shadows, pulled an arrow from his quiver, and quickly fired toward the ground at their feet.

The first man jumped back, spun around wildly. In a low voice, he hissed, "Someone's out there. Go, go, go, go."

The three poachers tore through the woods toward their truck. Rafe trailed them from a safe distance. Swearing and panicking, they tossed their guns into the bed, then climbed over one another, trying to get into the cab.

One screamed when he found the enormous vinyl NO TRESPASSING sign crammed behind the steering wheel, blocking them from getting into the cab. Rafe smirked.

The man yanked it out, tossed it on the ground, and got inside. The truck whipped around so hard it nearly hit a tree. Rafe pulled another arrow and shot it into the passenger-side door. A second arrow into the bed. A third arrow lodged deep in the bumper, right in the middle of the paper dealer plate, through the hole in the capital letter D.

With the woods his and his alone again, Rafe turned and headed back to the abandoned hunting blinds. With his bow and quiver strung over his back, he picked up the smoke bombs and dropped them in a bottle of water one of the poachers had left behind.

The smoke made his eyes water, and the scent was so acrid he had to retreat into the woods. From out of nowhere, the mother black bear appeared. She rose on her back legs, raised her front legs, and roared.

Instinct screamed at him to run, but something more ancient than instinct, a memory of a time before fear, held Rafe in place. He raised his arms over his head, made himself large, and roared even louder. A primal cry meant to save them both. A bear that mauled a human would be hunted down and killed, and her cubs would be left motherless before winter.

She went quiet and dropped down onto four paws again.

He waited for her to turn, to run away, but she remained. She stared at him with dark and shining eyes.

Then she bowed her noble head to him, bowed like a commoner to a king. What could he do but nod at her, accepting the bow, though he didn't know why, only that he knew he must.

The bear turned and trotted away to join her cubs.

Rafe watched her go, terror still gripping his heart. He ran back down the hill, through the tangle of trees, roots, and rocks . . . sliding on his back down a quick, hard drop, down a ravine into the muck of a muddy creek bed, and up the other side . . .

Finally, he reached the red spruces at the bend and collapsed by the rhododendron where he'd rested before.

He panted to catch his breath. Maybe he just needed to sleep. Sleep deprivation made people see things. That's all it was. Bears didn't bow, and if they did bow, they wouldn't bow down to him.

Rest. Just rest, he ordered himself, as he sat down on the ground with his back to the tree trunk. A few feet away, his little robin with the odd white feather in his wing pecked at the leaves, seeking out his breakfast. Rafe could bring him some mealworms or seeds later, a thank-you for the warning about the rat snake in his path. He'd always liked birds, and they seemed to like him, never flying off even when he passed too close to their nests.

The robin shook his feathers out, giving himself a dust bath. Rafe started back down the path to his cabin.

A hawk dropped out of the sky like a falling bomb.

"Shit!"

At the sound of Rafe's cry, the hawk flew off, talons empty.

Panicked and in pain, the robin spun in circles, unable to fly. His right wing with the white feather was bent in two, clearly broken.

Rafe knew what he had to do, what he should do. Grab the bird and twist its neck. The end. But he couldn't.

Instead, he pulled one of his dad's old handkerchiefs from his back pocket. Careful of the broken wing, he gathered the tiny bird into his hands and wrapped the unbroken wing against its body. The fractured wing hung limp.

"Shit, shit, shit." This was his fault for scaring off the hawk. He didn't want to see the robin eaten, but he knew better than to take sides in the woods. He'd lost a red-tailed hawk her breakfast and maybe killed a robin for nothing.

Cradling the bundled bird against his chest, Rafe began jogging the rest of the way to his cabin. What could he do? Take the robin to the bird center in Morgantown? Would it even survive the trip?

He made it back to his cabin and used his elbow to push open the screen door. He cupped the bird against his chest. Its small warm body beat like a heart in his hand.

Rafe tossed his bow and quiver onto the sofa. With his free hand, he opened the closet door, grabbed a shoebox, and dumped the contents—dozens of postcards—on the floor. He took it to the kitchen and grabbed a clean dish towel. Gently, he wrapped the towel around the bird and placed it in the box.

Still alive. The robin's black bead eyes were bright and wild. A miracle it hadn't died of shock. Blood dotted the white handkerchief. Puncture wounds from the hawk's talons.

Rafe whispered to himself, to the bird, "Don't die, okay? You'll fly again," as he placed the lid on the box.

The robin whistled one small, hopeful note.

With the box steady in both hands, he walked out to his driveway, pausing when he heard tires in the distance. The road to his cabin was gravel, and the scrape and rumble of a car carried for miles out here. It wouldn't be his mother. She always called before coming. The cops after him for chasing off the poachers? No, not a cop car. A gray SUV.

Holding the box, he walked to the edge of the drive and gazed down his mountain at the road.

The car snaked its slow way up the long S-shaped road just as morning broke over the summit of Starcross Hill and the pink and gray sky turned blue. It appeared on one turn, disappeared on the switchback, and then appeared again.

Rafe backed up as the car neared, backed all the way up to the porch, and waited. The engine turned off. He didn't recognize the car, but he recognized the driver. He would have known him at five hundred yards in the blinding sun or the dark of night.

Jeremy got out. He paused briefly, then closed the door.

On the porch, the shoebox still in his hands, Rafe watched as Jeremy came toward him and stood at the bottom of the steps. He wore jeans and a black jacket over a white T-shirt and sported a neatly trimmed beard. What was Rafe supposed to feel now? Relief wasn't right, but if not that, then what?

"What's in the box?" Jeremy asked, nodding toward the shoebox. No hello. They were long past hellos. Rafe stared at him. He looked like Jeremy, except the beard was new, and his red hair was turning to the same rust color as the robin's red bib.

"Robin," Rafe said. "Hawk got him, but I accidentally scared her off. His wing's broken. No time to talk. He'll be lucky to make it to the bird rehab place alive." He stepped off the porch and started for his truck. "Hang in there," he said to the bird. "You'll be all right."

"Let me look. Please."

It was quicker to give in than to argue, and had he ever heard Jeremy Cox say "please" before?

Rafe gave him the box.

Carefully, Jeremy lifted the lid, dropped it on the ground, and scooped up the bird with one hand. Still alive, Rafe saw. Jeremy tossed the bottom of the box aside and quickly unwrapped the bloody handkerchief from around the bird's small gray body. Rafe wanted to stop him, but it was too late.

The robin sat calmly on Jeremy's palm. It shook its head like it was waking from a dream, then spread its wings and flew away into the woods.

"It had a broken wing."

Jeremy said, "You sure?"

Rafe had been sure. He would've bet his life on it two minutes ago. "Probably just in shock."

"Maybe."

In a huddle of pines, a robin began to sing.

Rafe looked at Jeremy. "Okay, so what the hell are you doing here?"

"I need to talk to you."

"No."

Without a word, Jeremy turned and walked back to his car. Giving up already? Not likely. He opened the back door, took out a brown paper grocery bag, returned, and set it down at Rafe's feet like an offering. He even held out his hands, palms up.

"I had a TV gig in Kentucky."

Rafe toed the bag like a snake might be inside it. Glass rattled. He looked in and saw white bottle caps.

"Ale-8." Rafe's aunt lived with her husband and horses outside Lexington, Kentucky, and this was their local swill, as she called it. He'd spent every spring break with her as a kid, took Jeremy with him that one year they were best friends, and they'd drunk the stuff all week like water and wine.

"Remember when we drank so much of it that spring break, your aunt made us start buying our own?" Jeremy asked.

Not an offering then, but a bribe—the chance to taste being fourteen again.

"They make it in cherry now," Jeremy said. "Wild, right?"

"God damn." The memory of sweetness made Rafe's mouth water. But still, he hesitated.

"Rafe," Jeremy said. Just that. Just his name. But it wasn't his name. Nobody called him "Rafe" but Jeremy. Bank tellers, teachers, and dentists called him "Ralph." His mother called him "baby" and always would. And his dad had called him "son" in the same way people said "Mr. President," because the office mattered more than the person holding it.

But he was Rafe, in his own mind anyway. When Jeremy called him that, it was like hearing his true name spoken for the first time in fifteen years.

"All right," he said. "You can have ten minutes."

Jeremy reached into the neck of his T-shirt and pulled out a silver chain with a small oval medal pendant. Rafe knew exactly what it was. A St. Hubert medal.

Then Jeremy reached out and lightly tugged the silver chain around Rafe's neck, pulling the medal out from under his shirt. St. Anthony.

Caught like a robin in a hawk's grip. They had traded medals in the hospital. Jeremy wore his. Rafe wore Jeremy's.

He wanted to kick Jeremy out, send him packing, punish him for the silent treatment. But he couldn't do it. In fifteen years, you can stack a very long line of dominoes, a line so long you can't see where it will end. But someone has to kick the first domino over if only to hear that rapid-fire *clickclickclickclickclick* as they fall. They can't stay standing forever.

The bear. The bird. And now Jeremy. Was everything falling down or falling into place?

Rafe said, "Okay. Fifteen minutes."

· ✳ ·

CHAPTER FIVE

RAFE LET JEREMY into his cabin.

"Be right back. I'll put these away," Rafe said. He carried the grocery bag to the little galley kitchen and stuffed it into the back of the fridge, hiding it from himself. He left the door open a minute more and breathed the chilled air into his lungs.

Jeremy was here. Here in his cabin. Here on his hill. Jeremy, who he hadn't seen in person in fifteen years, was in his living room right now. He'd imagined this moment a million times, but now that it was happening, he didn't know what to do. Punch him in the face for abandoning him? Kick him out? Hug him until it hurt?

He had to pull himself together. He'd terrorized three heavily armed poachers this morning and faced off with a black bear. He could handle one conversation with Jeremy Cox.

But whatever Jeremy wanted from him, Rafe told himself, he wouldn't do it. Not unless Jeremy paid up in answers to the questions he'd asked fifteen years ago.

He slammed the fridge door shut and went out to the living room. Jeremy had found the postcards on the floor. He squatted and sifted through them.

"You kept the cards I sent you," he said.

Rafe bent down, grabbed a thick handful of the postcards, and tossed them into the wastepaper basket by the closet. He wished he'd cleaned them up before Jeremy saw them. Not that it mattered. There was no hiding from Jeremy Cox.

"Selling them on eBay. Since you're so famous now."

"Funny. You know how hard it is to mail a postcard from Pitcairn Island?" He grabbed the postcard from the can, waved it in Rafe's face, then tossed it back in the trash.

"I needed the shoebox for the bird," Rafe said. "And you're wasting your fifteen minutes."

"Did it start already?"

"One minute ago." Rafe pointed at his wristwatch. "So talk fast."

Jeremy was over the postcards already. He'd stood up and turned his attention to the murals Rafe had painted on the walls, the ceiling, even the wooden staircase that led up to his loft bedroom. His mother said it looked like Bob Ross had dropped acid—trees gone mad, impossible mountains, strange valleys. He'd painted it so that every time you walked into the room, you saw something different.

"Did you ever remember anything from when we were missing?" Jeremy asked.

"Nothing," Rafe said.

"You sure?"

"Yeah, why?"

Jeremy faced him. "How much time do I have now?"

"Thirteen minutes. Good time to tell me why you're here."

Jeremy went to the window and looked out. Nothing to see out there but the trail that led deep into the woods.

"What is this place?" Jeremy asked. "Starcross Hill? Some kind of nature preserve?"

"You want to waste your thirteen minutes asking me about my place?"

"Talk fast. Use lots of words in a short span of time. Go."

"It's just a hill. About a thousand acres. Some old-growth forest, so you have to keep an eye on it. I don't own the hill itself, but Dad bought the cabin for hunting after he retired. Now it's mine. I get to use the land in return for keeping an eye on it."

Jeremy turned away from the window. "You like it here?"

He shrugged. "Yeah. It's about the only thing Dad and I ever agreed on. He said he wanted to die out here. He got his wish."

"I'm sorry." Jeremy sounded almost sincere. Rafe didn't buy it.

"Are you?"

"Sorry for you."

Jeremy turned away from the window and pointed at the east wall, where Rafe had painted a sprawling spring woodland. Under the canopy of the pink and mossy green trees, animals ran, leaped, and danced— a silver tiger, a golden wildcat, snow-white deer, and smoke-gray foxes.

"Nice paint job," Jeremy said. "Different. More people should have hallucinogenic murals in their houses."

"I can paint over them if I ever sell the place."

"You'll paint them over my dead body," Jeremy said.

Rafe hated that he liked that, hated it enough that he pretended he hadn't heard Jeremy say it.

"You made this too?"

Jeremy stopped at the fireplace mantel to examine a carved wooden crow.

"Yeah."

"When did you start sculpting?"

"It's just whittling."

"This is not whittling. This is a sculpture. Did you teach yourself or what?"

If Jeremy was awed by one little crow carving, he would lose his mind over the sculpture garden in the back of the cabin.

"I started a few years ago," he said, "when painting didn't, I don't know . . . it wasn't enough anymore."

"No, I get it," he said.

A framed photograph sat on the mantel next to the crow, Rafe's parents on their honeymoon in 1989, back when his dad had a motorcycle, long hair, and a beard, and his mother wore sundresses and cowboy hats.

"Your dad looked good with a beard. You don't," Jeremy said.

"You sound like Mom. She won't even let me in the house until I shave."

"Your mother was always the brains in the family. How is she?"

"She's good."

"I sent her flowers after the funeral."

"I know. She appreciated that."

Without being invited, Jeremy sat on the sofa beside Rafe's bow and quiver.

"You're still shooting with your dad's bow?"

"It does the job," Rafe said. He stayed standing, not wanting Jeremy to get too comfortable.

Jeremy drew an arrow from the quiver. He looked at the broadhead tip and then at Rafe. "What were you hunting out there? Dragons?"

"Poachers."

"You didn't kill them, did you?"

"They were baiting a mother bear and her cubs trying to fatten up for winter. I just scared them off."

Jeremy eased the arrow back into the quiver. "Then I admire your restraint."

He reached for the chain on the old lamp with the taped-up cord but instead picked up a red trolley toy. He smiled.

"You still have this?" Jeremy spun the trolley's wheels.

"Of course."

"Mum kept mine too."

During the six months of their disappearance, the police had asked their mothers to make public pleas. Go on TV, they said, and talk about the boys. In case they'd been kidnapped, that was the point of the exercise. Rafe's mother had held up picture after picture, including a Polaroid of him watching *Mister Rogers' Neighborhood*, mesmerized, wearing only a diaper.

When they were finally found, Joanne Rogers, Mr. Rogers's widow, sent the signed trolley toys to the hospital with a note welcoming the boys back home. People worldwide sent them gifts: clothes, videogames, teddy bears, money for college. The red trolley to the Land of Make-Believe was the one gift Rafe kept.

"I guess you heard Mum died. Stroke—"

"Yeah, I'm sorry," Rafe said. "Dr. Cox was always nice to me."

"You never used to call her Dr. Cox. She was always Mum to both of us."

"That was a long time ago," Rafe reminded him.

Jeremy spun the wheels again, set the trolley back down, and met Rafe's eyes.

"I thought you were going to art school. Didn't you apply a few years ago?"

Rafe didn't ask how Jeremy knew that. Every year on November 18, the anniversary of the day they'd been found, their mothers called each other. Rafe's mother would've told Dr. Cox, and Dr. Cox would've told Jeremy. During those first few anniversary calls, Rafe had asked to speak to Jeremy, but he would never come to the phone. After the third anniversary, Rafe had stopped asking.

"I was thinking about it, but then Dad died."

"So?"

"So? So, I didn't go." Rafe checked his watch. "Next question. You're running out of time."

"Why do you care? It's my time."

"Because I know you want something. I want you to tell me what it is so I can tell you no."

"Why would you tell me no? Spite?"

"Can you blame me? Fifteen years ago, I begged you to tell me what happened in the woods, and you refused."

He waited, expecting excuses, explanations. Instead, Jeremy shrugged. "No, I can't blame you," he said. "I would be as pissed as you are if the roles were reversed."

"Ten minutes. What do you want? Tell me now, or I'm going to set my watch five minutes fast."

Jeremy leaned forward, rested his elbows on his knees, and looked up at Rafe, still standing.

"I need your help."

"My help?"

"With a case. A missing girl in the woods."

"You don't need my help. You've never needed my help."

"I need it now. She went missing in the Crow five years before we did. Thirteen years old. Shannon Yates. Do you remember hearing about her? Happened before Mum and I moved here."

"Maybe?" Five years before they went missing? He would have been nine or ten years old. He probably had overheard something, but he'd been too young to process it. "What about her?"

"Her sister wants me to find her."

"She still alive?"

"I think so. Still in the Crow."

"How is that possible?"

"She is very, very well hidden. More than off the grid. There is no grid where she is."

Possible? Maybe. There were hills and hollers in West Virginia so remote you couldn't even find them with a map. And Red Crow State Forest was huge—fourteen thousand acres. And it butted up against Monongahela National Forest, nearly a million acres . . . If there was anywhere in the United States someone could hide out for twenty years, it was in the deep, dark woods of West Virginia.

"You've been to remote places before. So why me? Why now?"

"To find this girl . . . this particular girl? I need someone I trust to go with me."

"So why me?"

"You're the only person in this entire world I trust."

Rafe was stunned into silence. All these years, not a word, and now Jeremy was here declaring Rafe was the only person in the world he trusted? If his high school girlfriend had called him out of nowhere and proposed marriage, he would have been less shocked.

"Me?"

"Nobody else here. What do you say?"

Rafe took a deep breath. "I say . . . I'll go."

"You will?" Jeremy's eyes widened in surprise.

"Yeah, if you tell me right now what happened when we were lost in the woods. Do it fast. You have seven minutes left."

Rafe held up his watch.

Jeremy sighed and sat back on the couch.

"Nothing's changed. I couldn't tell you fifteen years ago. I still can't tell you now."

"Can you at least tell me why you can't tell me?"

"The truth is too dangerous to tell."

"Even to the person you trust most in the world?"

"Especially to the person I trust most in the world."

"Makes no sense."

"It does to me. But . . . I can promise you this much—by the time we find this girl, you'll know everything."

"But you can't tell me now?"

"No."

"And you can't tell me why you can't tell me?"

"No. But I wish I could. So much, Rafe. So much it hurts."

"You have to tell me something, Jay."

Jeremy pointed at the armchair across from the sofa. Reluctantly, Rafe sat down.

"I'm sorry," he said. "I'm sorry I disappeared on you. There were a hundred news vans in the hospital parking lot when we got back. You remember?" Jeremy asked. Rafe nodded. "Mum wanted to get me out of there as fast as possible. There was no time for long goodbyes."

They had said goodbye, though Rafe had convinced himself Jeremy was leaving for a few weeks. Two or three months at most. Not fifteen years. Back then they could barely go fifteen minutes without talking to each other.

"I get it. I do get it. But those vans were gone after a week. You could have called me. You could've written."

"I could've, yes, but I had two choices. Either lie to you about what happened or say nothing. I don't like lying to you. I *hate* lying to you. That left silence."

"I'd rather you lied than give me fifteen years of silent treatment."

Jeremy met his eyes. Then he smiled. "We were abducted by friendly aliens and had a grand old time flying through space and time. There were musical numbers and Orion dancing girls. How's that?"

Rafe glared at him. "You're right. The silent treatment was better."

"Thought so."

"I needed you," he said. "You get that, right? I needed your help, and you never gave it to me. You know how many times they've put me in the psych ward?"

"Three," Jeremy said simply. "Three times. When you were seventeen, you stole your dad's truck while sleepwalking and drove off the road right before exit seven on I-68. When you were twenty, two people walking their dog found you wandering in a daze by Cheat Lake Road. And when you were twenty-two, you ran your car into a ditch and woke up in the backyard of my old house. Diagnosis—dissociative fugue states. You go to sleep in your bed, and you wake up miles from home. Do you really think it's pure coincidence you keep trying to get back to the Crow? And apparently, if you hadn't noticed, your subconscious wants to take me with you."

Rafe was stunned into silence. Jeremy knew everything, all of it.

"How did you—"

"Mum," Jeremy said.

"Right. Right."

"Have you had one of your spells since your father died?"

Rafe looked away.

"I'll take that as a no," Jeremy said. He met Rafe's eyes again. "Interesting you stopped running in your sleep when he was gone."

"After Dad died, I moved out here. I sleep better in the woods. Don't blame Dad when it was your choice not to come back."

"Come with me. Help me find this woman in the Crow. And I swear on my life, you will know everything you want to know."

"Tell me what I want to know, and I'll help you."

"It can't work that way."

Rafe sighed. "Then it can't work." His head was spinning from going around in circles with Jeremy.

"Would it help if you took a swing at me?" Jeremy asked. "One good hard punch. I'll be the first to admit I deserve it. Go on. Stomach. Ribs. Jaw. Don't care."

Jeremy stood up and held out his arms, waiting.

Rafe almost did it, almost punched him right in the gut. Only fair.

When Jeremy had disappeared from his life so suddenly, it had felt like a gut punch. Still did.

"You're out of time," Rafe said. "You can go now."

Jeremy looked at him, then smiled and bowed like a knight to his liege.

"Yes, Your Highness."

In Fairness . . .

IMAGINE IF SOMEONE from your past showed up on your doorstep after fifteen years of silent treatment and asked you to go into the woods with them? Would you go? Yeah, I didn't think so.

· ✳ ·

CHAPTER SIX

WAITING FOR JEREMY to call took Emilie back to those terrible days of waiting for her mother to get medical results from this test or that test, tests that would answer the question, Would she have a mother in six months? A year?

Now she wondered, Would she have a sister in a day or a week? Ever? Or never?

A dozen times a day, she clutched her mother's St. Agatha medal to remind herself that Jeremy had found it when she couldn't. Physical proof of his abilities, yet she still struggled to believe that her sister, presumed dead for twenty years, was out there somewhere, alive.

She didn't know what to do with herself while waiting for the call except pack. But what to pack? When she'd asked Jeremy what she should take, he'd given her a cryptic and somewhat terrifying reply.

"Imagine your house is on fire. Take only what you'd save."

Then he'd driven off after promising to call her when he had news.

What would she save in a fire?

Pictures of her mother, of course. She had a thousand pictures of her and her mother on her phone, but her favorites were the framed photographs from her childhood, which hung on the walls and sat on the mantels all over the house. She chose two photos. The first one of her mother, a youthful-looking forty-nine, holding screaming baby Emilie on the day of her adoption. Emilie might have been crying in the photo, but her mother's smile was radiant.

The other picture she chose was from her elementary school's annual Fall Festival. Emilie had been in the fifth grade, and she and her mother dressed up as "Identical Twins" for the school's Halloween contest. Matching pink dresses. Matching pigtails with pink bows. Matching smiles. They'd only won third prize, but the real prize was hearing so many people tell them how much they looked alike even though Emilie was a pale blonde and her mother a brunette.

Yes, those were the two photos she'd save in a fire. The only other things she put in her backpack were a change of clothes, a toothbrush, her makeup bag, and everything she could fit that had belonged to her sister. Shannon's old books, her poem, her little toy knight, her moonstone in the velvet bag.

And, of course, she would take Fritz with her.

Finally, on the afternoon of the second day of waiting, Jeremy called.

"Hey, any news?" She knew she should've eased in before asking him straight out, but she couldn't wait another second.

"Time to go."

"What? Did Rafe say he'd help?"

"No, he didn't. But he'll change his mind. He already has. He just doesn't know it yet."

"I don't even want to know what that means."

"It means it's time to get in your cute little Prius and drive to Rafe's house. We'll meet him there."

Emilie looked at her bag. This was nuts. She was going to go into the woods with not one but two very strange men to find a girl who disappeared twenty years ago? A girl who the police said was dead.

"Are you sure it was my sister you saw? Shannon Yates? That's what she said her name was?"

"Well, no, she went by another name."

"So maybe it wasn't her?"

"It was her."

She walked into the living room and knelt in front of Fritz's cage. He was sound asleep in his favorite tunnel. Looking at him gave her the smallest shot of courage. She had saved his little life. Not as impressive as saving all the girls Jeremy had, but Fritz was alive because of her, and only her, and that was something

"I looked you two up on Reddit, and they say Rafe has PTSD and a lot of mental problems."

"Reddit says a lot of things, including but not limited to the theory that we were abducted by the Mothman, sex traffickers, and/or Scientologists. What happened to all your books on courage? Did you return them to the library?"

"I want to be courageous, I swear. I just would prefer to be courageous inside my house."

Fritz came out of his nest and trundled up a ramp to her, gave her fingertips a love bite. She slipped him a chew stick, and he happily munched away. It must've been so strange for him being picked up and carried out of his old life and then finding himself in her house with no explanation. Must have felt like Dorothy being caught in a Kansas tornado and landing in Oz. Except he was much better off in Oz than in Kansas.

"I'm doing it. I'm doing it," she said.

"You're being very brave. Good job."

"I'm not brave. I'm just very susceptible to peer pressure."

"Either way, I'm proud of you."

She sighed heavily and rubbed her forehead. "What do I do?"

"I'll give you directions—"

"I have Google Maps—"

"Rafe's place is off the map. I'll text you the directions. Print them out. When you get lost, just wait. I'll find you."

"Okay," she said. "Wait. *When* I get lost?"

But he'd already hung up.

Emilie dressed for hiking—boots, leggings, sweater, hoodie, beanie hat with a pom-pom because at least she'd look cute when she died of exposure, she told Fritz. She put her bag in the car and Fritz into his carrier. She looked at her house one more time. How easy it would be to call this whole thing off . . . She could send Jeremy a text that said, *Never mind. If my sister is alive, she can find me. Thanks, but no thanks.* Then she'd go back in the house, unpack, and get into bed to sleep for a few days or weeks.

Sounded nice. Until she woke up and realized she was all alone in the house with only a rat to talk to. If her mom were here, she knew what she'd say . . .

"Mom, I'm scared."

"I know, Emmielou. But scared is a feeling, not an excuse."

All right. She would do it scared then.

Emilie got into her car, buckled her seatbelt, and drove away without another look back.

She followed Jeremy's directions to the letter, taking Route 50 and crossing over the Ohio River on the Blennerhassett Island Bridge into West Virginia.

At first, she didn't notice any difference between Ohio and West Virginia, but after a few miles on the Northwestern Turnpike, it started to get . . . *odd*. She couldn't put her finger on why, only that when she drove over the Ohio River and crossed the border, she felt something shift in the air. Was it the elevation? West Virginia was a mountain state, and it felt like she was driving closer to the sky. But it was more than that. The shadows were heavier here, the sky grayer, the wind wilder. Or was she imagining it?

And the beauty . . . if she'd known how beautiful these mountains were, these endless rolling hills all shades of October, she would have come every year. It didn't even look real. It was almost too beautiful to be trusted, too breathtaking to feel safe.

And she did get lost, of course. Although she was looking carefully, driving very slowly, she missed the turn-in to Rafe's road twice. Eventually, she found the hidden entrance. The trees were thick here and overhung the road like sentinels guarding it from outsiders.

The eerie feeling, like she'd wandered into a different world, only increased when she reached an ivy-covered cabin squatting in the middle of a forest. No cars anywhere, but she tried the front door anyway. Her whole body shook with nerves when she knocked. No one answered, so she walked around to the back.

There, she found a wooden privacy fence with an arched entrance wide enough for two men to pass through side by side. She'd only meant to stick her head in and shout "Hello?" but then she'd seen what she'd seen.

Tigers. Horses. Crows. A fox. A condor. A unicorn. All carved from wood and brightly painted so it felt like she was walking into an enchanted zoo. Stacked stones formed ivy-shrouded portals. Mossy paths led to staircases that led to nowhere. A wooden footbridge fit for a cat spanned a silver pond the size of a child's swimming pool. From a pole curved like a sickle, a crescent moon hung down, wearing a smile on its face.

Emilie went into the strange garden as if led by unseen hands and found herself standing at a statue of a girl carved out of the trunk of a long-dead tree. She stared at it for a long time, marveling at the resemblance.

She sent Jeremy a quick text saying, *Okay, now I believe you.*

THE MAIL DIDN'T COME to Starcross Hill, so Rafe had to drive to the nearest town of Kingwood to pick it up. Two days after Jeremy had come and gone, he went to the post office and opened his box. Almost empty. Nothing there but a single postcard from Jeremy.

The picture was of Morgantown's riverfront—the old brick buildings perched dangerously close to the Monongahela River, nothing but a few trees and one natural disaster away from falling into the dark water. On the back, Jeremy had written "436."

No street name was necessary. Rafe knew those numbers. They were the house number of Jeremy's old house on Park Street.

And this wasn't just a postcard. It was an invitation.

Accept it or not? If he went, what would happen? Another useless argument that ended in a stalemate? But if he didn't go, he'd always wonder if he'd been too cowardly to face Jeremy. Neither sounded very good to him, but he had enough regrets not to add another to his tab.

So he drove the twenty-five miles from Kingwood up to Morgantown. Although he hadn't lived there in years, it was still home. Cub Scouts. Boy Scouts. Eagle Scouts. Church. Trips to the hardware store on Maple with his father. If he hadn't made himself accidentally famous by getting lost, he might still live around here. He and Jeremy had both planned on attending WVU. Jeremy could get in free, since his mother taught music there, and Rafe had heard they had a great art program. They'd imagined their futures together back then. After high school, they'd go to college, move into the dorms, and room together, of course. That was the plan. Sometimes he still wondered where he'd be if they hadn't gotten lost, if they would've been able to stick to the plan. It was too late. The past was gone and there was no finding it.

Rafe drove past the school on the way to Park Street. Forty-five degrees out, and the college kids were in shorts and hoodies. Ghosts of a past life he hadn't gotten to live.

He continued down High Street, past the coffee shops and the ridiculous bronze statue of Morgantown's favorite native son, Don Knotts, dressed as Barney Fife, then past the Hotel Morgan, where he painted rooms every summer. Best view of the Monongahela River in the whole town.

Coming back home was never easy. He'd learned to keep his head down, to mumble his name so no one would put two and two together and ask, "Wait, are you *the* Ralph Howell? The kid who got lost?"

Because that's who he would always be to this town—one of the lost boys. Lost and left behind. After they were found, Jeremy's mother spirited him away to England, where she had family, and Rafe went back to high school alone. He'd never gotten started on his future. He hadn't been able to picture one without Jeremy in it. Sometimes, he thought he was still waiting for his life to begin.

And maybe that's why he hung a left and went up to 436 Park Street. Because it felt like this might be his last chance to start again.

Rafe pulled in front of the house, the Big Blue Monster, as Jeremy called it. Good name. Three stories. Sky-blue paint. Gray stone chimney. Five bedrooms for two people—Jeremy and his mother, Dr. Mary Cox, classical pianist and professor of musicology at WVU.

It was a beautiful old house, and Rafe had been dazzled by it as a kid. Even their mailbox had impressed him back then. A black pedestal box with a man riding a horse on the front and the word LETTERS in brass above. And he'd only ever seen windows like that in Catholic churches. He'd had to ask Dr. Cox what those odd windows were called. Lancet windows. Named for lances. Like swords. Sword windows.

The sword windows were all dark. A few years ago, someone had tried turning Jeremy's old house into a B and B, but now the Big Blue Monster was up for sale again. A realtor's lockbox hung on the front door. Rafe peered through a window and saw it was empty of furniture, empty of everything except for a card table covered in flyers and business cards in the music room. It looked wrong. No piano where Jeremy had practiced every day at his mother's command. No sofa nearby where Rafe would sketch or do homework while listening.

And there was no Jeremy here either.

Maybe Rafe had been crazy to expect him to be waiting on the front porch, but he was disappointed anyway. Rafe tried to ignore all the news stories about Jeremy's near-miraculous ability to find missing girls, but deep down he'd almost believed that he could find anyone anytime. And if Jeremy really had that power, then he'd know Rafe was there and waiting for him.

His dad had tried to warn him. Years ago, his father had said being friends with someone like Jeremy was a bad idea. They came from different worlds. Too different. Rafe was a coyote. Jeremy was a purebred poodle. You didn't see coyotes and poodles running around together, did you? Coyotes didn't belong in fancy houses. Poodles wouldn't survive a night in the woods. Poodles did tricks. Coyotes survived. A cruel thing to say, but the fact was . . . Jeremy and his mom did own a poodle. Her name was Martha, and Rafe had loved that dog as much as she'd loved him. He'd loved this house. After school, he'd walk over every day with Jeremy to do their homework together. Dr. Cox served them scones with clotted cream and hot tea with milk. Thanks to her, he knew hot tea should be made in a kettle and teapot, never the microwave. He knew the difference between a concerto and a sonata. And he knew he'd rather be a poodle in a warm house than a coyote in the cold, dark woods.

But maybe his dad was right. After all, he wasn't in a warm house. He was outside and alone with no Jeremy in sight.

Just in case, he rang the doorbell. No answer. Of course not. When he turned to leave, he saw someone had left a package on the porch, hidden so no one would see it from the street. A large flat rectangle wrapped in brown paper and twine. Rafe's initials were scrawled across the paper in black Sharpie.

Jeremy had been here.

Immediately, Rafe knew it was a painting. Nothing else came in that shape. A gift? A peace offering? He thought he knew what it was. Jeremy's mother had owned a print of Franz Marc's *The Foxes*, and Rafe had been enamored of it as a kid. Two red foxes, geometric, almost cubist, filled the canvas. The artist had used the same red for both foxes, so there was no telling where one began and the other ended. He remembered Dr. Cox saying, "You could do that someday." Jeremy had rolled his eyes and said, "Someday? He can already do better than that now."

Rafe had never forgotten that, because a fourteen-year-old kid doesn't forget something like that.

Even now, his own art was heavily influenced by Marc's bright colors, his strange animals, his wild lines. With his pocketknife, he cut the twine and carefully peeled back the paper.

It wasn't *The Foxes*.

It was one of Rafe's own paintings, made years ago in art therapy. The therapist told him to draw or paint the dreams he had on the nights he went into his fugue states. This had been one of them.

An expressionist painting of Jeremy, age fourteen, sitting at his mother's piano in this very house. An ordinary enough scene but for the red crow perched on the edge of the piano's open lid. In the dream, the red crow would listen to the piece until it was over. Then it would fly out the window. Jeremy would then turn to him and say, "Time to go."

But how did Jeremy get this painting? Rafe had tossed all his old therapy art years ago. And why give it back to him now?

To get his attention, obviously. It worked.

He could almost hear Jeremy's voice in his head, the voice from the dream . . .

Time to go.

Rafe grabbed the painting and carried it back to his truck. He drove straight to his cabin.

When he arrived, a white Prius covered in bumper stickers that said things like ADOPT DON'T SHOP and WHO RESCUED WHO? sat in his driveway. Not Jeremy's car. From the size of her footprints, he guessed a girl.

He followed her tracks—she'd stomped right through the brush—into his fenced-off backyard, and there she was, a young woman with long blond hair dyed pink at the ends. She wore boots and leggings, a sweater, and a jacket like she was about to hike for days. He didn't want to scare her if she was just lost.

He walked up to her, but she kept her back to him.

"Hey, you need help?" Either she didn't hear him or didn't care that she wasn't alone anymore. Her gaze was transfixed on his wood carving of the girl with the crown of antlers.

"Are you Rafe?"

"Yeah, who are—"

She turned and looked at him. Then he looked at the carving of the girl.

She pointed at the sculpture. "My name's Emilie. And that's my sister."

"Are you sure?" he asked. She held out her phone to him, displaying a photograph of a girl wearing the same clothes with the same eyes and the same Greek nose.

"She's sure," Jeremy said.

Rafe turned around, and there was Jeremy, who must have been right behind him on the road.

"You got the painting," Jeremy said. A statement, not a question. He walked over to them.

"I got it."

"You can still punch me if you want," Jeremy said. "If it'll make you feel better."

"It would," Rafe said. Fifteen years of loneliness, anger, helplessness . . . it came out in one punch to Jeremy's ribs. A good punch. All knuckle.

Jeremy stumbled forward, and Rafe caught him and lowered them both to the ground. Behind him Emilie gasped.

"Tell me one thing," Rafe said into his ear. "One thing about when we were gone. One thing I can believe."

After a labored breath, Jeremy said, "We were gone so long because you didn't want to come back."

Yes, he could believe that. He stood back and held out his hand. Jeremy took it, and Rafe pulled him to his feet.

"All right, come in," Rafe said. He looked at Emilie, staring at him in shock. "You too."

Elsewhere

YOUR STORYTELLER HAS IT on excellent authority that while all this was going on, a queen in a faraway kingdom—as far away as *And they lived happily ever after* is from *Once upon a time*—knelt on the floor of her library surrounded by splintered wood and shattered glass. A red crow landed on a purple velvet cushion where, for fifteen years, a book had rested inside a locked treasure box, but now the box was empty.

"What news, my spy?" the queen asked.

The crow sang the queen her secrets.

"Oh, not him. Anyone but him. I was afraid of that." She sighed heavily, wearily. "But who else would want to steal it but him?"

The crow sang another song full of secrets, for in this world, crows didn't simply caw. They saw. They saw, and they sang of what they saw. And the song the crow sang was one that said the world was about to change. Lost ones were coming home, but before they could feast in celebration, they must fight.

CHAPTER SEVEN

RAFE GOT THREE BEERS from the fridge and a bag of frozen peas for Jeremy. He lay stretched on the sofa, and Rafe tossed him the peas.

"Here," he said. Rafe wasn't proud of himself for how hard he'd punched Jeremy. But no denying, it had been a good punch.

Jeremy lifted his shirt to reveal a red bruise. "Ah, nice. It's like that red storm on Jupiter."

"It's not nice." Emilie glared at Rafe. "You don't go around punching people when they annoy you."

"Princess?" Jeremy said. "Welcome to West Virginia."

"I miss Ohio."

Rafe looked at her and said, "I'm sorry."

"Are you?" she asked. She was perched on the arm of the sofa by Jeremy's head. Behind her, he mouthed, *Say yes.*

"Yes?" Rafe said.

"Good. Because you could have broken his ribs, okay? Not cool."

"Did I break anything?" Rafe asked him.

"Just a flesh wound. How's your hand?"

"Been better." Rafe flexed his fingers. "Gonna need at least a week off jacking."

"Hey," Emilie said. "A lady is present."

"Sorry. Old joke. Blame him." He pointed at Jeremy.

"Freshman English," Jeremy said. "Mrs. Melby asked for an example of rewriting a sentence so it didn't end in a preposition."

Rafe said, "This jackass raised his hand and said, 'Tonight in the shower, I will off-jack.'"

Jeremy snorted a laugh but flinched. He caught his breath and said, "Two days in detention for me, and one day for him because he laughed so hard, that jackass fell off his chair. Totally worth it."

"And you two are the jackasses I thought could help me find my sister?" she said. "What was I thinking?"

Rafe wasn't laughing anymore. "Your name's Emilie?"

She nodded. "Emilie Wendell."

"I can't help you find your sister, Emilie," Rafe said. "I don't remember anything about when we were lost in Red Crow."

"As long as you're with us," Jeremy said, "I'll handle the rest. Okay?"

Rafe glanced at Emilie. "Can you give us a minute?"

"No," she said. "Absolutely not. And you can't make me."

"Do you have any Tylenol in your car?" Jeremy asked her.

"If I get it for you, will you throw it at him?" she asked, pointing at Rafe.

"Please," Jeremy said.

She sighed heavily, then stood up. Rafe would have laughed at the stern look on her face, but he didn't want to hurt her feelings. "Don't touch him. Don't lay a hand on him. He can't find my sister if he's broken."

"No promises."

"Promises," she demanded. "I don't know how to hurt people, but I can learn. No more punching Jeremy."

He raised his hands in surrender. "I promise I won't punch him." He looked at Jeremy. "I like her."

"Thanks," Emilie said, glaring. "The jury's still out on you."

She left, letting the screen door swing shut so hard it sounded like a gun going off.

"They must not have screen doors in Ohio," Jeremy said.

"Where did you get that painting?"

Jeremy sat up and tossed the frozen peas onto the coffee table. "Your mother rescued it from the bin and sent it to Mum. She wanted me to have it."

"I tossed it for a reason."

"I don't care," he said. "You shouldn't throw away something valuable or meaningful just because you think it's worthless. You don't get to decide that."

"Why do I think we're not talking about my painting anymore?"

"Because you're smarter than you look," Jeremy said.

"You could've brought it here. Any particular reason I had to drive all the way to your old house to get it?"

"I wanted you to remember that we're friends. Or at least remember I was never your enemy. I promise, staying away from you was the last thing I wanted to do, but I wasn't given much choice."

"Right, right. Secrets. State secrets."

"Bigger than state secrets. Much bigger."

Rafe tried to muster up the old anger and bitterness, but it was gone.

"You really think this girl who's been missing twenty years is alive out there?"

"Yes."

"And we knew her?"

Jeremy didn't answer. He simply pointed in the general direction of Rafe's sculpture garden.

"Okay, we knew her," Rafe said. He couldn't pretend otherwise. "How do you know she's still alive?"

"Gut feeling."

"That could be the bruised rib."

Jeremy snorted a laugh.

"Can you answer this?" Rafe said. "Simple yes or no. The reason you can't or won't tell me about what happened when we were lost . . . Was it because I was a coward out there?"

"No." Jeremy said that word loudly, clearly, and forcefully. Rafe stared at him. Jeremy leaned forward and met his eyes. "Jesus, Rafe, you were anything but a coward. You won't believe me, so I don't know why I should bother saying this, but listen to me, Rafe . . . You were the opposite of a coward. When we were gone, you were . . . heroic, courageous to a fault, nobler than any prince of this world dead, alive, or still to come. God, if anyone tried calling you a coward, that would be the last word I ever let them speak."

Rafe didn't speak at first, only sat silently to absorb the shock of Jeremy's speech. Who talked like that? *Nobler than any prince of this world* ... No one talked like that. Maybe in another world, another time. And about him? A country kid with a country mom who wore long skirts and no makeup, hair not just long but Pentecostal long? And an electrician dad who showed up to school meetings in his sweat-stained uniform shirts with his name stitched on the breast pocket? Him? A boy named Ralph Stanley from Nowhere, West Virginia.

"You're right," Rafe finally said. "I don't believe you."

"I tried." Jeremy sat back on the sofa.

"What do you need me to do?"

"Come with us to the Crow. That's it."

"That's it?"

"I can't do this without you."

"Can't or won't?"

"Let's just say even if I could, I wouldn't. Would you go back there without me?"

"I wouldn't go back at all."

"Why not? Didn't it ever occur to you that going back there might help you remember?"

"Dad said—"

Emilie chose that perfectly imperfect moment to return to the cabin, a bottle of Tylenol in her hand. She gave a nervous smile and then passed the pills to Jeremy. He didn't open them.

"Dad said what?" she asked. "And whose dad?"

"His dad," Jeremy said, pointing at Rafe with his beer. "My dad's been dead since before I was born."

"Oh, yeah, I'm sorry. It was a car accident, right?"

"Car? Yes. Accident? No. Leaving the car running in the garage wasn't an accident."

Rafe smiled behind his beer as Emilie stared at Jeremy, her jaw scraping the floor.

"You asshole," Rafe said.

"It's true," Jeremy said. "Not my fault the internet got it wrong."

"I'm sorry," she said. "I shouldn't have—"

"Don't feel bad," Rafe told her. "He pulls out the dead dad card whenever he wants pity."

Jeremy, shameless, only grinned. "Hey, it works. You can get your membership card now too."

"I don't want it," Rafe said. "You know, when we were lost, Dad went to the Crow every single day. Two hours before work, he was searching for us. After work, he'd be there until sundown. Long after the search-and-rescue volunteers went home, he was still there. The one thing he asked me was to never ever go back."

Jeremy leaned forward. "You're forgetting the part where he's the reason we got lost in the first place."

"What? How?" Emilie asked.

"We got into a fight the night before," Rafe said. "Just a stupid fight. And that's not why we got lost. You told the cops we got turned around trying to find the Goblin Falls."

"First," Jeremy said, ticking off on his fingers. "It wasn't a stupid fight. He tore your sketchbooks to shreds and slapped you so hard he left a bruise on your cheek."

"What?" Emilie sounded horrified.

"It was nothing."

"Second, we did get lost because we were looking for the Falls, but the reason we were looking for the Falls is we were trying to miss the bus back to school on purpose so Mum would have to pick us up, and you could stay the night at my house. You didn't want to go home. You told me you never wanted to go home."

"I was fourteen."

"You don't owe your father anything," Jeremy said. "Rafe? You know that, right?"

Rafe didn't want to talk about this, not to anyone but especially not to Jeremy and this woman he barely knew. Still, he knew it was easier to answer and get it over with than to argue.

"Four years ago, I was out here with Dad, helping him clear some vines. Porcelain berry. Pretty, but it's invasive."

He remembered piling all the vines into the clearing and creating a giant glowing bonfire. He could still smell the acrid scent of the burning bushes. His dad looked haggard, more than usual.

Can't let stuff like this take root, his father had said to him. *It'll take over the whole damn woods if you don't get it out.*

I think we got it all, Rafe said because he had to say something.

His dad was quiet before saying, *It's good to have your help out here. Sometimes, I forget I almost didn't have a son.*

I'm right here, Dad.

And the fire popped, and the acrid smoke rose, and maybe something in the air made his father brave enough to say it . . .

"That day, Dad said, 'I want you to know, son, I regret the things that happened before you got lost.' I said I appreciated that. Then he said, 'Did you ever get around to forgiving me for that?'"

"What did you say?" Jeremy asked.

"I said, 'Not yet.' You can guess what happened next."

Emilie said, "He died."

"My last chance to forgive him, and I didn't do it. Now you two are sitting there asking me to break the promise I made him. The one thing he asked me was that I never go back to the Crow. That place was cursed ground to him."

Rafe waited for Jeremy to make his argument. He knew it was coming. He knew it would be a good one, but before Jeremy could say a word, Emilie spoke up.

"If you heard Jeremy was lost in the Crow again, and no one else could find him, you'd go then, right?"

"That was a low blow," Rafe said.

"Would you like some frozen peas?" Emilie asked.

He laughed softly. The kid was all right. "I'll make you both a deal. If Mom is okay with it, I'll go."

"That's fair," Emilie said. "Yes?" She looked to Jeremy.

Jeremy shook his head. "Complete waste of time."

"It's his mom, Jeremy," Emilie said. "Do you even have a heart?"

"Not at the moment," he said, his tone steely. "What if your mother says no?"

"Mom has all of Dad's old maps of the Crow. Even if Mom says she doesn't want me to go, they might help you all navigate the park. Best I can offer."

"All right, we'll go to your mom's house right now," Jeremy said. "You can get her blessing—which she'll give you—then we'll all head out in the morning. Yes? Yes. Everyone say yes."

"Yes," Emilie said.

"No," Rafe said.

Jeremy glared at him. "No? Wrong answer. Try again."

"She won't let me in the house. I told you I'm banned from the house until I shave and get a haircut. And don't think I'm joking. I'm not joking."

"Then maybe—here's an idea—shave and get a haircut," Jeremy said with a nuclear blast of sarcasm that nearly peeled the paint off the walls. "The world will thank you. I will thank you."

Rafe had no desire to shave, no desire to get a haircut. "I can shave tonight, but the haircut might have to wait until tomorrow. It's already—"

"I can cut hair," Emilie said.

"You can cut hair?" Rafe asked.

"Back at the vet's office where I worked, I did some dog grooming. Human hair isn't much different, right? Oh, forgot to ask—is it okay that I have my rat with me?" She reached into her hoodie pouch and produced a small white rat with gray spots.

"His name is Fritz," Jeremy said. "That was Stevie Nicks's first band."

Rafe looked at Jeremy, at Emilie, back at Jeremy.

"I never should've let you two in my house."

· ✳ ·

CHAPTER EIGHT

NERVOUSLY, BUT PRETENDING not to be nervous, Emilie laid out her comb, her shears, and a couple of hair clips on the counter in Rafe's tiny bathroom. He sat on the edge of the bathtub, watching her warily.

"You brought hair-cutting scissors with you?" he asked. He didn't bother to keep the confused amusement out of his voice. Frankly, she didn't blame him.

"You see these?" She pointed at her bangs. "These require constant upkeep. Constant. I keep a good pair of scissors in my glove box."

"Are you going to give me bangs?"

"I'm thinking poodle cut."

"I like poodles," he said. She was relieved he had a sense of humor about the whole thing. All she wanted was to do a decent enough job that he didn't cry when he looked at himself in the mirror. She never had to worry about that with the dogs.

"So . . ." she said as she started running her fingers through his hair, trying to figure out her plan of attack, "do I call you Ralph or Rafe? Or Mr. Howell?"

"Mr. Howell's my father. You can call me Rafe. I like it better than Ralph."

"Who wouldn't? Sorry, that wasn't nice. Did Jeremy tell you I have trouble self-censoring? Can you soak your hair now?"

"I guessed." Rafe turned the shower on. "I'm going to take my shirt off. Don't freak out."

"I can handle seeing a shirtless guy without fainting," she said, rolling her eyes. Men. In the medicine cabinet mirror, she saw Rafe raise his eyebrows. Then he pulled his T-shirt off and tossed it on the floor.

She didn't scream, but she did gasp. "Oh my God."

"Warned you." Rafe stuck his head under the hot water. She turned around and stared, scissors and comb and haircut forgotten.

On his back, between his shoulder blades, were pale pink scars, lots of them. Thin and long and nasty-looking. They were healed, but still . . .

"What happened?"

"No idea. Happened when we were lost in the Crow. Bobcat, maybe? Or not. Jeremy says he doesn't even know."

"I . . . I've seen a lot of dog scratches and cat scratches. Even big ones. That's not . . . that is not that."

"Barbed-wire fence? Fell on something?" His voice was muffled with his head hanging upside down. She wanted to touch the scars but didn't dare. They reminded her of something, but she couldn't put her finger on what.

"You really don't remember getting those?"

She was scared just looking at them. What was out in the woods?

"No."

He sounded casual about the whole thing, too casual. He sounded like someone trying to pretend he wasn't bothered by his inability to remember what he'd suffered to end up with those scars.

He turned off the water and sat down on the edge of the bathtub.

"You ready?" he said.

That was a clear hint he wanted to change the subject.

"If you are."

"I am. Maybe."

"You can hold Fritz if it would help."

He laughed a little. "Sure."

She gently scooped Fritz out of her hoodie pocket and passed him to

Rafe. She watched for a second, making sure he wouldn't drop him or anything, but Fritz sniffed his hands and nibbled his beard.

"You hate the beard too, buddy?" Rafe asked him.

"He chews everything," she said. "But yes, he does hate the beard. He told me so."

Rafe lightly rubbed Fritz's head and ears. Emilie was starting to warm up to Rafe, though he still made her nervous enough that she regretted volunteering for this mission. Too late now.

She clipped a bath towel around his shoulders and ran her comb through his straw-colored hair.

"I'll just take off a few inches. Nothing drastic, okay?"

"The shorter it is, the happier Mom will be."

"Is she super strict or something?"

"Nah. She'd be okay if she thought I was growing my hair long because I wanted it long. She thinks the hair and the beard are a cry for help."

"No comment."

Rafe lifted Fritz, so they made eye contact. Or as much eye contact as you could make with a sniffing, shuffling, wriggling fancy rat. "Your mother's a little rude."

"Don't listen to him, baby. He doesn't know what he's talking about. You can put him in the tub to run around. He needs the exercise."

"Sure," Rafe said and gently sat Fritz in the empty bathtub, where he proceeded to run tiny rat laps.

"Ready?"

"Go for it." He sounded like a man facing a firing squad. The hair meant something to him. Freedom? Safety? A disguise?

"Let me guess—nobody recognizes you with the long hair and the beard?"

He gave a soft, bitter little laugh. "There's nothing worse than being famous in a small town. For years, I couldn't go in the hardware store without ten old guys giving me the evil eye, whispering behind my back about the hoax me and Jeremy pulled on the whole state. I just wanted to be a nobody again."

"Wait, a hoax? Are you kidding?"

"A lot of people don't want to believe two kids could survive in the woods that long. Doesn't help that I can't remember how we did it, and Jeremy skipped town three days after they found us."

She ran her comb through his hair again, snipping more length away.

"It must have been hard going through that without Jeremy. I mean, facing all those dirty looks alone."

"It wasn't fun," he said. She imagined that was a massive understatement.

"Jeremy says he had a good reason for staying away. Maybe he did?"

"Maybe. It would just be nice if he'd tell me what that reason was."

"Yeah, he is kind of annoyingly cryptic."

"Never used to be like that. He'd tell me everything."

"What was he like back then?"

"You would not have guessed 'savior of missing girls' would be his career path."

"You mean the guy who made jack-off jokes to his English teacher?"

"All day, every day. Never a dull moment with him. He called our vice principal 'Il Duce' to his face. He stole that from *Gilmore Girls*."

"Jeremy watched *Gilmore Girls*?"

"We both watched *Gilmore Girls*. I liked Rory. He liked Lorelai."

"Why doesn't that surprise me about him?" She took off another two inches. The hair fell in golden clumps onto the dark wood floor.

"People still talk about us like we're a team. The news called us 'The West Virginia Lost Boys.' Plural. I guess I thought we were a team too. Guess not."

Emilie was starting to think the only thing sadder than a lost boy was a lost man.

"The West Virginia Lost Boys sounds like a killer bluegrass band." Emilie went back to work, combing and snipping, combing and snipping. "If you want to know what I think, and I admit you probably don't . . . I don't think you ever hated Jeremy. You, you know . . . you missed him."

"Don't tell him that."

"Don't tell me what?"

Jeremy appeared in the doorway. Emilie saw Rafe eye him from under the curtain of his wet hair.

"That we know you're eavesdropping," Rafe said.

In what was clearly faux outrage, Jeremy said, "I was just coming to ask if you wanted me to put your gear in my car? You know, on the very slim off-chance you go with us tomorrow."

"He's sarcastic," Emilie whispered.

Rafe whispered back. "You noticed?"

"You want me to pack your gear up or not? I'd like to get going before it's midnight."

"Sure. It's—"

"I can find it," he said and disappeared from the doorway.

"He was definitely eavesdropping," Emilie said.

"I knew it. You almost done?"

"Two more seconds."

She set her comb and scissors down, then ran her fingers through his hair. She'd cut it to his ears. Shorter but not shorn. Even damp, it had a soft wave.

"Good enough? I hope?"

He stood up and looked in the mirror for a long time while Emilie cleared up clippings off the floor with a towel, then retrieved Fritz from the bathtub before he made a nest out of Rafe's hair.

"Not bad," he finally said. She sagged with relief.

"Oh, thank God. I was kind of out of practice."

He only smiled and said, "Give me ten minutes. I'll meet you two out front."

He pulled a shaving kit from under his sink.

"Good luck finding your face."

He took a deep breath and met his own eyes in the glass. "I'm in there somewhere."

Emilie left him in the bathroom and went to find Jeremy.

"Jeremy?"

"Upstairs, Princess," he called down to her.

She started up the stairs to the loft. "Rafe says he'll meet us in ten minutes. And we need to have a talk right now about this 'Princess' thing— Wow."

"Wow is the right response," Jeremy said, glancing around Rafe's bedroom, which merited a wow or two. Especially the bed.

"I guess I shouldn't be surprised he has a crazy bed," she said. "This whole cabin is wild. Did he do all of this?" She ran her fingers over the bedpost, carved like the sinewy branch of a tree. All four posts were carved like tree branches, and the tall headboard bore a scene of stags running through a forest. The picture window by the bed showed the sun beginning to set over the mountain.

"He's a man of many talents," Jeremy said as he reached behind the headboard and pulled out a large bow and a quiver of arrows.

"Whoa. He sleeps with his bow?"

"Old habits die hard." Jeremy sat on the bed with the bow in his hands. A black hard-shell case lay across the scarlet quilt next to him.

"This is absolutely incredible." It wasn't just the bed, but the walls too were covered in more of his murals. It looked as if they were sitting in a tall tree and fireflies with golden wings were flashing among the enormous leaves. "Bet this impresses all the girls."

Jeremy looked up at her sharply.

"What? You don't think he brings girls back here? I would if I were him."

He went back to unstringing and unscrewing the pieces of Rafe's bow and putting them into the case.

"Hadn't thought about it."

She didn't quite believe him.

"You have a girlfriend?" she asked.

"No girlfriend. No boyfriend. No petfriend."

"Sounds lonely."

"Maybe I'll rescue a rat or two from a dumpster," he said.

Emilie winced. "Um . . . I kind of need to tell you something. I sort of lied about that."

"Carry on. I'm intrigued."

"Fancy rats usually like other rats. Fritz . . . does *not*."

"Loner? Rebel?"

"Exactly. He had a couple cage-mates, but Fritz didn't like them. He would start fights. Remember I told you his owner got fed up one day and brought him to the vet's office to be euthanized for aggression? Which seemed unfair, you know? Getting killed over a bad roommate situation?"

"A little extreme," Jeremy said.

"That's what I thought, too, but I didn't say anything. Not my job. But then when I was carrying him back to prep him for the procedure, he nuzzled against my chest and fell asleep." She held Fritz to her chest and he nuzzled against her just like he had that day. "I couldn't do it. So I snuck him out the back door, got in my car, and drove home with him. I told you I quit my job when Mom got sick. I didn't. They fired me. Fritz's owner even threatened to call the police."

"Arrested for Grand Theft Fancy Rat." He laughed as he latched the bow case.

"It's not funny. I got fired from the only job I ever wanted. And that's not even the worst part. My poor mother, sick as a dog from chemo, had to drag herself off the bathroom floor to write Fritz's old owner a big check so he wouldn't press charges against me for stealing his kid's rat. The rat he was going to have euthanized anyway!"

"I'm still laughing," he said. "You could've told me that before."

"Well, in fairness, I did rescue five kittens out of the dumpster, so that part was half-true." She gently stroked Fritz's ear. Since her mom died, he'd been her only company, her only family. "I was worried you'd think I was crazy."

"I don't think you're crazy. And I'm very proud of you, Princess."

"Hey, enough with the 'Princess,' okay? I know I'm weak and spoiled and generally useless to society, but you don't have to rub it in."

"There's nothing wrong with being spoiled. But where did you get the idea you were weak?"

"If I had been kidnapped and dragged into the woods like my sister was, I wouldn't have been strong enough to fight him and get away. And if I did get away, I would've gotten lost and starved to death, not hidden out in a shack in the woods for twenty years."

"You would have died of dehydration long before you starved, I promise."

She ignored that. "My sister must have been so brave to have survived all this time . . . I'm not brave. I want to be brave like her. I want to look death in the face and boop his nose."

"You want to 'boop' death? These are the actual thoughts you think?"

She stuck out her finger and booped the imaginary nose of death. "Boop."

With two fingers he pointed at his eyes. "Focus."

She leaned forward and met his eyes. "I'm focused."

"On my honor, I only call you 'Princess' out of respect," he said. "I'll stop if you want, but I think you should get used to it."

She sat back and considered it. "You can keep calling me Princess then. If it makes you happy."

"Ecstatic."

She heard footsteps on the stairs and turned to see Rafe standing at the top of the steps.

"Ready if you two are," he said. "Meet you at the car." He started to leave.

"Wait a stupid minute." Emilie got to her feet. Rafe sighed and turned back around. The expression on his face indicated he knew exactly what was coming. "Oh. My. Lord. You are so . . . pretty. Holy cow."

He wasn't pretty. He wasn't remotely pretty. He was beautiful. Even in his ratty work pants, battered-all-to-hell hiking boots, and a white T-shirt with a faded red-and-black flannel over it, he looked like he'd walked out of a painting of knights, kings, and fair damsels. Now short and almost dry, his hair revealed soft blond waves. Strong jaw. Full lips. The profile of a poet. The sharp eyes of a hunter.

"You're staring," he told her.

"Staring at your freaking perfect face," Emilie said. "I don't think those old guys at the hardware store were giving you the evil eye. I think they were checking you out."

"Help," Rafe said to Jeremy.

Jeremy narrowed his eyes at him. "Maybe we should have kept the beard."

Rafe glared at him, then gave him the middle finger, which only made Jeremy smile.

"Can we go, please?" Rafe said. "If we get there in time, good chance Mom will feed us."

"Let's go." Jeremy shoved Rafe's bow case into his hands and went down the stairs.

Still standing at the top of the stairs, Rafe watched him walk away. Emilie watched him watching Jeremy.

"How did you two meet?" she asked, trying to keep her voice lightly curious, not nosy.

Rafe shrugged. "School."

"Oh, come on. There's gotta be a better story than that."

"Sorry." He started down the stairs.

Emilie scoffed. "It's a good thing you're pretty because you are a crap storyteller."

The West Virginia Lost Boys

IGNORE RAFE. THERE IS a better story than that. Here's the short version.

August 2006, the first day of high school.

Ralph Howell—he wouldn't become Rafe for another ten minutes—took a desk in the back row, the next-to-last seat on the right. He opened his new single-subject notebook and sketched a coyote on the inside cover. Hunched over his work, shading in the gray fur with his new mechanical pencil, he didn't notice someone watching.

"Wow. Nice."

Ralph glanced up. Leaning across the aisle from his seat in the last desk on the right was Jeremy Cox. The Jeremy Cox. They'd gone to different middle schools—if you could call the religious "academy" Ralph had attended a school. Still, Ralph had heard all about Jeremy from friends of friends of friends. Jeremy was British, which practically made him a celebrity around there. British, big fancy house, money. Rafe wasn't sure he trusted that "nice." Boys did not pay other boys compliments unless it was to salute a good burn or clap ironically if some genius dropped his lunch tray. It sounded like he'd meant it, though, both the "wow" and the "nice."

"Dog, right?"

"Coyote." He was a fourteen-year-old boy who'd gotten caught drawing animals in his notebook. To redeem himself, Ralph said, "I hunt them."

"For real?"

He shrugged to say yes, but no big deal. "Dad's been teaching me to hunt since I was a kid." A deliberate choice of words, implying that while he had been a kid once, he wasn't one anymore. The girl in front of them made a disgusted sound. "I got one this summer. Took him down on my own. He was killing our chickens."

All true, except for the part about taking the coyote by himself. Dad had helped. A lot.

"That him?" He pointed at Ralph's notebook.

"I guess."

"I like it. Better than mine," Jeremy said, showing off his artwork on the front page of his notebook. He'd drawn what any teenage boy saddled with the last name Cox would've drawn.

Rafe shouldn't have laughed, but he did. Jeremy put his notebook away, grabbed Rafe's, and studied his coyote drawing.

"How do you kill coyotes? Shotgun?"

"We're bow hunters," Ralph said with quiet pride. "Dad thinks it's cheating to use a gun on an animal. Guns are for other people." That was a joke his dad made all the time.

"I like that. Give the animals a fighting chance. Sounds more fun to shoot arrows anyway."

Jeremy didn't have much of a British accent. He must have lost it living in the States the past few years, but to Ralph, he did sound smarter than everyone else.

"I'm Jeremy."

"Ralph," he said.

Jeremy winced like he'd tasted soap. "No. Unacceptable. That's a redneck name. At least say it right." He lifted his chin and, in a voice eerily like Scar's from *The Lion King*, said, "Thou shalt pronounce thy name Rafe."

"What?" Sounded like he'd said *rave*.

"Rafe," Jeremy said again. "Rhymes with *safe* or *chafe*. Like *rage* with an *f*. Got it?"

"*Rafe*," he repeated. He liked it. He didn't know why he liked it, but he liked it. Maybe he just didn't want to be a Ralph anymore. Maybe he never had.

"Much better. You hunt a lot?"

The spine of the girl sitting in front of them stiffened dramatically, almost melodramatically.

"Every weekend, pretty much. Almost deer season."

The girl couldn't take it one more second. She spun around in her chair to honor them with her opinion.

"Hunting is gross," she said. "What's wrong with you two? Why would you want to go out and kill defenseless—"

"You a vegetarian?" Jeremy asked before Ralph could muster a defense.

"No, but—"

"Then shut up, Mabel." The girl's name was not Mabel. "You think your pet pepperoni pizza shot itself in the parking lot behind Blockbuster?"

A question that made less sense the more one thought about it.

Jeremy twirled his finger, warning her to spin her nosy little self around to the front of the class again.

"Sexist." She huffed and whirled away.

Jeremy's mouth fell open. He raised his fists and shook them as he silently screamed at the back of her head. Ralph had to wonder if all British people were like this.

Tantrum over, Jeremy tapped the girl on the right shoulder. She looked back at him, haughty as a duchess.

"I am not sexist," he said. "I am an asshole. There's a difference. Get it right."

With a roll of her eyes, she faced forward again. Really, what could she have said to that? *Sorry?*

The bell rang. Their teacher, Miss Farris, strode into the classroom, and everyone got quiet.

Jeremy jotted something on a scrap of paper and passed it to Ralph when Miss Farris turned her back.

Would your dad teach me to hunt?
Sincerely,
> *The Asshole (Who is not sexist because I'm an asshole to everyone equally)*

Before Jeremy, Ralph had felt like an outsider. There was no reason for it. He was, seemingly, just like everyone else. His grades were good enough. He was fine. He was acceptable. But telling himself that never did erase the sneaking suspicion he didn't belong. And then . . . Jeremy. It wasn't like Jeremy belonged either. He stuck out like a sore thumb, but he didn't care. He wasn't living in their world. He lived in his own world, and Rafe wanted to live there too. For the first time in his life, he was glad he didn't belong.

He replied,

Yeah. This weekend?

And the note was signed,

Rafe

Before they were the West Virginia Lost Boys, they were just boys.

CHAPTER NINE

WHEN THEY TURNED DOWN the long gravel drive to Rafe's mother's house, he spotted her beat-up red F-150, which had been his dad's beat-up red F-150, parked in its usual spot in front of the garage. She was home. The garden lights in the flower beds around the porch were already glowing, but no romantic lighting could make the old house with the ancient putty-colored vinyl look good. It was ugly, ugly enough that the first time he'd had Jeremy over, Rafe had tried distracting him by pointing out the woods attached to the backyard, ten acres with a little stream through it. To that, Jeremy had said, "Awesome," and it sounded like he meant it. Then when Jeremy's mother came to pick him up, he'd complained about having to go home.

They'd been friends for less than a week, and Rafe would have given him a lung, kidney, or both if Jeremy had wanted them.

Jeremy parked and turned off the engine.

"Wait," Rafe said as they started to get out of the car. "Don't tell my mom about Red Crow. Let me tell her."

"What if she asks?" Emilie said.

"Lie," Rafe said.

"I'm not lying to your mother," Jeremy said.

"You lied to your mother all the time," Rafe countered.

"Yes, but that's my mother. Very different."

"She'll know anyway," Emilie said. "Moms always do."

"Now I know why my parents stopped after one," Rafe said.

Emilie's mouth fell open. "Hurtful," she said.

"It'll be all right," Jeremy said. "Bobbi will be too happy to see me to even care why we're here."

"She doesn't like you that much," Rafe said but had a feeling he might be right. "Just let me handle it."

"Fine." Emilie flung open the car door. "But I'm telling you, she'll know."

As the three of them got out, the front door of the house opened. Rafe braced himself.

"If that's my son, he better look like my son." His mother yelled loudly enough everyone in the whole holler probably heard her.

"I look like your son," he called back, walking toward the porch. His mother wore an apron over her jeans, and the sleeves of her floral-print shirt were rolled up. They must have caught her baking something for church.

"We cleaned him up for you, Mom," Jeremy said from behind him.

Rafe was still mad at Jeremy, probably always would be, but he couldn't help but smile at his mother's reaction to Jeremy's voice. She gasped softly, put a hand over her heart, and ran down the porch steps. Jeremy met her at the bottom. She threw her arms around him, holding him tight.

Emilie crept up next to Rafe and smiled nervously.

"She always did like him better," Rafe said loud enough for his mother to hear.

"You hush," his mother said. "This is my redheaded stepchild, and I'm going to hug him tight if I want to." She patted Jeremy on the back and said softly, "I'm so sorry about your sweet mama. Mary Cox was a great lady."

"Yeah, she was," Jeremy said.

She grabbed him by the face. "Don't you ever stay away so long again, so help me God." She kissed his forehead like she was blessing him. Then she pointed at Rafe. "You neither, Junior."

Emilie covered her mouth to hide a laugh. But his mother still heard it.

"Now, who's this pretty girl?" she said.

"Emilie." Emilie raised her hand in a nervous wave. "Hi. I'm with Jeremy. Not *with* him with him."

"Jeremy's helping Emilie find her sister," Rafe said. "They need a place to crash tonight."

"You poor thing," his mother said to Emilie. "I'm Bobbi. You all come in and we'll get dinner on."

Just that easy, Rafe thought as they filed into the house. But as they went inside, Emilie turned around and mouthed to him, "She knows."

Moms

WHEN YOU READ fairy tales, you'll learn fast there are only two types of mothers you'll meet in those stories. One—good and dead. Two—bad and alive. Fathers usually fare better. They live longer. However, without their wives around, they tend to make very poor decisions. Snow White had a good and dead mother. Then her father remarried her wicked stepmother. Cinderella's father also exercised very poor taste when looking for wife number two. The father in "Rumpelstiltskin" took parental bragging to a whole new level when he swore to all who would listen that his daughter could spin straw into gold. One imagines if his wife had been alive, she would have quickly shut those rumors down by explaining to all and sundry that she'd married a narcissist.

There is a third type of mother in fairy tales, neither good and dead nor bad and alive, and though a rare figure, she does have a part to play in some stories, including this one.

That would be the fairy godmother, of course. Sometimes she doesn't even have to do magic to bestow a gift upon a worthy young prince or princess.

Sometimes the godmother is just a good mother.

And Emilie was right. Bobbi knew.

· ✳ ·

CHAPTER TEN

RAFE STOOD IN THE kitchen doorway, watching the chaos, three people at one kitchen counter. His mother bustled around happily, giving orders. Emilie was making the salad dressing. Jeremy chopped onions while wearing Rafe's mother's old apron that read, KISS THE COOK! with big red lips on the front.

Turn back the clock fifteen years, put Rafe in Emilie's place, and it could have been any Friday night when Jeremy slept over their freshman year in high school. The kitchen even looked the same as it had since it was built in the aesthetically challenged seventies. Yellow counters and yellow table. Brown checkered wallpaper. An oval rag rug lay atop the brown linoleum, which his mother mopped daily.

He should've been helping, but Emilie had taken over his job, and there was nothing for him to do. It felt good to stand back and watch his mom having fun. She loved guests, loved meeting new people, and loved cooking for anyone who was hungry. She loved Rafe's friends, always had, and she loved Jeremy most of all.

While the three of them threw dinner together, Rafe had the chance to slip away and find the maps. He was ninety percent sure everything had been stored in his old basement bedroom, another time capsule. He'd moved into this bedroom at eight years old, and when he left at eighteen, the tractor wallpaper was still on the walls. An old desk bought at a garage sale was still in the corner. The same twin bed he'd slept in his entire childhood still sat under the window.

The box of maps was either under the bed or in the closet. He got on his knees on the rug but found only a few boxes of old Christmas decorations under the bed. Closet then. He went to the closet and opened the door. On the shelf above all the winter coats, he found several plastic storage bins.

He took them out and piled them up by the bed. He sat down on the edge and pulled off the first lid.

Sketchbooks. All his old sketchbooks. He knew he needed to be looking for the maps, but he couldn't help himself. He took the books out and checked the inside covers for the dates penciled there. In his sloppy teenage penmanship, he found *October 7, 2006*, scrawled inside the cover of one book. That was the month he and Jeremy had started spending all their free time together. He rarely looked through his old sketches. He didn't mind the art, but he avoided the history. Especially from that year with Jeremy before they were lost. He opened the sketchbook to the middle and found a sketch of Martha, Jeremy's poodle. Another one of Jeremy's old house decorated for Christmas. A sketch of a breakfast Jeremy had dubbed *Still Life with a Tudor's Egg & Cheese Biscuit.*

After that, several pages of nothing but sketches of Jeremy sitting at the piano.

So many good memories from that year they'd been inseparable. If only it could be this easy to get his missing memories back. Open a book, turn the pages, and there they are ...

He heard footsteps and looked up. Jeremy stood in the bedroom doorway. Rafe immediately shut the book.

"Dinner ready?" he asked.

Jeremy said, "Not yet. But I want to give Emilie an archery lesson after dinner. Any chance there's a kids' bow in the house? She can't use mine. It'll kill her."

"You still hunt?" Rafe asked. True, that year they'd been friends Jeremy had gotten pretty good with a bow. His father, for all his faults, had been a great teacher. But he never expected Jeremy to keep it up.

"You don't want to know the answer to that."

"I asked."

"No, I don't hunt anymore, but if I'm looking for a body, I'll take my bow with me in case coyotes or vultures are—"

Rafe didn't need to hear another word. "Yeah, I get it. Shit. How are you sane after all that?"

"Who said I was?"

"True." Rafe caught himself staring at Jeremy. "I guess you can't tell me how you do it, right?"

"Right. Wish I could. Come with us tomorrow, and I will."

"I'll talk to Mom after dinner," he promised. "I think her bow's in the shed. It's only twenty-five pounds."

Jeremy nodded but didn't leave. After an awkward silence, Rafe said, "I haven't found the maps yet."

"They'll turn up." Jeremy peeled himself off the doorway and came inside, sat down on the floor among the boxes.

"What's all this?"

"My entire childhood in pencil sketches."

Jeremy dug out a sketchbook that looked different from the others— thicker, beat-up pages sticking out from the binding at odd angles.

"This is the one your dad ripped apart," Jeremy said. He opened the book to a sketch of himself, aged fourteen, sitting on the front porch of his mother's old house on Park.

"Yeah," Rafe said.

Jeremy flipped through the pages.

"Who taped it back up? You?"

"Had to have been, but I don't remember doing it."

"What's the last thing you do remember?" Jeremy asked.

"I don't remember the day we got lost," Rafe said. "I remember most of the day before, but . . . not all of it. I remember asking to stay the night at your house. Then all hell breaking loose."

Asking to stay the night at Jeremy's had been a mistake. His parents had a strict no-school-nights rule, but Rafe had argued the next day wasn't *real* school, just an end-of-year field trip to Red Crow State Forest. His mom had said yes. His father had said no. When Dad said no, it was no.

So, Rafe had been sullen and silent during dinner, picking at his mother's meatloaf. His dad returned this silence with surliness.

"What do you do at his house that's so much better than what you can do at ours?"

Rafe knew better than to answer that.

When he'd eaten as much as he could stomach, he'd taken his sketchbook out of his backpack to work on a drawing he'd started that weekend.

"Son, stop doodling and help your mother with dishes."

Doodling? Rafe did not doodle. He drew. But did his father ever once call it drawing or sketching or art? No. Always doodling.

"I'm busy," Rafe said. "Why don't you help her for once?"

Fifteen years later, he could still hear that chair hitting the floor and still see his mother's face, more shocked than he was when his father leaned across the table and smacked him so hard his eyes watered.

His mother gasped. He could hear the gasp right now, ringing in his ears. Chair scrape. Chair hitting the floor. Slap. Gasp.

But that wasn't all. His dad grabbed his sketchbook and flipped through it. He didn't like what he saw. Burning with shame, Rafe watched his father tearing the pages out of his sketchbook. He couldn't do anything but sit miserably at the kitchen table and beg his dad, *Stop, please, please stop it, I'm sorry. I'll do the dishes. Please . . .*

His mother had sent him to his room, not as a punishment. He knew that even then, that she was trying to protect him. He'd run in here, slammed the door, and locked it.

Jeremy had listened without comment to the whole story.

"That's it?" he finally asked. "The last thing you remember?"

"That's it. Locking my bedroom door. I don't remember anything after that until November, when I woke up in the ambulance."

"And your father had the balls to blame me for us going missing after he did that to you."

"He was trying to protect me."

"From what? Colored pencils?"

"He just didn't want me getting my hopes up, thinking I could be an artist for real."

"That is bullshit, and you know it."

Rafe said nothing, only flipped through his October 2006 sketch-book. When he found the sketch he'd been looking for, he carefully tore it from the binding.

"You want this one?" It was the sketch of Jeremy's mother looking out at her garden. Jeremy took it and looked at it for a long time.

"Thank you. I'll keep it with the other one."

"What other one?"

He didn't answer. He took out his wallet and opened it. Tucked inside, folded into the size of a credit card, was a piece of paper, held together by tape. Jeremy unfolded it and held it out to him. Rafe took it, studied it. Nothing special about it really. Just one of a zillion sketches he'd done of Jeremy at his house that year. In it, Jeremy lay stretched out on his mother's baby-blue antique sofa in the music room, reading something, probably homework. He was shirtless in the sketch, but otherwise it was nothing but an innocent drawing of his best friend doing homework or at least pretending to do homework. Yet, while the other pages of his sketchbook had been ripped in half, this one had been torn into a dozen or more pieces.

"Where'd you get that?"

"You gave it to me the day we got lost," Jeremy said. "You were upset, and when I asked what happened, you showed me this."

"Guys? Dinner's ready!" Emilie called out from the steps. Jeremy stood up and went to the door.

"Coming!" he called back, but he didn't leave just yet. "You forget how well I know you. We're like old cellmates. We know each other's crimes."

Rafe met his eyes. "What crimes?"

"We both know why your dad tore up your sketches. And it wasn't because he didn't want you going to art school." Jeremy started to leave, then called back over his shoulder, "Oh, and the maps are in the bottom of the closet."

CHAPTER ELEVEN

KATNISS EVERDEEN HAD MADE it look so easy, but shooting arrows was not fun.

"All right," Jeremy said, "this time, slacken your fingers and release the arrow. Let the string and the arrow do the work."

Emilie pulled another arrow out of the quiver and nocked it—she had just learned that term. After nocking the arrow came the hard part. Putting it on the rest and then pulling back the string without it flying off and landing on the ground. She'd done that twice already. So far, so good. The arrow still sat on the rest. She pulled back the string, which wasn't merely awkward but also painful, even with a shooting glove on. Then she released the arrow.

You release arrows, you don't fire them, Jeremy had told her sternly. *They are not guns. The only firepower in archery is the fire inside the archer.*

Fire, release, shoot, it didn't matter. Her arrow landed in the grass again.

"I suck at this," she said, nodding.

"You do," Jeremy replied.

"Is that your pep talk?"

"I also sucked at this once. I no longer suck at it. You, too, could be just like me. With practice."

"At least I look cool. Love the glove and the arm thingie."

"That's called an arm guard."

"Does it come in pink?"

"Let's focus on your aim before we start customizing your gear. Again."

She pulled another arrow and nocked it. Before she released it, he gently positioned her elbow six inches higher and back. Was her spine supposed to arch like that?

"Now try."

"Why are we doing this again?"

"Good excuse to get out of the house so Rafe can talk to Bobbi about Red Crow. But also, it wouldn't kill you to know how to defend yourself."

"Defend myself? Against what?"

"The unknown. Now try again. Pull back. Anchor. Don't release. Just let the string slip through—"

She tried again. Emilie didn't hit any of the circles on the target, but she did hit the target. Her arrow smacked the black circle, then fell out and onto the ground.

"I hit it! Horribly, but still!" She lifted her hand for a high five.

"No high-fiving," Jeremy said. "When you make a good shot, you say, 'West-by God!-Virginia!'"

"West, by God, Virginia?"

"No, it's West! By Gawd! Virginia!" He put ludicrous emphasis on the *God* in a mock West Virginian accent that was not flattering to West Virginians or any other people on planet Earth.

She tried it again. "West—by God!—Virginia! Better?"

"Much. Now shoot the target again and try to make it stick this time."

She released her arrow two feet to the left of the target. "I quit."

"Don't quit," he chided. "You want to boop death, remember?"

"Gotta be an easier way to boop death than this. Jeremy?"

He seemed to be elsewhere. He was looking up at the sky. Here in the country, miles from any town, the stars were out in full force. The stars and the old beat-up moon. The air was crisp and smelled lightly of distant smoke from a fireplace. He breathed in and smiled.

"On cold nights like this, we'd sit by the fire and read to each other until it was time for bed. Just the three of us. We were halfway through *The Wonderful Wizard of Oz* when we left. Your sister's probably still waiting for us to come back and finish reading the story."

Emilie's stomach ached with longing. She wanted to sit by the fire with her sister and read books out loud, wanted it so much it hurt.

"I hope she likes me," Emilie said.

"She'll love you. That's one thing you don't have to worry about. Come on. Let's go dig your arrows out of the garden."

"So Rafe's dad taught you how to do this?" she asked as she found one of her arrows in the high weeds.

"He did. I must've shot about ten thousand arrows the first month we were friends. I was trying to catch up with Rafe. He was better than his father by fourteen. Not that either of them ever admitted that."

"How'd you and Rafe meet? I asked Rafe, and he just said"—and here she lowered her voice an octave and made herself sound a little surly—"'School.'"

"Was that your Rafe impression?" He yanked an arrow out of the ground.

"School," she said again, trying to sound even more like Rafe. "I almost had it there. *School.*"

"Uncanny."

"So?"

"First day of high school. We sat next to each other in World Civ."

"Best friends immediately?"

"Stuck together like glue," he said as they walked back to the shooting line. "Everyone thought we were the odd couple. Everyone but us."

"Why odd?"

"Let's put it this way," Jeremy said. "I have a great-uncle who's an earl. Rafe has an uncle in prison named Earl."

She laughed.

"We didn't care about any of it, though. Mum was a music professor at WVU, concert pianist. Bill was an electrician, very blue-collar and proud of it. He didn't even want Rafe to go to college, much less art school. When Mum started encouraging his talent, telling him she could help him if he wanted, his dad wasn't happy. Thought we were putting ideas in his head."

"Some ideas are good to have in your head, aren't they?"

"It was more than that. He liked it better at our house. Never wanted to be home." He smiled, and Emilie could tell he was replaying a treasured memory. "I remember the first time Mum made me practice piano when he was over . . . Humiliating. I told him he could go upstairs and play Xbox or whatever until I was done. He didn't want to. He sat on the sofa in the music room, sketching in his notebook while I played. That became our after-school routine. I'd play piano while he sketched me or Mum or our dog. He'd never heard much classical music before, but in two weeks he was addicted to it. Ludovico Einaudi released his album *Divenire* that year, and we listened to the CD so much Mum had to buy a second one so we'd stop stealing hers. Rafe's favorite was track six, 'Primavera.'"

"So . . . you were best friends in high school, and then you got lost together but not really because you said you could've come home but didn't want to. Hmm . . ."

She shot another arrow and missed the target again. But she didn't mind. She was getting much, much closer to hitting the target she was actually aiming for . . .

"*Hmm?* What's *hmm?*" he asked.

"If I got lost, I'd want to go home. But you said you two didn't. Therefore, I hmm." She raised her bow. Jeremy took her elbow in hand and moved it up a few inches again.

"If you'd met Rafe's dad, you'd know why he didn't want to go home. No hmm necessary."

"That bad?" She shot another arrow, and at least this time, it hit the white of the target. And it stuck.

"Bobbi told Mum that the day after Bill's funeral, she went out and adopted a cat."

Emilie had met the cat, a brown tabby named Big Al, who had his own chair at the kitchen table. Luckily, he showed no interest in Fritz, asleep in his carrier. Too fat and happy to go hunting.

"Lonely?"

"She'd wanted a cat or dog forever, but Bill wouldn't allow it. If they had pets in the house, Rafe might not want to hunt animals anymore."

"Poor Rafe." She lowered her bow. "Sometimes in school, somebody might try to make fun of me for not having a dad. And I would be like, 'I met your dad. I'm good, thanks.' Your turn?"

"My turn."

"Thank God."

She stepped away to let Jeremy take her place on the line. He nocked an arrow.

"Hmm," she said again.

He turned and glared at her. "Now what's *hmm*?"

"Can I ask a question?"

He eyed her sternly, and she knew he was onto her. "Only if it's archery related."

"Um, it is," she said. "It is archery related in every respect."

"Go ahead."

"So . . . when did Cupid's arrow first hit you? The day you met Rafe, or was it later?"

He froze momentarily, then pulled back at the string and released the arrow. Gold.

She waited. And waited. He looked at her.

"Day we met. The second we met. For me anyway."

"Gay? Bi? Pan? Fun at parties?"

"That is not even remotely archery related. And I prefer the term *unisex*."

"Unisex?"

"Like a T-shirt. Fits both men and women. Plus, T-shirts are tops."

Emilie groaned and punched him in the upper arm. "That was inappropriate. So so *so* inappropriate."

"You asked," he said. He didn't even have the decency to rub his arm and pretend her punch had hurt.

"What about Rafe?"

"Why don't you go ask him yourself if he's gay, bi, or fun at parties?"

"I will *not* be doing that."

"Smart. But yes, to answer your question, he likes girls. And me, for some reason."

Emilie muttered, "I can think of a few reasons."

"Thank you," he said. "So what gave me away? The Subaru?"

"Exhibit A—you did not appreciate it when I made a joke about Rafe impressing girls with his big sexy bed. Exhibit B—when he showed his face after shaving, you looked like . . . you know, in the movies when the vampire finally sees the sun after centuries of darkness? Like that. No, even better." She breathed in dramatically. "Like in the live video for 'Silver Springs' in 1997. You know, when Stevie turns and starts singing the chorus directly to Lindsey, and the stage *melts* at the savagery?"

"The *savagery?*"

"When Rafe came out without his beard, you looked like you could have eaten him with a spoon. That, my friend, was savagery."

He gave her a look but didn't answer. He shot his arrow. It hit the line between the red and the gold. Not quite the center, not quite a bull's-eye, but pretty close.

"What about Rafe? Was he in love with you too?"

Jeremy pulled another arrow and took a breath. "When we were gone those six months, yes. But only then. With Rafe's dad . . . Well, his dad was one of many, many reasons we didn't want to come back home."

He shot another arrow. It hit the gold. Then another. Gold.

"I knew it," she said. "I totally knew it. Stevie and Lindsey. They went to the same high school too. Ah, this is amazing. Rafe is your Silver Springs." She wanted to pat herself on the back.

"Rafe is not my overpriced D.C. suburb."

"No, no. That is not what the song's about. The song is about how when two lovers are in a band together, even when they break up, or the band breaks up, they're still joined together because of the beautiful music they made. You, sir, are Stevie Nicks. And Rafe is your Lindsey Buckingham."

"At least I'm Stevie in this bizarre fantasy of yours."

"I love you so much for that," she said, giving him a hug he didn't seem to enjoy very much, but he took it without complaint. She let him go.

"Wait, if you've been in love with him for literally ever . . . why didn't you come back and visit him? He's pretty pissed you—"

"I did." Jeremy released another arrow. Gold again.

"You did."

He pulled another arrow from the quiver and straightened out the feather things on the end. Not feathers, he'd told her. The fletching.

"When he was twenty-two, Rafe got in a car accident. He was driving to the Crow in his sleep and ended up in a ditch. He'd had a few incidents before, but this time, they decided to commit him to a place called Brook Haven."

"Mental hospital?"

"Yeah. I took the first flight I could find and drove to Brook Haven straight from the airport. He could only have one visitor at a time, and Bobbi was back with him. Bill was in the waiting room. He wasn't happy to see me. Called security and had me kicked out. He blamed me for us getting lost. Easier than blaming himself."

"You should tell Rafe you tried to see him. He should know."

Jeremy shook his head as he nocked his arrow.

"Rafe took his dad's death hard. It's harder when there's unfinished business. I shouldn't have gone anyway. Tempting fate."

"I'll tell him if you—"

"No, you won't. And that's more than enough about me. What about you? Boyfriend? Girlfriend? Anyone you're leaving behind in Ohio?"

"Oh, me? Nobody. Ever."

"Ever?"

"I just want a family again," she said, "not boobs and boners in my face. Priorities, man."

Jeremy looked at her, then said, "Agree to disagree."

He pulled back the string again—

"Oh no." She gasped as a realization hit her quick as an arrow in the guts. "He doesn't remember it. If Rafe doesn't remember anything from when you two were lost, and that was when you two were together, then he doesn't remember . . ."

Jeremy drew back the string.

"I don't know what's worse, that he doesn't remember I'm in love with him or that he doesn't remember he was in love with me." Jeremy smiled, but it was so fleeting she wasn't sure if she'd seen it or not. "At least I can still play 'Primavera.' I can play it from memory. If I had to, I could play it blindfolded."

He sent his last arrow flying. Gold.

· ✳ ·

CHAPTER TWELVE

MOM WASHED THE DISHES while Rafe dried. Through the window over the kitchen sink, he saw Jeremy and Emilie taking turns shooting arrows from the five-yard line. He couldn't hear what they were saying to each other, but every now and then, Emilie would laugh, and they could probably hear it in the next county.

"They're having fun out there," Mom said, scrubbing the caked-on crumbs from the pie plate. Dinner had been fried pork chops topped with caramelized onions, salad, and apple pie for dessert. Why hadn't he cut his hair and shaved his beard off months ago? He knew why. Because every time they were together, Mom would tell him to call Jeremy.

"Sounds like it."

"It's been nice to see your face again. Forgot how much you take after me." She gave him a wink. "What made you change your mind?"

"Maybe I just missed your pie."

"Oh, sure, that's gotta be it," she said with subtle sarcasm. Emilie's laugh rang out again.

"I can handle these on my own. You ought to go out there and show 'em how it's done. You know you want to."

He did want to, but he was afraid to go out there. It felt like his father was watching him, making sure Rafe did what he was supposed to do— help his mother with the dishes.

"Go on." She'd caught him staring out the window and lightly elbowed him. "Go have fun."

"Dishes are more fun," he said.

"If you say so." She glanced out the window again. "That Emilie is a sweet girl. Quite a talker."

How long had he and Jeremy been alone downstairs while Emilie was up here with Mom? Long enough to wreak havoc.

"Lord, what did she say?"

"Nothing much. She said she'd hired Jeremy to look for her sister, a girl named Shannon Yates."

He knew that tone of voice, that look. She was fishing for something.

"When your son goes missing in a state park, you learn the park rangers' names pretty quick. You learn their wives' names, their kids . . . You put your hands on their shoulders sometimes," she said and reached out and put her hands on Rafe's shoulders, "and you say things like, 'Mike, tell me the truth. Are we ever going to find my son?' And they say things like, 'I don't know, Bobbi. We've never found Shannon Yates, and we've been looking for her five years now.' And you never forget that name because you know what Shannon's family's going through because you're going through it too."

Rafe met her eyes. This was the most they'd talked about his disappearance in years.

"They need me to go with them," Rafe said. "Not want. Need."

His mother slowly nodded. "I see."

"If you don't want me to go with them to the Crow, I won't." He glanced out the window to where Jeremy was showing Emilie how to keep her elbow high enough.

"I'd be happy if you never left this house, but that's my problem, not yours."

"I feel bad even thinking about going—"

"If you want to help that girl find her sister, I'm not going to stop you. I'm not going to enjoy knowing you're out there, but I'll survive it. Survived worse."

"Dad made me promise to never—"

"He's gone, baby. Let him go."

Her dismissiveness caught him off-guard. "Do you even miss Dad?" Rafe demanded.

"Do you?" She turned to him, waiting for an answer, hands still in the soapy water. He looked out the window. "I shouldn't have said that," she said, scrubbing a plate although it was already clean. "You're just a lot more forgiving than I am."

"No, I'm not."

She opened her mouth, then closed it again. Whatever she was going to say, she didn't let herself say it. Instead, she smiled brightly.

"Stay here. I got something for you." She took the dish towel from him and dried her hands off before tossing it back on the counter.

It was only a minute until she returned, carrying something in a large black case. He already knew what was inside it.

"Mom."

"Open it. Early Christmas gift."

Heart racing slightly, Rafe took the case from her, laid it on the kitchen table, and opened it, revealing a sixty-inch White Stag takedown recurve bow made of hand-carved marblewood.

"Mom. You didn't have to do—"

"Oh, but I wanted to. This is the right one, isn't it? The one you were gonna buy? Right size? Right arrows? Right poundage?"

"This is it. This is exactly it."

He'd ordered this bow at the archery shop in Kingwood four years ago. Then his dad had died. Nothing to do but cancel the order and use the two grand he'd saved for it to help cover the funeral expenses. He'd forgotten how much he'd wanted it until now.

Quickly, he assembled the bow and strung it.

"I love it," he said.

"A few steps up from what you've been using."

"I've been using Dad's." Rafe's father's bow was a forty-year-old Arrowsmith Shrike. A great bow, but it had never felt like a perfect fit. This one, though . . . he wrapped his fingers around the grip . . . They were made for each other. He couldn't wait to show it to Jeremy.

"Now you have your own. You take it with you tomorrow to the Crow."

"Are you sure? You swear?"

"I don't want you to go back to the Crow. But if you want to help Jeremy and that girl, you should do it."

He ran his fingers over the supple limbs of the bow, tracing the veins of the woodgrain. Outside, Emilie groaned, followed by another of her bubbling laughs. He wanted to be with them, but guilt still held him back.

"How come you never blamed Jeremy for us getting lost? Dad did."

He could see her hesitate before answering. "I was too busy blaming your father," she said. But then she smiled softly and nodded her head toward the backyard. "Now go show 'em how it's done."

Rafe walked out to the backyard. Jeremy lowered his bow when he saw him coming.

"Thank God. I'm shooting for shit tonight. Come show Emilie how to do it right."

"He's lying. He got six in the gold," Emilie said to him.

Rafe joined them at the shooting line and peered down the lawn at the target.

"Were you shooting with buckshot?"

"I'm not used to shooting this close," Jeremy said.

"You could throw them into the target better than that," Rafe told him.

Emilie shook her head, tsk-tsking him. "This is not a supportive learning environment."

"Very sorry," Rafe said, although he wasn't. He'd missed roasting Jeremy's aim. "I apologize for saying the target looks like a drunk guy threw arrows at it from a moving car."

"You didn't say that," she said.

"Meant to."

"Just shoot, Robin Hood." Jeremy gestured toward the target, then took Emilie by the arm and moved them back a few feet.

"Not from here." Rafe started walking off. Jeremy and Emilie followed him as they passed the twenty-yard line, the thirty-yard line, the forty-yard line . . .

"No way," Emilie said. "Are you serious? Are we in another zip code?"

"If this were the Olympics, we'd be way out there." He jerked his thumb over his shoulder to a line even farther back. He pulled an arrow and nocked it. "You need a stabilizer and a sight to shoot from there, though. But we practiced for hunting, not contests. If you're good at forty yards, you're amazing at twenty. Unless you're Jeremy."

"That would hurt my feelings if I had any," Jeremy said. But Rafe saw him wink at Emilie for some reason.

Rafe ignored them both, then released his arrow with a *zzzt*, which landed with a satisfying thud in the gold inner ring.

"West—by God!—Virginia!" Rafe and Jeremy shouted in unison.

"Wow, you people really do say that." Emilie peered down the field. "Was that a bull's-eye? I need binoculars to see that far."

Rafe shrugged. "Not quite, but close." Rapidly, he put four more arrows into the gold. His bow already felt like an extension of his arms. It belonged to him in a way that his father's bow never had. He pulled a sixth arrow and nocked it.

"New bow?" Jeremy asked. Rafe shot his arrow. Gold. He held out his bow and let Jeremy take it. He whistled in appreciation. "Fit for a king."

"From Mom," Rafe said as he took it back. "In case I need it in the Crow tomorrow."

"You're coming with us?" Emilie asked, dancing in place, which warmed his heart.

"I won't say Mom's okay with it, but she's not going to stop me."

Jeremy said, "I knew it. But I'm glad she gave you her blessing."

"So glad you're coming with us," Emilie said. "You're kind of scary, but I think that'll work in our favor."

"Am I scary?" he asked Jeremy.

"I'm not afraid of you."

"Maybe not scary," Emilie answered. "Intimidating? Mainly because you don't talk constantly, and I do not relate to that at all. Also, you are holding a weapon."

"So are you," Rafe said.

"Yeah, but I don't know how to use mine."

"Show Emilie how you kill the spider," Jeremy said.

"What's a spider?" Emilie asked. "I assume you don't mean an actual spider. Because I object to the senseless killing of spiders. Unless it's two A.M. and one's on my bed."

Jeremy pointed at the target, squinting one eye. "That little cross in the middle of the gold is the spider. We used to play a game where we'd try to hit it in one, dead center, from forty yards. You kill the spider in one, you win the world."

"Killing the spider at forty yards in one shot is practically impossible," Rafe reminded him. "You can't even see it from here without a sight."

"If it's an impossible shot," Jeremy said, "why did your father spend his entire life trying to make it?"

"Why not try? Even if you're off-center, it's still ten points," Rafe said.

"I still can't see it," Emilie said. "Let me look." She jogged down the field toward the target, chanting, "Don't shoot me, don't shoot me, don't shoot me . . ."

Rafe looked at Jeremy. "You think she wants me to shoot her?"

"You can kill the spider in one. I know you can. You know you can."

From the target, Emilie waved her hand and whistled for them.

"This thing?" She pointed at the tiny cross inside the very center ring.

"That thing!" Jeremy replied.

"No way!"

"She's right," Rafe said. "No way. If Dad couldn't do it—"

"I've seen you do it."

Rafe looked at him. "When did I—"

"Twice," Jeremy said. "Once when we were missing. But the first time, right here." He pointed at the shooting line under Rafe's feet. "You stood there, took one shot, and killed the spider."

"That never—"

"It happened. It was a perfect shot. I knew you'd done it the second the arrow hit the target. Even your dad knew. Your dad knew, and you saw what I saw—his ego dying right before his own eyes, being outshot by his fourteen-year-old son, who liked to draw sketches of poodles. It killed him that you made that shot, so you said, 'I think it's off-center.' Then you ran down the field to the target, and I was right behind you, Rafe. I was there. I saw you pull out the arrow. I saw you tear the paper to hide the evidence. And you yelled back to your father, 'It was off-center, Dad!'" He rolled his eyes in disgust. "I don't know who I was more pissed at—you for lying to make him feel better or your father for looking so relieved."

"I remember that day, and I missed it. By a hair, yeah, but I missed it."

"You didn't miss it." Jeremy looked at him, wouldn't look away.

Rafe couldn't stand Jeremy's eyes on him like that. He couldn't stand the weight of expectation. It was easier when nobody thought he could do anything special. Now he wanted to kill the spider. He wanted to be as good as Jeremy thought he was. But he wasn't.

"Try to kill the spider. Just try it," Jeremy said. "Dare you."

"Dad always said you were a bad influence."

"Holy crap, that's a long way," Emilie said as she jogged back up to them. "What's going on?"

"I bet Rafe that he could kill the spider in one. I've seen him do it before," Jeremy said.

"Not a chance. I'm out of breath just walking there and back."

"Try it," Jeremy said. "Nothing to lose."

Rafe gave in. "Anything to shut you up."

He moved into position. He knew there was no way he could do this, but he wanted to try because what if he could? It was his father who'd taught him how to use a bow and arrow and shared with him the secret of archery.

Put your heart where you want your arrow, son, Put your heart there first, then aim for your own heart.

Rafe put his heart into the target right where he wanted it, then he released his arrow.

Emilie gasped softly. "I think you got it. Did you get it?" She ran down the yard to the target. Rafe started after her, Jeremy following. But he already knew the verdict.

"Off-center," Rafe said. It hit off-center because of course it did. Because it was an impossible shot now and always and forever. "Told you so."

Rafe pulled the arrow from the target and slid it back into his quiver. Jeremy said, "You'll get it next time."

CHAPTER THIRTEEN

EMILIE WOKE FROM strange dreams that left her head spinning. From the window of the tiny guest room, she saw the gold and silver fingers of dawn climbing over the tops of the mountains and stretching into the sky. If Ohio had mountains, she thought, she would've gotten up a lot earlier every morning.

Awed, she watched the sunrise until she heard the soft scuttling sounds of a wide-awake fancy rat who wanted his breakfast. She unzipped the top of Fritz's large mesh pop-up tent, and he happily scurried into her hands and up her arm.

She kissed the top of his head and carried him to the kitchen to get his breakfast.

Rafe was already awake and dressed in dark hiking pants, a long-sleeved gray T-shirt, and a blue-and-black plaid flannel shirt on top. She hadn't quite cut his hair short enough, so when he leaned over the map, a lock fell across his forehead. Easy to see why Jeremy was so hung up on him, even after fifteen years apart. She didn't even have any interest in Rafe, and it was hard to keep her eyes off him.

"You're staring again," he said without looking up at her.

"Just admiring my handiwork," she said. "You look chef's kiss," she said, then kissed the tips of her fingers.

"You know, you don't have to say every thought out loud, right?" he said.

"Yes, I do."

She smiled, then got Fritz his chopped apples and pellets. As he ate, she studied the map Rafe had spread across the table.

"That's Red Crow? Bigger than I thought," she said.

"Looks smaller to me," Rafe said.

"What do you mean?"

He ran his fingers over a section of the forest. "This is where we went missing. There's a desire trail to a place called Goblin Falls."

"What's a desire trail?"

"That's when people make their own unofficial trails. But everyone knows about it. We knew about it. Jeremy told the police that's where we went off-trail. A few hikers say they saw us on that trail too. And that was the last time we were seen. Twenty-four hours later, we'd vanished from the park. Which makes no sense."

She looked down at the map that read RED CROW STATE FOREST TOPOGRAPHICAL MAP in the corner. Someone had drawn circles all over with pencils. Search areas?

"Why not?" she asked.

"You see this?" He tapped a line on the map and ran his finger down it. "River. Leads right to a main highway. And here? Trails. Trail here and here. You can get lost in a place like that, but you can't stay lost. You either die from injuries or exposure or dehydration or . . . you find one of, God, *fifty* trails and walk out in a day or two."

"You were injured, right? Head injury?"

"I had an MRI. No signs of head injury. Even a healed one. And Jeremy wasn't hurt. He could have gone for help."

"He said you all stayed away because you didn't want to come home."

She gave Fritz his applewood stick, which he happily munched on, oblivious to the turmoil around him. She envied the little guy.

"Right, right," Rafe said. "But say we were hiding in the woods. Not lost but hiding. Where were we all that time? There's no cave system in Red Crow. The park's been mapped a thousand times. Dad even had satellite photos. Detailed ones." He pulled one out from under the map and looked at it. "No houses, shacks, shanties, lean-tos, tree houses . . . And the first search-and-rescue parties were thorough. See?" He made a circle on the map with his hand. "This is as far as we could have gotten in twenty-four hours, and every inch was searched. They should have found us. They were right on top of us in that park, and we were . . . what? Invisible? And where were the bones?"

"Bones?"

"I went from five-four to five-nine. I put on twenty-five pounds when we were missing. Jeremy put on thirty and was almost six feet tall by the time we left. That happens to teenagers, but not when you're starving. If we were hunting out there, where were the bones? Dad never found a single deer carcass, a dead rabbit, not even a snare or a spear or the remnants of a cooking fire."

"People have hidden out in the woods. That guy in that park in Oregon—"

"Yeah, but no one was looking for him. As soon as they started looking, they found him in a day. God, I would kill to remember . . ." He ran a hand through his hair, exhaled hard. "'We are saddened to report that all avenues of discovery have been exhausted in the search for Ralph Howell and Jeremy Cox. There will be no further searches of the area. We ask everyone to keep the Cox and the Howell families in your thoughts and prayers. Thank you.'"

It sounded like he was reading from a cue card.

"What was that?"

"On June thirtieth, the police announced they were ending the search to find us. Their tactful way of saying they thought we were already dead."

He pulled a sheet of paper out from under the map, a photocopy of the news story.

"Your dad kept this?"

"He kept it all. He never stopped searching. But where the hell were we?"

She was hesitant to say it, but she thought he could handle it. He was already asking the questions.

"Searching behavior," she said softly.

"What?"

"Jeremy told me about a thing called 'searching behavior.' When people are grieving someone they lost, they'll go on long walks or long drives. Even when someone's died, they'll search because they feel like they have to do something. He said a lot of the time, it's guilt." She ran her hands over the whole of the map, the size of a kitchen table for four. "That's a lot of searching."

"A lot of searching, a lot of guilt?" he asked her.

She wanted to say yes, but this time, she managed to keep her mouth shut.

"He should've been furious with me. I went missing for six months. Not six hours. Six months. I talked back to Mom, and he slapped me and ripped up my sketchbook. I got back from being lost, and he didn't even yell at me. All he said was 'You're home. It's over. Let's pretend it never happened. Don't look back.' And he never hit me again."

For the first time since she came into the kitchen, Rafe met her eyes.

Then he looked past her, over her shoulder. She turned around in her chair.

"Did I miss a meeting?" Jeremy stood in the doorway, arms crossed in front of his bare chest. He had on hiking pants but nothing else. His rust-colored hair was slicked back with water.

She looked at Rafe, who was looking at Jeremy. Staring, in fact. Well, even she could see Jeremy had very, very nice arms. The shoulders weren't bad either, even she had to admit that.

"You got up early," Emilie said into the awkward silence.

"I had bizarre dreams," Jeremy said.

"Me too," she said.

Rafe looked up at them both, brow furrowed.

"You too?" Emilie asked him.

Rafe nodded. "We were all in a ship. The front, whatever it's called, was carved with a dragon."

Emilie sat up straighter, now more awake than if she'd had a gallon of iced coffee.

"We were sailing toward the edge of the world."

Jeremy said, "And we were going to fall off."

It was quiet a moment, then Rafe said, "We wanted to fall off."

Silence filled the kitchen. Emilie cuddled Fritz to her chest for comfort. Jeremy put his hands on her shoulders. Rafe rested his chin on his fist. His blue eyes were open wide in confusion and wonder.

In a church whisper, Emilie said, "Mom was in my dream. She kissed me goodbye and told me she was proud of me."

"Mum was in mine. She said, 'Have fun, my love, but watch your back.'"

They both looked at Rafe.

"Dad was there," he said so softly it was almost like he was confessing to a crime.

"What did he say?" Jeremy asked.

"He said he'd never forgive me if I left Mom."

Emilie was afraid to ask, but one of them had to say it. "What are you going to do?"

Rafe looked down at the table without answering, then met Jeremy's eyes again and said, "We don't need the maps, do we?"

"I never actually said we did. All we need is you."

Something passed between them in the look they shared. Like they were daring each other to be the first to jump off a cliff.

"Okay," Rafe said. "I guess Dad will just have to get over it."

· ✳ ·

CHAPTER FOURTEEN

A HALF HOUR LATER, they all gathered on the front porch. Rafe's mother seemed resigned to their leaving. She stood in her slippers and flannel bathrobe, a stern look on her face as she gave them their marching orders.

"All right, kiddos. I don't like letting you go," his mother said, "but I know you've got to do it. I know what it's like to have someone I love in those woods. I know what it's like to bring them home again. You promise me with all your heart you'll be safe as you can."

"Promise," Jeremy said.

"I promise," Emilie said.

Rafe nodded. "Of course, Mom."

"Good," she said and took a shuddering breath. "Now, presents. You got your new bow, baby, so this is for you, Red." She pulled a plastic baggie from her robe pocket and gave it to Jeremy, who took it with a smile. "That's an antique, but it would have gotten you two home in five hours back then."

"Is that a Nokia?" Emilie asked, eyes wide with awe. "I've heard about those."

"They'd survive the end of the world," Jeremy said.

"Still works to call 911," Bobbi said. "Fully charged and waterproof."

Jeremy tucked it in his pocket.

"For Miss Emilie." From her other pocket, she pulled out a pale leather sheath with a large knife in it. "That was Bill's old hunting knife, good as new." Emilie was almost shaking as she took the knife from Bobbi.

"Will I need this?" she asked.

"You better take it," Bobbi said, "and hope you don't need it. But you'll be glad you've got it if you do."

"Right. Thank you."

Bobbi took another shuddering breath. Rafe couldn't imagine what his mother was feeling now, allowing her son to walk back into the woods that had taken him from her before, and all to help a girl she barely knew.

"All right. You three hit the road, hit it hard, and come back to me before the rest of my hair goes gray."

With that, they were dismissed. Bobbi walked them all to the car. Each of them got hugs and kisses on the cheek. The longest hug was for Rafe, who hated to let her go. But he knew if he didn't, she never would. He pulled back and she released him.

"It'll be okay," he said. "Might be a good while before we come back, but we'll come back."

"I know," she whispered. "I hope I know."

Bobbi let Rafe go and then turned without another word and went back into the house, shutting the door fast, like if she didn't, she might come back out and stop them.

The three of them got into Jeremy's Outback. The roads between home and the Red Crow State Forest were all terrifying switchbacks hidden in shadows. Nobody but natives could drive well on West Virginia roads. Forty-five country miles could take ninety minutes if you didn't know what you were doing. And Jeremy clearly didn't know what he was doing.

"Grandma was slow, but she was old," Rafe said. "My beard's going to grow back by the time we get there."

Emilie snorted from the backseat. "You are driving in a rather snaillike fashion."

Jeremy glanced at her in the rearview mirror. "Can it, Prius." He looked at Rafe. "Can you do better?"

"So much better it's causing me physical pain."

"Aren't you the man who literally got arrested for driving in his sleep?" Jeremy asked.

This should have hurt Rafe's feelings. It didn't. It felt like old times, actually. Old times he'd missed, though he would never admit it out loud.

"I'm awake now."

"Fine." Jeremy slowed and turned onto the nearest side road. Rafe got out, and they switched places.

They started off again on a particularly treacherous winding road kids at their high school had nicknamed "Slaughter Alley." Rafe took it fast and loose like he had a thousand times before.

"I want to get there too," Jeremy said, melodramatically clinging to the door. "But I'd like to get there alive."

Rafe couldn't stop grinning. "I learned to drive on these roads. You learned to drive, I don't know where . . . Wait, did you ever learn to drive?"

"I never should have talked to you in Miss Farris's class," Jeremy said. "My original sin."

"Do they have Subarus in England," Rafe said, "or are you guys still on carriages?"

"Just drive, redneck," Jeremy said.

"That's an offensive term," Emilie said from the backseat. "You should apologize."

"What? Redneck?" Jeremy said. "Not if I'm being literal. Check the back of his neck."

Rafe tilted his head forward so Emilie could look, and that was the exact moment Jeremy slapped the back of his neck.

"Ah, I'm driving, asshole."

"That was for punching me."

"Are we there yet?" Emilie said from the back.

It felt like a party in the car. A celebration. They couldn't get to the Crow fast enough. He felt the slightest tug in his stomach like a rope was tied around it and someone somewhere was pulling the rope. The closer he got to the park, the harder the pull. There was no turning back now for any of them.

Finally, Rafe pulled into the Red Crow State Forest parking lot. When he turned off the engine, the gravity of what they were doing seemed to hit everyone at once.

"Guess we're here," Emilie said quietly.

"Now what?" Rafe asked Jeremy.

"First, no phones." Jeremy held up his iPhone before tossing it in the glove compartment. He held out his hand to take theirs.

"What? Why?" Emilie asked. "There's stuff on there I wanted to show my sister."

"Tough. No phones. The Nokia is all we're going to take. You both will thank me later."

Rafe gave his up without a fight. He was done fighting.

"Come on, Princess." Jeremy wagged his fingers at her, motioning for her to hand it over.

"I have pictures of my mom on my phone," she said as she reluctantly gave it to him.

"Sorry," he said. "But safety first." He slammed the glove box closed and got out of the car. Rafe took a breath, then got out after him and opened the door for Emilie.

"Okay, anybody watching?" Jeremy asked as he opened the back hatch.

Emilie wrapped her arms tight around her middle like she was trying to hold herself steady.

"I don't see anybody," she said.

Rafe didn't either. They were alone. Jeremy took out a bag and unzipped it. A long black bag that Rafe assumed held a tent or something. It didn't. It contained a short sword.

"I'll explain later," Jeremy said as he strapped on a scabbard or whatever it was called and sheathed his sword.

"I thought you were joking about the sword fighting," she said. "People don't sword-fight. Who sword-fights?"

"I do," Jeremy said.

Strangely, Jeremy looked right with a sword. And Rafe was glad he had one. He got out his bow and his quiver and slung them across his back.

"Got your knife?" Rafe asked Emilie. She took it out of her pocket and held it up. "It goes on your waist. Got a belt?" She didn't, so Jeremy dug one of his out of his overnight bag and stabbed a hole through the leather to fit her smaller waist. She held up her shirt while Rafe fastened the knife to the belt and strapped the belt around her waist.

"Tight enough?" Rafe asked.

"Perfect," she said. For some reason, Jeremy was watching this exchange intently, almost smiling.

"What?" Rafe asked him. "What's wrong?"

"Déjà vu," Jeremy said. "Ignore me. We better go."

A few drops of rain fell.

"It's going to start raining," Emilie said. "That going to be a problem?"

Jeremy shook his head. "No. We ready?"

A story came back to Rafe, an old story he'd heard in church as a kid. The story went like this: A town suffered a terrible drought. The drought grew so bad that the church pastor called for everyone to come together to pray for rain. No one came. No one believed. Then he saw a girl walking up the church stairs carrying an umbrella.

The girl had an umbrella because she knew it would rain.

And Jeremy had a sword.

You don't bring a sword into a park unless you think you will need a sword. And if Jeremy thought he needed his sword in the Crow, either he was crazy or . . .

Something was out there.

"Rafe?" Jeremy's voice broke through his trance.

"What?" Rafe asked.

"You all right?"

He wasn't. He absolutely was not all right. Something stirred in his blood. He looked around him, saw the peaks and slopes of the forest hills, deep and dark. When he was a little kid, those hills had fascinated him, frightened him. He'd gotten into his head those rolling hills were sleeping giants covered in thick green animal pelts, giants who'd wake one day and take the world back for themselves. He'd outgrown his fear of them, of course. Now it was back.

Jeremy put his hand on Rafe's shoulder, stopping his trembling like a finger on a tuning fork.

"Something's happening," Rafe said. "I . . ." He rubbed his face. "What's happening?"

"Time to go."

He took a deep breath. "What do I do?"

"Just walk," Jeremy said.

Emilie said, "Where?"

But Rafe already knew the answer. He pointed to a trail. "There."

They walked across the parking lot to the start of the path. Rafe hesitated only a second before he stepped off the pavement and onto the soft brown dirt of the forest floor. He stood still, very still, as he felt something like electricity begin to course through his feet.

He took another step forward. Red and gold leaves skittered across the path in front of him. The dark forest beckoned like the song of the Pied Piper.

Emilie crept forward, peered down the trail and then back at Jeremy.

"What's out there?" she asked. "Something's out there. I thought—"

"What?" Jeremy asked. Rafe looked at her. Was she feeling the same strange pull he felt?

"I thought I heard someone call my name," she said.

Jeremy smiled. "Better go and answer them."

· ✳ ·

CHAPTER FIFTEEN

THE WIND WAS COLD and rain dampened her clothes, but Emilie didn't complain. She didn't know what lay ahead of them, only that if she wanted to find her sister, she would have to go there. So she went along, like a needle in a record's groove. They hiked in near silence for nearly an hour until Rafe came to a stop for seemingly no reason.

"What's wrong?" she said, her voice hushed as if they were doing something more dangerous than had ever been done before.

"We go here." Rafe pointed to a narrow dirt path off the trail.

"That's it," Jeremy said. "That's the way to the Goblin Falls. I remember coming this far."

They stepped off the trail and made their way down the path. Rafe led. She followed. Jeremy brought up the rear, even catching her once when she stumbled over a tree root.

"You all right?" he asked as he put her back on her feet.

"Terrified and happy. I don't know why."

He smiled. "I do. Keep going, Princess."

Where Rafe was leading them, she had no idea. He didn't seem to either, only that he followed his nose or his feet or his gut. They passed the Goblin Falls, a small rock formation where water trickled gently over the sides, and kept going and going, until they reached a steep hill. It seemed there was no way up, but Rafe wasn't deterred. He led them around the base until he found a hidden path, maybe a deer trail or something, that zigzagged up the hillside.

Carefully, the three of them made their way higher, higher, and finally, a few yards ahead was another, even higher ridge. Rafe went up and over it first, then turned around and reached out his hand for her. Behind her, Jeremy held her steady while she took Rafe's hand. He pulled her up, and she scrambled over to a plateau. Jeremy came last, but they all made it.

After pausing to catch her breath, Emilie stood up, looking around.

"Weird," she breathed.

Rafe nodded. "Very, very weird."

Here, the trees seemed older to Emilie, larger, thicker, taller. She saw enormous maple trees and oaks with bent and twisting branches. A sacred grove. That's what this place was. She almost expected to see druids in white robes. Bonfires. Chanting. Ancient magic.

And in the center of the grove stood a strange tree. The tree seemed to rise forever, spread forever, the emperor of all trees. The trunk was as wide as a small car, with a hollow in it like the mouth of a screaming ghost. Or a door.

"God . . ." Rafe breathed, not saying the word like an oath but a prayer.

"Jeremy?" Emilie said. Her voice shook. "What's happening?"

She turned and found him standing under the emperor tree, gazing up at a branch.

"Look," he said.

A bird perched on that branch, scarlet as a cardinal, big as an eagle. But it wasn't a cardinal or an eagle, but a bird she'd never seen before.

"That's a crow," Rafe said. "That can't be a crow."

Emilie didn't know much about crows but knew they didn't come in red. She covered her mouth with her hands.

"No way," Rafe said. "That's . . . that's impossible."

"Nothing's impossible," Jeremy said quietly. A wild wind rose and whipped their clothes, their hair. Emilie stared into the hollow of the tree. It beckoned her.

Above their heads, the red crow spread its great crimson wings and took flight.

It flew into the door in the tree. It didn't come back out.

"We have to go in together," Jeremy said.

"Jay, are you sure about this?" Rafe asked.

"Surer than I've ever been in my life."

"All right," Emilie said.

And Rafe said, "Okay."

Jeremy said, "Ready? Steady? Go."

Holding hands because that's what you do when you're scared and don't want to be alone in a strange, dark place, the three of them stepped out of the world and into another.

Wonderland

"WHY, SOMETIMES I'VE BELIEVED as many as six impossible things before breakfast," said the White Queen to Alice in *Through the Looking-Glass.*

Fair warning: If you've never believed any impossible things before, now is a good time to start.

CHAPTER SIXTEEN

RAFE WOKE FACEDOWN in soft leaves. He groaned, then pushed onto his back. He felt like he'd slept for days and dreamed a thousand dreams. Waking was a long, slow climb out of the bottom of a deep well.

He blinked his eyes open. Something seemed off with his vision. The forest looked wrong. In his mind, he crawled back to the last thing he remembered. The hill. The top of the hill in Red Crow. Emilie, Jeremy, and him.

And a red crow.

A red crow in Red Crow.

A red crow like the one he'd painted so many years ago.

A dream? Did he have a head injury? These were not West Virginia trees. If he could trust his eyes, then these trees soared a thousand feet too tall, the trunks a hundred feet too thick. But they weren't like the pictures he'd seen of the sequoias in California. Those were ancient and massive evergreens. These trees had leaves every color of Easter—pink and green and blue and yellow and white. They looked like the trees he might have scribbled as a child, five different fat Crayola markers to color one tree. Yes, these were a child's imaginary trees made real somehow.

And it wasn't raining. Only a wisp of white cloud danced across an electric-blue sky.

Overhead, something flew from one tree branch to another. Enormous wings, like a small airplane. It landed on a tree branch a hundred feet in the air and perched like a bird. Golden wings. Black beak and legs. Ten feet tall or more. A condor? There were no condors in West Virginia.

So either he was still dreaming . . .

Or this wasn't West Virginia.

The great golden condor leaped from the branch, and the flapping of its enormous wings set a breeze blowing through his hair.

"Holy . . ." Rafe scrambled to his feet and watched the bird disappear into the sky.

The forest was real. But how could it be real?

Rafe took a deep breath and inhaled something extraordinary, a scent like dew or some sweet perfume he'd never breathed before. It smelled pure, unpolluted. Whatever this place was, there were no factories, no cars spewing exhaust, no coal mines or coal plants. He was, he knew, smelling air the way it was supposed to smell.

He took a step toward one of the enormous tree trunks and touched it. It felt gritty and real, like pine bark. He turned a circle. A giant loomed above him, but it was only a stone statue of an old man half-hidden by sea-green moss.

Maybe he laughed. Maybe he cried. Maybe both. He found a rock outcropping, ran up the side, and stood atop it to see deeper into the forest. A gentle mist rolled across the ground. Overhead, the red crow sat on a branch and cawed.

"Did you do this?" he asked the crow.

"Shh . . ." Jeremy's quiet voice came from behind him. "You'll wake the unicorn."

Rafe spun around and saw a small white unicorn asleep, its head resting in Jeremy's lap.

A unicorn.

In Jeremy's lap.

He sat with his back against one of the enormous trees, and the unicorn, which was no bigger than a Shetland pony, let out a soft breath as Jeremy stroked its white mane and graceful neck. Its single horn shimmered like pearl.

In a low voice, Jeremy said, "I have your bow and quiver, but I think we dropped a backpack outside the tree. Emilie's over there. She hasn't woken up yet." Rafe glanced over, saw her small form curled under Jeremy's coat. "She will soon. You were asleep over an hour."

Asleep. Rafe's mind latched onto the word. Asleep and dreaming? It looked like his dreams—the trees, the stone statue, and Jeremy—but he never remembered his dreams like this, only the most fleeting images. No, not a dream. He'd been dreaming for fifteen years. Now he was finally awake.

Something hooted above him. A brown owl with a black face gazed at him placidly. The black feathers formed a perfect circle, making it look like a bird with one enormous eye.

"Cyclops owl," Jeremy said.

Rafe covered his mouth with his hand and breathed through his fingers.

"Rafe? You all right?"

Cyclops owl. Condor. Unicorn.

"Jay." Rafe got one word out. It was all he could manage.

"They're lazy as house cats," Jeremy said. "We might be here all day. I don't mind. I've missed this." He smiled and twined his fingers into the unicorn's white mane. "When I was a kid and Mum and I flew on planes, I would look out the window and see the clouds under us. I wanted to touch them. Mum said you wouldn't feel anything but water vapor, but I didn't believe her. They had to feel like something." He stroked the unicorn's long neck again. "This is what clouds are supposed to feel like."

Rafe couldn't stop gazing all around him, drinking in the beauty like a man who's crossed the desert on his knees drinks water from an oasis.

"I painted all this. I carved it," he said to himself. He spun, looked at Jeremy.

"I wasn't painting my dreams. I was painting my—"

"Memories." Jeremy nodded.

"This is what you wouldn't tell me?"

"Couldn't tell you."

"Why?" The agony of fifteen years of loneliness, of wondering, of wandering, of waiting for an answer he thought would never come could be heard in that one single word, that question that was the biggest question of all.

"Because if I told you, we never could have come back."

"What?"

"Look around, Rafe. This is magic. Real magic. Magic plays by its own rules, and it doesn't like to answer questions. Magic brought us here. It let us go home again. It let us come back. If magic imposes rules on you, you follow them, no matter what."

"You couldn't tell me?"

"No, but I can now."

Rafe sat down on the ground a few feet from Jeremy and the unicorn.

The unicorn snorted softly through its nostrils. A unicorn snore?

"Once upon a time in West Virginia, two boys were lost in the woods. But not for six months. We were lost, but only for a day and a night," Jeremy said. "You were upset. You'd fought with your dad the night before, and you didn't want to go back home. We thought if we missed the bus on purpose, we could get Mum to pick us up, and it would be so late in the day you'd just spend the night at our house. That was the plan."

Rafe had heard this much of the story before.

"You and your father had gotten into it before, but this felt different for some reason. You weren't just angry. You were scared."

"Of what?"

"Going home," Jeremy said. Rafe nodded for him to go on. "We were trying to find the Goblin Falls. They're not on any trail, but we'd heard you could find them if you followed a certain game trail. We thought that would be a good enough excuse to explain why we'd gone off-trail. And that's how we got lost. And we were lost. Completely, stupidly, utterly lost. It was about five in the evening when we realized we had no idea where we were. So, of course, we panicked and did everything wrong."

Jeremy told him everything about that day, how they followed the game trail, thinking it would lead to somewhere with people. It didn't. They found a high hill and climbed it, thinking they could see the trail. They couldn't. Huddled together for warmth, they slept on the hill.

Jeremy gently stroked the sleeping unicorn's horn with the backs of his fingers. "By morning, you were in bad shape, barely able to speak. You got dehydrated so fast, I thought we'd never get home alive. It's the most scared I've been in my life." He raised his head and looked up and around, then smiled. "Then I saw this red bird on the tree branch. I thought I was hallucinating. It looked like a crow. It called out to us and then flew into the hollow of the tree. Somehow I knew we were supposed to follow it. So we did, and then . . . we were here."

"Here? Right here? Where's here?"

"The kingdom of Shanandoah," Jeremy said. "Not like the river in West Virginia. You spell it with an A. Shanandoah, named for Shannon Yates."

"My sister," Emilie said.

Rafe looked over his shoulder. Emilie had woken up and now stood clinging for dear life to the side of one of the trees.

"We never called her Shannon. Never knew that was her name. Here, she's known as Skya. This is her kingdom."

"What do you mean this is her kingdom?" Rafe asked Jeremy.

"I mean, she's the queen. Queen Skya."

Emilie dropped slowly to her knees.

"I'm sorry I pushed you away at first," Jeremy said to Emilie. "For years, I'd worried someone would ask me to find a missing girl in the Crow, and I'd have to tell them no without telling them why."

"You don't have to explain," Emilie said. "This . . ." She looked up at the tree that seemed to rise a mile into the sky. "This explains everything."

"Skya didn't tell us much about her life before she came here, but she did tell us about you. She said she had a baby sister who'd been adopted somewhere to someone. She didn't even know your new name. Here, you're known as the Lost Princess of Shanandoah."

"Me," Emilie said. "That's me? Oh my God, that is me."

"You." He stroked the unicorn's long neck again, then looked at Rafe. "The first time, we woke up right here. Well, somewhere over there." He pointed toward a gently flowing stream. "I didn't even notice the trees at first, only the water. It was fresh and clear, so I got you some to drink, and you started to come around. I had never been so happy in my life to see your eyes open." He paused for a breath. "Then the Bright Boys found us. Terror, even holy terror, draws them like moths to a flame."

"Bright Boys?" Emilie asked.

"Hard to explain them," Jeremy said. "The queen calls them her immortal mortal enemies. They look just like teenage boys, but somehow you know they aren't. The teeth are too sharp. They eat fear. They could smell the fear all over us. We must have looked like a feast to them. I don't remember much. We probably both passed right out. Then suddenly . . ." A look almost beatific, like a saint in an old painting seeing a vision, passed over Jeremy's face. He didn't smile. He didn't need to. His eyes glinted as if a candle burned behind them. "I heard a hunting horn. I'd never heard one before except in movies, but I knew that's what it was. I woke up to the sound. Then all these girls with swords rode in on horses and started killing the Bright Boys left and right. It was incredible." Jeremy laughed. "Even scared shitless, I remember thinking, *I like these girls. I hope we can be friends.* By this point, we were tied up together on the ground, so all I saw at first were two feet in brown boots. Then this one girl looked down at us and smiled. She said, 'You two look a little lost.' That's how we met Skya. Your sister," he said to Emilie, "saved our asses." He looked at Rafe again. "The next thing I remember is being in the palace, and you were with the healer getting the cuts on your back cleaned up. Then there was wine and pie and I don't remember much else from that first day except we decided if we were dreaming, we didn't want to wake up."

"It was the Bright Boys who gave me the scars?"

"I didn't see it happen, but Skya said they could be vicious like that."

Rafe closed his eyes and let his head fall back in relief. Now he knew where his scars came from, finally had an answer to a question that had plagued him for years. And it was a much better story than a bobcat or barbed wire. He almost laughed. A little part of him had been afraid it was something . . . but it wasn't. That's all that mattered.

Rafe opened his eyes.

A tear landed on the unicorn's face.

"Sorry, milady," Jeremy said to the little creature. "Go back to sleep."

"I've never seen you cry before," Rafe said.

"Yes, you have."

Rafe moved closer, as close as he dared. Without touching the unicorn, he leaned forward and, using the cuff of his shirt, wiped the tear off Jeremy's face.

"Thank you," Jeremy said.

"This place is where we were those six months?" Rafe asked. Jeremy nodded. "Why did we leave here?"

"That's a long story and the Bright Boys are probably already on their way here. But the short answer is you." He nodded toward Emilie. "Skya always left an empty place for you at the table." Jeremy looked at Rafe, met his eyes. "I was going to go back home alone, but you wouldn't let me leave without you. So Skya took us to the Witch of Black Wolf Cave. She's the one everyone goes to when they need magic. The witch told Skya it was too dangerous to send us both back, dangerous for Shanandoah. One of us says there's a magic kingdom through a door in the woods, and they think, 'Oh, he's crazy.' Two of us say it? Maybe they go and look."

"What did she do?"

"She divided the memories in half. I would remember this place and everything that happened here, but she took away my memory of how to get back. Red Crow would be like the Bermuda Triangle for me. And from you, she took all your memories of this world. But she let you remember—"

"How to get back," Rafe said. "That's why I drove here in my sleep?"

How often had he woken up in his truck to find he'd driven halfway to Red Crow? Six times? Seven?

"How did she make me forget everything?"

"She gave you a book. A sketchbook with a silver lock on it, like a diary. You had to draw in it everything you needed to forget. You shut yourself up in your room and drew all day and all night. The next morning, we rode to the Painted Sea and boarded the queen's ship. We sailed a day and a night and another day to the farthest shore. Then we changed into our old clothes. What was left of them anyway. Our shoes didn't fit anymore. I was given a map of Red Crow. I had to burn it. That's how I was made to forget the way back to the door in the tree. Then you shut your book and locked it with the combination. You passed out." Jeremy snapped his fingers. "When you woke up, all your memories of our time here were gone."

Rafe nodded but didn't speak. That was it. That's exactly what it had always felt like . . . that he'd locked up his memories, and if he'd only had the key . . .

"The spell came with one rule," Jeremy said. "One ironclad rule that could never be broken—I couldn't tell you. If I told you, we'd never be allowed to come back. Before you locked your book, you looked me in the eyes and said, 'Whatever I do, whatever I say, no matter how much I beg you, don't tell me anything.'"

Rafe closed his eyes and exhaled. "God. Jay . . ."

"But I wanted to tell you. A thousand times a day, I wanted to tell you. But I couldn't. I didn't want to lie to you, and I couldn't tell the truth, so the only other option was to stay away from you." The unicorn lifted her head for a chin scratch. "They love having their chins tickled. On the worst days, the days I wanted to tell you the most, I told myself if we ever wanted to scratch unicorn chins again, I needed to keep my big mouth shut. Right, milady?"

She bleated softly, just like a toy trumpet.

"I know," Jeremy said to the unicorn, talking the way everyone does when addressing a small animal or a baby. "You're exactly right."

"What did she say?" Rafe asked.

"She said you should pet her."

"I don't want to scare her."

"You won't scare her."

Rafe held out his hand to the unicorn and waited.

She turned her regal head and pushed her velvet nose into his outstretched palm. His fingertips brushed the shimmering horn, and he felt a laugh bubble up in his soul, but he kept it inside. He stroked her silky jaw and her ears and neck and yes, yes, it did feel like holding a cloud in his hand.

Jeremy said, "Welcome home, Rafe."

"I'm sorry. I'm so sorry, Jay."

"You don't have to apologize."

"Yes, I do."

All his anger at Jeremy, all the bitterness, which was simply another name for loneliness, fled like shadows at the touch of the sunlight.

"Is there more?" Rafe asked.

"A little more," he said. "It's all in your book of memories."

"Then let's go find—"

Suddenly, a hundred or more unicorns appeared in the clearing. White unicorns, silver-gray unicorns, black unicorns with golden eyes ... Rafe inhaled and froze in fear and wonder and awe. The unicorn in Jeremy's lap raised her head and blinked. One large unicorn stepped forward and snorted his mild displeasure.

"Better run along, milady," he said. "Don't get us into trouble with your father."

The unicorn pushed her snout once more into Rafe's palm. One last pet. One last scratch behind the flickering ear. With a light and sprightly leap, she rejoined her family. At some secret signal, the herd ran off together deep into the woods.

Jeremy stood up and handed Rafe his bow, his quiver. A few white strands of the unicorn's mane dusted his shirt.

"How did you survive fifteen years without . . ." Rafe waved his hand at the world, the impossibly beautiful world. "This?"

Jeremy gave him a little rueful smile.

"You don't want to know."

Jeremy

IF YOU ACTUALLY DO want to know how Jeremy survived those fifteen years, read chapter seventeen. If you don't, you can skip it, and we'll meet again after, in chapter eighteen. But I would read it if I were you.

P.S. If you noticed Emilie suddenly seemed to disappear from the last chapter . . . good eye.

· ✳ ·

CHAPTER SEVENTEEN

A YEAR AND A HALF before he found Emilie—or, more accurately, before Emilie found him—Jeremy was on a flight: LAX to Sydney. A teenage surfer had disappeared from the beach, and Jeremy knew she'd fallen asleep on her board and was drifting farther and farther out to sea with every passing minute. The Australian Navy was looking for her and would, he prayed, find her before his plane landed.

Fifteen-hour flight. He needed distracting. *Outdoorsman* magazine had asked him to write a piece for them—"Top Ten Tips for Surviving if You Get Lost in the Wild."

If only he'd had a list like that for surviving the real world after having gone to another world. As the plane flew across the Pacific, Jeremy came up with the list he wished someone had given to him . . .

Jeremy Cox's Top Ten Survival Tips for Those Who Have
Gone to Other Worlds and Come Home Again

1. *Learn how to lie.*

Two days after they came back, Jeremy was still in the hospital, although he wasn't sick. That was the problem, actually. Everyone expected him to be sick. He'd been missing six months in the woods. He should've had any number of illnesses and/or conditions. Malnourishment for starters. Injuries. Lyme disease (the woods were full of ticks, after all). Tooth decay. Dysentery. Scurvy.

But Jeremy and Rafe were in perfect health. More perfect than when they left. Taller, stronger, bright eyes and clear skin, Jeremy was the picture of youth and vigor. Rafe, too, though everyone thought he had a head injury, since he remembered nothing about the past six months. When the police asked Jeremy how Rafe got the scars on his back, he told them, "I don't know. We passed out and when we woke up, something had attacked Rafe. Bobcat, maybe." The "something" made it feel less dishonest. But if he said, "Monsters in the form of boys ambushed us in a magical kingdom," they would never have let him out of the hospital.

Still, it became clear the doctors were not convinced Jeremy and Rafe had been lost in the woods for six months. Kidnapped then? Except what kidnapper ever returned a child in better condition than he took him? Jeremy said quite plainly to all who would listen that they were lost in the woods but had survived on their own. No one kidnapped them. No one harmed them.

"As many churches as you have in this bloody state, you'd think you all would know a miracle when you saw one," Jeremy's mother told them. "Stop asking why and let me take my son home."

The doctors and police finally gave up. They didn't know how to investigate or diagnose miracles.

So Jeremy was to be released the next morning, which gave him one last chance to see Rafe alone. He pretended to sleep until he knew from the deep quiet on his ward that everyone else was sleeping. He snuck out of bed and into Rafe's room across the hall. Lucky break. Bill wasn't there, only Bobbi, dead asleep in the chair by her son's bed.

Rafe wasn't sleeping either. His eyes opened as Jeremy slipped into the room. Without a word, he moved over, making room for Jeremy in the narrow hospital bed. In the quiet, they whispered so softly they were almost communicating telepathically.

Mum's taking me out of here at dawn. We're going to hide out with my grandparents in Oxfordshire for a few weeks.

Then you're coming back?

Soon.

Jeremy saw something glinting silver around Rafe's neck. He held it up to the little shaft of light in the room that seeped in from the street-lights in the parking lot.

Some priest gave this to Mom. She gave it to me.

Mum gave me hers too. Yours is better. It has a stag on it.

Want to trade? I've actually heard of your guy.

Quietly, in the dark, they traded heavenly protectors. Jeremy sent his heart with St. Anthony to watch over Rafe.

Bobbi stirred a little in her sleep. They were running out of time.

I still don't remember anything. They're going to run more tests on me.

Don't be scared. There's nothing wrong with you.

What happened, Jay? Did something bad happen? Is that why—

Nothing bad happened. We were gone. Now we're home. That's all. I have to go.

Jeremy wanted to kiss Rafe goodbye. He'd kissed him goodbye so many times he almost didn't know how to say goodbye without kissing him. He would have to learn.

But you'll come back soon, right? Rafe asked again.

Soon as I can.

And nothing happened out there?

No, nothing. We were just lost, that's all.

One conversation, two minutes long, five lies.

2. *Accept that there really is no coming home again.*

It wasn't until they were at his grandparents' house in Kingham, Oxfordshire, that Jeremy's mother told him Martha had died while he was gone. She said all the comforting things a mother was supposed to say—*She was a very old dog . . . She didn't suffer . . . No, no, it's not your fault she died . . .* But he didn't really believe any of that. Martha loved him, yes, but she loved Rafe even more. And if any animal in the world can die of grief, it was a dog in love with a boy who was never coming back.

His grandmother fussed over him, and even promised him a new dog. She acted like he had simply gone on an extended holiday, nothing more.

"This must be a shock to you, leaving the States and coming here after all you've been through."

It wasn't a shock to him. Once, he had woken up in a medieval palace, in a bed with posts made of braided willow trees with a red crow named Aurora perched on the footboard, and a girl called Queen Skya offered him pie and wine. He remembered his first taste of Shanandoah—the pie was rainberry and lemon with sea salt, served with spiced wine in silver goblets. The memory made his mouth water.

When you have drunk spiced wine with a queen and a crow, nothing can shock you anymore.

His mother was English to the bone. Whatever trauma she'd been through while he was gone, she kept it to herself. Only once did he see past the "Keep Calm and Carry On" smoke screen. A few days after coming to his grandparents' house, he sat at their upright piano in the drawing room and played "Primavera" from memory, played it perfectly.

Only when he'd finished and seen his mother in the doorway staring at him in near horror did he realize the mistake he'd made. No one went six months without playing piano then picked up a piece that complex without missing a note. And there were no pianos in Red Crow State Forest.

But there were pianos in the Moonstone Palace, in the queen's private salon. Skya loved to hear him play nearly as much as Rafe did. If anything, Jeremy was better now than before they'd disappeared.

"I would practice in my head when we were lost," he said. A lie. "I didn't want to get behind."

She nodded, pasted on a smile. "Sounded lovely. Well done, my love."

They never spoke of it again.

3. *Learn to live with boredom.*

Jeremy was enrolled at a school close to his grandparents' house. Not a boarding school. His mother couldn't bear the thought of it. But it was a good school. They even had a fencing team. He knew how to sword-fight—Queen Skya's Valkyries had taught him—but fencing with a foil was different enough that he only seemed like a natural to his fencing master, not some sort of mad prodigy. Fencing kept him sane. It felt like he was keeping his skills sharp for the day he would return to Shanandoah.

He didn't forget his quest to find the missing princess but didn't know how to begin quite yet. Queen Skya had warned him the gift she was giving him would help only if and when the lost princess was ready to be found. Could be tomorrow. Could be ten years or never.

Until then, he simply had to go on with his life.

One day at school, a girl named Lily lost the opal ring her grand-mother had given her for her sixteenth birthday. Weeping, she stood before the class and described the ring, offering fifty pounds to anyone who found it.

Other boys in his class laughed and snickered. Some of the girls too. But Jeremy would have wept, too, if he'd lost Rafe's St. Hubert medal, which he wore night and day, never taking it off, even in the bath.

Opal ring, gold band . . . Jeremy pictured it on Lily's finger. Then, out of nowhere, like a flash of lightning inside his brain, he saw it in her bag. He plucked her bag off the floor, stuck his hand into the bottom, and pulled out the ring. It had slipped inside a torn seam.

Lily gasped and ran to him, tears gone, all smiles, all hugs.

"How did you know?" she asked. The look in her eyes was awed. He didn't like it. It was a taste of things to come.

"Mum lost a ring in her bag once. It was loose on her finger and fell off. Lucky guess."

Lily became his first girlfriend, but it didn't last very long. A month or less. He was still in love with Rafe. And relationships, he was quickly learning, required honesty. Jeremy couldn't tell Lily the truth about anything. Even the question *How are you?* required a lie. He always said he was fine. Eventually, she caught on to the fact that she was doing all the talking, and he was only pretending to listen. Not her fault. She was a lovely girl, but his heart was far away.

"You can tell me anything," she said one night. "I promise you can." She'd wanted them to sleep together, but letting his guard down scared him too much. Would she figure out he'd done that before and want to know the who and the when and the where?

"There's nothing to tell," he said. Another lie. There was everything to tell. Nobody could begin to understand how it felt to be the only person on the planet who knew the best way to lure a mermaid to you was putting candles into paper boats and setting them adrift. Mischief makers, the mermaids surface to blow the candles out. Rafe had caught one and made her tell him a secret. She told him the secret, whispering it in his ear. Then she kissed him square and deep on the mouth.

"You can catch me anytime, beautiful boy," she said before she swam off, leaving him wide-eyed and blushing.

"Fess up, dollface. What secret did she tell you?" Queen Skya demanded.

"She said someone on this boat was in love with me."

"Not me," Queen Skya said. "Ask them." She pointed at her Valkyries.

"Not me," said each of the seven Valkyries.

Jeremy pointed at Aurora, who betrayed him by flying off the boat, leaving only him as the culprit. So he admitted it, and he would remember Rafe's smile ten times a day until he died.

"You miss someone in America, don't you?" Lily asked. She was wearing a T-shirt with a mermaid on it.

Finally, a question he could answer honestly. "Yes."

Then she broke up with him, which was a relief. He could only pretend to enjoy watching movies in her bedroom so much before he lost his mind and screamed, *I have fought battles with demons cloaked in human form. I have swum with mermaids and parlayed with giants and hunted snow deer on hidden mountains with queens and princes! No, I do not want to watch Harry Potter with you again!*

"Hope she's pretty."

Jeremy only laughed. Rafe was very, very pretty, yes. Even mermaids thought so, and they were notoriously hard to impress.

4. *Be prepared. There will be people who don't believe your cover story.*

He picked Magdalen College and studied English. His mother thought he was following in his long-dead father's footsteps. Thomas Nigel Cox had graduated from Magdalen with a first in Classics and English. But no, going to Magdalen was a private joke between Jeremy and the universe. It amused him, being a student where C. S. Lewis, creator of Narnia, had once been a Fellow.

He played the part of a university student well enough until the day a tutor's daughter went missing. She was only three years old and wandered from the back garden into the woods behind the house, and by the time Jeremy heard the news, she'd already been missing two days.

Her name was Petra, and when Jeremy called her name inside his mind, he saw her curled up asleep, deep inside a rotting log.

It took him one hour to find her.

When the police asked how he did it, this time he told them something more like the truth.

"I was lost once as a kid. I suppose I know where to look."

He saved the girl, but the price was high. His face was all over the news. A reporter with *The Times* put two and two together. The headline read, FORMER LOST BOY FINDS LOST GIRL.

After that, Jeremy went into search-and-rescue full-time. The princess he was supposed to find didn't want to be found, apparently. But maybe if he looked for enough girls, he'd find her by accident.

He didn't charge much for finding missing girls unless the parent or partner hiring him was rich, and then he charged through the nose. By the time Jeremy was twenty-three, he'd already found nine missing women and girls and two bodies.

A wealthy couple in Short Hills, New Jersey, offered him ten grand to find their ballerina daughter who had "eloped" with her dance master. Standing in the foyer of their seven-bedroom house, Jeremy said he'd take ten up front and ten when he found her. They liked that he said "when" and not "if," so they paid him in cash.

The ballerina daughter, age sixteen, and her kidnapper were a few hours outside of Vegas when Jeremy caught up with them at an IHOP.

He nursed a black coffee while waiting for the police to come and arrest the dance teacher. The girl looked exhausted, with dark circles under her eyes, long hair barely brushed, her eyes darting around the restaurant as if seeking someone to see her, to save her. He met her eyes and nodded, hoping she would understand he was there to help her. She looked away.

While waiting, he wrote a postcard to Rafe that read simply, *23 September 2015—Las Vegas.*

As he dug the postcard stamps from his wallet, his phone buzzed.

Someone had posted something to his Facebook page. Jeremy hated social media as much as he needed it as a cover. Occasionally, he posted safety tips so he'd seem like any other outdoor influencer—hug a tree; wear wool socks, not cotton; always travel with matches—instead of a freak with magic powers on a quest to find a missing princess.

Reluctantly, he opened the app to read a new comment from someone calling themselves Johnny Cosmic. The comment was one word—*Liar.*

Jeremy deleted the comment immediately. As a rule, when someone tried to start something with him online, he'd ask himself three questions:

1. Do I know if this person is over the age of twenty-one?
2. Do I know if they're mentally stable?
3. Do I know if they're under the influence of drugs, alcohol, or a cult leader?

If the answer was no to any or all of these three questions, he'd delete the comment. These were also the three questions he'd ask himself before sleeping with someone.

Mr. Cosmic wasn't done with him, unfortunately. He posted a photo. Jeremy squinted at it, not sure who he was seeing or what. Then he knew.

Rafe. A picture of Rafe's naked back. Jeremy recognized those long pink scars that ran from his shoulder to his hip. In the photo, Rafe appeared to be sound asleep on white sheets.

The caption to the photo read, *This is not what a bobcat attack looks like. What is Ralph Howell hiding? Admit it! You were never lost.*

Jeremy took a screenshot seconds before Johnny Cosmic deleted the comment and picture himself. Even the account was gone.

He stared at the screen. Was this a recent picture? He couldn't see much of Rafe's face, only in profile a little, his straw-blond hair falling over his cheek. And who took it? Someone he was sleeping with, obviously. Call him sexist, but he had trouble believing a woman would take pictures of her lover's scars while he was unconscious. A man then? Jeremy ignored the stab of jealousy, sharp as a sword point in his stomach. Well, it wasn't like he'd been an angel all these years.

Then Jeremy saw what he hadn't seen at first, distracted as he was by Rafe's body, so vulnerable and exposed in sleep. A wristband. A white wristband. Plastic from the looks of it, with black type on it.

A hospital wristband. Brook Haven. A nurse or an orderly or another patient had recognized Rafe's name. One of the West Virginia Lost Boys "truthers" who believed there was more to the story than two fifteen-year-old boys lost in the woods for six months.

Jeremy hated them for two reasons. One, because they pulled insane and evil shit like this on Rafe. And two, because they were almost right.

Finally, the police arrived. Two uniforms. Jeremy subtly pointed out the girl, and the cops nodded, walked up to the table, and, five minutes later, the dance master was in handcuffs. Jeremy tried not to think about what would happen next to the girl. Her family would want to celebrate, to pretend everything could and would go back to normal. But it wouldn't. He would tell them that "normal" and "back to normal" were two very different things.

Then he sent the screenshots to the lawyer he kept on retainer just in case Johnny Cosmic was more than an internet troll. At least once a week, someone contacted him online, taunting him, *Tell the truth. We know you were abducted by aliens. We know.*

If only it were that simple.

5. *You'll be lonely. Just don't let it make you stupid.*

Ten years after they went missing, Jeremy gave in and went back to Morgantown to see Rafe. Although Jeremy had gone no-contact with

Rafe, apart from the postcards, his mum filled him in every time they spoke, so he knew exactly where and how to find him. At the Hotel Morgan, painting a block of rooms like he did every summer.

Jeremy checked in to the hotel, and the next morning, he waited at the bar, where he had a good view of the elevators. Rafe arrived at eight. He wore old canvas trousers covered in splotches of white paint, a gray V-neck T-shirt, and work boots. He looked thin, tired, the older brother of his teenage self. The older brother who didn't sleep last night or the night before or the night before that.

Often, Jeremy wondered if his memory had exaggerated the strange beauty of Rafe's eyes, that weird ice blue almost like a husky's. But no. His eyes were exactly like Jeremy remembered. Rafe glanced vaguely in his direction once without a flicker of recognition. Jeremy was in a new Tom Ford suit, wearing glasses he didn't need and a beard he was still getting used to.

Rafe waited for the elevator, and it took everything within Jeremy not to stand up, go to him, grab him by the shoulders, and say, "Don't you know who you are? You haunt the nightmares of monsters. Old men take off their caps when someone speaks your name. You painted the portrait of a queen, and it hangs in the Great Hall. Don't you remember?"

But no, of course, he didn't remember.

Then the elevator door opened, and Rafe got in, then the door shut. He was gone.

Jeremy took the stairs up to his room, stripped out of his clothes, and then laid naked on the cold tile floor. He didn't vomit, but it was a close call.

They'd stayed at this hotel once, he and Rafe. His mother had been given a free night in one of the suites when she agreed to play piano for a friend's daughter's wedding. She gave the room to him and Rafe and slept at home in her own bed. They stayed up until four in the morning eating, talking, never even turning the TV on because, whether they would admit it or not, they were both hoping something would happen. It didn't, because no one on earth was more chickenshit than a boy in love with another boy who doesn't know he's in love with him.

The only reason Jeremy knew Rafe was also hoping something would happen was because, eventually, they'd fessed up. One night, he, Rafe, and Queen Skya had played Shanandoah-rules croquet by lantern light in the courtyard behind the palace.

Every wicket they missed, Skya said, they had to tell her a secret. So Jeremy offered the embarrassing confession that he didn't want to learn how to hunt. He just wanted an excuse to hang out with Rafe. Then Rafe missed and said he had purposely forgotten to pack a T-shirt that night they were staying at the Morgan, so maybe Jeremy would give him one of his. He slept in the shirt every night for a week.

Skya said purposely forgetting a shirt and then sleeping in said shirt for a week counted as two embarrassing confessions. Rafe said, "Well, damn," then missed his next wicket to even things out.

After that, they all started missing their shots on purpose. Jeremy. Rafe. Skya.

Jeremy's secret—he'd been in love with Rafe from the moment he saw him.

Rafe's secret—he hadn't been in love with Jeremy from the moment he saw him. It had taken more time, like a painting he wanted to get just right. He couldn't rush it. But the day he started to fall—before he even knew he was falling—had to have been the first time he sat in on Jeremy practicing piano. Why else would he sit there thinking he never wanted to be anywhere else with anyone but Jeremy?

And Queen Skya told them her secret that night, that as much as she loved Shanandoah, she'd often thought of leaving it to find the lost princess. Her mother, who'd given birth to her at fourteen, had brought home a new baby when Skya was ten. A little girl with lungs like an opera diva. But her mother had gotten flakey again and started disappearing for days at a time. Her aunt Marie, who had taken Skya in, said she couldn't handle another child, and her sister was given up for adoption. For one beautiful month, Skya had a sister.

But she hadn't gone back for the simple reason that she was afraid to. This was her kingdom, after all. It needed her more than her sister did, didn't it?

Or did it?

That night they had a slumber party, piling like a litter of exhausted puppies onto the queen's silken pillows. They'd crossed the border into the hidden country of each other's hearts, and they couldn't bear to leave again.

Jeremy wiped tears from his face. Coming home to see Rafe was a massive mistake. Obviously, Rafe was suffering, but Jeremy could do nothing about it. In Shanandoah, Rafe had made Jeremy promise not to tell him anything so they could go back someday. Jeremy's loyalty was to the boy even if his love was for the man in paint-splattered clothes who didn't notice him sitting twenty feet away.

It was the last time Jeremy let himself try to see Rafe.

6. *Accept that there's no rational explanation for what happened but have fun trying to find one anyway.*

When Jeremy was twenty-eight, he returned to Oxford to visit his mother. She was having a difficult year as Jeremy's father had died by suicide when he was twenty-eight. It was hard, she said, to wrap her mind around her son now being older than her husband.

On his first night back in town, he found himself at the pub where Thomas Cox and Mary Turner met thirty years earlier as students— The Eagle and Child, though Mum always called it The Bird and Baby. He wanted to sit at the table where they'd had their first date, but someone had beaten him to it.

A beautiful woman sat alone at the table. She saw him looking her way and smiled.

"Am I in your spot?" she asked.

"You might be."

"I'll fight you for it."

"Not mine, actually," he said. "My parents', I think. Their first date."

"You can join me." She pointed to the empty chair across from her and moved her piles of books out of the way. He took his pint and walked over.

Her name was Chi, and she was thirty-five, from Victoria Island in Lagos, Nigeria. He assumed she knew as much about West Virginia as most West Virginians knew about Lagos—it exists, and people, supposedly, live there. About this, he was very wrong.

"Ah, beautiful place," she said. "I visited once. The mountains, wonderful . . ." She fanned herself as if overcome by the memory of beauty.

She laughed when his response was a slightly baffled "Why?"

"The observatory."

"Green Bank," he said. He glanced at the books and academic journals. "You're an astronomer."

"Physicist. Well, cosmologist. The fun sort of physics. No one makes science-fiction movies about Bernoulli's principle of fluid dynamics."

Her laugh was like a bell ringing. They were going to be friends. More than friends?

He introduced himself as Jeremy Turner. He let her do most of the talking and learned her family had moved to London when she was ten. Now, twelve years later, she sounded as English as Mary Poppins, though, like him, she could switch accents when she felt like it.

"Tell me something I don't know about the universe," Jeremy said.

"No one knows what ninety-five percent of the universe is made of. How's that?"

"That's a lot of universe to have gone AWOL," he said. "Do you think parallel universes exist?" He'd always wondered if that's what Shanandoah was, but who could he ask? "Other dimensions or planes of existence?"

Her eyes gleamed with mischief as she reached across the table and lightly chucked him under the chin. "Oh, my Jeremy, you watch too much *Doctor Who*."

The flirting was more than welcome.

"You know what this place is?" He pointed around them at the pub— the dark wainscoting, the ivory-yellow walls covered in pictures and plaques.

"A . . . pub?"

"Not just a pub. It's the pub where C. S. Lewis and J.R.R. Tolkien used to fight about their imaginary worlds," he said. "They had a writers' club that met here, the Inklings."

"I've never read them. I like books by girls." She smiled defiantly, as if daring him to tell her she should read them. He didn't.

"Just made me think of Narnia," he said. "Imagine you're looking for a shirt in the back of your closet and end up in another universe. Possible?"

She shrugged elegantly. "No evidence of it, but . . . why not? We thought Einstein was mad when his theories said there were regions of space so dense they collapsed into themselves and formed black holes. Now we've found them. Could there be other dimensions? A multiverse? I wouldn't be surprised."

"So there might be another universe where I stayed at my table instead of coming over to yours," he said, pointing to a now-empty table across the room.

"Precisely."

"Which do you like better? That universe or this one?"

"This one," she said with a smile. "By a light-year."

That was a good answer.

One night in bed, he asked her, "Are wormholes real?"

"Jeremy, this is your pillow talk?" He loved the way his name sounded in her accent. He called her Chi-Chi, which she found equally charming.

"Just looking for an emergency escape route," he said, happy to be where he was for once.

They were in her flat, her bed. He liked sleeping at her place. And it made his mother deliriously happy that he was finally dating someone she was allowed to meet.

"Wormholes . . . it depends."

"On what?" He expected Chi to say something about math or GTR, which is how cosmologists, he'd learned, casually refer to Einstein's general theory of relativity.

"Depends on whether the universe is infinite."

"Let's say it isn't."

"Very well," she said in a crisp tone. This was her tutoring voice. "In a finite universe, it's impossible anything should exist."

"Anything?"

"The world. The universe. You. Me. Us. The likelihood of life existing, thriving, and then developing consciousness? Infinitesimal. So infinitesimal, this world is statistically impossible. Yet"—she fluttered her hands as if the world were a prize on a game show—"here we are."

"But if the universe is infinite?"

"Then yes. Yes to everything. Infinite universe equals infinite outcomes."

"Unicorns?"

"Yes?"

"Dragons?"

"Yes, yes!"

"Infinite monkeys typing infinite *Hamlets*?"

"Yes, in an infinite universe, wormholes have to exist. All possible worlds exist. In fact, there are no possibilities in an infinite universe, just eventualities."

"What do you think it is? Finite or infinite?"

"Oh, I don't know what I think, but I know what I want. I want an infinite universe." She rolled onto her side to face him. "Think about what it means if literally anything is possible. We could be anything you can think of."

"Anything?"

"This entire universe we're in right now could be tiny, fitting in the palm of some being's hand so far beyond us, we're like ants to a giant. And the giant keeps us in jars on her windowsill. We're a computer simulation. We're characters in a storybook left on a train by a girl late for dinner. We're a dream an ancient god is dreaming, and any minute now . . . he will wake. Ask any question in an infinite universe, and the answer is yes. Always yes."

All worlds are possible? Jeremy wanted to believe there was a world where he and Rafe never left Shanandoah, a universe where they're still there, riding out with Skya on their horses, Freddy and Sunny, killing Bright Boys, hunting snow deer and drinking sweet rainberry wine, climbing the great spring trees to watch the firemoths come out and flash their autumn-red wings . . .

THE LOST STORY 155

In an infinite universe, he and Rafe haven't spent the last thirteen years apart. That's the universe he wants to live in, a universe where he could say to Rafe, "Do you miss me as much as I miss you?" or "Do you love me as much as I love you?" and the answer is yes, yes, forever yes. Even if that universe existed only on the pages of a book written by a storyteller in another world in another time in another dimension. Did it matter?

He and Chi parted ways very amicably when he was called back to his work. When she asked him if they'd meet again, he reminded her that if the universe were infinite, they undoubtedly would, which made her smile when she kissed him goodbye.

In an infinite universe, all stories were true stories.

7. *When you begin to question your sanity, remind yourself that the fact that something impossible happened doesn't mean it didn't happen.*

It had been almost fifteen years since Jeremy left Shanandoah, since he'd lost Rafe, and he still hadn't found the missing princess. Maybe he never would. Maybe she'd be lost forever and so would he.

Then his mother died of a stroke, died so fast he wasn't able to make it home to tell her goodbye.

In his grief, he sleepwalked through his mother's wake, forgetting the names of her colleagues and students as soon as they introduced themselves. Later, he'd remember only one person he met that day. A woman in dark blue shook his hand and said, "Jeremy, dear, I know your mother was so proud of you. She told me all the time."

"Thank you," he said for the thousandth time.

"I also knew your father, Jeremy. I was at his funeral too. Shame."

He turned back and looked at her. "You were?"

"So young. I'm so glad you're doing so well. We were all a bit worried."

"Worried about what?" he asked.

"Oh, it's hereditary, they say. Schizophrenia. But you're quite well, obviously. A hero even. It's . . . Well, it's good to see you. Only wish it was under better circumstances and—"

He left. He just left her standing there, prattling on. His father had schizophrenia? His father had schizophrenia, and his mother had never told him? Depression. That's all that was ever said about it. That he was overworked and depressed and no one would publish his books, and in a weak moment, he drove his car into the garage and left it running.

He sat on his mother's sofa with his head in his hands. Why? Why wouldn't they tell him? And then he knew. The woman in blue had told him why.

Hereditary.

His mother didn't want to scare him.

He'd found two different women with schizophrenia. Their families and doctors had told him what to expect when he encountered them. Delusions. Delusions of persecution. Evil creatures were out to get him. Bright Boys? Delusions of reference. Something normal happens, and you think it's happening just to you and for you? A former missing child with a special talent for finding other lost people? Delusions of grandeur. In another world, he served a queen who sent him on a quest?

Delusions and hallucinations and it was hereditary . . .

Jeremy didn't leave the house for a week. He barely ate, hardly slept. It explained everything, didn't it? That's why Rafe didn't remember Shanandoah. Because they never went there. They were lost in the woods or maybe they had been kidnapped? Those scars on Rafe's back . . . not from the Bright Boys but from some maniac who'd held them in his basement?

He tried to remember hunting in the woods or banging down doors or anything other than Queen Skya, the Moonstone Palace, putting his sword into the bellies of Bright Boys and watching them turn into smoke and waft away.

What was real? Was any of it real? Did Rafe ever even love him? Or was all that a delusion too?

On the seventh day, someone rang the doorbell. He didn't want to answer it but then came a knock. Another knock. Jeremy crawled off the floor and went to answer it.

A man in a suit looked at him like he'd seen a ghost. Did Jeremy look that rough? Probably. When was the last time he'd showered?

The man, properly English in every way, plastered on a bland expression and introduced himself as the administrator of his late mother's estate. Certain property had been put into storage for Jeremy, and he was delivering it. He pointed to a small white moving van parked in the drive.

Two young men carried in a large wooden crate and set it in the living room. Jeremy signed some forms without reading them, and then he was alone again.

Even in his despair, he couldn't help but be a little curious. He found a hammer and used the claw end to pry open the crate.

On top of a pile of straw, he found a note from Bobbi Howell of all people. Rafe's mother? What the hell would she have shipped all the way to Oxford in a wooden crate?

Dear Mary,

These are for Jeremy. Ralph painted them in art therapy. He put them out with the trash, but I know he'd want Jeremy to have them. You know our boys. Can't admit how much they need each other. I don't even know if you should show them to Jeremy. Would it make it better or worse? I swear they're like those twins in stories that step on their own toes and punch their own faces so the other one feels it.

I wish I could see you again, Mary. You're the only one in this world who knows what it's like to lose one son and get back a different one.

Love you.
Bobbi

Jeremy dug through the straw and packing material and found that the crate contained paintings. He lined them up along the walls.

They were all of him.

Age fourteen or fifteen, sitting at his mother's piano at their old house on Park. He could almost hear the music coming out of it . . . "Primavera" by Ludovico Einaudi. And a red crow is perched on the open top.

Another painting . . . Jeremy kneels before a young queen holding a sword on the stone steps of a palace.

Another . . . Jeremy in dark leather armor facing off against a silver tiger.

And another . . . Jeremy walking a sorrel stallion through a field of rainberry blossoms.

The style was wild and expressionistic. He could almost see the paint moving like wind across water.

Rainberries don't exist. Not here. But they exist in Shanandoah.

Jeremy hung the painting of himself playing the piano over the fireplace in his mother's music room. He sat at her baby grand and played "Primavera" by memory. He couldn't even picture the notes on the sheet music. It was simply muscle memory, the same muscle memory Rafe used to paint red crows and rainberries. Shanandoah wasn't a delusion. It was real. Somehow, Rafe still remembered rainberries. Not his mind, no, but his hands. His heart. Like the music was in Jeremy.

When he woke up the next morning, he had an email from a TV show wanting to tape a segment in Bernheim Forest in Kentucky. Kentucky, next-door neighbor to West Virginia.

He wrote back and said he'd do it.

THE PLANE LANDED. His phone buzzed with a hundred missed calls and text messages saying the Australian Navy had found the girl. She'd drifted farther than they'd anticipated and they'd only kept looking because Jeremy had suggested the correct search area. He visited her in the hospital. Her skin was blistered from the sun and her voice rasped from the severe dehydration, but her smile when he walked into her room was bright as the Sydney sun.

Her first words were "Will you marry me?"

"I don't surf," he told her.

"Trust me, I don't either anymore."

Saving the girl who could make a joke marriage proposal five hours after facing certain death made finishing his top ten list a lot easier.

It went something like this . . .

8. *Never forget, the price of magic may be high, but it's worth paying.*
9. *If you forget, see number eight.*
10. *If you forget again, see numbers eight and nine.*

· ✳ ·

CHAPTER EIGHTEEN

ONLY AFTER THE UNICORN herd had disappeared into the forest did Rafe and Jeremy notice Emilie was gone.

She'd been sitting by a tree about fifty feet away from them. They saw the tree, but there was no Emilie.

"She was right there," Rafe said. "We were talking . . . She was there, then—"

"Emilie!" Jeremy shouted, his voice echoing through the forest loud enough to rattle the leaves on the great red trees. "Maybe the Bright Boys took her? They usually aren't that clever, but maybe they grabbed her when the herd ran past." He swore violently. "God, they must have been waiting for us. They must have known we were coming."

"Can you feel her?" Rafe asked. "Can you find her?"

Jeremy closed his eyes. He shook his head.

"Nothing," he said.

"She's dead?" Rafe demanded.

"No, she's . . . I can't feel anything. At all. It's like she's hidden. Somehow. Or I can't . . . It's gone. I can't sense her, Rafe. I don't know why."

"Dammit." Rafe bent over and caught his breath. "This is my fault. I wasn't watching out for her and—"

"It's not your fault. We were separated from her for thirty seconds, and they got her."

A small voice in his head taunted him, telling him this was what he'd put his mother through. Coming here had been a mistake.

Jeremy started to say something but stopped and held up his hand.

Rafe felt it before he heard it. The ground rumbled.

"The herd?"

"Horses. Someone's coming." Jeremy drew his sword from his sheath. "More than one. Get ready."

Rafe felt a deep and eerie calm settle into his body. His heart rate slowed, and his hands didn't shake as he nocked an arrow onto his bowstring. The sound of horse hooves grew louder . . . louder. The ground shook harder. He waited.

Out of the misty shadows emerged horses and their riders. Women, all of them, in tunics and leather armor. Rafe counted seven as they galloped into the clearing and reined their horses to a halt. He scanned them for weapons and saw swords and bows.

As if sharing one mind, he and Jeremy took their positions back to back, protecting each other as the riders arrayed themselves in a half circle facing them.

From the corner of his eye, Rafe saw Jeremy lower his sword. The one in the center of the circle dismounted. A tall Black woman in dark leather armor with red gauntlets on her wrists faced Jeremy.

"It's all right," Jeremy said to Rafe. "Stand down. They're with us."

"Are we?" the woman said. "State your name and your business, and we'll see about that."

"Tempest, it's me," Jeremy said.

"Weapons down," she ordered.

Rafe looked at Jeremy, who nodded. Slowly, Jeremy laid his sword on the ground. Rafe put his bow down and his quiver and felt immediately naked without them.

"Name and business," the woman said again.

"Business? The queen's business, always. And name? Jeremy? Red? Hello?" He pointed at his head, his face. "Is it the beard?"

"Prove yourself." She stood before him and pulled her sword, pointed it at him. Rafe took a step forward, but Jeremy moved in front of him, putting himself between them.

"Whoa, wait a minute." Jeremy held up his hands, pleading peace. "What's going on?"

"You could be a Bright Boy," she said. "We've been overrun with them lately."

Jeremy touched the tip of the sword of the soldier he'd called Tempest, then held up his finger to show blood trickling from the cut.

"No smoke. See?"

"So you're not a Bright Boy," she said. "Doesn't prove you're our Red."

"What do you want?" he demanded. "Driver's license? Passport? Library card?"

"You send a card to a library?" said one of the other women, the palest one with white hair.

Rafe felt like a drowning man. Who were these women? What were they talking about? They were all heavily armed with swords on their hips and knives strapped to their boots. He could grab his bow off the ground, but it would be useless in such close quarters. Even if he used an arrow as a spear, he'd get run through with a sword before he could pull one from his quiver. He had to stop this somehow.

He stepped forward and held out his hands.

"I swear Jeremy is who he says he is. I'm Rafe. But none of that matters. The queen's sister is missing. She was just here with us, and now she's—"

It happened fast, but Rafe saw it in slow motion . . . Tempest turning toward him and bringing her sword down as if to cut off his head. Before he could even think of ducking, Jeremy grabbed his sword off the ground and blocked the killing cut.

The sound shocked his ears, the clash of metal against metal.

"Not bad," Tempest said. She wore the slightest smile. "Might be our Red. Might not. Let's keep going."

"Back up, Rafe," Jeremy said.

"What? No. You can't—"

All at once the other six women, still on horseback, pulled their swords and pointed them at him. Rafe froze, looked at Jeremy, who only took a breath.

"Guess they can," Jeremy said.

"Disarm me," Tempest said, "and I'll know it's you. Only you ever could." She pushed her sword into his blade.

"Tempest, it's been fifteen years."

"Then pray you have a good memory."

She fell back but only to strike at him again. Rafe had no choice but to watch as Jeremy parried blow after blow from her sword. It seemed a dance of sorts, and both fighters knew all the steps. Their swords crossed again and again, metal glinting, sparking. Rafe watched in terror and awe as Jeremy wove and ducked and spun out of reach of Tempest's blade. Then he suddenly changed tactics, going on the offensive, pushing her to fall back. And they must've been enjoying the dance, as they kept breaking into a smile.

Although he knew nothing about sword fighting, Rafe could tell they were equally matched, both masters, both shockingly strong and agile. This was Jeremy? Rafe looked at him with new eyes. No, not new. The same awestruck dazzled eyes that had once watched Jeremy playing piano in his mum's music room.

"I don't want to do this," Jeremy said to Tempest. They were both breathless, sweating hard.

"Yes, you do," she said. She swung her blade low and Jeremy put his sword tip onto the ground to block it. As soon as her blade crossed his, he raised it in an arc, using his superior height to knock it out of her hands.

The sword landed on the ground with a soft clatter.

"All right, I did want to do that," Jeremy said, panting. He sheathed his sword. "Now do you believe me? Jeremy? Red? Hello? Hugs all around? Wait, I forgot. Valkyries don't hug."

"One hug," she said. "Since it's been so long."

She smiled and stepped forward as if to hug him, but without warning, she pulled a knife from her sleeve and pressed the point against the center of his chest.

Jeremy slowly raised his arms a little higher.

"This hurts my feelings," he said.

"Now I know it's you," Tempest said. "You always let your guard down too early."

"It's a personal problem. I'm working on it."

"Work harder." She put her knife away again, then held out her hand. Jeremy took it and she gave the slightest smile. "Stand down, Valkyries." The other six women sheathed their swords at once. Still wary, Rafe knelt and picked up his bow and quiver from the ground.

"Jay?" Rafe said. Jeremy turned to him. "Who the hell are you?"

Jeremy grinned and the grin turned into a grimace. He wiped sweat off his forehead. Rafe tried to stop staring at him, but it seemed mostly impossible even with seven heavily armed Valkyries, whatever those were, surrounding them.

"Obviously, I left a few things out. I'm a—"

"Dismount!" Tempest ordered.

The Valkyries leaped lightly off their horses and onto their feet, then put their right fists over their hearts and bowed their heads toward him.

"Your Highness," they said in unison.

He stared at them, then looked at Jeremy for answers. "Wait. What's going on?"

Jeremy said, "So that's what I forgot to tell you. Slipped my mind."

"What slipped your mind, Jay?" Rafe demanded. "What?"

"That's you. They're talking to you," he said. "In Shanandoah, you're a prince."

Introductions

VERY EVENTFUL DAY, YES? Magical kingdom. Jeremy in a sword fight. Emilie's disappeared. Rafe's just found out he's royalty, which is the least of his problems, as he needs to know where Emilie is, and also, he can't seem to stop looking at Jeremy (don't blame him), which he's finding both confusing and annoying (also don't blame him). Under these circumstances, I assume no one wants to wait for elaborate introductions. The seven women on horses are known far and wide as the Valkyries. They're the queen's cavalry and her guard.

Tempest is their leader, already described, but no matter how glorious you imagine her, she is even more so in person.

The other six are as follows:

> Ember—*redhead, temper to match*
> Winter—*she's the pale one with white-blond hair*
> Gale—*dark brown skin, brown hair, griffin tattoos on both arms*
> Torra—*the tall, glowering one with the crossbow*
> Rebel and River—*the olive-skinned black-haired twins who rarely*
> *speak with anything other than their swords*

We now return to our crisis-in-progress.

· ✳ ·

CHAPTER NINETEEN

RAFE WAITED FOR the laugh, for the punch line. No. Nothing.

Jeremy was looking not at him but at the leader, at Tempest.

"He doesn't have his memories back yet," Jeremy said. "Go easy on him."

"I'm a prince," Rafe said in disbelief.

"Yes, Highness. I'm sorry you don't remember that, but I promise you, the rest of us do." Tempest spoke those words, but all the Valkyries nodded in agreement.

"You can freak out about it later," Jeremy said. "We need to figure out what to do now. We should probably—"

"Probably?" Rafe said. Finally he shook off the bewildered daze he'd been in since waking up in this world. "Emilie's gone. While you two were playing Jedi knights, whoever has her was getting away. You all have horses. Can you track? We need to hunt them down, now, and get her back ten minutes ago."

This speech was met with silence.

"I thought you said he didn't remember he's a prince?" Tempest said to Jeremy.

"He doesn't."

Tempest gave him the slightest of smiles. "Are you sure about that? Sounds like our prince."

"Still bossy," Ember said.

"Focus, please," Jeremy demanded. "Where's Skya? We brought her sister and—"

"The queen is on her own mission," Tempest said. "One I'm not at liberty—"

Rafe said, "Someone has Emilie. Is anyone going to help us find her, or do we have to go ourselves? I'm ready to go. Ten seconds until we get a good answer or I'm leaving. Ten—"

Tempest said, "The queen asked me to tell you both, 'Thank you for bringing her sister to Shanandoah. You have fulfilled your promise in full. The princess is no longer your concern or obligation. Please accompany the Valkyries to the palace forthwith.'"

"Skya said that?" Jeremy said. "Was she high at the time?"

"I'm paraphrasing," Tempest said. "She left us a note for you."

She held out a sheet of linen paper. Jeremy took it and unfolded it.

Jeremy read from the paper, "'Stop arguing with the Valkyries, asshole, and do as you're told.—Skya.' Okay, that sounds more like her."

"No, no, I'm arguing," Rafe said. "Emilie is—"

"No longer your concern, Highness," Tempest said. "And if you wish to know more and why, we must go to the palace. You are both under the queen's orders."

"I'm not leaving until—"

"Rafe," Jeremy said.

"No, no, I'm not—"

"One minute, please, Highness." Jeremy took him by the arm, and they stepped away from the Valkyries.

Rafe had had enough of orders. "Highness? Seriously?"

"Better get used to it. Rafe, listen, if Skya told us to go to the palace—"

"I don't know Skya, but I know Emilie. We can't leave her out here—"

"You do know Skya," he said. "You do. And you love her and you trust her with your life. Tempest knew who I was from the first second she saw us. She knew me, and she knew you. That whole song and dance with the sword fight was to buy time for some reason, and apparently it was Skya's reason. We need to go to the palace anyway. That's where your book is."

Rafe stepped away from Jeremy and faced Tempest. "Just tell me one thing, please."

"Anything, Highness," she said.

"Is Emilie safe right now?"

"None of us are safe right now. That's why she was taken. But this should give you comfort, Highness. Right now the princess is safer where she is than she would be with you two."

Some of the terror and fury left Rafe's body at that news.

"Whether you can believe it or not," Jeremy said, "these are our friends."

The funny thing was that Rafe could believe it. He wanted to believe it anyway.

Rafe took a breath. "Is the palace close?"

"We have to ride," Tempest said.

"Where are *our* horses?" Jeremy asked her.

"At the palace," she said.

"You knew we were here. Why didn't—"

"You want your horses? Come back to the palace," Tempest said.

"What are your names?" Rafe asked them.

"Rebel," said one and bowed. "River," said another. One by one they each said their name with a bow.

"I'm not a fan of the bowing," Rafe said.

The smallest Valkyrie, the pale one called Winter, said, "You never were, Highness." In lieu of a bow, she gave him an awkward curtsy, which he found painfully endearing.

"All right. Let's go," he said. And if he hadn't quite believed he was a prince before, he did when every one of them, Jeremy included, immediately scrambled to obey.

"Mount up," Tempest cried out.

Seven horses for nine riders, so Rebel and River rode together, leaving a horse for Jeremy. Rafe assumed he'd ride with one of the others, but

Winter offered him her horse, a brown mare dappled in white spots like a newborn fawn.

"Take mine. I'll ride with Gale," Winter said. "Her name is Sparrowhawk."

"I don't know how to ride," he told her.

Her white eyelashes framed eyes so pale they were almost pink. They widened at that statement, and she shook her head.

"It'll come back to you at once," she said. "Just like bossing us around."

"Sorry about that."

"Don't be, Highness. It's your job."

She handed him the reins and mounted her horse. Her complete confidence in his abilities unnerved him as much as it comforted him.

Everyone was ready but for him. Instinct led him to put his left foot in the stirrup. He did and hopped up, throwing his right leg over the saddle.

"Like riding a bike," Jeremy said. "If the bike could bite you. Let's go. You lead," he said to Tempest.

She ignored him. "Your orders?" Tempest asked Rafe. He looked at Jeremy, who only shrugged as if to say, *Don't look at me. You're in charge.*

"Um . . . Lead the way?" Rafe said.

"Yes, sir." To the others, she said in a commanding tone, "Ride on."

With a kick of her heels, Tempest shot off down the path.

Rafe looked at Jeremy. "You a prince too?"

"What? Me? No."

"Oh, yeah, because that would be ridiculous."

"It would," Jeremy said. "I'm a knight."

HOOVES AND EARTH. Sweat and snot and flying chestnut mane. Rafe leaned in, clung to Sparrowhawk's mane, all on instinct. It felt like when he painted or carved . . . his body remembered what his mind couldn't. He did know how to ride a horse. Knew how and loved it. The exhilaration, the speed, the wind in his face, and the incredible power of the animal under him. Grief and joy warred in his heart. Joy of rediscovering what he'd lost. Grief when he thought of the past fifteen years and what he'd missed out on. After all, you didn't have to be rich to own a horse in West Virginia.

They passed through the forest in what felt like the blink of an eye. From forest to river's edge and then along the banks of a river flashing silver and gold in the evening light. Finally a village or something appeared in the near distance.

Tempest called for a halt, and they reined in the horses and trotted across the stone bridge.

Sweating and tired, Rafe was grateful for the small break.

"What's happening?" he asked Jeremy, who trotted his horse over to him. It was strange to see Jeremy so comfortable in the saddle, like he was born on a horse.

"Water break for the horses."

They rode into the town. Everywhere Rafe looked, it was like seeing a page from a book of fairy tales. Small colorful cottages, thatched roofs, stone bridges, and cobblestone streets, old women sweeping the dust from their front porches with witch's brooms. A blacksmith's shop. A bakery. Children, free and fearless, running barefoot from house to house. He smelled chimney smoke and the sweat of horses. The setting sun over the distant hills turned the clouds to watercolors.

"Where are we?" Rafe asked Jeremy.

"Sleepy Creek," he said. The clopping of the horses' hooves on the cobblestone was a sound Rafe had heard only in films. But it was exactly the same. "We're halfway to the palace."

Jeremy swung his leg over the saddle and dropped to the ground, then grabbed both horses by the bridles and led them to the water.

Rafe dismounted Sparrowhawk with a groan.

"God—" he said with a half-strangled scream as pain spiked up his entire body, from his feet to his neck. If his muscles had been twigs, they all would have snapped. "Ahh . . . that is . . . not good."

"Don't worry," Jeremy said, patting Sparrowhawk's panting chest. "It only hurts the first time. That's a lie. It hurts every time."

"Highness?" A small voice spoke behind him. Rafe turned and saw a woman of about forty years old wearing a green velvet gown that wouldn't have looked out of place at a Renaissance Faire.

"Me?" he said. He would never get used to it.

She stared at him with wide eyes.

"Prince Rafe? Is it you?" she asked.

"I . . . yes?"

The woman ran off, calling out, "The prince has returned! And our knight!"

Quickly, a crowd formed around them, a few dozen men and women, some with children perched on their shoulders or babies in their arms. They were all dressed like characters from books or old paintings except they were all ages and races, as if someone had gathered lost souls from every corner of the globe and dropped them into this old English village and said, "Welcome home."

Impossible, wasn't it? The uncanny feeling passed quickly when Rafe saw their eyes full of fear and hope.

The townspeople wanted nothing from him but to shake his hand and pat his shoulder. Jeremy's too.

Welcome home, Highness. Oh, we've missed you, Sir Jay. Come to dine with us when you can, gents. We'll roast a goose for you and have a dance.

Rafe caught himself smiling, greeting them like old friends.

"Highness?"

He turned toward a soft voice from behind him. The girl who'd spoken had a smudge of flour on her cheek, as if she'd run there from baking something.

"It's really you?" she asked.

"Really me?" he asked. "I hope so."

"You're Prince Rafe?" Then she looked up at Jeremy. "And the Red Knight?"

"We are," Jeremy said, answering for him.

She clasped her hands as if in prayer and hopped on her toes.

"You don't remember me, I know, Highness. It was so long ago. Mama said you rode two villages over at night to fetch the midwife when I was being born breech and brought her back just in time to save us both. Mama asked you to name me."

Rafe wanted to remember so badly it hurt. He wanted to remember that night ride and the panic he must have felt and the beautiful relief of returning in the nick of time. He wanted to remember hearing the baby's cry, holding her, and naming her. What would he have named a baby girl?

"You've forgotten. It's all right," she said. "It was such a long time—"

"*Firefly*," Jeremy said into his ear, which activated a very old primal memory.

Rafe said, "Kaylee?"

A smile wide as the horizon spread across her face. "You do remember."

He couldn't take that smile from her. "How could I forget?"

"Time to ride," Tempest said. "Back to your homes!" she cried out to the crowd. "The Bright Boys are on the prowl. Don't let your children out of your sight!"

Kaylee gave him one last shy smile before stepping forward suddenly and kissing Rafe on the cheek.

"They always say it's good luck to kiss a prince," she said, then ran away before he could say anything, even goodbye.

As some townspeople filed off, many lingered a moment to shake Rafe's and Jeremy's hands. A few women gave them quick embraces. All of them called him *Highness, Your Highness, My Prince, Prince Rafe*.

When they were gone, Rafe turned to Jeremy. "How did you forget to tell me I was a prince here?"

"I also forgot to tell you I was a knight."

Rafe glared at him. "You're a bad knight."

Jeremy only grinned. "That's not what she said."

"Asshole."

"That's Sir Asshole."

Jeremy mounted his horse and it danced a circle.

"Let's go. Sun's about to set."

With a barely suppressed cry of pain, Rafe mounted his horse again. Rafe and Sparrowhawk took up the rear, racing down the road that led to the Moonstone Palace, named, he assumed, as it rose white as the moon in the distance.

The red sun fell hard and fast, and the horses and their riders cast long shadows across the fields. The golden light of the setting sun and the brilliant blue of the sky turned the meadows and hills into a van Gogh painting. He couldn't help but slow his horse to a walk just to take it all in. The other riders raced on, and for a moment he was alone with his wonder.

"I was a prince here," he said to himself as he gazed at this new old world of his. "I am a prince here."

"More fun bein' a king."

The voice came from everywhere and nowhere at once, a smirking sneering evil voice.

A small gray cloud like a dust devil twirled in front of his horse, and poor Sparrowhawk reared up and tried to kick it, but there was nothing to kick.

Then the dust cloud solidified and took the form of a boy of about fifteen or sixteen.

At once, Rafe knew what Jeremy had meant when he said the Bright Boys look just like boys, except you know immediately they aren't for no reason you could name. The boy or whatever it was wore dirty gray rags wrapped around him like a mummy. His pale face was sickly looking, and when he—it—grinned, the teeth were too many and too sharp.

"Remember me?" the thing said. "Ah, no you don't. Still don't have your brain back. That's all right. Never needed one m'self. Name's Ripper."

"What do you want?" Rafe demanded. "Tell me now."

The Bright Boy feigned shock and dismay, putting his hand over his mouth and batting his eyelashes.

"Ain't you a tyrant," he said. "I don't work for you, remember? Just here to deliver a little message. My king wants you to come pay 'im a visit over in the Ghost Town. Sooner better than later. Much better. Your knight'll survive the night better, if you know what I mean." The creature mimed unslinging a bow from his shoulder, nocking an arrow, and shooting it toward the riders in the distance.

"Who's your king?" Rafe asked. "What does he want with me?"

"Just wants ya. I don't ask questions. But, uh . . . hurry up, little prince. He said if I get you before tomorrow night, he'll let me try on your crown."

The gray thing turned to smoke and then was gone.

·✳·

CHAPTER TWENTY

NO TREES. NO UNICORNS. When Emilie opened her eyes again, she saw the sun setting over distant hills. She lay on her side in a patch of silver-gray wildflowers. Slowly, she sat up, trying to get her bearings. Before her, only a few yards away, a blue river wound slowly toward those hills. She'd never seen a blue river before. Blue like a tropical ocean.

It seemed she was alone now. Alone and sitting on the bank of a blue river, the sun overhead sinking toward the horizon, and behind her, a full moon rose, white as snow and far too large.

A red crow landed on a rock a few feet from her. It preened its breast feathers and then looked placidly at her with its large black yet eerily wise eyes.

"Hello," Emilie said. "Where am I?" The crow said nothing.

"The Bluestone River," came a voice from behind. "We'll camp here for the night."

The red crow took off in a flutter of red wings, and Emilie spun around at the sound of the voice.

A woman with long blond hair pulled back in a braid stood about twenty feet behind her. She wore a loose white tunic, brown leather vest, brown riding pants, and boots. A bow was slung over her shoulder, and a quiver too. In her hands, she carried a brown felt hat, upside down, like she was about to pull a rabbit out of it.

"Dinner," the woman said. "Nuts and berries. I'll catch a few fish, too, if you're hungry. Even if you're not, I am."

The woman walked toward her. Emilie could only stare as she came closer and set the hat down on the ground in front of her. She didn't look at the hat, only at the woman's face and not even her face. Her eyes.

The woman ignored her staring and walked to the bank of the river, then waded in up to her knees.

"Stay quiet," she said as if Emilie were at all capable of speech.

Emilie watched the woman take an arrow from her quiver, and with careful aim, she stabbed at the water. When she brought the arrow up, a foot-long fish with shimmering blue and silver scales hung on the tip.

"You know how to start a fire?" the woman asked her.

She brought the fish over and laid it on the rock.

Finally, Emilie spoke. "No."

"No?" The woman arched one eyebrow.

"I've had an easy life," Emilie said.

"No shame in that. I'd rather you have an easy life than a hard one," she said as she squatted down by a pile of twigs in the center of a ring of stones.

"Skya."

No question mark. Emilie knew who she was. She'd known the very moment she looked into her eyes. They had the same eyes. Mourning dove gray. Maybe she was thirty-three now and not thirteen like the pictures, not a teenager like Rafe's carving in his sculpture garden, but Emilie did know her sister when she saw her.

"Emilie, right? I heard my knight call you that."

"Your knight?"

"Jeremy," she said.

"He's a knight?"

"Yes, and Rafe is my prince."

Emilie stared at her. "Serious?"

"Serious? Shanandoah isn't a kingdom that takes itself too seriously. But if you mean are they actually princes and knights, then yes. And I'm the queen here."

Emilie rubbed her temples. "This is a *lot* to process."

"Take your time." Skya ate a handful of nuts and berries from her hat and offered it to Emilie, who took it but didn't eat.

She had a thousand questions but hardly knew where to begin.

"How did I get here? I was listening to Jeremy and then I felt a tap on my shoulder—"

"That was me. I blew sleeping powder on you and carried you off."

"Oh, great. Now I've been kidnapped. Sorry. That was insensitive."

Her sister didn't seem offended. "Not kidnapped. Rescued. You were ten seconds away from being snatched by two Bright Boys with burlap bags. More were on the way."

"Bright Boys? Are Rafe and Jeremy safe?"

"They're as safe as we can hope for right now. They're with my Valkyries. While I'm away from the palace, my prince can serve in my place."

"*Your* prince? Possessive much?"

"They swore their undying allegiance to me over fifteen years ago. They are as much mine as I'm theirs. My prince. My knight. I am their queen. Always. Even in other worlds."

"Am I your princess?"

"You haven't sworn your undying allegiance to me. But you're *a* princess."

"And you're Skya," she said again. "Not Shannon."

"No one has called me Shannon since I came here. I never liked that name. Or, more like, I never liked the woman who gave it to me. But I loved my initials—S.K.Y. Add an A, and you get Skya."

"It's pretty," Emilie said. "Very regal. But the kingdom's called Shanandoah?"

"In school we studied the rivers of West Virginia—Monongahela and the Shenandoah. My teacher said that *Shenandoah* was a Native American word for 'daughter of the stars.' Sounded pretty. So I just changed the spelling to make it mine. But that's what you get when you let a thirteen-year-old name a kingdom."

Skya knocked two stones together, and sparks flew at the twigs and slivers of wood shavings inside the stone ring.

"So this is your kingdom, and you're the queen. And there are people here?"

"Of course there are people here. Ten thousand last count."

"Are they like . . . *people* people? Or like elves?"

Skya snorted a laugh.

"What? I woke up to see a unicorn in Jeremy's lap, but I mention elves and that's too far?"

"You're right. Fair point. I just know them so well. Cady, who makes the bread for the palace. Olin, our farrier. Daisy, who keeps the aviary. It would be like if I asked you if your mother was an elf and your grandmother a fairy."

"Mom was a tax attorney. Very boring and well paid. She would have much preferred to be an elf," Emilie said.

"She took good care of you?"

"Great care of me. Best care of me. Zero complaints. Until she died. I did complain about that."

"I'm glad she took such good care of you. I wanted to send Aurora to find you but had no idea where to send her. I worried about you." A tendril of smoke danced around the twigs and wood. Skya bent down and blew on it.

"You were worried about me? I thought you were dead in the woods. I hired Jeremy to find your body."

She scoffed and blew on the fire again. "He wishes I would let him find my body."

That was it. Emilie had enough of being polite. "Skya. What happened? Seriously? How—"

"I don't know," she said. "One minute I was in Red Crow Forest. Next minute I was following an actual red crow here. All these tough-looking girls with swords rode up on horses and hailed me as their queen. I was only thirteen years old. Thought I'd died and gone to heaven. Then I thought I'd gone to heaven but skipped the dying part. Then I realized I hadn't died and this wasn't heaven, but it was, you know, *almost* heaven." She smiled to herself.

"Oh. Well, that's good."

Skya blinked. "That's good?"

Emilie swallowed. Her mouth was so dry she wanted to drink the entire blue river, fish and all.

"You hear about bad things happening to girls. And even when the men get caught and go to jail, what do the girls get? They just have to go back to school. If they're lucky, I mean. Some of them go to the morgue." She looked at Skya. "I always thought a girl who went through something like that at least deserves her own castle or maybe a private island or something."

"I don't have a castle. I have a palace. That looks just like a castle."

Skya blew on the smoke again, and the first red flame sparked to life.

"Can you teach me to do that?" Emilie asked, nodding toward the fire.

"It takes a long time to learn. We don't have much time."

"Wait, why not?"

The fire was beginning to glow hot. Skya tossed some dry leaves on it, then sat back and let it burn.

"We have a problem," Skya said. "I have to handle it."

"What? Where?"

"There's a place called the Ghost Town. That's where the Bright Boys live. Not a nice place. I'm heading out in the morning."

"Why?" Emilie moved closer. She'd hoped when they met there'd be hugs and tears and laughing, but apart from throwing a blanket over her and carting her off, her sister hadn't so much as held her hand.

"Two days ago, a Bright Boy named Ripper got into the palace and stole something very precious. They do that sort of thing, and it's a game of keep-away. I always get it back. I rode out immediately after it and ran into Ripper at the border of the Ghost Town. Usually, we just fight it out. I always win. The Bright Boys always die. Then they waft away to the Ghost Town and come back to life. Then I kill them again. But he didn't want to fight me. He wanted to keep it."

"What was it?"

"Doesn't matter. But first, I have to get you to safety."

Emilie's stomach dropped. "Why did you rescue me and not Rafe and Jeremy?"

"Because they can take care of themselves," she said. "And you're my sister. You're my responsibility, like it or not."

"I'm not sure I like it."

Skya laughed.

"Sorry," Emilie said. "That was mean. Thank you for saving me from the Bright Boys. They sound terrible."

"They are. But don't be afraid. Aurora is watching out for them."

"I'm not afraid now. With you." Emilie wasn't being nice. She meant it. Her sister had speared a fish, cleaned it, started a fire, and all after rescuing Emilie from a forest full of monsters.

"Good."

"So what happens now?" Emilie asked.

"We'll camp here tonight. Tomorrow morning, we'll ride to the Painted Sea. There I'll put you on my ship. It will take you to the middle of the sea, where no one can reach you or harm you. The Bright Boys don't go near water if they can help it. That's the only way to kill them."

"What about you?"

"I'll go into the Ghost Town and do what I have to do. If I don't come back, then you'll have to decide whether to stay and rule my kingdom or return to your own world. But that's a choice only you can make."

"Wait. If you don't come back? You think you might not make it out of there alive?"

Emilie trembled, and her chest tightened like a giant fist was squeezing it.

"I have no choice. There is someone very, very dangerous in the Ghost Town who can't be ignored."

"Does he want to kill you or something? Take over the world?"

"He wants to hurt my prince. He's done it before. I can't let him near Rafe. I have to go alone. You understand?"

Slowly, Emilie nodded.

"Something you need to know about Shanandoah. There are no kings here. Never have been. Never will be. If something happens to me, Rafe can rule as prince regent, but he can never be king. I can't ask you to stay and rule if I'm killed but—"

"Stop, stop. Please," Emilie begged. Skya went silent. Emilie took a breath. "I just found you."

"I might come back."

"You might not."

Skya shrugged. "Shit happens."

"Is that how queens talk?"

"It's how queens from West Virginia talk. Eat. You need to eat. Long day tomorrow."

Emilie reached into the pouch of her hoodie and pulled out Fritz, who was none the worse for wear. Luckily, he could sleep through a hurricane and/or being gently abducted.

"Who's that?" Skya asked as Fritz woke up and began to run up and down Emilie's sleeves.

"Fritz. He's my fancy rat. I don't have anyone at home to take care of him, so I just brought him with me." She picked up a small handful of nuts and let Fritz eat them out of the palm of her hand. When Fritz finished eating, he started to explore, racing through the grass, sniffing, then hopped over to her and wiggled in circles.

"He likes it here," Emilie said. "He only does that when he's happy. Nice to see. He's had a hard life. Lonely. Lashes out when other rats try to get close to him. He's only hurting himself really."

"Maybe he just hasn't met the right rat yet," Skya said. "That's what I tell Granny Apple when she asks me when I'm getting married."

Aurora returned and landed on Skya's shoulder with a flutter of feathers.

Then the bird hopped off her shoulder and walked toward Fritz, tilting her head left and right, examining the tiny creature. Then she opened her beak.

Emilie snatched Fritz away and held him to her chest.

"Aurora, don't eat my sister's friend."

"Please," Emilie said. The crow fluttered back up to Skya's shoulder.

"Kids," Skya said. "What can you do?"

Emilie smiled when Skya called her "sister" but didn't say anything. She released Fritz from her grip and let him play in the tall grass.

"Maybe I could go with you," Emilie said. "I could help."

"Can you use a sword?"

"No."

"Bow and arrow?"

"Jeremy tried to teach me, but I wasn't very good."

"Then you can help by doing as I say so I won't have to worry about you. Eat. Sleep. Then tomorrow, get on the ship—"

"And do nothing while you go alone on a suicide mission. Right. Got it."

Skya almost cracked a smile. "Don't be a brat."

Emilie ate a few of the berries, hardly tasting them. Then she laid the blanket on the ground. She stretched out on her side with Fritz curled up in her hoodie pouch.

"I thought you'd be happy to see me. Like, hug me or something?"

Skya tossed a log onto the fire, and it hissed and crackled. "I can't."

"Why not?" Emilie asked.

"I might not let go."

"Then don't let go."

"I have to be queen before I can be your sister. Now get some sleep."

Emilie tried very hard not to cry herself to sleep, and she succeeded. Almost.

· ✳ ·

CHAPTER TWENTY-ONE

RAFE URGED SPARROWHAWK into a gallop. As the final pink and red rays of the day's sunlight streaked across the sky, they reached the Moonstone Palace.

He rode into the courtyard, then halted. He was too dazzled to do anything but stare. The palace looked more like a medieval castle. A tower at each corner of the palace stood four stories high, banners flying. The white stone exterior shimmered red and gold as the sun set. And here, the bustle of the courtyard, women in armor guiding horses to stone stables, and steps that led to two enormous doors, big enough to ride an elephant through. He didn't even notice Jeremy come up to him until he spoke.

"Rafe? You all right? You disappeared," Jeremy said.

He looked down. Jeremy held Sparrowhawk's bridle. By torchlight, sweating, hair damp, face dirty, he looked like a stranger, like a soldier. No, like a knight.

Rafe said, "We have another problem."

Quickly, he told Jeremy about his encounter with the Bright Boy who called himself Ripper.

"There are no kings in Shanandoah," Jeremy said. "That doesn't make any sense. He didn't say what he wants with you?"

"Only that I have to come as soon as possible or else."

"God, I hate Bright Boys," Jeremy said. "Bad enough they terrorize you, but they're also incredibly annoying."

His eyes were bright with fury and frustration, but also, Rafe could tell, a touch of bloodthirsty pleasure.

"You want to kill them?" Rafe asked.

"So, so much," Jeremy said.

"Who are we killing?" Tempest asked. Rafe dismounted his horse and faced her.

"Bright Boys," Rafe said. "One showed up and demanded I visit his king in the Ghost Town. Can you translate that?"

She growled like a wolf, then said, "I can. Unfortunately. Let's go to the queen's salon, and I'll tell you everything I . . . I'm allowed to tell you."

"Give us five minutes," Jeremy said to her. Then to Rafe, he said, "Come on. First things first."

Rafe gave the horse over to a stable girl and followed Jeremy up the stone steps of the palace and through the open front doors. He stopped abruptly, seized by a sudden and overwhelming sensation of déjà vu. It nearly knocked him to his knees, this feeling of familiarity, like walking into his mother's house and smelling the perfume of his childhood again. He turned a slow circle.

An iron chandelier dripping with white candles revealed intricate tapestries hanging on the stone walls. Unicorns and griffins danced around maypoles and red stags raced across meadows knee-high in rainbow-hued wildflowers. Arched entryways led to darkened rooms with beamed ceilings. He walked to one door and looked in. A banquet hall held long tables and the largest fireplace he'd ever seen. He could have stood inside the hearth.

A grandfather clock in a sitting room gave a low chime of the hour, and Rafe knew he'd heard that sound before.

"Jay . . ." he breathed. "This is . . ."

"Home," Jeremy said from behind him. "Right? Feels like coming home."

Rafe raised his hand to touch a silk wolf embroidered into one of the tapestries. A delicate black beast that bowed to a young woman wearing a crown of antlers. "Home sweet home."

"Come on. We'll take the tour later. This way," Jeremy said. He waved him on and Rafe followed.

"Where are we going?" he asked.

"To find your book. I'm guessing it's in the library. Good place for a book, right?" Jeremy was almost running down the hallways, though Rafe kept stopping every few steps to take it all in. Every time they passed a torch it would flicker to life. When they reached the library, another chandelier overhead suddenly lit up with dozens of burning candles. Rafe turned in a circle. Books sat in dark wooden cases as far as the eye could see. He inhaled the scent of leather bindings, old glue, paper and ink.

"All right . . ." Jeremy said as he checked podiums and plinths and display cases. "If I were a magic book full of memories, where would I be—"

"It's gone. Stolen."

Rafe turned around and saw Winter standing in the doorway.

"Stolen?" Rafe's stomach fell through the floor.

She walked to a red curtain and pulled it back to reveal a niche in the stone wall. Shards of glass lay on purple velvet.

"A Bright Boy broke in and forced the lock two days ago, shattered the glass box into a million pieces. Somewhere in the Ghost Town, there is someone or something calling himself their king. He wanted your memories," Winter said. "We don't know why, only that Queen Skya is pursuing him there. She swears she will bring the book back to you, but until then, you both must stay in the palace and not leave again until it's safe."

"Why?" Jeremy asked, stepping toward her. "We always fought by her side. Why would we let her fight alone now?"

"Because she knows who this king is." Winter dropped the curtain. "He's an old, old enemy of the prince's, and she says it's too dangerous for the prince to face him."

"Who?" Rafe demanded. "I have an old enemy here?"

"I don't remember anyone," Jeremy said. "Everyone kills Bright Boys. They can come back to life, but they usually don't hold grudges. Like Skya says, they're all wheel, no hamster."

"I would say if I knew," Winter said, "but I only know what Queen Skya told us."

"Could your memories have been erased or locked away too?" Rafe asked Jeremy.

"I don't remember that, but I suppose I wouldn't." Jeremy shook his head. "What about Emilie? Can you tell us where she is?"

Winter sighed. "The queen is taking her somewhere safer. I know nothing else." She knew nothing else, but it seemed she wanted to say something else. She opened her mouth but closed it again.

"On the ride here, Ripper showed himself to Rafe and said the king wants to see him," Jeremy told her.

"That is exactly what Queen Skya fears most," she said. "This pretender king is a dangerous foe. He defeated you before, and she won't let you risk your life again. You know the queen," she said to Jeremy. "There's no arguing with her when she's made up her mind. Though I fear—"

"What?" Jeremy said.

"I fear she won't be able to defeat him alone."

"The Valkyries can't help her?" Rafe asked.

"We can't pass into that place," she said. "We're made of light and the darkness there is poison to our kind. We're like fish drowning in air. We would go if we could. But now you've heard her orders, and there's no more I know to tell you." She met Rafe's eyes. "I am sorry, Highness. During the summer you were among us, we would all ride the countryside and make camp under the stars. By the fire, we would all take turns telling stories. I liked the stories you two told the best, the one about the handsome spy and the man who was also a bat and would fight crime? They are dear memories to me. And we spoke of them often during those long years without you both."

She looked at Jeremy. "You remember where your rooms are, don't you? Nothing has changed. The queen has kept them for you as they were."

Winter bowed her head and walked out of the library.

Rafe stood very still and quiet while Jeremy dragged his hands through his hair and made an angry circuit of the room.

"We told them James Bond and Batman stories," Rafe said.

"Yeah, well, we didn't have the plot of *King Lear* memorized yet, and you can't do much better than *Batman Begins* for a campfire story."

"It doesn't make sense. Why would someone steal my memories?"

"I don't know, I don't know . . ." Jeremy said. "And I don't know who the king is. Never heard of him, but I want to eat his dinner, his daughter, and then burn his mother's house down while he watches."

"She said he's an old enemy of mine? Maybe someone I fought without you—"

"No." Jeremy shook his head. "We were always together. Always. You never fought any king or any pretender king or anyone who defeated you." He exhaled. "Maybe one of the Bright Boys got ambitious?"

Jeremy sat down in the deep sill of a large arched window that overlooked a courtyard. Rafe went over to him. The moon was full and white and bright. Too full, too bright. It looked too close and smooth, untouched by a billion years of meteor strikes. A different moon than theirs. A younger, more innocent moon.

"What is the Ghost Town?"

"The Ghost Town? Lost souls roam there, people who get stuck and can't move on. Worse than the damned, Skya said. The damned are resigned to their fates. The ones in the Ghost Town want to claw their way out, and they'll claw anything. That's why the Bright Boys live there. It's a feast of fear for them." He glanced out the window, though there was little to see. "Skya must have hidden Emilie somewhere safe. Otherwise I could find her."

He rubbed his forehead, and Rafe wanted to comfort him but didn't know how.

"Why was it so hard to find her all those years? You could find everyone else."

Jeremy raised his face. "The gift only let me find the lost. Lost people. Lost things. Even bodies because the families wanted them back. But there was a catch, or maybe you could call it a failsafe to keep me from abusing the power—if something or someone didn't want to be found, I couldn't find them. Emilie didn't want to be found."

"If you can't find her now, maybe she's where she wants to be."

"God, I hope so."

Jeremy stared up at the strange moon. He looked young again in that light, like the boy Rafe used to know.

"What's wrong?" Rafe asked him.

"I didn't want your homecoming to be like this. There was so much I wanted you to remember."

"Then tell me."

A slight smile played across his lips. Jeremy stood up.

"Better. I'll show you."

· ✳ ·

CHAPTER TWENTY-TWO

JEREMY AND RAFE WALKED through the torch-lit palace corridors.

They took a different route this time—wider hallways, fewer rooms. Instead of tapestries on the walls, someone had painted murals.

Jeremy stopped and raised his candle to illuminate one particular section of the wall. "Look familiar?" he asked.

Rafe squinted. A silver-and-purple dragon fled across an arched bridge, pursued by a small black rabbit. It looked more than familiar. It was like seeing his own face in a mirror.

"Mine?" he asked.

Jeremy waved his hand to indicate the entire wall of the corridor, at least ten yards long and completely covered in wild paintings of this strange kingdom.

"All of them are yours," he said. "You painted this entire hallway for Skya."

"Why?"

"She loved your work. Your first royal commission. Not bad for fifteen, right? Come on. This way."

Jeremy jogged as if he couldn't wait to show him whatever lay ahead. Rafe ran after him, but as they reached the arched doorways, Jeremy suddenly stopped.

"Wait, let me show you something first," he said. "Stay here and watch."

Rafe waited behind the threshold, watching, curious, as Jeremy walked into the throne room. He stopped a few yards in and turned to face him.

"Okay, now come in," Jeremy said.

Confused but willing, Rafe started forward. As soon as he stepped across the threshold, the torches on the walls flickered to life, and the grand room was suffused with warm and flickering light.

"The throne room torches only light up when the royals enter," Jeremy said. "Elitists."

"This is unbelievable," Rafe said as he turned a slow circle, trying to take it all in . . . the mosaic tile floor that depicted a scene of a dragon ship on a turquoise sea, the lancet windows in the high walls, the ceiling like a medieval cathedral . . .

Rafe imagined the room flooded with sunlight. It must have been dazzling.

How did we ever leave? he wondered again. He knew why, to find Emilie, but how . . . and then he remembered how he was able to leave. He'd wished his memory of this place away. But what about Jeremy?

"How did you leave this place?" Rafe asked.

"How or why?"

"Both."

"I'll tell you later. Over here."

Rafe followed Jeremy to the throne. An incredible piece of art, it appeared to be a living tree with branches twisted to form the arms, back, and seat. Jeremy placed his hand on the back of the throne like he was comforting an old friend. Then he stepped forward and pointed to something on the wall.

"You see that arrow behind the throne?" Jeremy said.

Rafe looked up. An arrow with red fletching was stuck into the wall a few feet above the throne.

"The Bright Boys love trying to scare Skya to death," Jeremy went on. "They brought a red sleeper spider out of the Ghost Town and let it loose in the throne room. By the time we'd spotted it, it was too late. It was on the wall, only two feet above her head and getting closer. They're incredibly deadly. They will sting you while you're standing and you're dead by the time you hit the ground. And you can't get near them either. You can't move a muscle or they'll jump like lightning and strike. The only way to kill one is from a distance . . ."

He pointed to the arched entryway.

"We were all hiding there in the doorway, terrified and helpless. We couldn't take a step into the throne room without risking Skya's life. The whole time, she sat completely motionless on the throne, knowing if she so much as sneezed, she would die. Aurora, Skya's pet crow, was going to catch it and eat it. She's fast enough to do it, but the poison's so strong, even eating it would kill her. You stopped her, Rafe. You ordered her to stand down. Then you asked her to give you two pinion feathers. You took them and fletched an arrow—"

"No," Rafe said. "No way." He shook his head. There was no possible way . . .

"You had one shot."

"Not a chance." His heart hammered in his chest.

"If you missed, the spider would have jumped and stung Skya, and she would have died. So you ordered us to stand back, far back, so none of us would have to see it if you missed—"

"Shut up."

"And they all did what you said because there was nothing else to do. Except I couldn't let you see that alone. So I stayed at your side. At least I could help you if you had to cover her body and carry it to the chapel."

Rafe's eyes were hot with tears, and he didn't know why.

"I remember watching you nock your arrow. Your hands didn't shake. You were a rock because you had to be, because Skya had to be."

Rafe closed his eyes, begged his mind to give up the memory so he could believe the impossible words Jeremy told him.

"You raised your arrow," he went on. Rafe opened his eyes. "And then like it was any of the other ten million shots you'd made . . ." Jeremy snapped his fingers. "Bull's-eye. You dropped your bow. I can hear it clattering on the floor right now. It's in my ears."

Jeremy tilted his head as if hearing an old favorite song playing on some distant radio.

"Skya ran to you and grabbed you and held you. Her eyes were so wide . . . God, I remember it like it happened five minutes ago. The Valkyries saw her, and they just . . . they fell onto their knees. But no one said anything. You'd think we'd all shout and scream and dance around, but it wasn't like that. Joy is quieter than people think it is. Especially the joy of getting back something you thought was lost forever."

Jeremy took a deep shuddering breath. His voice was almost normal when he spoke again.

"The robin's wing was broken, Rafe. Wasn't it?"

"What do you—"

Jeremy said, "You healed the robin."

"I did?"

"Yes, you healed it because that's how Aurora thanked you for saving her and Skya. She granted you dominion over birds. Give a bird an order, and it will obey you—in this world or any other."

Deep in Rafe's soul, he knew this was true, that when he told the robin not to die, that he must live and fly again, the robin obeyed him.

"I wish you could remember your coronation," Jeremy said, his voice wistful. "It was two days after you saved Skya. By then the whole kingdom knew. Even the white stags left the forest to stand an honor guard around the palace. No one had ever seen anything like it before. Everyone said it was proof you were a true prince of Shanandoah. Skya never let anyone take the arrow from the wall so no one would ever forget the courage of Prince Rafe, savior of the queen, savior of the kingdom."

Rafe stared at the arrow in the wall. His arrow?

"Impossible shot," Jeremy said, raising his hand to touch the fletching of the arrow, like people touched the toes of bronze statues for luck. "For everyone in the world but you. Even your dad. Then again, it was the second time I'd seen you kill the spider. Can you see the legs?"

Rafe could see them. Eight tiny red legs sticking out from the hole the arrow's tip had left in the wall.

"In our world, you were the prince, and I'm the nobody," Rafe said.

Jeremy snorted. "Who told you that absolutely idiotic falsehood?"

"You know you were. Fancy house. Rich mom. Piano in the music room. Come on. Your mother even called you her little prince."

"She also called me a git, a twat, and Ginger Spice. Doesn't mean anything. You were the one who could hunt, fish, shoot bows and arrows, make art . . . I was a spoiled brat. You were Robin Hood, Prince of the Woods. When Skya made you the prince of the realm, it was not a surprise to any of us. Least of all me."

But Rafe was barely listening now. He gazed at the arrow in the wall. He *was* a prince here. Even the torches in the throne room had recognized him. What would a prince do at a time like this?

"Whatever's out there, it wants me," Rafe said. "I can't let Skya face that thing alone. I have to go—"

From the doorway of the throne room, Winter spoke.

"You're not allowed to leave. Queen's orders."

Rafe looked at her. "Yeah, but the queen's not here. And I outrank you. Don't I?"

"Good point," she said and smiled.

"Can I order you to tell us what we should do?" Rafe said.

Winter considered this. "If you were to give that order, I would say you should ride out tonight for the Ghost Town. The moon is full and it's bright as day. It's an easier ride to the entrance at the Devil's Tea Table, but the gate at the Angel Windows is by Granny Apple's orchard, and she'll help you."

"We can use the help," Jeremy said.

Winter whispered behind her hand. "You should probably order me to pretend this conversation never happened."

Rafe whispered back. "Consider it an order."

"What order, Your Highness?" she asked and disappeared from the doorway.

When they were alone again, Rafe said, "I have to tell you something.

That thing, Ripper, threatened to kill you. Specifically you. Maybe you shouldn't go—"

"When Skya made me her knight, I vowed to guard you both with my life. I meant it then, and I mean it even more now."

"If you're guarding us, who's guarding you?" Rafe asked.

Jeremy opened his mouth, but before he could speak, a clock in a tower began to toll the hour.

Whatever he was going to say was lost.

Lost Words

WELL, NOT REALLY. I know what he was going to say. If the bell hadn't interrupted, he would have said, "You guarded me, day and night. Not because you had to but because you wanted to." That's all. Not quite a confession of love, but near enough to one that it would have made Rafe wonder what else Jeremy wasn't telling him.

Then again, Rafe was already wondering that.

That's what Jeremy would have said had the bell not tolled. What he wanted to say was something else . . .

"You did, night and day. Not because of any vows you made but because you were in love with me as much as I was in love with you. Oh, by the way, I was very, very in love with you."

Maybe not those exact words, but something like that anyway.

· ✳ ·

CHAPTER TWENTY-THREE

THEY SPLIT UP. Jeremy went to get some provisions while Rafe went to the stables. Rafe had asked him how he would know which horses were theirs. Jeremy said, "You'll know," before disappearing down a hallway.

In the courtyard, Rafe followed his nose to the stables. It was dark inside the barn, scented with hay and horseflesh. He lit an oil lamp and carried it past the stalls.

Peering over the tops of the stall doors, he found all the horses sleeping. Brass plaques on the stall doors gave each horse's name.

A spotted pinto horse was named Beans, and a pretty Appaloosa was dubbed Loosey-Goosey. A black stallion—Blackjack. A fog-gray mare—Quicksilver. He reached the stall of a horse with a golden coat named Sunny of a Gunny. What were those called? Palominos?

The Palomino raised his head and snorted. He bucked twice, so Rafe stepped back, scared he'd terrified it. But then the horse whinnied, and it was a jubilant sound. He put his long neck over the stall door and lowered his head as if trying to bow.

Rafe's hand shook a little as he reached out to stroke the horse's forehead.

"You know me?" he said, and the horse answered by nuzzling his neck. He pulled away but only to open the latch on the stall door and go inside. Sunny nearly knocked him over in his excitement to sniff him from head to toe, to nibble at his clothes and hair.

"All right, all right," Rafe said with a soft laugh. "You know me. Wish I knew you."

Sunny rested his long heavy neck over Rafe's shoulder and sighed with contentment as he was stroked for the first time in years by his boy.

"I painted you once. I didn't even know I was painting you. Thought I was ripping off Franz Marc's *Little Yellow Horses*. But I wasn't. It was you. My brain didn't remember you but my paintbrush did."

In his own painting, a red horse and a golden-yellow horse rested against each other while the sun set behind them.

Was the red horse in his painting also here?

"Wait here a sec," Rafe said. He picked up his lantern and went to the next stall.

The brass plaque said the horse's name was Reddy Freddy.

A golden horse named Sunny. A reddish-copper horse named Reddy Freddy.

"Rafe?" Jeremy called out.

"Down here. I found them," Rafe said as Freddy put his head over the stall door and lightly nipped his shoulder.

"Hey, no biting," Rafe said.

"He gets that from me," Jeremy said. "Ah, there's our lads. Hey, laddie, missed you." Jeremy's horse, Reddy Freddy, nearly broke the stall door trying to get to Jeremy.

"Hold on, Freddy. Calm down." Jeremy went into the stall. "Here we are. I'm home." He leaned against Freddy's side, rubbed his long neck all over. "Love you too."

"We have horses," Rafe said in wonder. "We have horses that . . . match our hair."

"Gifts from Skya. And these are not horses. These are Shanandoah mountain chargers. They're strong as Clydesdales, fast as Arabians, and can live a hundred years. They love rocky terrain, stomping Bright Boys to death, and they're massive whores for dried rainberries. Right?" he said to Freddy. "I said the magic word? *Rainberries?*"

Freddy snorted in happiness as Jeremy took a handful of berries from his pocket. Then he gave another handful to Rafe for Sunny.

"You raided their kitchen?" Rafe asked.

"It's our kitchen, Rafe. We live here."

"I've been here five hours," Rafe said as his charger lapped every last berry out of his hand, "and I already know I would die for this place."

"Please don't," Jeremy said like he'd forgotten they were joking with each other.

Rafe, taken aback by how serious Jeremy sounded, said, "I'll try not to."

"Good." Jeremy nodded as he scratched Freddy under his chin. "Because if you die it'll kill me." He smiled, the old Jeremy again. "Skya would really kill me."

Jeremy opened the stall door and in one swift movement mounted his horse. "We might make it by morning, but don't come crying to me when your ass is screaming at you."

"If my ass starts screaming, I'm crying about it to everyone." Rafe got on Sunny's back and again felt the muscle memory, the déjà vu he'd felt before, but a thousand times more so. This was his horse. They belonged together.

"One word of warning," Jeremy said. "I'm your knight. If we get in a fight, I will fight to protect you, not myself. That's how it works."

"Right, because I outrank you."

"You do," he said. "Not that I ever let it stop me."

"Stop you what?"

But Jeremy only gave him a roguish wink and rode out of the stables.

"What's he not telling me, boy?" he asked Sunny, who only whinnied impatiently. "Not telling? See if I give you any more rainberries."

Skipping Ahead

RAFE AND JEREMY rode hard. Emilie slept miserably. We'll skip ahead to the next morning if you don't mind.

· ✳ ·

CHAPTER TWENTY-FOUR

THE SUNRISE WAS DIFFERENT in Shanandoah. It came with musical accompaniment. As the sun rose and turned the sky from purple to pink to blue, the night breeze turned to wind. Somewhere, somehow that wind blew through the distant trees, making them sing like wind chimes. The chiming of the trees woke the birds, and they began to sing along with the wind. First, one bird carried the melody, then another thousand birds accompanied it. The song echoed off the distant cliffs and amplified it. Emilie had never heard any music so strange and ethereal, and she had to wonder . . . was the world singing because the sun was rising, or was the sun rising because the world was singing?

She sat on her horse blanket by the Bluestone River and watched, rapt, and when the sun had risen, and the music stopped, she didn't know if she'd been awake for minutes or hours or years.

"It never gets old," Skya said. Emilie had sensed her sister standing behind her, watching the sunrise with her, but neither had said anything. Neither had wanted to break the spell.

Emilie wiped her face. "I've never heard a sunrise symphony. This happens every morning?"

"Just here in the valley. I wanted you to hear it."

"I'll never forget it. Thank you," Emilie said.

Skya lightly tapped the top of her head. "Come on. We need to go. The ship will be waiting for you."

Emilie stood up and followed Skya to her horse, a big black-and-gray-spotted charger named Morgan. Skya took a hunting knife out of her saddlebag and stuffed it into her belt.

"That's not how you do it," Emilie said. "It's supposed to go through your belt loops." Emilie showed her the hunting knife on her hip.

"Ah, this is why I need my prince," Skya said with a wistful sigh. "Rafe always put my knife on my belt for me the right way."

"I can do it for you. Since Rafe's not here, I mean." Emilie took the knife in its sheath and fed the end of her sister's belt through the loops. Skya buckled her belt back on nice and tight. "Good enough?"

Skya tugged her knife. It stayed on. "Thank you. Good as when Rafe did it."

Emilie wanted to hug her sister, almost asked for it, but she was afraid of the answer.

"Better go," Skya said.

"If you insist."

Emilie rode behind her sister on Morgan's back. Once they left the valley, Emilie spotted a white gull flying overhead. The air was lightly scented with salt. They were getting closer to the sea.

"You know, since I helped you with your knife, I was thinking maybe I could go with you and just hold your sword and stuff? Like a caddie? Do queens have caddies?"

"You're annoying," she said. "Did you know that?"

"I always thought it was the job of the baby sister to annoy her big sister. I'm just doing my job."

"Guess what?"

"What?"

"You're very good at your job."

Skya spurred her charger into a gallop. There was no more talking after that.

They rode for several hours. Even scared and heartbroken, Emilie couldn't help but marvel at the sight of the Painted Sea as it came into view. She even got Fritz out to show him, though he was less impressed than she was.

The shore of the Painted Sea was swirled with colors like a child had spilled their jar of rainbow sand everywhere. Pinks and blues and greens and purples. The water was so clear she could see through it like a window. Small silver dolphins and lazy rays played in the surf. A line of enormous elephant-gray boulders jutted out in the water, forming a pier. And at the end of the dock waited a ship. A magnificent dragon boat like something from the pages of a child's book on Vikings.

Emilie spotted a small crew aboard the ship, bustling about, preparing to leave and take her away with them.

Skya brought her horse to a halt at the top of the hill.

"You sure you don't want to come with me?" Emilie asked. "We can just hang out on the boat instead of you getting yourself killed?"

She was hoping to make Skya laugh, but it didn't work.

"I love this place," Skya said. "This world is mine the way my heart is mine. It's part of me, and I would defend it the way I would guard my own heart. If I don't come back, I hope you will stay and rule and let this place into your heart."

"Run a kingdom. I don't know. With Mom gone, I barely remember to pay the electric bill. I don't think I can do that. I think I'd fail everyone."

"I understand," Skya said.

Emilie instantly regretted what she'd said, but it was too late to take back.

"If you do decide to leave," her sister went on, "the way back is different than the way you arrived. Tell the captain to take you to the farthest shore. When you step off the ship, you'll see a cobblestone path in the sand. Follow it until you reach a door in the desert. No wall. Only a door. Go through it, and you'll be home again."

"Will I forget this place like Rafe did?"

"No. You'll never forget it no matter how much you wish you could."

Morgan, made for steep climbs, carried them easily down the winding path to the beach below. Then Skya dismounted and helped Emilie down.

"Say goodbye to Morgan," she said. "We'll meet the ship at the end of the pier."

Emilie stroked the magnificent horse's mane, then hugged her long neck. Slowly, she pulled away.

She couldn't believe she was doing what she was doing. But it had to be done.

When they reached the beach, Skya stopped and reached inside her tunic. She handed Emilie an ancient, barely decipherable Polaroid. Emilie peered at it through the cracks in the photo paper and saw a skinny blond girl holding a doll in her arms. Except it wasn't a doll but a baby.

"I loved holding you," Skya said.

Emilie stared at her. "I didn't know we ever met."

"No?" Skya smiled. "You lived with us for a month. Mom showed up with you when you were about ten days old. She was wrecked. She tried to pick you up and almost dropped you. And you were so tiny, but you, man . . . kid, you could scream. I got so tired of hearing you scream that I put on some music, turned it up, and pretended we were rocking out. Like magic, you calmed down. That was my whole life for a month, you and me, singing and dancing. Our favorite song was 'Landslide.' You would fall right asleep when I sang it—"

Emilie's heart leapt like a stag.

"'Landslide'? Stevie Nicks? I love Stevie Nicks. She's my lady and savior."

"Oh," Skya said. "Funny. We didn't have a lot of music in the house, but I had an old Fleetwood Mac cassette. It was the only music that worked on you."

"You gave me Stevie."

Emilie looked at the photograph again, the old, fading Polaroid. Emilie realized that if Skya had it here with her, that meant she'd had it on her when she disappeared. "I thought I might get to keep you if I could get you to stop crying. But Aunt Marie came to me one day and said it was time to tell the baby goodbye. You were going to go to a new home.

We took this picture in the lawyer's office. We couldn't afford a babysitter, so they took me to watch you while they were doing all the paperwork. I didn't want to let them take you, so the receptionist lady took the picture to distract me. She was the one who told me that as your big sister, it was my job in the world to keep you safe. And the safest place for you would be where you were going. And I thought about how scared I'd get when Mom would show up out of nowhere, middle of the night, drunk or on something. Bringing creepy guys around . . . And I knew that lady was right. It was my job to keep you safe, and the safest place for you was far away."

Emilie wanted to speak, but maybe for the first time in her life, no words came out.

"I'm going into that place without you for one reason," Skya said. "There are mermaids in the sea and unicorns in the forest and giants in the wild desert reaches . . . that's how magical this place is. But as magical as this place is, the Ghost Town is just as dangerous. And if you were to get hurt there or die, the magic would be gone and a thousand mermaids and ten thousand unicorns and a million giants wouldn't be able to bring it back to me.

"So you're getting on that ship, right?"

And Emilie said, "Right."

Skya started forward along the pier, and there was nothing for Emilie to do but follow her. The sea breeze smelled like salt and rain clouds, and the sun was warm but not hot. The enormous powder-white gulls barely had to flap their wings to stay aloft.

As they made the long final walk down the pier, Skya went on.

They were at the dragon ship now. "Please . . . get on. And I promise you I'll do everything I can to come back alive. Then we can be sisters, okay?"

"Okay," Emilie said. Her sister had made up her mind and nothing would change it. Emilie had made up her mind too. "I'll get on the ship."

"Good. Thank you."

Emilie got on the ship.

The captain and her crew of three began to pull ropes, raise sails, and turn wheels. The ship caught a strong breeze, and soon it was moving away from the pier.

The ship turned toward the sea, and Emilie moved to the stern. On the pier, Skya stood stock-still and staring, her pale blond hair whipping in the wind. She looked so alone. Too alone. No one should ever be that alone.

The gulf between them widened. Ten yards. Twenty yards.

Skya watched her go, and Emilie watched her watching.

All right. She would give her sister something to watch.

She ran up to the side of the boat and dove off into the water.

The sea was warm, but it still wasn't easy swimming fully clothed back to the pier. But nothing was going to stop her from getting back to her sister. Luckily, Emilie had spent twenty summers in St. Croix with her mother. She swam with all her might and reached the pier, where Skya was already kneeling down on the rocks to pull her up.

"Have you lost your mind?" Skya demanded, gray eyes blazing blue and red.

"Sorry. I forgot Fritz."

"What?"

Emilie pointed at Morgan. "I left Fritz's pouch in Morgan's saddlebag. Oops."

"Oops? That wasn't an accident. Don't lie to me. What the hell are you thinking?"

"I'm thinking you're my sister, and I'm not going to let you go into that place all alone."

Skya grabbed her as if to shake her, but instead she hugged her so hard it hurt.

"At least if something terrible happens to you," Skya said, "nobody can say I didn't try."

Emilie laughed softly. "You tried. You can't defeat a baby sister with her mind set on something."

"All right, Brat. Let's go then."

They started up the pier toward Morgan.

"I like being 'Brat.' Better than 'Princess.'"

"Come on then, Brat. And don't think for one second you're getting a towel. You can air-dry."

Emilie, because she had little to no ability to keep her intrusive thoughts to herself, said, "Was that a test? Did I pass a test? Were you testing me? I think that was a test."

"I wasn't testing you. But if I was testing you, it's safe to say you passed."

"You were totally testing me."

"Hush, Brat. If you're coming with me into the Ghost Town, there are things you need to—"

A loud, piercing caw alerted them both to Aurora's return. The red crow landed on Morgan's saddle horn. She cawed again, and Skya's shoulders slumped.

"What?" Emilie asked.

"Aurora says Rafe and Jeremy snuck out of the palace and are going into the Ghost Town on their own, which is the exact opposite of what I wanted them to do."

"Well, shit," Emilie said.

Skya nodded. "Exactly. Time for a new plan." She got into the saddle and held her arm out for Emilie.

"New plan?" Emilie asked as she settled in behind her sister. "We didn't even have an old plan."

"I'll think of something," Skya said. "I always do."

· ✳ ·

CHAPTER TWENTY-FIVE

IN THE ALMOST-LIGHT of the hour before dawn, Rafe and Jeremy rode through fields and glades and into wild ivy-thick ravines, then traced the edges of a high ridge that overlooked a verdant green valley. Jeremy pointed west.

"Granny Apple's orchard is over there. You see?"

Rafe looked into the sunlit valley filled with row after row of apple trees. A whitewashed stone cottage was half-hidden under ivy.

"That's her house," Jeremy said. "Pretty small. She might put us in the barn. Can you handle that, Your Highness?"

"You've seen my cabin. I can handle it."

"I like your cabin. It's rustic."

"That's a nice way of putting it."

"I can be nice."

"When?"

Jeremy grinned, though his eyes were red with exhaustion. "Upon request. Come on."

Rafe followed Jeremy down into the valley.

As soon as they dismounted their horses, the door opened. A woman, wrinkled as a dried prune, waved a sunburnt hand at them.

"Come in, children. Leave the horses be. Granny will see to them."

They went to the front door, and she looked them both up and down.

"About time you got handsome," she said to Jeremy.

"Gingers are late bloomers," he admitted.

To Rafe she said, "You were always handsome. But you need a bath."

Rafe didn't disagree.

"We're going into the Ghost Town," Jeremy said. "I was told you'd help us."

"Oh, I'll help you, all right. Someone's got to. But first, you sleep and you eat."

"We don't have time," Rafe said.

"Make time or you'll be goners before your boots hit that cursed ground."

Rafe and Jeremy looked at each other.

"Okay," Rafe said. "One hour?"

"Two," Granny said and neither of them had the energy to argue.

The cottage had a small second bedroom, where she sent them to sleep while she tended to the horses. It was a cozy room fragrant with the drying wildflowers that hung from the rafters and with clean, cold water in the basin.

"Better than the barn. Perks of being royalty, I guess," Rafe said as he splashed fresh water on his face.

Jeremy fell backward onto the bed, fully clothed. "Fun. Straw mattress."

Rafe crashed next to him. "You think Granny would give us an extra pillow?"

"I wouldn't push our luck." Jeremy rolled onto his back and patted his chest. "I'll be your pillow."

Maybe it was exhaustion, maybe it was something else, but Rafe took Jeremy up on his offer without hesitation. He rolled onto his side, threw his arm over Jeremy's stomach, and laid his head down on his chest.

"Better?"

"Old times," Rafe said.

"What is? You used to sleep on straw?" Jeremy asked.

"I was thinking how this is just like it used to be. Back before we were lost, you know. Crashing in your giant bed. Talking all night when we were supposed to be sleeping."

"Exactly the same. Except I have a beard. Literally the only difference."

"And I'm not scared."

"Not scared of the Ghost Town?"

"Not scared of my dad."

Jeremy was quiet a moment, then said, "I never told you this, but I . . . I tried to see you when you were in Brook Haven."

Rafe raised his head and looked at him. "Brook Haven? That was eight years ago. What happened?"

"I walked in. Your dad saw me and lost his mind."

"Did Mom—"

"No. She was back with you when it all happened. She didn't know I was there either."

Dad kept Jeremy from him? The one person he'd wanted to see more than anyone else in this world or any other, and his father kicked him out.

"Why?"

"Why didn't I tell you?"

"No, why did you come to Brook Haven?"

"To get an oil change. Why do you think I went? To see you."

"You couldn't tell me anything. So why—"

"Because I was going to tell you everything."

"But—"

"I would have done anything to help you. Even give up this world if that's what it took."

What could Rafe say to that? Jeremy was willing to give up this world to help him sleep a little better at night? Why? He was almost afraid to ask, so he didn't.

"Thanks for trying," Rafe said, at a loss for any better words than that.

"Should've tried harder."

"No, I wouldn't have believed you even if you'd told me everything. And we wouldn't have been allowed to come back."

Rafe laid his head down again and Jeremy put his hand in his hair, stroking it softly. Why did this feel so natural to him, so easy? He yawned and rested his arm lower on Jeremy's stomach before catching himself.

"It's all right," Jeremy said. "You can stretch out."

"I don't want to hit your bruise."

"I think it's better."

Rafe sat up, then lifted Jeremy's shirt. The bruise had turned purple.

"It's not better." Rafe winced.

"Badge of honor."

That's not what Jeremy had called it before. What had he called it? The red storm of Jupiter. Rafe made an orbit of it with his fingertips, as if to quiet the storm.

"No excuses," Rafe said. "I'm sorry." Before, when Emilie had made him apologize, he hadn't meant it. Now he did.

"Forgiven. If it makes you feel any better, that night at Brook Haven, I punched your dad."

"What? Are you kidding me?"

"Right hook." Jeremy raised his fist in a power salute.

Rafe remembered something. "He did have a black eye around that time. He said he slipped on ice in the parking lot and hit his forehead."

"He hit my fist."

"Did he hit you first?"

"No. He was bellowing at me, and I couldn't help myself. I clocked him. I clocked him and said, 'That was for slapping Rafe.'"

Rafe looked at him. He could've kissed him for doing that. He almost did. As a joke, of course.

"You did that for me?"

"I'd say yes to get on your good side, but the truth is, I did it for me." He grinned wickedly. The smile faded and he said, "I used to 'look' for you in my mind all the time. This gift I have? I could sense where you were. I did that more often than I should admit."

"Thought you could only use it to find lost people."

"You didn't remember this world, but deep down you knew you belonged here. I think you were lost without this place. Admit it. Don't you feel you belong here?"

He did. But was it because he was in Shanandoah or because he was with Jeremy?

Granny rapped on the door. "I hear talking! I need to hear snoring!"

"Yes, Granny!" they called out. He and Jeremy met eyes and laughed as silently as they could. Jeremy put his finger over his lips.

Rafe moved closer, laid down again on Jeremy's chest.

"Your heart is going really fast. You okay?" he asked in a whisper.

"I'm good," Jeremy said. "I'm perfect."

In seconds, they fell asleep. They woke midmorning and Granny was waiting for them with breakfast. Bread and fresh butter, hot tea, eggs, and cheese. Ravenous, they ate without speaking and didn't hear the door open and close again until a basket of apples landed on the table.

They looked up at Granny, forks suspended in midair.

"You're going into the Ghost Town, you need apples," she said.

"We need . . . apples?" Jeremy said. "Fiber?"

"Eat one," she said. Rafe picked an apple out of her woven basket and took a bite. "You taste that?"

"It's good," he said. "Delicious. They taste like . . ."

"Light," she said. "These are Golden Sun apples. They are full of sunlight. So much sunlight they turn the color of the sun. Where you're going, there's no sunlight. No good light. You take the light with you."

Rafe took another bite. The taste was so familiar.

Why could his hands remember this world when he painted or carved something? Why could his body remember how to ride horses and his tongue remember the taste of the golden apples, but his mind couldn't remember a single moment he'd spent in this world with Jeremy?

"You're a prince. You're a knight," Granny said. "In the Ghost Town, you both are dinner. If you don't want to be eaten alive, you'll do what I say."

"Yes, ma'am," Rafe said. Jeremy silently nodded.

"Take these. You keep the apples until you need them. You stay together, because if you get separated, you may never find each other again. Or worse, you'll think you've found each other, but you won't like what you've found. Stay together. Say that to me."

They looked at each other, then repeated, "Stay together."

"That place casts a dark spell. Don't think you can't fall for it. Anyone can fall for it. If one of you sees the other begin to fall, do whatever it takes to snap him out of it. Better to lose a hand or an eye than your whole soul to that place. Do whatever it takes. Say it."

"We'll do whatever it takes."

"Good," she said. "Watch for sleeper spiders. They live there too. And the Bright Boys are at their strongest in that blighted place. Only dunking in water can kill them for good, but there's no water in that place, so there they are truly immortal. Worse, they can and will trick you. Everything will try to trick you. Don't be fooled. Don't believe your eyes. Say it to each other."

"Don't believe your eyes," they repeated.

"The Ghost Town changes form, changes name. I don't know who or what you'll find there, but whatever it is, it'll haunt you if you let it. Don't let it. The ghosts can't die, but they can kill you, so they have the high ground. Don't trust your eyes. Trust your heart. You have hearts, and they don't, so there, *you* have the high ground. Now go. The sooner you get in, the sooner you get out. If you get out. Now promise me you'll get out. Say it."

"We promise," they said again.

"Tricked you," she said. "That's not a promise you can make."

With that terrifying statement, she left them alone. Rafe looked at Jeremy across the table.

"Now I'm scared," Rafe said. "You?"

"Scared shitless and witless."

Rafe finished his apple with one more bite. If he died in the Ghost Town, at least he'd go out with the taste of Shanandoah sunlight on his tongue.

CHAPTER TWENTY-SIX

THE ROCK FORMATION AHEAD of them looked foreboding for reasons Rafe couldn't explain to himself. At first, he thought it was the high wall of an old cathedral or something, like in photos he'd seen of medieval ruins. But then, as they got closer, he saw it wasn't anything man-made. A high natural wall, fifty feet or more, with three empty holes, tall and narrow. Like doors or . . .

"The Angel Windows," Jeremy said, answering the question Rafe hadn't asked.

"Why are they called that?"

"They say because only angels are brave enough to go in there. But even they're afraid to use the front door."

"We go through those? There's nothing but fields behind them."

"It's hidden. It's not just a town for ghosts. The town itself is a ghost." Jeremy brought his horse alongside Rafe's, and they trotted to a halt, the rock formation only about a hundred paces ahead. "We have to walk through them. And we can't take the horses. I wouldn't do that to them anyway."

They rode to the Windows and dismounted.

"We'll be back soon, lads," Jeremy said as he gave both horses head scratches and more berries. "Head to Granny's house. She's got apples for you both."

The horses stubbornly refused to budge.

"Typical," Jeremy said.

Even with his bow and a quiverful of arrows, Rafe already felt woefully outgunned as they walked to the rocks. He stood before the tallest of the three Windows. Looking through it, all he could see was more of the same world, more Shanandoah. A field of violet flowers, yellow butterflies, and enormous rocks strewn all over with no discernible pattern, as if some ancient structure had collapsed eons ago and the world had reclaimed most of it.

"Ready?" Rafe said.

Jeremy took a long breath, then said, "To quote the great lion Aslan, 'Further up and further in.'"

Rafe started up and into the Window, but Jeremy put his hand on his shoulder and stopped him.

"The knight goes before the prince," Jeremy said.

"Is this a chess rule or something?"

"It's the Jeremy rule."

"Granny told us to stay together. Remember the creepy kitchen chanting exercise? We go at the same time. You can go through that one." He pointed at the opening next to him. "I'll give you a half-second head start. Okay?"

"Acceptable."

Rafe started forward again, but Jeremy's hand on his shoulder stopped him.

"What—"

Jeremy kissed him. Nothing but a quick kiss on his cheek, but still a kiss.

"It's good luck to kiss a prince, remember?" Jeremy said. "Old wives' tale here, but I am nothing if not willing to forgo logic and reason if I get to kiss somebody." He looked into the Window. "And we need all the luck we can get."

Rafe froze, overcome by a sudden wave of déjà vu, just like the sensation he'd felt walking into the Moonstone Palace for the first time. Except that wasn't the first time he'd entered the palace. Jeremy's kiss felt exactly like walking into the palace. Both felt like coming home. Both felt like they'd happened a thousand times before.

"Rafe?"

And this felt familiar too. The flush of warmth, of happiness, of courage. The courage from the kiss felt more familiar to him than his own name.

"Any benefits to kissing a knight?" Rafe asked.

"Several. Undying gratitude. Extra Christmas present. He'll follow you anywhere."

"Good to know."

Before Jeremy could say anything more, Rafe climbed through the Angel Window and landed in a nightmare.

The Ghost Town

IN SHANANDOAH, THERE ARE two entrances to the Ghost Town—the one Rafe and Jeremy took through the Angel Windows and the stone gate at the Devil's Tea Table, which Emilie and Skya were taking at about the same time.

In the Real World, for want of a better name, there is only one way to get into the Ghost Town, and that is to die with unfinished business.

* ✳ *

CHAPTER TWENTY-SEVEN

WHATEVER RAFE HAD EXPECTED to find in the Ghost Town, it wasn't this. Morgantown, West Virginia. Or the shadow of it. Rafe recognized the city the way you recognize a dinosaur at a museum, by the shape of its skeleton. The bones of the shops and the spine of the street were still there, but the flesh of the city was gone, eaten away by something.

There was no sun, only black clouds chasing one another across the bitter sky. Angry clouds but no rain. All was dust beneath his feet. No rain had ever fallen here. Nothing to wash the ash away.

He might have cried at the sight of it if he hadn't been so scared by the sheer terrible wrongness. Seeing his hometown like this—he'd bought his favorite boots over there, had coffee with a girl once there, taken a job painting hotel rooms just down there—it was like seeing the body of a friend left for dead on the side of a road.

A faded billboard that once had read WEST VIRGINIA had been defaced. The W and the E were blacked out, and other letters scrawled over them.

Now the sign read—

LOST VIRGINIA.

"Jay," Rafe breathed, but he wasn't there. He turned around, looked back at the Angel Windows. They were empty and black. "Jeremy?"

Nothing. No answer. No Jeremy. Granny had warned them, and Rafe had already lost him.

Afraid to go but too afraid to stay, he slung his bow over his back and made his slow way down the broken hill that had once been High Street. He took what was left of the sidewalk, watching every step as he tried to avoid the black moss and sinister mold growing up through the cracks. He could hear the nearby rushing of the Monongahela River, too loud in the deep silence of this dead or dying city. And then, another sound. A rockslide somewhere and the unmistakable sound of something hitting the water. The river's name meant "sliding banks," but he'd never actually heard the bank slide into the water before.

And yet, he almost managed a smile at the sight of one familiar face. The statue of Don Knotts, Morgantown's favorite son, sat in its place of honor outside the old theater. But when he reached it, he saw old Don's face contorted into an open-mouthed scream.

Rafe stepped back.

A pile of gray leaves had gathered at the statue's shoes. A woman's face, dirty, sallow, rose out of the leaves. Not leaves but rags. A woman in rags.

Rafe backed away a few more steps, pity warring with terror. He could have sworn it was only leaves.

"Have you seen the moon?" she rasped, her voice like broken glass. "I lost the moon."

"What? How do you lose the moon?" he asked.

She looked up at the angry, hateful sky.

"You lose the moon the same way you lose hope," she said. "One day, you look up, and it's gone."

She sank into herself again, and when a foul-smelling wind blew past, she turned back into dead leaves and was scattered along the street.

The leaves crunched under Rafe's boots as he walked away, all that was left of the woman who'd lost the moon.

Heart pounding, he touched his pockets and found the apples still there. One in each pocket. He wished he'd brought a peck.

Movement ahead caught his eye. Jeremy. He stood at the bottom of the hill, outside the hotel, before turning and running up a side street.

"Jay! I'm here! Up here!" The joy in his voice was probably the first time this place had heard anything like joy.

Heedless of leaves and the shattered street, Rafe ran as fast as he could, but by the time he reached the intersection, Jeremy had disappeared again.

Rafe turned circles, then ran up the block and around it, then returned to what was left of High Street. He stopped in front of the Hotel Morgan. From the top floor, he might be able to see where Jeremy had gone. He started forward.

The sidewalk cracked under his feet. Shifted sideways. He nearly fell, but he managed to race across the street. The sound grew louder, cracks like cannon fire, and when he stopped and turned, it was just in time to see the hotel crumble to rubble and slide into the river.

Slowly, as if every step could cause another earthquake, he walked up a street that once was called Pleasant, but here someone had changed the sign to read UNPLEASANT STREET.

Finally, he found fresh boot prints that had to have been Jeremy's. He followed them over a bridge. He knew exactly where Jeremy was headed. His old house. This was the way to Park Street.

Whatever disaster had befallen downtown, Park Street had been mostly spared. But even though the grand old houses still stood, and the brick streets were mostly unbroken, an air of calamity hung heavy over the neighborhood like radioactive fallout.

The colors of the houses, once white or blue or yellow or green, had all faded to a sickly gray. Something had eaten a large hole in the side of the big white house on the corner. Rafe watched, mesmerized, horrified, as a brown snake, fat as a barrel, long as a school bus, pushed into the hole.

If Rafe had been more scared in his life, he couldn't remember when.

He ran off toward Jeremy's old house. There it was, the Big Blue Monster. Still blue in places.

The screen door hung open and *clack-clacked* against the frame. Instinct told him to go in the back door. If this was a trap—and it felt like a trap—he wouldn't walk straight into it.

He went around to the back and crept carefully in through the kitchen door. He avoided looking at anything too closely. Things were in the sink that shouldn't have been in the sink, and before he turned corners, he heard the scuttling sounds of creatures scurrying away to hide.

No Jeremy on the main floor or in the abandoned rooms on the second floor. By the time Rafe was on the narrow staircase to the third floor, he was shaking. The third floor, Jeremy's floor. The bedroom, the full bath, the sitting room. Jeremy's own private kingdom.

The old steps creaked dully under his feet, and that sound made him forget for one single second this wasn't Jeremy's real house.

"Jay?" he called out.

"We're in here."

We?

Rafe swallowed, nocked his arrow again, and pushed the door open with his elbow.

He stepped into the past, into Jeremy's old room just like he remembered it. The same elegant wainscoting along the walls, the old brick fireplace painted bright white, the print of Franz Marc's *The Foxes* still hanging over the mantel. Except someone had broken the glass in the print's frame and sliced the picture up with some kind of knife or razor. Spatters of brown on the white brick made it appear as if the painted foxes had bled on the walls.

Rafe kept moving, clutching his bow tight in his sweating hands. There it was just like he remembered it—the king-sized bed tucked under the eaves, the antique Amish double-wedding ring quilt still on top.

He moved into the room carefully as a soldier crossing no-man's-land.

"I'm here," Jeremy said quietly.

Rafe found him sitting on the floor at the foot of the bed, his sword on the rug next to him.

And on his lap lay a small white poodle, seemingly asleep.

"Jay?"

"I saw my father," Jeremy said. He wouldn't look at him. Jeremy's eyes stared blankly out the window.

"Your father? Your dead father?"

"I thought it was him. He looked like him. He wanted to tell me why he—"

"What?"

"Why he killed himself two months before I was born."

Jeremy stroked the dog's fur mindlessly. It looked just like Martha, the Coxes' toy poodle, the dog who had been dead for fifteen years.

"He told me he killed himself because he saw the future, saw that I would run away from Mum and break her heart. He couldn't stand the thought of being a father to a son who would do that, so that's why he left us. I could tell he was a Bright Boy, but you know the crazy thing? That didn't make it any easier to kill him."

"Jay."

Jeremy glanced over at the sword. "Nice of them to make me do it in my old room."

"Where are your apples?" Rafe asked.

"My father wanted one."

"You had two."

"I ate one. I had to so I could kill it."

"Look at me." Rafe knelt in front of Jeremy, snapped his fingers, and met him eye to eye. "This is the Ghost Town. Granny told us there'd be temptations here. Lies. Monsters. We can't let it get to us."

Jeremy gave a little laugh. "At least Martha's here. Aren't you, my sweet girl?"

He scratched the dog under her chin, and she raised her head and gave a little whine of pleasure.

"God, I missed this stupid dog," Jeremy said. "She loved you. She worshipped the ground you walked on. She always slept with Mum unless you were spending the night, then she had to sleep with us. Remember?"

Rafe did want to remember, and he did want to pet her, but he didn't do it.

"Jay, Martha was a good dog. That's what I remember about her. Why would a good dog be here in this awful place?" He touched Jeremy's face. His skin felt clammy and cold to the touch. His hazel eyes had darkened to the dull brown of dead leaves. "That's not Martha."

"Let me pretend it is," Jeremy said. He stroked the dog's soft ears with his fingertips.

Rafe got out an apple and held it to Jeremy's lips, but Jeremy turned his head away.

"Just give me a minute. One more minute."

"Jay, no. Eat the apple. One bite. Please."

Jeremy closed his eyes and laid his head back, petting the false Martha.

Rafe was losing him. He couldn't lose him. He'd lost him before and wasn't going to let it happen again.

So he took a bite of the apple. Then another. Then another. He filled his mouth with the taste of sunlight until the sweet golden juices dripped down his chin. He held one bite of apple in his mouth, then he put his hands on Jeremy's neck.

He kissed him. Hard.

At first, it seemed to have no effect, but then it was like a drowning man breaking the surface to breathe again. Jeremy's lips parted, and Rafe pushed the last bite of Golden Sun apple into his mouth. Jeremy swallowed it whole, then took Rafe's face in his hands, tilted his head back, and, with his tongue, drank from him every last drop of sunlight.

Light makes heat, and there was so much heat in their kiss that Jeremy's hands grew warm on Rafe's skin. The apple kiss was working. Working like magic. It wasn't merely a good kiss. It was too good. Jeremy kissed him like he knew how, like he'd had years of practice, like he had something to prove and knew he could prove it.

They might have kissed forever, except Martha, who had never once growled in her long and gentle life, began to snarl. Rafe pulled back and took out his hunting knife.

He said to Jeremy, "Close your eyes."

Before he could dispatch the beast, it disappeared into a puff of smoke. Rafe stood up, grabbed Jeremy, and pulled him to his feet.

The smoke materialized in front of them and became a leering Bright Boy with ashy skin and smelling of sour milk.

"That felt nice," it said to Jeremy. "You have good hands. Lucky prince," it said, sharp teeth smiling at Rafe.

Jeremy went for his sword, but the creature was standing on it. Rafe held his arrow like a spear, ready to strike, but the Bright Boy held up a white flag he produced from thin air.

"You can't kill me when I wave this," the Bright Boy taunted.

"Who says?" Rafe raised the arrow.

Jeremy said, "Talk fast."

"The King of Lost Virginia awaits your presence. Follow the Blackwater River. Go now or stay here with . . . *that*."

He jerked his head toward the bedroom door. Rafe heard footsteps and slammed the door shut and latched it.

"Darling? It's time for dinner."

A woman's voice, English, loving. Jeremy's mother.

"Hurry," the Bright Boy said. "Don't keep the king waiting."

"Love? Why's the door locked?" The thing knocked harder this time.

"Oh, in case you decide to run off instead of coming to see the king . . ." The Bright Boy pulled something off his neck, something silver, and tossed it to Jeremy. He caught it and looked at it.

"This is Emilie's St. Agatha medal," Jeremy said.

The Bright Boys had Emilie.

Without thinking, Rafe rushed forward to spear it with his arrow, but the creature blew like a storm wind through the window and was gone.

CHAPTER TWENTY-EIGHT

THE DOOR RATTLED on the hinges. Whatever was out there wanted in and wanted in now.

"Is Rafe staying for dinner?" it asked. "He's very welcome to."

Rafe put his hands on Jeremy's shoulders, met his eyes. "It's not her."

"I know. When did Mum ever cook for us?"

"Boys? What's going on in there?"

Something banged hard against the door, like a shoulder.

"Go," Rafe ordered. "Now!"

Jeremy didn't hesitate this time. He grabbed his sword, sheathed it, and clambered out the window into the dead sycamore tree in the backyard.

"I know my son is in there," the thing roared like a demon. "Give him back!"

Rafe nocked an arrow, then took a breath. He popped the latch and shot at the first head that came through the door.

While the monster flailed in fury, Rafe escaped out the window and down the tree.

He landed on the ground, and Jeremy hauled him to his feet. They ran even as Mary Cox's old rose vines grabbed at them, stabbing their legs with vicious thorns.

They ran as fast as they could over streets that made no sense anymore. The bricks crumbled to dust even as they raced across them. Ahead, Rafe saw a river that shouldn't have been there, a black and raging river wide as a two-lane highway. A rope bridge spanned it, and across the river, he saw a dirt road. That must be it, the way they were supposed to go.

Jeremy went across the bridge before Rafe could stop him. He made it easily, but Rafe didn't trust it.

Carefully, he started across the swaying bridge. He told himself not to look down, but he did and saw Jeremy in the water, flailing and fighting the current, an arrow sticking out of his back.

"Rafe!" the Jeremy in the water screamed. "Help!"

"Come on, Rafe, I'm here," Jeremy called out to him from the bank on the other side of the bridge. "Don't fall for it like I did. I'm right here."

But what if he wasn't? What if that was the fake Jeremy on the other side of the bridge and the real one was in the water begging for his help?

Jeremy on the bank started back across the bridge, but a board broke under his boot.

"Stop!" Rafe called to him. "You said water kills Bright Boys."

Jeremy in the river reached up his hand.

"Rafe, it's not real water, remember?" Jeremy said from the end of the bridge. "It wasn't a real dog or a real house, and it's not real water."

He wanted to believe that, but what if he was wrong? There had been a brief moment when he and Jeremy were separated when he stayed in the bedroom to fight the thing behind the door. What if—

He remembered something.

"How do you sing 'Country Roads'?" Rafe called out to the Jeremy on the other side of the bridge.

The Jeremy in the river called back, "What?"

"The real Jeremy Cox has his own version of 'Country Roads.' How does it go?" Rafe called out. The real Jeremy knew every word to John Denver's "Country Roads," West Virginia's state song. Knew it and had his own special version of it.

"Rafe! I'm falling!" The River Jeremy clung to a rock in the water, holding out his hand. Rafe could reach it if he lay down on the boards and stretched out—

"It's not 'Blowing like a breeze,'" Rafe said. "It's—"

The Jeremy on the bridge called out to him, "'Blow me like a breeze!'"

Rafe ran the rest of the way across the bridge and looked back in time to see the River Jeremy sink into the water, which wasn't water at all but an evil-looking black oil.

Jeremy grabbed him as he panted to catch his breath.

"That was brilliant," Jeremy said.

"I always liked your version of the song better," Rafe said. "Come on. Let's go."

Sword and bow at the ready, they walked fast along the path that ran parallel to the river. Even though they knew not to be fooled, the river continued to taunt them with bodies in the water and cries of the drowning.

"What is this horrible place?" Rafe said under his breath.

"Skya said it was the place lost souls passed through. A place between . . ."

"Between what? Heaven and Hell?"

"Between your last breath and your last chance."

An ax flew past them and the blade struck a tree. Sap, thick and red as blood and smelling of copper, poured from the trunk like an open wound.

Rafe wanted to run but was frozen in place. A Bright Boy stood ten feet away dressed in ragged graveclothes and smelling of dead things. He strode to the tree and pulled the ax from the trunk. The blade glistened brown and wet.

"Good move, Prince. Smart. You're very smart," he said. "That trick won't work next time, though."

"What do you want?" Rafe demanded.

"What does Chopper want?" the thing asked as he circled them, moving closer like a shark in the water. "Chopper wants you two to hurry up. That's all. Chop-chop." He took his ax off his shoulder and started to swing it.

Jeremy shoved Rafe out of the way as they ducked, but by the time the ax blew over their heads, Chopper had disappeared.

. . .

RAFE LAY ON HIS back on the scarred ground. Jeremy hovered over him.

"You all right?" Jeremy asked, looking around, assessing the danger.

"You're fast."

"Tempest is a good trainer in the knightly arts of keeping your prince alive." Jeremy grabbed Rafe's hand and yanked him off the ground.

"You just saved my life," Rafe said.

"You saved mine back at the house. New meaning to giving someone the kiss of life. Ready?"

"Not yet." Rafe wasn't ready. He could feel this place getting to him. He'd almost died. Jeremy had almost died. If he was going to die, he wanted to know everything now. "Tell me the truth."

"About what?"

"Back there, that wasn't our first kiss. Right?"

Jeremy looked at him. "No, it wasn't."

"When were you going to tell me?"

"Now, I guess. I was going to tell you at Granny's, but I chickened out."

"When we were here before, we were, what? Fooling around? Experimenting?"

"In love," Jeremy said simply. "If you can believe it. Maybe you can't."

Rafe grabbed him by the back of the neck and pulled him down for another kiss. No excuse this time. No Bright Boys around. A kiss for the sake of kissing.

And then Rafe let him go. "Come on. Now I really want this stupid book back."

"Let's get it back then." Jeremy held out his hand. Rafe took it and they started off down the dark road that ran along the black waters.

They walked on for what felt like hours. That terrible sense of déjà vu crept up on Rafe again. The hills, the curve of the road, the empty houses . . .

"I know where we are," Rafe said.

"This is the way to your house."

Jeremy held his hand tighter.

They found the gravel drive and walked toward the house. It looked like home with the porch swing and his mother's flower bed out front. Home but not home. The flowers were all dead, long dead and decayed.

He felt the darkness coming for him now. He didn't want to go in there.

"Rafe?"

"Mom was right. I don't miss Dad. I'm glad he's gone. He made everything so hard. It didn't have to be hard. Who cares if I liked to draw at the kitchen table? What did that have to do with him? When I was little, Mom got me a book from the library. *How to Draw Animals.* I was trying to draw a wolf, and Dad saw me and shut the book. He made me go outside with him. 'Forget all that,' he said. 'I'll teach you how to hunt wolves.'"

Rafe took a step back, then another. "There aren't even wolves in West Virginia. The hunters killed them all over a hundred years ago." He didn't even know what he was saying, but he knew he couldn't go in there. Even if Emilie was there. He couldn't go in there at gunpoint because what if—

A light came on in the window. The front door opened. The Bright Boy who called himself Ripper came out and waved. More Bright Boys . . . they all rose from the ground, poured out from the trees, all of them grinning, baring their fangs, all in gray rags. Ripper sauntered down the porch steps toward them.

Jeremy tried to move in front of Rafe, but Ripper raised his knife.

"About time," Ripper said. "King's been waiting. But first, let's lighten your load."

The Boys surrounded them, and Rafe and Jeremy had their weapons taken from them. Even worse, the Bright Boys found the last Golden Sun apple in Rafe's pocket. They took it like it was a grenade and tossed it onto the ground. The one called Chopper took his ax to it, and that was that. They were on their own with only the light they had left within them.

Unarmed, they were marched toward the front door.

"This is my house," Rafe said to Ripper, whose sharp fingers were digging into the back of his neck. "Let Jeremy go. He—"

"No," Jeremy said. "Not a chance. Don't even think about it."

"You heard 'em, pretty boy," Ripper said in a cruel, mocking tone.

Jeremy only said to Ripper, "Didn't I cut your head off once?"

Ripper pulled his stained collar down to reveal the black thread stitches that encircled his neck.

"Sewed it back on." Ripper kicked Rafe in the ankle to make him stumble. Jeremy struggled against the two Boys holding him, trying to fight his way free. "Take him away."

"No!" Rafe screamed as they dragged Jeremy away from him and around the house.

"Sorry," Ripper said. "King wants you alone."

Ripper knocked on the door but didn't wait for a reply before pushing it open. In a parody of Rafe's mother's singsong voice, Ripper called out, "Honey, we're home!"

"Kitchen!"

No. No. No. Rafe knew that voice.

Ripper shoved him into the kitchen.

And there was his father sitting at the table and looking just as he'd looked fifteen years ago, in those last days before Rafe went missing, and he'd aged ten years in six months.

Brown hair with streaks of gray. Big, strong, and scowling like always, lines around his mouth not from smiling but from smoking. He wore his work shirt, gray pinstripes smelling of oil and dust, a patch on the breast pocket that said DECKER ELECTRICAL, and under it in cursive, his father's name. *Bill.*

The table was covered in things that didn't make sense—a fork, a razor blade, a knife, and a small welding torch.

Rafe took his chance, lunged forward, and grabbed the fork. He jammed it into the thing that looked like his father, just in the arm. He wanted smoke to pour out, but no . . . nothing. Not a Bright Boy. Something else. The fork fell from Rafe's hand and clattered onto the floor.

"No," Rafe breathed.

"Sit down, son," his father said.

He sat because the Bright Boys made him and because the man in front of him really was his father, and when his father said sit, Rafe sat.

Yes

IN CASE YOU WERE still wondering, yes, that really is the lost soul of Rafe's father.

· ✳ ·

CHAPTER TWENTY-NINE

EMILIE WAS BACK HOME in Ohio, back in her bedroom, and only fourteen years old. Stevie sang "Dreams" to her through her speakers, and the scent of fresh-baked bread wafted up from the kitchen below her, where her mom was cooking dinner. Their dog, PawPaw, lay asleep and snoring on the rug while Emilie folded her laundry. PawPaw didn't even flinch when she stacked her folded T-shirts along his back, almost half of them Fleetwood Mac tour shirts.

And she wasn't afraid of anything.

With her eyes closed, she kept singing and remembering all her favorite days, especially the easy days, the lazy days, the days when she didn't know the definition of fear.

It was working. Skya had told her to do this as they traveled into the Ghost Town. The Bright Boys ate fear, her sister had warned her, and with a gleam in her eyes, she'd said, "Starve them out."

So far, it was working. Although they'd trapped her in a cold basement room, all concrete and wood paneling, she was safe. Her memories of happiness had kept the Bright Boys away from her. The more she sang, the more the boy-shaped parasites slunk off, seeking easier prey. That morning, she'd jumped off a moving ship into a strange ocean and swum fully clothed to the rocks and told her sister, the queen, she would

not leave her. Brave and stupid felt good on her. A good fit. This fake
king of a dead world was not going to win, not without a fight.

The floor vibrated with approaching footsteps. Emilie smiled at the
fear and sang to it. She raised her voice and belted out the chorus just as
the door opened. One of the boys half threw, half pushed Jeremy inside.
He landed in a heap on the concrete floor. She was on her feet and at his
side in an instant.

"Jeremy? Jeremy? You okay?"

She grabbed him by the shoulders, pulled him into a sitting position,
and rested his back against the wall.

"Been better," he said with a grunt of pain. His nose trickled blood,
but otherwise he seemed to be in one piece, more or less. "Can you help
with this?"

He held up his wrists. They'd been tied tight with a cut-off length of
electrical cord.

"Oh my God, Jeremy, no . . ." She started to panic as she frantically
worked at the cords.

"Deep breaths. Stay calm," he said. "They love to freak us out."

"Why did they do this to you?" she asked between slow breaths.

"For touching the king's son," he said. "I'm lucky they didn't cut them
off. And other things."

"I can't. They knotted them." She tried pulling and tugging . . . nothing
worked. Jeremy's hands were turning red. They'd be blue soon.

She fought back tears. She needed music again, needed Stevie. No,
not Stevie.

"Hold on," she said. "I got it. I got it."

"Hurry," Jeremy said. "I'm losing feeling." She took Fritz out of her
hoodie pouch and set him on top of the bindings.

"Chew, baby, chew. You can do this, buddy. Pretend it's one of my
phone cords."

"Smart," Jeremy said as Fritz got to chewing, his sharp front teeth
making quick work of one cord, then another. "I love rats. Rats are my
new favorite animals. Don't tell the horses I said that."

Emilie laughed through her tears. "I won't. Promise."

Finally, Fritz snapped the last cord with a single bite. She hefted him into the air for a victory cheer while Jeremy flexed his hands.

"Good, thank you," he said. "They still work."

Fritz was exhausted after all that chewing, so she kissed him on top of his head and tucked him away again for safety. God only knew what the Bright Boys would do to him if they found him.

"Where's Rafe?" she asked as she helped Jeremy chafe his wrists and hands to get the blood circulating again.

"Kitchen. Something's up there pretending to be his father."

She lowered her voice and leaned close. "It is him, Jeremy. It's his lost soul."

He stared at her, eyes wide with horror. With a cry of fury, he got to his feet and pounded on the door. He kicked it so hard the wood splintered. Then he kicked it again. Again. It didn't give.

"Jeremy!" she called out. "Don't. Remember the fear—"

"This isn't fear," he said. "This is rage."

He kicked it again, but she could tell there was no getting through it.

"You're scaring me now," she called out to him. That worked. Jeremy turned around and went back to her. He sat on the floor, and she put her arms around him.

"Of course it's his father," he said. "Of course that bastard would haunt him even after he died."

He picked up the length of electrical cord and threw it across the room. Emilie rubbed his back, trying to comfort him. He turned to her and took her in his arms. Love was good in a dark place like this, Skya had told her. Love was their secret weapon.

"I know it's bad," she said, then lowered her voice even more, "but you have to focus, okay?" She pointed at her eyes to make him smile. "Skya needs us."

His eyes widened.

"Skya? She did find you?"

She smiled because even in this dank, evil city, having her sister was like having a one-woman army behind her. "Yeah. She tried to make me sit this one out. I wouldn't let her."

"Good," he said. "Brave girl." He kissed her forehead.

"We have a plan. That's why I'm here. I'm supposed to get a message to Rafe."

"What is it?"

"I don't know what it means, but she told me to tell him, 'Do it in one.' Does that mean anything to you?"

"No idea."

"Maybe he'll know. I have to get up there."

"Does Skya know what Bill's doing here?"

"He has Rafe's sketchbook full of memories. We peeked in the windows and saw it on the table. He's trying to open it, but he can't do it. My sister said only Rafe can do it."

"Why would he want his memories? He's dead."

"Skya says there's something in there he doesn't want Rafe to remember. But she wouldn't tell me, said she promised Rafe."

"He knows about Shanandoah now. He knows about us," he said. "So . . ."

"So what could his dad want Rafe never to remember?" she asked. "I mean . . . what's left? You were with him the entire time, right? You remember everything he'd remember."

Jeremy stopped and looked up, cocked his head to the side. "Not quite. He says he can't remember anything from the night before we tried to run away, and I wasn't with him then."

She moved right in front of him and sat knees to knees. "So his last memory before going missing was from the night before. What happened that night?"

Jeremy exhaled hard. "Uh . . . fight with his dad."

"Bad fight?"

"He destroyed Rafe's sketchbook. Shredded the drawings. Too many of me in there." He gave a bitter laugh.

"So that's Rafe's last memory."

"No," Jeremy said. "He says the very last thing he remembers is shutting his bedroom door after Bobbi sent him to his room."

"And nothing after that?"

"Nothing."

Emilie took Jeremy's hands in hers and studied the rope marks on his wrists. She glanced at the chewed-through electrical cord across the room, then at his wrists again.

The cord. A memory. The marks on his wrists.

Too many sketches of Jeremy. *Why did they do this to you? For touching the king's son* . . .

"Unfinished business," she said softly.

"What?"

"Skya says lost souls come here if they have unfinished business. This place is where they can finish it. It's their last chance to make things right."

He met her eyes and waited. She wasn't sure she was sure, but she was sure she had a very good idea.

"The scars on Rafe's back. I saw them when I was cutting his hair. They reminded me . . . At the vet's office, someone brought in this pit bull, Pumpkin. All three of us vet techs had to help because she was so reactive. Because she'd been abused when she was a puppy. Now I remember . . . I remember the scars on her. Long, thin pink scars. Her new owner said someone had tied her up and beaten her with—"

"What?"

Now she knew what Rafe's dad wanted with the sketchbook. He wanted to make sure Rafe never remembered that night. The night he beat him with—

She whispered, "An electrical cord."

This time, when Jeremy tried to kick the door down, she didn't try to stop him.

· ✳ ·

CHAPTER THIRTY

THEY SAT ALONE in the ghost of his mom's kitchen. No Bright Boys. Just him and his father. If it was his father.

If? No, it was. The crow's-feet around the eyes. The gray patches of hair by the temples. The dozens of healed scars on his arms from a hundred minor workplace injuries. The broad shoulders slightly stooped from a lifetime of manual labor but still strong as an ox.

But it wasn't his face or his shoulders or even his eyes that told Rafe this man sitting across from him was his real father or the ghost of his real father . . .

It was the fear, his oldest fear. Not death, not pain, not watching someone he loved suffer. The simple stupid terrifying fear he'd carried like gravel in his guts ever since he was a child. The fear of knowing he was in trouble with his dad.

"It's all right, son," his dad said, though Rafe hadn't apologized for stabbing him with the fork. "I know it's a surprise. A surprise to me too."

"You're alive. You're . . . younger. You're—"

He shrugged. "I'm here. Can't really explain."

"Try."

His father narrowed his eyes in a warning. Rafe quickly adjusted his tone. "Please."

"I wanted another chance to talk to you. I got it. Sometimes that happens. Don't ask me how it works."

"Why did you want to talk to me?" Rafe asked him.

"Why?" He seemed surprised by the question. "Because you're my son."

Rafe wanted to scream but didn't. He knew better, and the unwritten rules were tattooed onto his soul. Don't raise your voice to your father. Don't swear in front of your father. If you raise your voice and swear at your father, good night and game over.

"Dad. Please. What's going on? You're in Shanandoah's Ghost Town, and you have Bright Boys calling you the King of Lost Virginia. A king?"

"You call yourself a prince, don't you?"

"I don't *call* myself a prince. I *am* a prince. You are not a king."

"You always did think you were better than me."

"Never, Dad. I never thought that. I knew I was different, that's all. You're the one who took that as a personal insult." Rafe leaned forward, tried to reach out to the man his father used to be, the man who had wanted forgiveness, wanted to make peace. "The Bright Boys are evil. You saw my scars. You saw what they did to me."

His father actually looked a little sheepish about that. He lowered his voice and said, "It's getting lonely here. I keep expecting to walk in and see you at the table helping your mother shelling peas or cleaning the tassels off the corn. Those sorts of things you don't think about when you have them but miss most when they're gone. My wife in the kitchen. My son at the table."

"I'm here now."

"Good to have you. We ought to spend more time together."

Rafe gave up, lapsed into silence. He used to lose his mind trying to have conversations with his father. Nothing he said was right. He could never crack the secret code to get through to him. Everything Rafe said made things worse, and silence was always the only form of surrender his father would accept.

Now he saw this verbal smoke screen for what it was—a shield. He'd seen his father raise that shield a thousand times and it always worked. Rafe never dared to look behind it. Now he did.

"What are you hiding, Dad?"

His father brought his big meaty fist down onto the table so fast and so hard that the knife fell to the floor and the window rattled in the frame. Rafe jumped.

"I am trying to help you!" The voice. That fury. His father's shouting had been a weapon, a flamethrower. How many times had Rafe and his mother had to shrink away from it before they got burned?

"What the fuck are you talking about, Dad?"

He waited for the *good night and game over*, but it didn't come. His dad only sat there, staring at him, eyes wide with shock. Was that the first time in his life Rafe ever shouted back? Maybe.

After a tense silence, his father picked up the book in front of him. Black leather binding, cracked, faded, but locked up tight with a silver combination lock.

"You know what this is?"

Rafe knew. "My book of memories."

"That is *not* what this is." His father's tone was sharp as a knife. "This is . . . misery, son. Garbage. This is . . . You open this and let all that trash spill out, and you'll never—never—be happy again in your life."

"Trash? Are you serious?"

"Everything in this book is poison. It'll poison you against your home, against your mother, against me. You don't want any part of this, of what's in here."

"Why? Because I'll remember how happy I was in Shanandoah? I'll remember how happy I was away from you? Or is it because I'll remember how happy Jeremy and I were when we were—"

The fist came down again, harder, louder.

But Rafe didn't flinch. "In love."

"In love . . ." His father sneered in disgust. "Two ignorant boys prancing through the woods playing queens and castles. What do you know about love?"

"I know it's not whatever this is," Rafe said as he sat back in the kitchen chair. He tried not to look at the book on the table, the book that held the whole lost and beautiful story of his life in Shanandoah, his life with Jeremy.

"You don't know anything," his father said. "Nothing. But I know. And you can hate me, you can judge me, but I know what's best for you, and what's best for you is getting rid of this thing right now."

He tapped the cover of the book like it was a bad report card.

"So get rid of it," Rafe said. "What are you waiting for?"

For one brief—too-brief—moment, his father looked almost scared.

"You can't do it, can you?" Rafe asked. "You can't get it open and you can't destroy it. Only I can. Magic sketchbook. Little bit tougher to destroy than my old sketchbooks, huh?"

"Please, son." He took a breath. "Ralph, I'm trying to help you. All I want to do is help you. You open this and you'll never ... you'll never be able to not see what you see in here, and you'll wish you had. You'll wish it so hard, but it'll be too late for you. I want what's best for you and it's not in here."

Rafe waited for more. There had to be more.

His father reached into his breast pocket and pulled out his old chrome cigarette lighter. He held it out to Rafe, who took it, smiled.

"When I was a kid, I used to love the tricks you could do with this thing," Rafe said. "The way you could flick it open and closed one-handed, make the flame disappear. I thought when I grew up, I'd be able to do it too. Never bothered to figure it out."

"See? You looked up to me once, before that boy came along. Don't you want that? Don't you want good memories? Come on, son. Do it for me. Burn it and that's that."

Rafe held the lighter in his palm, then threw it across the kitchen so hard it shattered the window.

His father didn't look surprised. In fact, he looked like he'd planned for it.

"All right," he said, resigned. "Rip?"

Ripper's grinning face appeared in the doorway.

"Yeah, Boss?"

"Bring up the girl."

"Not the boy?"

"Saving him for later," his father said. "Go get her."

Rafe was on his feet at once. "Dad? Dad, don't do this. Please don't do this—"

"Too late, son."

His father took the book off the table and tossed it into his big red toolbox on the floor, then kicked the lid shut and locked it with his fistful of jangling keys.

Ripper and Chopper dragged Emilie into the kitchen. Her hands were tied in front of her and they'd gagged her with what looked like one of his dad's old blue handkerchiefs.

"Here she is, Boss," Ripper said. "And your knife. We took it off her when we caught her."

His father took the hunting knife and looked at it.

"How'd she get my knife?"

"Mom gave it to her," Rafe said.

"I didn't say she could do that."

"You were dead."

"Least I got it back." He put his knife into his belt. "Let her down, boys."

The Bright Boys put Emilie on her knees on the floor. Rafe got up again, ready for a fight, but Ripper grabbed him, put a knife to his throat.

"You wanna find out why they call me Ripper?" he asked.

"Stop that," his father said. "Not my son."

Ripper only laughed low in his throat, then leaned in close to whisper in Rafe's ear.

"Your daddy said I get to be prince when you're gone."

"Gone home," his father said. "Not gone. *Home.*"

"Home," Ripper repeated. "Right. Home."

He stepped back, wrapped his hand in Emilie's long blond hair, and held it hard enough that she cried out behind the gag.

"What should we do with her, son?" his father asked.

"Let her go," Rafe said. He couldn't believe this was happening, that his father had turned into this monster. But he could see the darkness in his eyes. This benighted place had gotten to him. Was there any light left in him?

"You'll destroy that book?" he asked. "You do that, I'll let her go. Easy as pie."

Rafe glanced at Emilie. Behind the gag, her eyes pleaded with him. Not to say yes, but to say no. She groaned a sound.

"Shut her up," his dad demanded.

Ripper grabbed her by the neck and slapped a hand over her mouth so that she couldn't get a single sound out. Emilie tried to bite at the hand that silenced her but she couldn't do it. What was she trying so hard to tell him? It didn't matter. Rafe had already made up his mind.

He said, "Okay, I'll—"

A single perfect red feather wafted through the hole in the broken window and floated on the air until it landed at Rafe's feet.

A red feather like the fletching in the arrow above the queen's throne. Rafe said, "I'll play you for it."

His father looked at him, eyes narrowed. "Play?"

"Let's kill spiders," he said. "You know, like old times."

"I already have the book. Why should I play to win something I already have?"

"We aren't just playing for my book." Rafe's mind whirled, thinking up terms, how to make it interesting enough to get his father to go along with it. "How about this? If I kill the spider, I get the book, and we all get to leave. But if you kill it . . . I'll destroy the book, and I'll . . ." He couldn't believe he was making this offer. He looked at the red feather on the floor again. "I'll stay with you. Here."

"You'll stay here with me? You and me?"

"You let Emilie and Jeremy go home, and I'll stay here with you until you, you know, move on."

"No running away the second my back is turned?"

"No running away."

His father thought about it, then said, "What if we both miss it?"

"Then you still win just for playing. If we both miss, I'll still destroy the book. I only win if I kill the spider." He faked a smile. "Come on, Dad. It'll be fun. And you were always a better shot than me, right?"

Slowly, his father nodded.

"Having you here sounds good to me," he said. "We'll have a good time." To Ripper he said, "Get our bows."

Ripper said, "This ain't a good idea, Boss."

"Do what I say," his father ordered.

The Bright Boy released Emilie. "I'll get your bows."

His father patted Rafe on the shoulder.

"I know you missed me, son."

CHAPTER THIRTY-ONE

RAFE STOOD IN THE dark and dank backyard as his father gave orders to Ripper about the target, the distance. It seemed there were no floodlights in this version of the house. Would they have to wait until morning? Rafe couldn't stomach the idea of spending a night in this place. He had to get Emilie and Jeremy to safety. At least she was there in the backyard with them, tied up but alive for now. Where was Jeremy? What had happened to him? Was he hurt?

He couldn't think about it.

Bright Boys began to mass in the yard. A dozen, then two dozen, more . . . they all carried lit torches like a mob of angry villagers hungry for a good witch burning.

What had he done? He was crazy to think he could win this game. Once, when he was fifteen years old, he saved a queen's life with a lucky shot. Now, years later, he had to do it again? And if he failed he'd have to stay in this place forever, this evil place two streets over from Hell?

Ripper nailed the paper target to the trunk of a skeleton tree forty yards from the line. Even by the light of so many torches, Rafe could barely see the spider in the center. They'd be shooting on pure instinct.

His father joined him behind the shooting line.

His father chuckled softly. "You and I both know how this ends already. And I've kept myself busy waiting for you to show yourself."

Rafe's mouth was dry when he answered, "You've been practicing."

"Not much else to do here."

One of the Bright Boys, a shorter one with a forked tongue and fangs like a snake, appeared carrying both Rafe's bow and quiver and his father's.

"Sire," the boy hissed.

Rafe took his own bow and clutched it tightly. The bow his mother had given him. What if he never saw his mother again?

"So how do we wanna do this?" his father asked as he checked his own bow. "Six rounds? Twelve rounds?"

Two Bright Boys stood behind his father. The squat one with snake teeth and a taller one with skin so pale he looked like a ghost in gray. But their eyes gleamed with satisfaction. They looked sated. They ate fear. That's why the Bright Boys had let a deadly sleeper spider loose in the throne room. Not to kill the queen but to create a feast of terror. And the ones by his father's side looked especially well fed.

His father was afraid. Petrified. These creatures weren't loyal, but hungry, and his father was an all-you-can-eat buffet.

Rafe looked around, caught Emilie's eyes. Although her hands were tied in front of her, she could still move her fingers. She held up her index finger, then nodded as if giving him a secret message. She or Jeremy must have a plan.

Rafe said, "One."

"One round?"

"One arrow."

"One arrow? Just one?" His father sounded aghast.

"Just one."

"No one gets it in one, son."

"So you win," Rafe said. "Right?"

"You can get it, Boss. We'll be mighty disappointed if you don't," said Snake Teeth.

"You can do it, Big Man," the Gray Ghost said.

"Go on," Ripper said. "We can't wait to see this. Show 'em why you're the king around here."

With the Bright Boys goading him on, his father had no choice but to step forward.

"I'll go first, son."

Rafe stepped back as his father stood on the shooting line. He pulled an arrow and nocked it. As a boy Rafe had loved watching his father shooting targets. Rafe wanted to be just like him. He'd wanted to be that good. Every day he practiced, trying to be that good. Strangely, the better Rafe got, the less his father seemed to enjoy their games. Rafe didn't understand it then. He did now. Trying to be as good as his dad was one thing. Being better than him was another.

His father drew his arrow. It seemed an eternity passed between the draw and the release. The arrow flew and hit the target with a soft thud.

"Dammit," his father said.

"You aimed," Rafe said. His father turned to him, fire in his eyes, but maybe it was just the torches of the Bright Boys. "You taught me to never aim."

"Just shoot, son."

"Two seconds, Boss Man," Ripper said. "Gotta make a little adjustment. Don't mind us."

Two Bright Boys emerged from the basement door, dragging Jeremy between them. His cheek was bruised, his shirt torn, but his eyes were still defiant.

Rage swelled in Rafe's heart, threatening to overwhelm him. But he couldn't give in to it, because now they were forcing Jeremy to sit under the target. On the ground, back to the trunk, the top of his red head touched the bottom of the blue ring. They didn't tie him to the tree, however. Why not?

"Even on my worst days," Rafe told his father, "I don't miss the bull's-eye by a foot."

"You think you can kill spiders. Kill a spider then, son."

In disgust and horror, Rafe watched Ripper's mouth open wide, wider, until his face nearly split in two. He reached down his own throat and pulled from his gut a spider. A red spider. A red sleeper spider.

Gently, he placed the spider on the target.

So that's why they hadn't bothered to tie up Jeremy.

Rafe stared down the line. Jeremy sat motionless, barely breathing. But though the Bright Boys were immune from the spider's venom, they still kept their distance from Jeremy as if they were repelled by him.

Jeremy wasn't afraid. That was why they didn't want to be anywhere near him. Fearlessness was poison to them. Love. Light. Trust. There was one and only one reason Jeremy wouldn't be afraid with a sleeper spider eight inches from his head.

He knew Rafe could make the shot.

Rafe pulled an arrow from his quiver. He nocked it. His only regret was the necessity of killing the spider, a creature that hadn't asked to be a pawn in this game.

He raised his bow. Now he remembered that day in the backyard so long ago . . .

"Remember that day we were shooting spiders, and I thought I almost got it, but I said it was off-center?" Rafe asked. "It wasn't off-center. I killed the shit out of that spider."

Then he released his arrow. He didn't even have to look. The silence said everything.

A voice broke the silence, one Rafe didn't remember but recognized at once as the voice of his queen.

"West—by God!—Virginia!"

· ✳ ·

CHAPTER THIRTY-TWO

QUEEN SKYA STOOD on the roof of the house, tall and fearless. With her bow she released arrow after arrow at the Bright Boys. They turned to dust before her arrows had even passed completely through their bodies.

Rafe felt a surge of pride that this was his queen, and he would have died for her with a smile on his face right then and there, if he didn't have so much to live for. He grabbed his quiver and nocked another arrow. He shot Snake Teeth as the Bright Boy ran toward him, club in hand.

From the corner of his eye, Rafe saw Jeremy get to his feet and yank the arrow from the target. With it he stabbed one Bright Boy, turning him instantly into a puff of smoke.

The few Bright Boys still standing scattered like roaches in daylight. Skya jumped down to the deck and untied Emilie. Rafe wanted to run to Jeremy, but there were too many of the monsters between them.

"Dad!" Rafe called out for his father, but he only sank to his knees in defeat. Rafe got off a few more arrows and it seemed the scent of courage was so noxious to the Bright Boys, they began to back off; some even ran into the woods.

Only Ripper showed any backbone. Twisted blade in hand, Ripper charged Rafe, hate in his inhuman eyes. He ran fast, too fast, and Rafe's quiver was empty.

"Son!" His dad stirred from his stupor and tossed him the hunting knife he'd taken from Emilie. It landed on the ground a few feet from him. Rafe dove for it, but when he reached out to grab the handle, Ripper was there, bringing down the blade.

Rafe pulled back his arm just in time to avoid getting it cut off. With his bow Rafe jabbed Ripper in the stomach, throwing him off-balance, then struck him again across the face with the wooden riser. Smoke escaped a hole in Ripper's cheek, but it wasn't enough to kill him. Ripper recovered, kicked Rafe in the stomach, and sent him sprawling onto his back.

No time. No chance to tell Jeremy goodbye. He would die without remembering the first time Jeremy told him he loved him, the first kiss, the last kiss before Rafe forgot what they were to each other.

Ripper brought the blade down but then stopped, inhaled, then coughed up a small puff of smoke.

Slowly, the creature turned around. The hunting knife . . . Rafe's father's hunting knife protruded from his back. More smoke seeped out from around the wound.

Rafe smiled, knowing Ripper would now see that his father had come to his defense, had saved him.

But it wasn't his father who'd stabbed Ripper.

Behind Ripper, Emilie stood tall, face set in stone, eyes pure gray steel. "Got you," she said.

Ripper stumbled; his chin fell to his chest. He was trying so hard not to die.

"Mean girl. Do you think I want to be like this?" he asked her. "The king said I could be a prince. I always wanted to be a prince."

"You're not a prince," Emilie said, then pointed at Rafe. "That's a prince."

Slowly, as if he could feel real pain, Ripper turned and looked at him. "They call me Ripper cuz I'll rip your heart out."

Emilie yanked the knife from Ripper's back. He spun, lunged at her, and she stabbed him again, this time in the chest.

"Not fair," Ripper said. "Not fair at all."

She tapped the tip of his nose. "Boop."

Then he turned to smoke and was gone.

Pride

GOOD JOB, PRINCESS. I knew you had it in you.

CHAPTER THIRTY-THREE

IT WAS QUIET AGAIN. The Bright Boys were all gone, turned to smoke or fled. Rafe glanced around, searching the yard for Jeremy. He had to see him, had to know he was all right.

"Jay!"

"I'm here, Rafe." Jeremy limped over to him from the trees, Skya at his side. Rafe scrambled to his feet and took Jeremy's face in his hands, examining him.

"You okay? You hurt?"

"I'll be fine after a bath and a bottle of wine. Maybe not in that order." He grinned. Rafe kissed him.

Emilie said, "Did you all see me kill that thing? I'm amazing."

"You are," Rafe said. He reached out and took her hand in his. "You saved my life."

She threw her arms around him and whispered into his ear, "Your scars. It was your dad. Night before you got lost. He used an electrical cord. I'm sorry."

Rafe pulled away and looked at her. "What?"

She met his eyes and gave him the smallest and saddest of smiles. He looked to Jeremy, who only nodded.

"I'll go get your book." Emilie went to his father, still on his knees on the ground, and held out her hands.

"Where is it?" she demanded.

He reached into the pocket of his old worn work jeans and pulled out the keys.

"Toolbox."

She took the keys and went into the house.

Rafe stumbled over to his father, stared down at him.

"We can go," Jeremy said. "You don't owe him anything. We can leave right now and never look back."

But Rafe couldn't do that. He stepped in front of his father and said, "Dad?"

"Yeah, son?"

"It's true?"

His father raised his head and Rafe saw in his eyes that it was.

Jeremy said, "I should've known. When we were lost in the woods, you got dehydrated so fast. Too fast. Like you were sick with something. If the cuts got infected—"

"He could've died," Skya said. She strode like a soldier toward his father, who knelt with his head bowed, like a condemned man waiting for the ax to fall.

Numb, Rafe listened as his queen told the story he'd never wanted to hear.

"Your son woke up the next morning, his back covered in open wounds, and instead of telling anyone and getting you thrown in jail, he put on two shirts and smiled through the pain. He was so ashamed of you, of what you did to him, he couldn't even tell his own best friend. I made him tell me, though. He told me and said he never wanted to go home again. The universe listens when a child says he doesn't want to go home. I listened."

"I'm sorry," his father said. "I'm so sorry, I am. You have to believe me."

Emilie came out and stood by her sister, the book in her hand. She held it out to Rafe, and he started to take it.

"Don't, son. Please?"

"Why try to stop me now?" Rafe asked. "I know what's in there."

"You know but you don't . . . you don't remember. I admit it. I went down to your room to talk to you. I just wanted to talk to you about—"

"About you shredding my pictures of Jeremy?"

"Yes, that. And when I saw you'd taped those pictures back together, I . . . I lost my mind. I lost control of myself. I lost . . . I just lost it," he breathed.

"So it was my fault?"

"I didn't mean it like that. You said you hated me. You said over and over again how much you hated me and how much you wished you lived with Jeremy and his mother, that they weren't a bunch of stupid rednecks like me and—"

"And you were forty and I was fourteen."

His father began to weep.

"I only wanted to protect you, son. I was afraid, afraid if people knew about you boys, they would—"

"Hurt me?" Rafe asked. "Dad, you're the only person I've ever been afraid of."

Jeremy stood by him, said nothing, but he was a shield, a wall, and Rafe felt safer, stronger just having him by his side.

"You used to let me win," his father said. "I thought maybe you were gonna let me win again."

"You're the one who taught me the secret of archery, remember? Put your heart on the target and aim for your own heart. You put Jeremy there. You made it too easy."

Skya stepped forward. "You are not a king and never have been," she said to Rafe's father. "You are a sad old man afraid of your own son. But when the moment of decision came, you gave your knife to my sister instead of one of your vile army. I grant you one final chance to mend what you tore to pieces. If you succeed, your soul will lighten. You may grow wings and fly from this place into the blue sky. Whether you find hawks or Heaven is not up to me. But I can say this: if you fail you will never feel the sun on your face again."

If he hadn't believed Skya was a queen before, Rafe believed it now.

To this speech, his father said nothing, only bowed his head again.

Skya turned to Rafe and smiled.

"My prince," she said.

"My queen," he said.

She smiled, and her eyes were the brightest lights to be seen in this dark place.

"You don't even remember me."

"I want to, though."

"I know. I'm not bad, right?" She chucked him under the chin. "Come on, gorgeous. I'm hungry, dirty, and my ass is so wrecked from riding I'm asking for a new one for Christmas."

Rafe laughed, and it felt like the sun was coming out, if only in his soul. They started to walk away, leaving his father on the ground, alone.

"I remember the day I started teaching you how to shoot arrows," his father said as they headed toward the path. "You were at the kitchen table, trying to teach yourself how to draw wolves. I said why draw wolves when I could teach you how to hunt them. Don't you want to go hunting? There's wolves here, son! We can hunt wolves together!"

"You want me to punch him again?" Jeremy asked.

Rafe said, "No."

"Son? Ralph?" his father called out. Rafe kept walking. "Rafe?"

Rafe didn't look back.

Reunion

LEAVING THE GHOST TOWN is like waking from a nightmare into your sweetest dream. No matter what horrors you left behind you, your spirit will sing. The joy of returning to the light of Shanandoah was eclipsed only by the happiness of being reunited. Jeremy and Rafe? Goes without saying they were beyond glad to see each other in the sunlight. Emilie and Skya too. But perhaps the sweetest, tenderest reunion was between Skya and Jeremy. Emilie and Skya had only met, had only just begun to know and treasure each other as sisters. And Rafe, of course, didn't remember Skya. But Jeremy did remember his queen, and she remembered her knight. Once they were safely out of the Ghost Town, Jeremy picked her up and spun her in his arms, which the queen allowed for approximately two seconds.

"Put me down, knave," she ordered. "This is conduct unbecoming a knight."

Jeremy set her down on her feet. "My insincerest apologies, my queen." Then he bowed deeply. When he stood up again, she groaned.

"Oh no. You got tall," she said. She looked at Rafe. "My prince, I told you not to let him get taller than me. How could you let this happen?"

Rafe only shrugged. "Like he listens to me."

(At this point, Jeremy may or may not have kissed the top of her head to rub it in, and she may or may not have retaliated by pinching him on the ass. Both parties deny this interaction ever took place, though eye-witnesses confirm it.)

Then Jeremy and Skya dropped the act and held each other for a long time. Not long enough to make up for fifteen years but close enough.

CHAPTER THIRTY-FOUR

THEY ARRIVED BACK at the palace late in the afternoon. Emilie gazed in awe at the towers, the turrets, the horses in the fields and paddocks, the endless beauty.

"Like it?" Skya asked.

"That's your house?"

"Palace. The Moonstone Palace. And it's not mine, it's ours."

Emilie liked the sound of that. Not the palace, though it was spectacular. *Ours.* She liked the sound of *ours* because *ours* sounded like she had a family again.

"Just please tell me it has hot running water. One of the Bright Boys coughed on me. It was like Satan's gravy."

"We have hot running water," Skya promised. "And very, very soft towels."

Emilie was taken to a large room, all marble and tile, with a pool that filled itself continually from a central fountain. The hot spring water soothed her sore muscles, and by the time she got out, she felt reborn. And the towels were, in fact, very, very soft, so soft that Fritz fell asleep in them.

After her bath, Winter gave her clothes to wear—a white linen tunic, a warm vest, soft brown leggings, and boots. They fit perfectly, like they were made for her. On the way up to her room, Winter pointed out the kitchens, the armory, the aviary, and the way to Rafe's and Jeremy's rooms.

"Where are they anyway?" Emilie asked Winter.

"The queen is punishing them for defying her orders and going to the Ghost Town after she told them to stay in the palace."

"What's the punishment?"

"She let them choose between beheading or being sent to their rooms without dinner."

"Oh," Emilie said. "Which one did they pick?"

Emilie's bedroom was in the south turret. She knew it was hers because on the arched oak door someone had put up a sign that read THE PRINCESS SUITE.

"You all just put this together for me?" Emilie asked.

"You've had a room here forever, Princess," Winter said. "The day after our prince and our knight left us, she began making up this room for you. She wanted it perfect by the time you arrived."

Emilie touched the sign, the white letters painted so carefully on the black wood.

"She missed me that much?"

"That much and more."

Slowly, Emilie opened the door. The room was round because she was in the turret. She turned a circle to take it all in . . . the large canopy bed, a herd of leaping racing chasing unicorns carved into the wooden headboard . . . with pale blue and silver curtains surrounding it . . . a wide balcony that looked out on the faraway mountains . . .

"We have this for your friend, Princess."

Winter whipped away a velvet cloth, revealing a gilded cage, five feet high and round as the castle tower. A spiral staircase led through tunnels. Ropes and toys and a silver food and water dish, rat-size.

"A rat palace," Emilie said. "Look, Fritz. This is for you." She took Fritz out of his fuzzy bath towel and let him loose in his new home. He immediately ran up and down the staircase, ate some berries, drank some water, used his litter, and collapsed into his nest to sleep.

"Good idea, buddy," she said. "Let's all eat, crap, and sleep. In that order."

"All your clothes are in here," Winter said, opening a wardrobe door. "Everything should fit you."

"How?" Emilie asked. "I just got here. And Skya's taller than me."

"That's how it works. It's in our story."

Something about that seemingly simple statement made Emilie's heart skip and her blood turn a degree or two colder.

She faced Winter. "What story?"

Winter took her down to the first floor and through a long corridor to a set of enormous double doors. Emilie pushed one open and found herself in the most magnificent private library she'd ever seen in real life or pictures. Rows upon rows of books sat on rows upon rows of bookshelves, their spines making a thousand rainbows.

She glanced at a few of the books and recognized some of the titles— *The Wind in the Willows* and *A Christmas Carol* and *The Princess and the Goblin* . . .

"These are all books from . . . where I'm from." She turned and looked at Winter. "What's going on?"

The door rattled and opened. Emilie barely recognized Skya at first. Gone was her leather armor, her torn and dirty clothes. She wore a loose gown of forest green with long flowing sleeves and her blond hair in a braided crown.

"I thought I heard voices in here," Skya said.

"Hello, Majesty." Winter bowed. "The princess wanted to see our story."

"I'll show her," Skya said. "Thank you."

After another bow, Winter left them alone together.

"What story is she talking about?" Emilie asked her.

"Over here." Skya crooked her finger and Emilie followed her to another door that led to a smaller room. "My private salon. Rafe and Jeremy and I would hang out in here on cold nights."

A beautiful room, intimate and cozy with a pale blue fainting sofa and large armchairs, and tapestries on the walls. One armchair sat at the corner of the rug by the fireplace, a side table next to it stacked high with books.

One of them was *The Wonderful Wizard of Oz*, a bookmark with an emerald-green tassel between the pages.

"I never showed this to them," Skya said as she pushed aside a tapestry to reveal a secret wall niche. On a bed of white velvet sat a golden box. "Don't remember why. Maybe I didn't know how to answer all the questions I knew they'd ask. I don't even understand it all myself."

With a key that hung on a cord at her waist, she unlocked the box.

Emilie looked inside and saw something she never dreamed she would see in this strange, magical kingdom.

"A Trapper Keeper?" Emilie asked, laughing in her surprise.

"Got it at the Goodwill on Hunters Way," Skya said. "Down from the Arby's." She took out the Trapper Keeper—the picture on the front was of a neon sun setting into a neon sea. She opened the Velcro flap with a satisfying *ssst*.

Inside the binder lay dozens of pages of notebook paper, slightly yellowed, and covered in a girl's looping cursive handwriting.

Emilie read the first line on the first page.

Once upon a time in West Virginia . . .

She looked up in surprise. "Skya? What is this?"

"When I was in the fifth grade," Skya said, "our teacher taught us about fairy tales. We were supposed to write our own. I'd never tried writing a story before, but once I started, I was hooked. I couldn't stop. Every other kid in the class turned in a one-page story. Mine was twenty."

"*Twenty?* That's a million pages to a ten-year-old. I couldn't write twenty pages now."

Skya smiled. "Mrs. Adler was amazed by all the work I'd done. She asked me to stay after school. I thought I was in trouble. But she handed me this mechanical pencil with a unicorn for an eraser, and she said, 'Here, take this. It's a magic pencil. If you keep writing . . . you can change your whole life.' I felt like King Arthur with Excalibur."

Emilie looked at her sister, trying to see the little girl in the face of the woman.

"Was it bad? Your life, I mean?"

"A kid shouldn't wish her mother away, right? The only good thing she ever did for me was bring you home."

She turned the pages slowly. The paper crinkled like an old Bible.

"Fifth grade, sixth grade, seventh grade, eighth grade . . . I'd work on this story every day. I'd skip lunch and go to the library and just write and write. I wrote until I had a permanent indentation on my finger." She ran her fingers over the paper. "And that unicorn pencil must have been magical because it never seemed to run out of lead."

With a shaking hand, Emilie turned the pages and read a few lines here and there.

Queen Skya had a pet crow named Aurora. This was no ordinary crow. Aurora was red, for starters, instead of boring old black. And she was a wonderful spy. You couldn't think of a single secret without that crow knowing. Even better, she could pass between worlds when she felt like it. She visited one forest in West Virginia so often, they named it after her . . .

The Bright Boys were the queen's immortal mortal enemies. Not truly immortal. You could kill them if you doused them in water, but usually it was more fun to shoot them with arrows and turn them to dust and smoke. Then they came back in a week or a month and you got to kill them again . . .

The day came when a star grew nightsick. It was made of light but lived in the dark, and when it couldn't take the darkness anymore, it fell a thousand thousand miles. When the star landed it broke into seven pieces. The seven pieces saw that the kingdom where they landed was beautiful and good, so they decided to stay. Each piece turned itself into a girl to fit in, though their hearts were forever made of the stuff of stars—iron, light, and fire. They called themselves the Valkyries because one of them had heard about them in a story a passing comet once told them, and they thought the word had a nice ring to it.

And the Moonstone Palace was a magic palace. Any book you would ever want to read would appear on the shelves of the library. Any clothes you needed hung in your closet, always a perfect fit. And the water in the baths was always warm and the towels were very, very soft . . .

The queen traveled three days to the Witch of Black Wolf Cave to beg a magic spell to find her missing sister.

"Here is the spell," the witch said, "and with it you can find a lost child or a lost trinket, but the one thing you can never find with it is that which does not want to be found. If your sister is not truly lost, there is a chance you may never find her."

"I know, but I have to try."

There were hand-drawn maps of the kingdom with place-names like Ravencliff and Apple Pie Hill. Lists of made-up imaginary animals too—the cyclops owl, snow deer, silver tigers, and the phantom fox . . . She'd drawn pictures of the creatures. The phantom fox was nothing but a pale outline with two black, staring eyes.

"Your story came true," Emilie said. "That's not how it works. Something happens and you write about it. You don't write about it and then it happens."

"I don't know," Skya said as she turned another page. "Sometimes you want a story to be real so badly, you almost believe wanting it can make it come true."

Skya put her hand lovingly on the cut stone walls. "You know why this place is called the Moonstone Palace even though it's a castle? I didn't know the difference between palaces and castles."

"I just . . . I can't believe it. Why? How?" Emilie flipped through the pages again, unbelieving and yet believing, because how could she not believe her sister's story had come true? She was standing in it.

Skya reached out and cupped the St. Agatha medal Emilie wore. Jeremy had gotten it back for her.

"Maybe someone was watching over me," Skya said. "A tenderhearted angel? Some patron saint? A friendly god of another world taking a stroll through our solar system?"

Skya released the medal. It fell softly against Emilie's skin.

Aurora fluttered down to sit on Skya's shoulder.

"Or maybe it was you all along," Skya said to her bird. "I was running from that guy in the park, and he grabbed me by my backpack. I could've just let it go and kept running, but it had my story in it. I couldn't let him have it. It was more me than me, you know?"

"What happened? Or do I not want to know?"

"He got me by the arm, started dragging me to the ground. But then . . ." She laughed and it sounded like church bells ringing on Christmas morning. "This huge red bird flew out of nowhere and started pecking at his face, his eyes. When he started to fall, the bird flew into the hollow of the tree, and I followed. I don't remember what happened next, but when I woke up, I was here. And I wasn't Shannon anymore. The Valkyries found me in the forest and said this . . ."

She pointed to a line in her story that read, *Hail, Queen Skya! We are your Valkyries if you will have us.*

"I just liked the word 'Valkyrie.' Wasn't even sure what it meant."

Emilie remembered something. The teeny tiny pencil sketch of the girl sitting at her desk . . .

"I saw your homework assignment about what you wanted to be doing in ten years. You didn't want to be a queen of a magic kingdom. You wanted to be a fantasy writer. You did understand the assignment."

Emilie turned another page.

The queen knew she could never leave her kingdom. It would not survive without her. If she wanted to find the lost princess, she would need to send a knight or a prince.

Or both.

Another page.

"*Remember this warning, my queen,*" *said the Witch of Black Wolf Cave.* "*Only three times may the door into this world be used. After that, it will lock from the inside. You can get out, but no one else may get in. For you can always walk away from magic, but if you turn your back on it, it may never offer you another chance . . .*"

"Three times," Emilie said. "What does this mean? Three times the door opens before it closes forever? Do you mean the door we came through? The door in the tree?"

Skya sat down on the sofa and laid her head on the arm.

"Now I remember why I didn't tell Rafe and Jeremy about the story."

Emilie carried the Trapper Keeper to the armchair, reading the pages before and after, trying to find a loophole or a correction or something . . .

"But if it's only three times, that means—"

Easy math. Skya came through. That was one time. Then Rafe and Jeremy fifteen years ago. Then they brought her through. That was three.

"Things always come in threes in fairy tales," Skya said. "*You have three days to guess the secret of the dancing princesses or you die. Three iron bands around the heart to keep it from breaking. Click your heels together three times . . .* I didn't know when I wrote that line that someday I would have to tell my prince that if he goes home again, he can never come back to me. And if he stays here, he'll never see his mother again."

Emilie's throat tightened with panic. "Change it. Change the story. Can't you erase it, write over it? Make it four times? Five?"

"Wish I could," Skya said. "I tried a hundred times. I tried changing everything in the story. I tried erasing death and pain and suffering and sickness. It wouldn't let me."

"Why not? It's your story."

"Not anymore," she said. "Now it's Shanandoah's story." She leaned back with a heavy sigh. "And it turns out you can't have a fairy tale without anything bad happening in it. Fairy tales need heroes. Heroes need dragons. Princes and knights need enemies. Life needs death. I wish it was easier, but it's not. Not even here."

Emilie wiped tears off her face and took a breath to settle herself. "But we can leave?"

"You can leave anytime," Skya said. "If the price of magic is too high for you, you can leave. The door might only let you in three times, but it will always let you out. That's how magic works. It will only give you so many chances to accept what it offers before it finds someone else who's willing to pay the price."

"So we can leave but we can never come back," Emilie repeated. "Do they know? I mean, they will go back eventually. Rafe promised his mom."

And Jeremy would go with him. She'd found a sister in Skya, but it felt like she'd also found two brothers in Rafe and Jeremy.

"I'll tell them," Skya said. "I didn't know how to tell them then, and I don't know how to tell them now, but—"

"I can tell them," Emilie said. "You don't have to do everything anymore."

"It's my story. I'll do it." Then she smiled. "You're starting to act like a real princess, you know? I'm proud of you."

"Great, I want to puke."

Skya laughed. Emilie closed the story, sealing it shut with the Velcro flap. She carried it back to the golden box. Skya came over and locked it inside with the key.

"I'm sorry, kid. I just wrote the story. I didn't make the rules." Skya put her arm around her.

"Maybe you could write another story? A sequel?"

"I haven't written a story in a long time. Been a little busy running a kingdom."

"But what if you tried—"

"Can't do it. Lost my magic pencil in the trunk of that guy's car. Lost my pencil, lost my stories with it."

"Maybe your stories aren't lost. Maybe they're just missing. Maybe . . . maybe we can find them?"

"Maybe." Skya kissed her forehead. "For now, let's just be happy together, all of us, for as long as we can. The end of this story can wait awhile."

. ✳ .

CHAPTER THIRTY-FIVE

MEANWHILE, RAFE WAS sleeping peacefully, more peacefully than he'd slept in fifteen years. He woke when he felt a shadow blocking the sun. He opened his eyes, propped himself up on his elbows, and saw Jeremy standing in the entryway to his balcony.

"Knock, knock."

"Nice outfit," Rafe said, blinking and yawning.

"I call this palace casual." Jeremy stepped inside and turned a circle in the last of the evening sunlight. He wore a light tunic with a black vest and black trousers. Cleaned up and polished, he looked more like a prince than Rafe did in his T-shirt and boxer briefs. He looked like a dream, like something he'd dreamed or painted or painted in a dream.

"Aren't you supposed to be in your room?" Rafe asked. "Queen's orders."

"Do you know how long it's been since someone sent me to my room?"

"I know your mother never did it."

"Never had to. I loved my room," Jeremy said. "Like yours better, though. This one, I mean."

Rafe had to agree. His bedroom was more than fit for a prince. An enormous bed with posts carved like animal heads—a wolf, a dragon, a rabbit, an owl. A tapestry on the wall embroidered with a maypole scene, a hundred children in white clothes dancing and twirling pink, blue, and gold ribbons. A painting of Skya on her ivy throne hung over the stone mantel. Rafe knew he'd painted it. He'd signed it in the corner.

But he knew Jeremy wasn't talking about the décor.

"It's not bad," Rafe said and stacked the pillows behind his head. Without realizing it, he'd re-created this room back home in his cabin, down to the carved posts on the bed.

"Let me guess . . ." Jeremy leaned across Rafe, almost laying on him as he reached for something behind the bed. For a split second, Rafe thought he was going to kiss him, but no. Jeremy pulled up Rafe's bow from the hook on the back of the headboard.

"You always slept with your bow," Jeremy said. "You still do."

He leaned over Rafe again and put it back on the hook, hiding it behind the headboard. Then he sat back on the edge of the bed.

"Asshole," Rafe said.

"What? I was just checking." Jeremy gave him an innocent look that Rafe didn't buy for one second. "Nice to see some things never change."

In the Ghost Town, they'd kissed twice. Not that he was keeping count, but two was an easy enough number to remember. All their secrets were out. They'd been much, much more than friends here, and yet it seemed Jeremy still didn't want to talk about it. Why?

Rafe noticed Jeremy glance at the black book on the table by the bed, still latched, its secrets shut up inside.

"Are you ever going to open it? You already know what's in there."

"Yeah, exactly," Rafe said, wincing. "Do you think I want to remember what Dad did to me?"

"Fair. Very fair. But I promise there's more good than bad in there."

Rafe raised his eyebrow. "Like what? If it sounds good enough, maybe I'll consider it."

Jeremy gave a low laugh. "All right, let me think." He pointed to the tapestry of the maypole dancers. "See that? They have that festival at Ravencliff on the summer solstice. These two beautiful girls made flower crowns for us and 'sold' them to us for a kiss."

"Not bad. What else?"

Jeremy moved a little closer to him on the bed. "Oh, you'll like this one. The queen liked to take us out on her dragon ship at night. When you're on the Painted Sea, you can watch the stars falling."

"Meteor shower?"

"Not here. Here the stars actually fall. And if you're fast enough and lucky enough, you can catch one with a net."

"I highly doubt that's true."

"If you open your book, you'll know . . ."

"Try again." Rafe was enjoying this game.

Jeremy's head fell to the side and he stroked his chin. In his eyes, Rafe could see him sorting through memory after memory, looking for the right one, the best one. Then he raised a finger.

"One night . . . about a month after we came here, Skya showed us that some of the trees in the Sweet Spring Forest had stairways carved inside them. Enormous spiral staircases, and you could go five hundred feet or more up the interior of the tree and then walk out onto the branches."

"And we did that?"

"We did. By ourselves. She said the heights made her too dizzy, but we wanted to try it. Then we got up there and sat on a branch. As soon as it was dark enough, the firemoths came out."

"Firemoths?"

"They're massive," Jeremy said. "Wings as wide as your hands." He held up both hands side by side, fingers spread to show the moths' wingspan. "And they flash orange, so when they all come at night, it's like Halloween up there."

"What about the bad memories?" Rafe said. "Or was it all falling stars and firemoths?"

Jeremy was quiet a moment, then he rose and went to the balcony. Standing in the arched entrance, he pointed to the distant mountains.

"One morning, I woke up early. The light was different. The air was different. I was standing on this spot and saw it had snowed in the mountains. That's when I realized how long we'd been here. From spring until almost winter. You woke up and asked me what was wrong. I didn't say anything. Then you wrapped the blankets around you and came to stand right here." Jeremy stepped sideways one foot. "You saw the snow and said, 'Almost Christmas.' And you smiled at me, and I knew you wanted to spend Christmas here. Every Christmas."

Rafe got off the bed and walked over to him, standing where young Jeremy had once stood while Jeremy stood where young Rafe once had.

"Then what?" Rafe asked.

"Finally you ordered me to tell you what I was thinking. In my mind I was picturing Mum all alone in our house, Mum and Martha, and it was Christmas, but there was no tree up. Just a cold quiet house and Mum not even playing carols on the piano. Because she wouldn't have any reason to celebrate if I was still gone. Lost her husband when she was twenty-nine, lost her son at forty-four. I almost lied to you that morning. That's how much I loved you. That's how much I wanted you to be happy. But an order was an order, so I told you the truth. I said—"

"Time to go."

Jeremy cocked his head at him. "You remember?"

"Only in a dream." How strange to find that so many of his half-forgotten dreams had been memories.

Jeremy crossed his arms over his chest and leaned back against the stone arch. "Nobody ever tells you that when you go to another world, that even if it's paradise, you'll still miss your mum and your dog." He sat on the balcony ledge. "Or maybe I finally realized what a selfish little shit I was being. This wasn't us staying out past curfew. We'd been gone *months*."

Rafe sat on the ledge across from him. "What did I say when you told me?"

"Well," Jeremy said, brightening, "never let it be said that my teenage self did not have excellent taste in boyfriends and princes. All you said was, 'Okay, we'll go home.' But that morning we didn't know what going home would mean. For us. I wonder sometimes what would've happened if we'd stayed."

"To us or our families?" Rafe asked. "Dad aged ten years while we were missing. Mom lost forty pounds she didn't need to lose."

"And Mum's medicine cabinet was full of pill bottles that weren't there before we got lost. I overheard my grandparents saying if I'd been gone another month, they probably would've lost her too," Jeremy said. He lowered his head but then gave a soft laugh, looked up, and met Rafe's eyes. "And you would be so sick of me by now, wouldn't you?"

Rafe laughed. "Good chance of that, yeah." He looked out at the mountains. No snow yet but soon. He could smell it in the air. "I always did judge people a little who stayed with their high school sweethearts."

Jeremy pointed a finger at him. "If you ever call me your high school sweetheart again, so help me—"

"Sorry, sorry." Rafe raised his hands in surrender.

"Look," Jeremy said and pointed. Outside the palace walls, a white stag and a red hart stepped lightly and gracefully through a pumpkin patch, sniffing out a perfect one for their dinner.

"Wow," Rafe breathed. The deer finished eating and dashed back into the woods.

"I took all this away from you because I was homesick."

"I could've stayed," Rafe reminded him. "I didn't have to go home with you. It was my choice."

His choice to go. Even knowing what his father did to him, Rafe still chose to go home. Why? Because he loved Jeremy that much? Or because he also had grown up enough to know he couldn't, as Jeremy said, stay out past curfew forever. Even for white stags and Skya.

In silence they watched the sun setting over the green and silver peaks of the distant mountains. The wind was picking up, crisp and cutting, and Rafe shivered.

"Come on," Jeremy said, standing up. "Either get back inside or put on some warmer clothes."

"That something that knights do? Tell princes to put on their jackets?"

"If the prince is stupid enough to sit outside in October in a T-shirt and his underwear, then yes."

Rafe got up and started to go inside. "You coming?"

Jeremy glanced over to the next balcony. "I should get back to my room before we get into trouble with Skya. She's not going to be happy until she beheads at least one of us."

"Or you could stay here and just get in trouble."

Jeremy raised his eyebrow. "Who's the bad influence now?"

They returned to the bedroom, where a fire had magically started in the fireplace. Rafe stood by it, warming himself. Jeremy, seated in the armchair, stretched out his long legs toward the fire. Rafe saw him look over at the locked sketchbook on the side table again. He didn't have to ask Jeremy why he wanted him to open it. Now he knew.

He turned away from Jeremy and held his hands out toward the flames. Easier to say it without looking at Jeremy.

"I fell in love with you here, didn't I?" Rafe asked. "I remember wanting to but being too scared, so it had to have been here."

Before they were lost, he remembered talking himself out of being in love with Jeremy, telling himself there was no point to it, that it was a stupid crush that would go away, that even if Jeremy felt the same—and why would he?—they could never do anything about it, so why bother?

"You did," Jeremy said. "Took you long enough."

"Being in this world, away from Dad, it must have felt like I could love you, that it wouldn't be wasted here."

"It wasn't wasted here. Not a drop of it. Love doesn't go to waste on Queen Skya's watch."

Rafe turned his back to the fire and faced Jeremy again. "And you and I, we—?"

Jeremy slowly nodded his head.

"A lot?" Rafe asked.

Jeremy nodded again.

"So my high school girlfriend Cassie in my truck wasn't my—"

Jeremy shook his head no.

"It was you and it was here."

Jeremy pointed at himself and then at the bed behind him.

Rafe took all that in. "Okay. Good to know."

The fireplace gave a satisfying pop. Another wave of déjà vu washed over Rafe as he inhaled the heady scent of the burning logs, like smoked brown sugar. He'd stood here before, smelled this scent before, felt this feeling before, that he was where he wanted to be with the person he wanted to be with and all was right with the world. *This* world at least.

"You could've told me."

"I *should've* told you," Jeremy said, "but that's a very awkward conversation to have with someone who hates you.' Oh, by the way, I know you think you despise me, but actually you were once *madly* in love with me, and we used to fool around in the Star Tower so much that Mira, the court astronomer, had the locks changed.'" He clasped his hands behind his head and shrugged. "Here's another bad memory you'll find in your book. We broke up. We had no other choice, since you literally forgot you loved me. And, it's no secret I haven't been a monk since then, and don't pretend you were either—"

"Monk*ish*," Rafe said. Then, "Except when I wasn't."

"But that doesn't change the facts."

"And what are the facts?"

He slipped his hand under his collar and took out the St. Hubert medal he wore. Rafe's medal around Jeremy's neck.

"I have always been in love with you, Rafe."

Rafe needed a moment to recover his ability to speak. "All this time?"

"All of it," Jeremy said. "Every minute. Every hour. Every day."

Rafe didn't know what to say except, "Why?"

"Why?" Jeremy laughed at that. "Why? Do you want the reasons in alphabetical order or by order of importance? Let's go with alphabetical, because my top ten is a little shallow."

"How shallow?"

"Number six is your eyes. Number three is your mouth. Number two, never mind."

"What's number one?"

"Because I remember who you are, even if you don't."

Rafe looked at him and waited for a punch line that never came.

"You mean that."

Jeremy nodded, then groaned softly. "God, it was easier going in the Ghost Town than telling you that." Jeremy looked away from him. "I know we had a nice couple of moments back there, namely when you forced your tongue down my throat along with half an apple. But I'm not asking for anything from you. I don't expect us to pick up where we left off. You deserved to know everything. Now you know."

Rafe took a deep breath, and said, "You're being very fair."

"I am a knight of Shanandoah. We have a code of honor. I don't remember all of it, but gallantry in matters of the heart was mentioned once or thrice."

"Do princes have to be gallant in matters of the heart, or can I just order you to kiss me until I forget who I am again?"

Rafe took perverse pleasure in seeing Jeremy dazed and dumbstruck.

"I suppose . . . uh," Jeremy said, then cleared his throat. "I suppose if I don't find that objectionable at all, then it wouldn't be, you know, *un-gallant* of you. To give your knight such an order, I mean. We do live to serve. Sort of the whole knighthood gig."

"Consider it an order then."

Jeremy sat up a little straighter, then put his feet on the floor, his hands on the chair arms, and pushed himself to his feet. He came to stand by Rafe in front of the fire.

Rafe laid his palm over Jeremy's heart. It pounded against his hand nearly as hard as his own heart pounded inside his chest.

"Might be fun to fall in love with you again," Rafe said. "I don't remember the first time it happened, so who knows . . . maybe it'll feel like it's the first time."

"*Two* first times? Now you're being greedy." Jeremy leaned close just as the sun sank behind the mountains and the night fell like a black curtain over the kingdom of Shanandoah. He whispered into Rafe's ear, "But I like the way you think."

And then Sir Jeremy proceeded—very gallantly, of course—to make Prince Rafe forget his name.

An Admittedly Infuriating Interruption

VERY SORRY, BUT WE'LL have to close the door here and give our knight and our prince their privacy.

After all, this isn't that kind of story.

A Less Infuriating Interruption (I Hope)

QUEEN SKYA, LONG MAY she reign, was so happy her prince and her knight had returned the lost princess to her that she declared fifteen days of celebration. Why fifteen? One day for every year she'd waited for Rafe and Jeremy to return. When you're a well-loved queen, you can do that sort of thing, and no one says you're being self-indulgent.

No time to tell everything wonderful that happened during those fifteen days, but I'll try to hit the highlights.

ON DAY ONE, the good people of Shanandoah gathered together on Halfmoon Hill. At sunset, the Valkyries—looking glorious and fearsome all in white—led a procession into the sacred grove and formed an honor guard.

Then came Rafe, wearing his finest dark green doublet and trousers (trust your storyteller—he looked to die for). Jeremy came next in his favorite black trousers, tunic, and vest, and Queen Skya wore a gown of deepest red. Rafe carried a bowl of water, Jeremy a bowl of fire, and Queen Skya a bowl of earth—the three elements of all creation. Then Emilie, wearing a humble linen gown, entered and stood in the center of the circle. Her hands were empty, to symbolize that she was willing to receive what the Creator would offer her.

Music played, soft strange pagan melodies, and when the song faded to silence, Jeremy began to speak. Although Emilie hadn't yet learned the ancient language of Shanandoah, the tongue of the one who laid the foundations of the world, she understood the meaning.

And Jeremy said, *No one knows the face of the Creator, but we have seen those giving hands at work in the rising and the setting of the sun and the shining of the moon and the dancing of the stars and the finding of the lost. One who was lost stands in our midst and we celebrate that she, at last, has found her way home . . .*

The words sounded like autumn leaves scattering in the wind.

ON THE SECOND DAY, the four of them rested and recovered from the blessing ceremony, which had lasted until long after midnight. The day was cool and crisp because October in Shanandoah is exactly what you want October to be. Far too cold for their usual game of combat croquet with the Valkyries in the back garden. As night was falling, the four of them retreated to Skya's cozy salon. Emilie lay on the rug in front of the fire. Rafe stretched out on the sofa. Jeremy took the armchair, and Skya sat at his feet on a silk cushion. As Rafe read aloud to them from *The Wonderful Wizard of Oz*, Jeremy took Skya's long hair out of its braid and gently rubbed her tender scalp.

"Can I get a head massage next?" Emilie asked her sister.

With a blissful smile on her face, Skya said, "Get your own knight, Brat. This one's mine."

"Ahem," Rafe said.

"Sorry, my prince," Skya said. "This one's *ours*."

Rafe finished reading and closed the book with a dramatic "The end."

They all applauded. Time for bed.

"What are we reading tomorrow night?" Emilie asked her sister as they went up the stairs to their rooms.

"One I picked," Skya said. "It's a story about two school friends who get swept into another world and then they have to help a prince who has forgotten who he is."

"What's it called?"

"*The Silver Chair.*"

. . .

ON THE THIRD DAY, Skya declared they'd been lazy long enough. It was only a matter of time before the Bright Boys reared their ugly heads again. After a morning spent receiving well-wishers who'd come to greet the new princess, they ate a hearty lunch, and then it was time for Emilie to practice her archery with Rafe and her sword fighting with Tempest and Jeremy. The sword fighting wasn't much fun, but with Rafe teaching her, Emilie finally managed to land a few arrows in the target. When one hit the blue ring and stayed in it, she remembered to cry out, "West—by God!—Virginia!" much to her sister's delight. She decided she would get very good at archery, no matter how long it took. When she told Rafe this, he passed on to her the deep secret of archery, that she must put her heart where she wanted her arrow, and then be willing to put an arrow into her own heart. There is no other way.

ON THE FIFTH DAY, the village of Beartown hosted a festival in honor of the return of the prince and his knight. Emilie was more than a little relieved to be out of the spotlight for a day. Although they did ask her to judge the pie-baking contest, which she was happy to do. Very, very happy to do that, thanks for asking and pass the pie. Rafe and Jeremy were fed and feted at the feast as the mayor and other villagers recounted the tales of long-ago feats of derring-do. (And yes, I realize this last sentence is a tongue-twister, but it's not my fault "fed," "feted," "feast," and "feats" sound so much alike.)

They toasted Rafe for saving the queen from the sleeper spider, of course, but also for riding three days to the Witch of Black Wolf Cave to fetch a cure for a child's blue fever, and Jeremy for scaring off a silver-backed tiger from Beartown with his sword and some very choice four-letter words he'd learned in his home country of Engle-land.

"We did all that?" Rafe whispered to Jeremy between toasts.

To which Jeremy responded, "We couldn't make out in the Star Tower all the time."

"Why not?" Rafe asked, then in front of two hundred villagers, Rafe kissed Jeremy, and the cheering was so deafening that Emilie had to shout to announce that the red rainberry pie had won the contest.

That very night, Queen Skya sent Emilie to bed early. She sat Rafe and Jeremy down in her salon and read them a story. Her story. All of it. Even the part about the door that would lock behind them if they left again.

They were shocked and sad, but otherwise they faced the news with courage and good humor. But that was no surprise to the queen. She'd chosen her knight and her prince well. They might be Shanandoah princes, Shanandoah knights, but they were also Mountaineers—one by blood and one in spirit—and they grow them strong in West—*by God!*—Virginia.

THE NEXT DAY, they rode out early to the Painted Sea and spent two days and two nights on the queen's dragon ship. At dusk, when the water was bloodred with the setting sun, they set anchor. Then they all made mermaid traps out of candle boats and set them floating on the water as they waited on rafts.

An hour passed before a mermaid took the bait. A silver-skinned young one with bright copper eyes surfaced and blew out Emilie's candle.

"Got you," Emilie said, as she tossed a ring of pink orchids around the mermaid's neck. "Now tell me a secret."

Captured fair and square, the mermaid whispered the secret into Emilie's ear, then turned around fast, slapped her in the face with her tail, and disappeared into the deep.

They all returned to the dragon ship.

"I thought you said they kissed you," Emilie said, dripping water on the deck.

"Well, one kissed Rafe," Jeremy said. "But who hasn't around here?"

Rafe rolled his eyes.

"What secret did she tell you?" Skya demanded. "Come on. Dish on the fish, sis."

But Emilie only smiled as she squeezed the water out of her hair.

"If I told you, it wouldn't be a secret."

. . .

ON THE NINTH NIGHT. Emilie had a dream about her mother and woke up crying. A few minutes later, Skya knocked softly on the door and then let herself inside. Without a word, she crawled into bed with her sister and hugged her.

"How did you know I needed you?" Emilie asked.

"A little bird told me."

Aurora perched on the end of Emilie's bed like a sentinel, guarding her from more sad dreams.

"Want to tell me about your dream?"

"No," Emilie said. She barely remembered it now anyway, only that in it, her mother was alive and with her in Shanandoah.

Skya stroked her hair and kissed her forehead.

"Want to tell me about your mother?" Skya asked. "The mother who raised you?"

"What do you want to know?" Emilie asked.

"Everything."

"Well, for starters, her name was Theresa, and she would've loved you."

ON THE TENTH DAY. Rafe and Skya holed up in the Star Tower and they refused to tell Emilie or Jeremy what they were doing.

"Queen stuff," Skya told Emilie when asked.

"Prince stuff," Rafe told Jeremy when asked.

"Bedeviling," Emilie said of the whole thing. Jeremy agreed with this assessment, so the two of them went off to do princess and knight stuff.

Of course, the queen and prince stuff they were doing wasn't particularly scintillating. Rafe was painting a gift for Emilie and Skya was needed to give her input.

"More pink," she said. "My sister loves pink."

"It's already so pink."

She watched him a while longer. "You are so talented at this, my handsome prince," Skya said, chin resting on his shoulder as he worked. "Why aren't you an artist?"

"I am. If you do art, you're an artist. You don't have to get paid for it. You're not paying me, right?"

"Only in love and adoration." She kissed his cheek. She watched, mesmerized, while he worked magic, taking a blank rectangle and filling it with beauty.

"If you had died in Red Crow that day," she said, "all the paintings you ever could have painted would have been lost. You kill an artist, you kill all their unmade art too. Why don't people think about that before they hurt each other?"

He dipped his brush in white paint and began to make a unicorn appear before her eyes.

"Sometimes I think art is stronger than we are," he said. "My favorite painter, Franz Marc, got his head blown off in World War One, but a music professor in Morgantown in 2006 had a print of his painting *The Foxes* in her house. I saw it and decided I wanted to do that. And I did. So that's immortality, time travel, and miracle working. Not bad for some paint and wood and canvas." He gave her a sidelong glance. "Your entire kingdom exists because someone liked your story. If I were you, I'd take that as a sign you oughta write some more stories."

"I haven't written a word since I was thirteen. Where do I even start?"

"You can start where I started my painting. I paint people I love. You could write about people you love."

She mulled that over as she watched him work.

"Write about people I love . . ." She hugged him from behind, and he stopped painting to rest his head against hers for a long, lovely moment. "That means I'll be writing about you."

He returned to his painting. "Just make me look good."

"Maybe I'll make you the hero."

ON THE ELEVENTH DAY, the Moonstone Palace hosted a Fall Festival in Emilie's honor. More food. More drinking. More games. Even an archery tournament. Emilie entered the beginners' match and won third prize, which was a dubious honor, as most of her competitors were between the ages of ten and fourteen.

After copious amounts of goading on Skya's part, Rafe entered the masters' level. The prize was a white pony with gray spots and a gray star on her forehead. When he inevitably came in first place, he brought the pony to Emilie and offered a trade—the pony for her third-prize ribbon.

When she was done hugging and kissing Rafe a few thousand times, she stroked her horse's nose and whispered her name—Rhiannon.

No one was surprised by this.

THE DAY OF EMILIE'S coronation grew closer and closer. Jeremy and Rafe set out to the Witch of Black Wolf Cave to secure the gift Skya wanted to give her sister. It was a long, long ride, so they had to camp in the woods and hunt and fish for their dinner. They nearly got themselves lost when the Green Lady took a liking to Rafe's pretty face and changed the path to lead them both to her home in the Big Dark Hollow, a particularly ancient and mysterious part of the old forest. The boys had quite a time getting out. I wish I could tell the whole story, since it involved a failed seduction by sentient foliage, and at one point Rafe literally had to say, "You're a lovely tree, but I'm in a relationship."

Alas, we're running out of time.

WHILE THEY WERE GONE, Skya and the Valkyries took Emilie to the source of the Bluestone River so they could bathe her in the holy waters. When they returned to the palace, they spent all evening trying to find a dress for Emilie to wear for the coronation. And this was the happiest Emilie had been in a very long time.

AND FOR DAY FIFTEEN . . . well, I think that deserves its own chapter.

· ✳ ·

CHAPTER THIRTY-SIX

EVERY SOUL IN THE wild and wonderful kingdom of Shanandoah had pressed inside the throne room to watch Queen Skya, wearing her crown of antlers, place a crown of silver and gilt leaves on the head of the lost and found princess.

To the beaming assembly, the queen called out, "I give you Princess Emilie, the Lion-Hearted."

The cheers were deafening. Prince Rafe and Sir Jeremy, in full regalia, stood behind their queen and the princess.

"I remember your coronation," Jeremy whispered. "Don't remember your full regnal name and titles, though. I think it was 'Prince Rafe, the Golden-Haired, Golden-Hearted, Hawk-Eyed Prince of Shanandoah.'"

"Mouthful," Rafe said.

"I'll say."

If the queen or anyone noticed Prince Rafe elbowing Jeremy in the gut to shut him up, they didn't say anything about it. Shanandoah, as it has been said, is not a kingdom that takes itself too seriously.

After all, one of the guests of honor at the coronation was a rat named Fritz, who watched from a silk cushion held by a Valkyrie. Did he know what was going on? Probably not, but he seemed to have a grand time chewing the tassels off the pillow.

After the ceremony, there was the giving of honors.

First, Jeremy was given a promotion from knight to baron. Rafe muttered, "Still outrank you, my *lord.*"

To which Jeremy may or may not have responded, "Bite me, my prince." All assembled agreed Lord Jeremy wore his new silver coronet well.

Rafe was given a promotion from prince to high prince, which just meant he got a slight upgrade in crowns.

And tiny Fritz was given his own dukedom for chewing through Lord Jeremy's bindings in the Ghost Town.

For even the smallest acts of courage and kindness performed by the tiniest citizens of Shanandoah deserve the highest of honors.

After honors came the best part, according to Emilie anyway. This was the giving of gifts to the newly crowned princess.

From Jeremy she received a music box that would play any song her heart desired.

She opened it a crack and "Dreams" began to play.

"Where did you get this?" she demanded.

"Traded my extra sword to a traveling wizard."

"Well, I guess there's no Amazon here, so that tracks."

Rafe was next. He gave her the painting—Emilie's official portrait. In it, Emilie sat on a pale pink armchair and was framed by an oval of animals—unicorns, rabbits, cats, foxes, and Fritz, of course, on a pink cushion on her lap. Even the frame was pink.

"I love it," Emilie said. "Now can you paint one of me and Skya together?"

He kissed her cheek. "I'll put you on my schedule."

Rafe and Jeremy watched very closely as Skya presented Emilie her gift. They had, after all, traveled days to fetch it for her.

Emilie opened an empty black velvet bag.

"Fresh air?" she asked. "Thanks, Sis!"

"Very funny," Skya said. "That bag holds your gift. You decide what you want your gift to be. If it can fit in that bag, you can wish for it and it'll appear."

"Like anything? Like a tiny snake that speaks Japanese or a DVD of *The Matrix?*"

"If it can fit in there, you can have it."

Emilie peered into the empty bag. "That seems really irresponsible."

Skya nodded. "Probably is. You don't have to decide tonight. But once you decide, you just hold the bag against your heart and say, 'Thank you for the—' and then say the gift."

"This feels like another test."

"I am not . . . Why do you think I'm testing you, Brat?"

"Probably a test," Jeremy said.

"I'll try not to accidentally blow up the world with it," she said. "Wait, can I swear my undying loyalty to you now?"

"If you want," Skya said. "No pressure."

"I want. And Fritz too."

"Lord Jeremy? Sword, please."

Jeremy passed his queen his sword. Emilie knelt, and Skya tapped her gently on her left shoulder, then her right. Then with a butter knife, she tapped Fritz even more gently on his left shoulder, then his right.

"Princess Emilie and . . . Fritz, do you swear your undying loyalty to me and the kingdom of Shanandoah?" Skya asked.

Emilie looked up. "What does that entail exactly? Shouldn't I read the terms and conditions?"

"I don't know," Skya admitted. "We just kind of do this one for fun."

"Then sure," Emilie said. "I swear. So does Fritz. I think. That might not hold up in court, though."

"Rise, Princess Emilie!" Skya ordered.

Emilie came to her feet and into her sister's arms. "Now you're *my* princess."

After the giving of gifts, there was only one thing left to do.

Party. The entire kingdom celebrated with singing and dancing and feasting and drinking and general madcap revelry long into the night. They all joined in—Rafe and Jeremy, Emilie and Skya, even the horses, Freddy and Sunny, who wore pink and gold ribbons in their manes.

While Emilie and Jeremy were sharing a dance, Rafe found Skya standing behind her throne, watching the scene before her with a smile on her face.

"Isn't she beautiful?" Skya said.

"That question also feels like a test," Rafe replied.

Skya laughed. "Dance with me, my prince."

"I'm a terrible dancer."

"I remember. But we'll try it anyway."

Like two nervous kids at homecoming, they put their arms around each other and swayed together.

"Aurora tells me you still haven't opened your book. Care to tell me what's stopping you?"

"Not really," he said, but since she was the queen, he told her anyway. "Every day I think this is the day, but then I don't. I'm happy here. Scared to risk that."

"You don't want to hate your father?"

Rafe took a breath, swallowed the sudden knot in his throat.

"I don't want to hate my mom."

Understanding dawned in Skya's dove-gray eyes, so like Emilie's.

"Oh, my prince."

"Dad said if I remembered everything, it would poison me against Mom. What if she knew and didn't do anything?"

She took his hand and led him away from the celebration into an empty corridor behind the throne room. With a sigh of relief, she shed her crown and set it on the head of a suit of armor. Then, under the light of a torch, she pulled back her sleeve and showed him her right arm. It was covered in faint white scars.

"Skya."

He ran his fingers up a jagged patch of pale white scar tissue that wound from her wrist halfway up her arm.

"Got these trying to get out of that guy's car trunk."

"I wish that never—"

"I know." She smiled softly at him. "You told me and only me what your father did to you. You told me because I showed you my scars first and told you how I got them. And I kept your secret, even from Jeremy, because I know what it's like to not want to talk about your scars."

He lifted her arm to his mouth, kissing her scars as Jeremy had kissed his in the deepest, most secret hour of the night.

Skya pressed her forehead to his. "My golden-hearted, golden-haired, hawk-eyed prince, I promise you this . . . you will not hate your mother. I could only wish for a mother who loved me like yours loves you."

He looked into her eyes and believed her.

"Can't remember, are princes allowed to kiss queens on the lips?"

"If you opened that book, you'd know it's not only allowed but also required."

He took her face in his hands and kissed her tenderly, as tenderly as he loved her.

"Very nice," she said. "Now go find Jeremy. I better not see either of you again until morning."

She was the queen. Orders must be obeyed.

EMILIE FOUND HER SISTER on the balcony staring up at the bright full moon.

"Great party."

"It's not all parties, you know," Skya said. "Sometimes it's a lot of work."

Emilie only shrugged. "I needed a new job anyway."

"When I was a kid, I read every single fantasy story I could get my hands on. In every one of them—Narnia, Oz, Clock Island . . . the kids who go to the fantasy world always go back home at the end of the story."

"I'm not going home. I mean, I have a crown now. Fritz has a dukedom. We're here to stay."

"You promise? Because it's a big decision. No going back. Literally."

"I don't miss anything back home but my mom, and she's not there anymore. Oh, crap, what about my house? My car? I gotta talk to Jeremy—"

She started to leave, but Skya grabbed her by the arm.

"Listen, please. I'm not kidding. This place is magical, but it's also dangerous. And there are no TVs, no telephones, no radios, no hospitals. Magic can't fix a broken leg if you fall off your horse. I just hope you don't regret it."

Emilie took her sister by the hands and squeezed them. "I'm staying. I decided. So get used to me."

Skya pulled her close and said into her ear, "I'm already used to you."

Emilie gasped.

"What?" Skya said. "You okay?"

"I just figured out what I want for my gift."

"You sure? You don't want to think about it first?"

Before she lost her courage, Emilie wrapped her fingers around the bag and whispered, "Thank you for the magical unicorn mechanical pencil with endless pencil lead just like the one my sister used to have so she can write another story."

Skya stared at her, wide-eyed. Emilie reached into the bag and pulled out the pencil.

"Now you have a pencil." Emilie gave it to her sister, her queen.

"I love you, Brat."

"Love you too. Can't wait to read your next story."

CHAPTER THIRTY-SEVEN

RAFE AND JEREMY CHANGED out of their finery into riding clothes. Then they quickly saddled Freddy and Sunny and rode out
into the forest.

But before they left, Rafe grabbed his book from his bedroom and
put it in the saddlebag.

Jeremy led the way to one of the larger trees in the great dark woods,
so enormous a stream had worn a tunnel through it. They took off their
shoes and waded through the stream and into the darkness inside the
hollow trunk.

"Watch this," Jeremy said. "You'll be very impressed and aroused."

"Can't wait," Rafe said.

Jeremy wrapped a dry cloth around the end of an arrow and set the
cloth on fire. Then he shot the arrow up into the tree.

The flame briefly revealed the tree's secret. Stairs.

A hundred, two hundred steps or more were carved inside the tree in
one long, seemingly endless spiral.

"See?" Jeremy said. "I didn't make that up."

Rafe followed Jeremy up the stairs, his fingers finding handholds
worn into the wall by ancient fingers.

Up they went, up and up forever, around and around endlessly. They
finally reached the top and Jeremy led Rafe out a knothole and onto a

branch, a branch as thick and wide as a small car. They sat and caught their breath. The forest floor was so far down, Rafe couldn't see it in the dark.

"Look," Jeremy said. "Here they come. Showtime."

Rafe peered through the branches and saw nothing. Darkness. A few stars. More darkness. Then a sudden burst of bright orange light in the distance.

At first, the orange light popped once every minute or two, then every thirty seconds or so, until every five seconds or less, that same strange orange light flashed and disappeared, then flashed again.

Firemoths. Dozens, then hundreds of them danced in the high branches.

One flew close. Yellow light came from the enormous wings, even bigger than a grown man's two hands. The yellow light plus the red leaves of the giant trees combined to make orange, filling the trees with the eyes of a thousand glowing jack-o'-lanterns.

"Wow," Rafe said. He spared a glance at Jeremy, saw the lights flash in his eyes. "I painted these on my bedroom walls."

"I noticed."

Rafe reached into his pack and took out his book.

"Hope I don't remember I'm afraid of heights."

Jeremy reached out and pulled Rafe back against his chest, holding him tight as a seatbelt.

"You remember the combination?" Jeremy asked.

"No, but I can guess it."

It was a three-number lock and Rafe put in the first three numbers that came to mind.

436 for 436 Park Street. Jeremy's old house.

The book opened for him right away. Magic.

"It's all right. You're all right," Jeremy said, and Rafe held on to those words like a lifeline even as he sank beneath the surface of an ocean of memories.

ARE YOU SURE you want to do this, my prince? You can stay. You can stay forever.

I can't let Jeremy go alone.

THE LOST STORY 289

The magic won't let you both remember. Not as long as the door is open. It's too dangerous for the kingdom.

I know.

And you won't be able to help Jeremy.

I know that too.

Then why go?

Because I . . .

THE BOOK WAS BLACK with a silver combination lock on it. Skya set it before him, her beautiful face grim with unshed tears.

How does it work?

Set the combination and open it. Don't tell anyone the combination. Make it something you remember from your old life.

436. Easy enough. Jeremy's house number.

Done.

Now draw in it or write. Whatever you put in the book, when you lock it, it will be locked away in your mind.

So it's still there?

Yes, but you won't remember it. It'll be as if it's behind a door you can't open.

So I just . . . draw things that happened, and I won't remember them?

Not until you open the book again. The witch warned you may dream of them, and when you wake you'll try to remember your dream, but it'll fall through your fingers like water and sand.

Easy enough to sketch the Sweet Spring Forest and the Castle Mountains, the Moonstone Palace, the Painted Sea, and the Bluestone River. But that wasn't all. He would have to draw Skya, the Valkyries, the unicorns and silver tigers, the baby he'd saved and named Kaylee, and hardest of all . . . he'd have to draw Jeremy. No, not Jeremy. He would always remember Jeremy Andrew Cox, his best friend from back home. He had to draw Sir Jeremy, the Red Knight. His knight. It was him he had to forget. His knight and their nights.

I'm sorry, my prince. I didn't want this either. But the rules are written into the world.

It's all right. I can do it.

Since he had to forget all his beautiful memories, he decided he deserved to forget his worst memory too. He drew a picture of an electrical cord in his father's hand.

LAST NIGHT HERE. What do you want to do?

One more trip to the firemoths before we leave.

Why? You won't remember them, and I can't tell you about them.

Jeremy's eyes so wide, his face so young, the sadness in his voice . . .

It's your favorite place. And you'll remember for the both of us. Just promise me something. One last order, I guess.

Anything.

I think it's going to be a long time before we can come back.

Maybe. Probably.

I won't remember I love you, so I don't know what'll happen. I won't ask you to, like, wait for me. You know what I mean.

I know.

But please, don't forget you love me.

Is that an order?

Pretend it is.

A kiss. The first kiss of their last night. Then a whispered promise in the dark.

Yes, Your Highness.

FINALLY, A CHANCE to talk to Jeremy alone.

You think we're dreaming? Rafe asked.

If so, we're having the same dream. This place is unbelievable. She said we could stay as long as we want.

I want.

JEREMY SAT AT THE feet of their queen, head in her lap as she stroked his hair. Rafe on the rug by the fireplace next to them, sketching them. Evening. Candles lit. Fire glowing. They tell one another stories.

He has never known happiness like this. If they could only stay this way forever.

Your turn to read, my prince.

What are we reading?

The Wonderful Wizard of Oz.

A HAND, IMPOSSIBLY STRONG, yanking him out the basement door to the shed. The shed, the shed, he hadn't been out to the shed since he was eight.

You think you're funny? You think this is funny?

No, no, it's not funny, Dad.

You taped that thing back together to be funny?

He can't tell him the truth. He can't. He can't say the book slid under his bedroom door, taped back together. Because then it's Mom out here in the shed. Better him than Mom.

Say you're sorry. Say you're sorry or you're gonna regret the day you were born.

Don't say it. Don't say it. He's got an electrical cord in his hand, and if Rafe says it—

I already do.

RAFE? THAT'S YOUR NAME?

Flat on his stomach in a bed softer than he's ever imagined . . . eyes slowly blinking open . . . the first question the only one that mattered—

Where's Jeremy?

A girl knelt on the floor by his bed. Seventeen? Eighteen? Pretty girl. Not beautiful. More like a Roman goddess than a beauty queen. An interesting face. He wanted to paint her.

In the other room waiting for you to wake up. You were really weak and running a fever. But you're doing much better now.

She touched his forehead and he thought of his mother. Was he dreaming all this? Soft bandages are wrapped around his chest and back. Nothing hurts anymore.

Are you hungry? I tried to give Jeremy some pie, but he's on a hunger strike until he sees you.

Pie sounds good.

I'll get Jeremy. We'll all have wine and pie by the fire.

She started to leave, and he didn't want her to go. He had so many questions, and it seemed she had all the answers.

Where am I?

I'll explain later after you get some food in you. My name's Skya. I'm the queen here.

You sound like you're from West Virginia.

I am.

There aren't any queens in West Virginia.

Oh, kid, you are not in West Virginia anymore.

Red Crow Forest. The day they were lost. But they weren't lost yet. Soon.

Rafe? What's wrong? Come on, tell me.

He can't say it, so he shows him. Not the cuts on his back. He could never show him that. He shows him the sketch instead, a dozen pieces held together by tape.

Shit, Jeremy says, and his hands shake as he holds the paper. *Your dad?*

Rafe nods.

Does he think we're—

Rafe closes his eyes, nods.

I'll tell him he's wrong, Jeremy says. *Or I'll . . . I'll say it was all my idea.*

Don't. A sob rises in his throat, and he swallows it. *Don't say anything to anyone.*

If his father would do this to him, what would he do to Jeremy? His father is a bomb and only Rafe can defuse him before he blows again and takes everyone with him.

Did he do that to your face?

Rafe doesn't answer, which is an answer.

You can't go home, Jeremy says.

I don't want to go home. He is the paper in Jeremy's hands. He is torn into pieces and barely held together by invisible tape.

Let's just, um . . . we'll stay out here and miss the bus, all right? Jeremy says. *I'll call Mum. She'll pick us up. We'll tell your Mom you're sick and too sick to go home. Stomach flu, something. We'll figure it out. Okay? Rafe?*

He's hot and everything hurts, but he pretends he's fine. He just needs to get away, that's all. Mom and Dad only fight about him, so if he's gone, she'll be safe.

I'm okay. Let's just go somewhere. Anywhere.

Where?

Far away as we can.

ARE YOU SURE *you want to do this, my prince? You can stay. You can stay forever.*

I can't let Jeremy go alone.

The magic won't let you both remember. Not as long as the door is open. It's too dangerous for the kingdom.

I know.

And you won't be able to help Jeremy.

I know that too.

Then why go?

Because I . . . we.

We what, Rafe? You can tell me anything.

We miss our moms.

Rafe closed his book.

AT DAWN, HE AND Jeremy watched the sunrise together through the trees. It took a long time for the red and pink rays to climb all the way over the distant mountaintops.

"Those are the Castle Mountains," Rafe said. "I remember that now."

"They are."

"The dragons live there."

"We never saw one, though," Jeremy said. "Skya says they're sleeping until a time Shanandoah needs them. I don't want to know what might wake them."

It was all true. They could catch stars in nets. He did ride all night to fetch a midwife to help bring Kaylee into the world. Jeremy had fought a silver tiger until it fled back into the woods.

"We did make out in the Star Tower all the time."

"Great view," Jeremy said. He smiled. "As if we ever looked at the view."

Breakfast was calling, so they made their way down the spiral stairs in the tree to the ground below. The horses were still half-asleep, but they woke up when Jeremy promised them they could have their rainberries and oats back at the palace. As they rode through the Sweet Spring Forest, the morning mist was so thick on the ground, it seemed the horses were wading through clouds.

After an hour, the mist dissipated. Rafe clicked his tongue once, and Sunny halted.

Jeremy rode to him. "What is it?"

He looked around him and laughed. "This is it," Rafe said. "This is where we woke up. Right here. I remember that rock by the river, the one that looks like a sleeping cat."

Jeremy nodded. "You're right. You remember?"

"I remember. I remember waking up soaking wet."

"You were dehydrated. I had to make you drink some water. For every drop I got down your throat, a few liters ended up on your shirt."

"That was when . . ."

"When what?"

"I saw you cry. You cried that day when you thought I was going to die," Rafe said.

"No. I cried when I knew you were going to live."

Rafe dismounted and walked over to the bank of the river. Sleek pink fish darted under the surface. Sugar trout, Skya called them. Savory and sweet when smoked over a campfire.

"What are we going to do?" Rafe asked. He didn't have to explain what he meant. Jeremy knew.

"Let's stay," Jeremy said. "We can stay forever this time."

"What about Mom?"

"What about Skya? What about Emilie? What about the kingdom? What about you being happy here?" Freddy nuzzled against Jeremy's back, bit at his tunic. "Yes, and what about the lads? We can't leave our horses."

Rafe leaned against Sunny's neck and rubbed his velvet nose.

"Jay, it was Mom."

"What was Mom?"

"Mom taped my sketches back together. It wasn't me. She taped them back together and slid them under the door of my room. I remember her saying, 'Baby? Here you go. I did my best.' She was whispering. You know why she was whispering?"

"I can guess."

"She was afraid of him too."

"I know your mother loves you. Wouldn't she want you to be happy?"

"She would want me to be happy. But I also don't want her to die of grief. And she will if I don't come home this time."

"Maybe . . ." Jeremy looked up to the sky. "Maybe Aurora? She can travel between all the worlds with or without the door. Maybe she can get a message to your mom and tell her you're all right."

"*Dear Mom, I'm all right and very happy, so I'm never coming home again ever. Love you. Bye.*" Rafe could only imagine how well that would go over with his mother.

"We don't have to decide today. Right? We have time," Jeremy said.

"Right. Good point. We have time. We have lots of time."

Rafe turned to Jeremy, raised his head to kiss him. And that's when an arrow struck Jeremy in the back.

Time's up.

· ✳ ·

CHAPTER THIRTY-EIGHT

JEREMY INHALED SHARPLY and started to fall. Rafe grabbed him, looked around in terror.

Back from the dead, Ripper stepped out from behind a tree and cackled.

"Told ya I'd rip your heart out!" he cried in triumph.

Rafe reached for his bow, but Sunny and Freddy were faster. They crossed the distance in seconds, it seemed, then reared up and kicked Ripper into the river.

As Ripper sank into the water, he cried out, "Not fair!" before dissolving into nothing.

Jeremy twitched in his arms, grunting in pain.

"Don't—" Rafe said, but it was too late. Jeremy twisted hard and yanked the arrow from his back. It had landed under his right shoulder blade, not the left, thus missing his heart.

"Jay? Jay, talk to me."

Jeremy collapsed onto his side in the fetal position, face white with pain.

"Can't ... breathe."

"Hold on. Just hold on." Rafe called the horses over. Freddy went down on his knees like a show pony and Rafe helped Jeremy onto his back. He mounted behind Jeremy to hold him as they rode. Though it was agony for Jeremy, there was no time to be gentle. They raced to the palace, and as he passed through the gates, Rafe called out for help.

Soon they were surrounded.

"Get him into the palace," Skya ordered. "Now. Carefully."

Rafe and the Valkyries lifted him—sixteen arms like a stretcher carried him to the queen's morning room. Ola, the healer woman, kicked them all out but Skya. Even Rafe and Emilie were made to wait outside. Behind the closed door, he listened. Jeremy coughed and it was a terrible liquid sound.

"He'll be all right," Emilie said. "I know he'll be all right. He has to be."

"How do you know?" Rafe barely knew what he was saying.

Emilie didn't answer, only held on to him. Jeremy's soft gasps of pain were music to his ears. They meant he was alive.

Then suddenly it was quiet.

"No," Rafe said. Just that. Only one quiet *no*. He started to fall. Only Emilie's arms held him up.

Skya opened the door.

"He's alive," she said. "They've given him something to ease the pain. But he doesn't have very long."

The words poisoned the air. Rafe could barely breathe.

"You mean he'll die?" Emilie asked. Her voice was sharp as a sword. "Jeremy can't die. No, no. That can't happen. There has to be something. There has to be—"

"The Witch?" Rafe asked.

"Too far," Skya said. "He won't make it that long."

"How long do we have?" Rafe asked her.

She stared at him. When she spoke, she sounded like a judge delivering a life sentence. Better, though, than a death sentence.

"Long enough to get him to a hospital," Skya said.

"Home," Rafe said. Of course. Home. Hospitals. Doctors. Surgeons.

"The Painted Sea—" he began. He remembered now how long it had taken them to get home the last time. Two nights and two days.

"No," Skya said. "He won't make the sea crossing either. There is another way out, much closer, but—"

"We'll take it," Rafe said. "What is it?"

Skya lowered her voice. "Your father's soul is in the Ghost Town. It would have made a tear between our worlds when he passed through. You can use it to get back home. A day's ride to the entrance. An hour or two through the Ghost Town."

"The Bright Boys will swarm us," he said. "I can't fight this fear."

"You can. It's not courage that repels them most. It's love. Love casts out fear."

He was sweating with panic. "You sure about that?"

"I read it somewhere. Sounds good, right?" she said, smiling through her tears. "Now go talk Jeremy into leaving. I'll get the horses saddled."

Rafe pushed open the door. The healer had Jeremy's shirt off and was wrapping his chest in white linen bandages. Jeremy's face was gray, and blood flecked his lips. She finished bandaging him and came over to his side.

"A hole in his lung, Highness," the healer said quietly to Rafe. "He's drowning in his own blood. This wound is beyond my powers."

"I understand," he said. "Thank you."

She walked out and left them alone together.

Rafe went down on his knees in front of Jeremy and wiped the sweat off his forehead. He couldn't seem to take a full breath.

"Verdict?" Jeremy gasped.

"You're going to be fine," Rafe said.

"Liar."

"You will. We're going home. You'll have surgery."

"No, we can't. If we leave, we can't—" He paused to gulp air. "Come back."

"I don't care."

"I do. You're a prince here. You're . . . You belong here. If I'm going to die, Rafe, let me die here—"

"Listen. Listen to me." Rafe put his hands on Jeremy's face, forced him to meet his eyes. "There's something I remembered that you forgot. I was lost. That day we met? The day you saw me drawing my stupid coyote in my notebook? I was already so lost. If you hadn't found me, I could've ended up just like my father. Do you understand that? And remember you said you could always sense where I was because deep down I knew

I belonged here, that this was home. That's not why. I wasn't lost because I wasn't here. I was lost because I'm lost without you. All this time, I've been lost without you, and you were the only one who could ever find me. And if you die, I will be lost forever."

Brothers. Lovers. Best friends. Partners in crime. Cellmates. Soul mates. There was no bond that bound hearts that did not bind theirs.

"You," Rafe whispered in his ear, "are my kingdom. Where you are is where I belong. And I did remember that I loved you all this time. I just forgot I remembered. I'll never forget it again. And as long as we're here, I outrank you, so when I say we're going home, you say—"

"Time to go."

"Right, right. Exactly," Rafe said. "Time to go."

From the doorway, Skya shouted, "Valkyries! Now!"

Everyone moved at once, bringing round the horses, blankets, water. Only Rafe and Jeremy stayed still and quiet in the eye of the storm.

"It wasn't—" Jeremy began, then took a ragged breath.

"What?" Rafe asked him.

"It wasn't a stupid coyote drawing. It was good."

Apologies

I'M SORRY ABOUT THIS.

To quote the queen, "I wrote the story. I don't make the rules."

· ✳ ·

CHAPTER THIRTY-NINE

SKYA, EMILIE, AND THE Valkyries rode with them, flanking them in case other Bright Boys tried anything else. They rode Rafe's horse, but Freddy ran with them, carrying no weight, so that they could change horses when Sunny lost steam.

The riding was hard for them all, hardest for Jeremy. Every bump left him gasping in agony. When they stopped to change horses, Jeremy leaned against a tree and coughed up blood. Rafe held him and gave him water. It was all he could do. Whatever this world was, whoever had made it for Skya and filled it with white stags and giants and impossible forests, they'd allowed in death and suffering as well. Maybe that was the rule. Maybe that was the deal. Maybe it was the price of magic. Maybe the price, sometimes, was too high. He didn't need unicorns and castles. He just needed Jeremy.

It took from morning to evening to make it to the Devil's Tea Table. The horses had taken them as far as they could go. Rafe held Jeremy steady as the Valkyries formed a circle around them so they could all say their goodbyes.

"Ignore everything you hear and see in there," Skya said. "Stay on the path. There's only one path even if it looks like there's more. I would go with you if I could, but the Bright Boys would come out of the wood-work to get me, and I'd only slow you down."

"I know," Rafe said. "We'll make it."

"Aurora will go with you. Follow her out as you followed her in."

Aurora flew overhead in low circles, cawing as if to say, *Hurry, hurry* . . .

Skya sighed, wiped her forehead. "So much to say and no time to say it. Your names are written on my heart. And I know my name is on yours. The day I forget either of you is the day my heart stops beating."

She took Rafe in her arms, but only for the briefest moment, long enough for him to say, "No matter what world I'm in, you are my queen."

"And you are my prince forever and always."

Then she took Jeremy in her arms, very gently, and whispered something in his ear. It must've been something nice because he managed a smile even through the pain.

Tempest left the circle to shake Jeremy's hand.

"I did it . . . again," he told her. "Let my guard down . . . too early."

"You're the only one who could ever disarm me," Tempest said. "I'm almost glad you're going. That's not true."

Then, for the first and last time in Shanandoah's recorded history, a Valkyrie hugged someone. She returned to her place among the guards.

Then Emilie went to Jeremy and carefully kissed his cheek. He could barely speak, but he managed a few words to her.

"Miss you already, Princess. Pet Fritz for me."

"I'll see you again," Emilie said.

"No, you won't."

"I'm a princess. What I say goes. I'll see you again. Thank you for finding us."

It was almost as hard to say goodbye to their horses. Rafe gave his beautiful Sunny one quick kiss on his nose while Freddy leaned against Jeremy or maybe Jeremy leaned against Freddy. Or maybe they just leaned against each other.

"Princess Emilie will take very good care of you," Rafe said to the horses. Emilie took them by the bridles.

"I will," she said. "I promise." And the horses bowed their heads as if in mourning.

With Jeremy's arm over his shoulders, Rafe half walked, half carried him past the rocks, and just like that, they were back in the ruins of Lost Virginia.

Two hills rose to the sky, and between them lay a broken cobblestone road, shrouded in fog. But as they took their first steps, the mists grew thicker, and soon they could see only three steps ahead, then two. But that was all Rafe needed to keep going. Skya had warned them that the path would seem twisted, confusing, turning in on itself, but they only had to keep on it to make their way out. And Aurora stayed close, cawing to them whenever they questioned their next step.

Around them, shapeless forms moved in the shadows but made no sounds. Once, something slithered across the path. Rafe couldn't tell if it was a snake or something much worse.

"I wish we'd brought apples," he said.

"I wish," Jeremy said, gasping between words, "we'd brought my Outback."

Rafe laughed and kissed his forehead. Jeremy was feverish and clammy. They were running out of time. Aurora cawed again, insistently. *Hurry, hurry.*

Redoubling his efforts, Rafe practically dragged Jeremy down the dark path. Skya had been right to warn them. They passed the same tree limb overhanging the way twice. Once on their right. Once on their left. But they kept going, remembering her warning.

"Need more water?" Rafe asked. Jeremy didn't answer.

But Jeremy had passed out.

"No, no, Jay, wake up." Rafe held him with one arm, lightly patted his face with his other hand. Slowly, Jeremy's eyes opened.

"Here," Jeremy said.

"I'll try to carry you," Rafe said. "Okay?"

It wasn't easy. They weren't kids anymore. Rafe took Jeremy by the wrist and dragged him across his back and shoulders, then pressed up with all his strength. A cry of pain escaped Jeremy's lips, but he said nothing else. Probably passed out again.

They weren't going to make it. They had to make it. They would make it. They couldn't make it.

Terror and hope went to war with each other in Rafe's heart. No telling which side would win.

For another mile or more he walked head down, eyes on the path, seeing nothing but his feet as he carried Jeremy step by torturous step. He tripped once, recovered. But when he stumbled a second time, he barely made it to his knees without dropping Jeremy.

As carefully as he could, he moved Jeremy off his shoulders to the ground. Rafe rested him against a tree stump.

"Jay?" Rafe wiped sweat from Jeremy's cold forehead.

Panting the words out, Jeremy said, "I'm done."

"No," Rafe said. "No. I can keep going."

Jeremy shook his head no again.

"Dammit, Jay." Rafe groaned, rubbing his face. "Don't give up. This can't be the end. I won't let it be the end of us. We just found each other again."

Resigned, Jeremy lifted his hand and touched Rafe's face.

"Go back to Shanandoah without me," Jeremy said. "Promise me."

"No, no . . . I won't go anywhere without you."

Jeremy gave a tired smile. "Born to be a prince."

Aurora landed on a branch above their heads, looked down with her bright black eyes. Even she seemed to have given up. Rafe wished he could order Jeremy to live again, to fly, the way he'd ordered the robin. If only the world could obey him, but no, only birds. Yet Aurora was no ordinary crow.

"Aurora," Rafe said. "We need help. Go find help if there's anyone who can help us."

She spread her wings and flew off into the Ghost Town wilds.

"It's going to be all right," Rafe said. "Aurora's getting help."

"Remember the first time . . . we were here . . ." Jeremy said, taking pained, shallow breaths after each few words. "You and Skya had a horse race . . . I was the prize."

Rafe laughed through tears. "I remember."

"Still wonder . . . what she would've . . . done with me . . . if she'd won."

"I asked her. She said she needed you to hang pictures in her room and clean out her closet."

"Glad . . . you won."

Jeremy's eyes suddenly widened. For one brief moment, Rafe thought he was gone, and in that split second his heart died.

"No, Jay . . ."

Something moved in the mists.

Rafe turned his head, saw the shadow moving closer, closer . . . He reached for his bow, his quiver. He would kill anything that came near them. But Jeremy touched his hand, telling him without words to stand down.

Why? Was Jeremy ready to die? If that's what he wanted, then they would die here together.

The shadow on the path drew closer. The darkness slowly took form.

Aurora landed on the ground next to them.

The mists swirled, then parted, and Rafe heard heavy steel-toed work boots on the path.

Work boots.

Rafe looked up.

"Dad?"

Without a word, his father went down on one knee and reached out for Jeremy.

"Don't," Rafe said, moving in front of Jeremy. "Don't touch him."

His father looked at him, held up his hands.

Jeremy said, "Let him. Last chance."

His last chance or his father's last chance? Both. And Rafe's last chance too.

Rafe looked up at his father, then nodded. His dad reached out again, gathered Jeremy in his strong arms, and lifted him up. He stood up and started off into the mists, down the path, his pace steady and unflagging.

Behind them, Rafe watched in quiet awe as the father who'd once beaten him bloody for drawing too many pictures of Jeremy now carried his lover through this evil world to safety.

Finally, a light. It was weak, diffuse in the fog. As they got closer, it grew bright, sharper, golden as the sun. They made it to another arched doorway, and outside the door stood a miniature forest.

Gently, his father put Jeremy on his feet. Rafe held him with both arms and guided him through the doorway.

Passing through this time was easier. In a few steps, they were out. Rafe lowered Jeremy to the ground outside the tree on the hill. He looked at his father, who was little more than a shadow in the hollow of the trunk.

"Dad, come on."

But his father only shook his head.

As if it took the very last of his strength, his father opened his mouth. Rafe knew what he would say, that he would ask if Rafe forgave him. This time he would say yes.

But his father only said, "Don't be like me."

Rafe said, "I'm not."

There were no trumpets sounding or angels singing. In the quiet of the morning, Rafe's father disappeared before his eyes. He didn't turn into a cold gray corpse or a puff of smoke. He transformed into a robin.

"Fly away," Rafe said. "The sky's waiting."

The robin spread his small gray wings. Aurora cawed at him, and together the two birds flew toward the sunrise.

No time to mourn again. Frantic, Rafe looked around, saw the pack he and Jeremy had dropped when they passed through the tree. Rafe dug into the pocket.

There it was, the old Nokia phone his mother had given him. And it still had a little charge left.

Rafe called 911, told them where to meet them.

They rested a moment. Rafe held Jeremy to his chest. He watched as the light from inside the hollow of the strange tree flickered like a candle, then died.

"We don't get to go back," Jeremy said.

"No, we don't."

The sun rose higher and turned the hills to gold, and there was nothing but beauty and magic and the endless wild rolling ocean of trees as far as the eye could see.

Jeremy smiled. "It's . . . all right. This is good too."

· ✳ ·

CHAPTER FORTY

JEREMY WAS AWAKE for a few minutes after the operation. The surgeon said he was talking, aware. All good signs. There was some concern about a head injury, since Jeremy couldn't tell them what day it was, so they were considering an MRI.

Rafe wasn't worried about that. He didn't know what day it was either.

While conscious, Jeremy had said he wasn't sure who'd shot him. Just a hunting accident, he'd said. The police would probably stop by to take a report. No one seemed troubled by their cover story. This was West Virginia. Hunting accidents happened all the time.

Finally, the surgeon asked if Rafe wanted to see Jeremy.

He did, yes. Yes, he wanted to see Jeremy. A nurse led him to the room where Jeremy had already fallen back asleep. She checked his vitals, then left them alone.

The room was lit only by the machines hooked up to Jeremy. They breathed and beeped and clicked and dripped medicine. Rafe pulled a chair right next to Jeremy's hospital bed. He wanted to take his hand, but it had an IV needle in it, so Rafe reached under the covers to hold Jeremy's ankle instead.

He was warm, alive, and breathing. He would heal. He would be himself again. They'd lost a whole world coming back here, but Rafe didn't miss it. He had Jeremy, he had the world.

Time passed. Eventually, Rafe's mother made it to the hospital. She opened the door a crack. Rafe waved her in. She entered, came over, and kissed Jeremy on his forehead.

"Mom?" Jeremy muttered in his drugged state.

"Yes, it's Mom," she said. "Now go back to sleep."

He nodded and did just that. She came to Rafe's side, put her arm around him, and kissed his forehead too.

"You okay?" she asked.

"I'll be okay when Jeremy's okay."

"Where's Emilie?"

"Safe. With her sister."

"Good. That's good to hear."

She didn't ask more questions, though he knew she wanted answers. He thought of her sitting at the kitchen table after his father had stormed off, piecing together his sketches with Scotch tape.

"I need to tell you something, Mom. About when we went missing."

"You can tell me anything."

He told her they had run away. He told her he was so pissed at Dad for, well, everything, that he ran for the hills and didn't look back. And Jeremy went with him because—

"Of course he did," his mother said.

They found a safe place to hide out, he told her. A girl they met helped them with food and stuff. They were okay out there, but the longer they were gone, the harder it was to imagine coming home again. Impossible almost. It was like they were living in another world.

But they did come home. Finally. He felt so bad about what happened that he blocked it out. Being back in the woods with Jeremy brought it all back.

"I'm sorry, Mom. I'm so sorry I did that to you."

She was quiet a long time, then said, "Deep down, I always knew you two ran off together. I think that's the only way I stayed sane that whole awful time." She fell silent again, then took a breath. "The scars on your back ... your father didn't—"

"No," Rafe said, the lie coming so easily he realized he'd planned it the whole time. "That was some barbed wire."

She looked him in the eyes as if not quite believing what she was hearing.

"You sure?"

"I'm sure, Mom. He did drag me to the shed but only to chew me out some more without you hearing."

"When I saw him tearing up your book, I thought . . . Ralph's next. First the book, then my son. I should've protected you better. I should've run away with you myself. If I ever stood up to him once—"

"It wasn't your fault—"

"It was," she said, and Rafe knew he would never convince her otherwise.

"How about this? I'll forgive you if you forgive me?"

"Done deal," she said.

"I want to forgive Dad too," he said. "I won't ask you to."

She was quiet for a long time, then she picked up her purse from the floor and dug through it.

"I don't know if I should show you this, but after your father died and we cleaned out the cabin so you could move in . . . I found this."

She passed him a piece of white paper folded into quarters. The paper had been folded and refolded so many times it had gotten soft. Carefully, Rafe unfolded the sheet and saw a few lines written in pencil.

"What is this?"

"Read it," she said.

In my dreams I'm young again.

A young father of a young son

My young son sits at the table

Teaching himself to draw Wolves from a book.

In the dream, I pat him on the back with one hand and close the book with the other.

Come on, I say, I'll teach you to hunt Wolves.

He puts his pencil down. He'd follow me anywhere.

Lesson one I say—find a wolf.

I wake up an old man in an old world

I want to call my boy, still young somehow to say I'm sorry I closed his Book of Wolves.

To say I'm sorry I was the only wolf he found.

Lesson one I'd say—don't be like me.

"Oh my God," Rafe said. "Dad wrote a poem." It was his handwriting, his missing commas, his voice. He pictured his father with his carpenter pencil, sharpened with a box cutter, scrawling these words on the back of the electric bill. "My father, Bill Howell, wrote a poem."

"He wrote me a couple when we were young, and he was trying to get my attention. I thought there'd still be poetry after we got married, but there wasn't. Maybe he knew he was going to die soon, and he felt like he had to say something to you but didn't know how."

She turned the page over to show that the bill was dated the week before he died.

"Wish he'd said all that to your face instead of writing it down."

"This is better. Can I keep it?"

"He wrote it for you."

Rafe folded the paper and slipped it into his wallet. He wasn't sure why he wanted to keep it. Maybe for the same reason he still wore Jeremy's St. Anthony medal. A reminder that sometimes miracles happen.

"Jeremy's going to need some help when he gets out of here," she said. "I'd be happy for him to stay at the house."

"He'll stay with me," Rafe said.

"At the cabin? You only have the one bedroom."

"I know." He waited for his mother to say something about that, but whatever she said, nothing would change his mind. Still, he barely breathed, the old fear rising up again. Then his mother gave a little chuckle.

"Your father would spin in his grave," she said, then rested her head on his shoulder. "Oh, let him spin."

· ✳ ·

CHAPTER FORTY-ONE

THREE DAYS LATER, Jeremy was released from the hospital. A full recovery would take months, but he would heal better at home, they said. They had said the same thing to Rafe's parents when he was in the hospital after being lost. But this time was different. Better.

This time when they left the hospital, they left together.

Rafe drove slowly down the back roads to Starcross Hill.

"Dude," Jeremy said, "Grandma was slow but she was old."

"You're not funny. And I'm going thirty."

"The speed limit's fifty."

"The limit's fifty," Rafe said. "You can go under."

"I'll die of old age before we get home."

Rafe gave in a little and pressed down on the gas, thinking of how often his father had scolded his mother for driving too slowly on the back roads. Precious cargo, she would reply.

They didn't say much during the rest of the trip. Jeremy was still exhausted from the pain and the painkillers. His color was better, though. He didn't look like a walking corpse anymore. When he rested his head against the passenger window and nodded off to sleep, Rafe eased his foot off the gas again. He didn't want to accidentally wake Jeremy when he took a tight corner.

They reached Starcross Hill by lunchtime. When Rafe turned onto the gravel drive, Jeremy woke up, wincing as he stretched.

Rafe pulled right up to the cabin so Jeremy wouldn't have to walk more than ten feet to the door. Inside, Jeremy eased himself down onto the sofa. Rafe went into the kitchen. He glanced out the window to his sculpture garden. A robin perched on the shoulder of the queen. But that didn't mean anything, he told himself. The woods were full of robins.

He opened the fridge and returned to the living room with two green glass bottles of Ale-8. The lids twisted off in his hand, and he passed one to Jeremy, kept one for himself. Then he sat on the sofa beside Jeremy and put his feet on the coffee table. Jeremy did the same.

They drank and it tasted like being a kid again.

"Sweet as you remember?" Jeremy asked.

Rafe said, "Sweeter."

One Last Postcard

AS SOON AS HE was feeling well enough to drive, Jeremy went on one final mission for his queen. She'd asked him to send a postcard for her. The postcard was addressed to a retirement community outside Venice, Florida. Luckily, a certain psychic pan-dimensional red crow was watching from a nearby palm tree as Deborah Adler set down her pickle-ball racket and opened her mailbox. She took out the postcard and smiled at the picture, an old-timey painting of the Shenandoah River. That brought back memories, not all of them sweet. She'd loved living in West Virginia until the horrific kidnapping of one of her favorite former students had broken her heart, and she moved away.

When she read the back, she put her hand on her chest and sank to the ground. Tears fell on the words written in a strange hand. A strange hand but a familiar name.

The postcard read, *Shannon Yates asked me to tell you, "Thank you for the unicorn pencil, Mrs. Adler. It really was magical."*

· ✳ ·

CHAPTER FORTY-TWO

RAFE WOKE FROM a deep sleep with a sudden start. Immediately alert, he lifted his head and listened, hearing nothing at first but a morning breeze, and Jeremy's soft steady breaths coming from the pillow next to him.

Slowly, he laid his head down again. Jeremy had gotten in late last night. He'd driven six straight hours from New York, where he'd helped locate a boy who'd wandered away from his family hiking the Appalachian Trail. To hear Jeremy tell it, he carried the boy out of the woods, handed him over to his weeping mother, patted the kid on the head, and got into his car and drove away before anyone could even shake his hand.

"You pulled an Irish goodbye on terrified parents?" Rafe had asked him when he'd dragged himself through the door at midnight, tracking Bellvale Mountain mud all over the floor.

"They got their son back. And I wanted to come home." A kiss put an end to the discussion.

Rafe would've gone with him, but he was halfway through building an addition onto the cabin—an art studio, a master suite, and a screened-in porch that would eventually look out onto the sculpture garden, which Jeremy had taken to calling Little Shanandoah.

He was also supposed to be adding stables so he and Jeremy could get a couple of horses. Starcross had perfect riding trails, and yet something held him back. He knew it was stupid, but he didn't want any horses other than Sunny and Freddy.

As much as he missed the lads, he missed their girls a thousand times more. Jeremy talked about Emilie almost every day, and Rafe felt like a part of him was missing without Skya. A prince needed a queen to serve, right? He almost wished he could forget again, but even if he could, he wouldn't. The pleasure of the memories was worth the pain of knowing that was all Shanandoah would ever be to them—a memory.

If only he could've brought something back with him. They'd left in such a hurry, they'd forgotten Jeremy's sword and his own book of memories. But, he comforted himself, he did have a Shanandoah baron sleeping next to him almost every night, and you couldn't do much better than that for a souvenir.

Something tapped on the window. Three soft *taptaptaps*, then silence, then *taptaptap* again. Tree branch? Polite woodpecker? Whatever it was would wake Jeremy any minute now if Rafe didn't put a stop to it. Jeremy had already stirred in his sleep and dropped his arm across Rafe's chest. Luckily, he'd had plenty of practice escaping from Jeremy's arm trap. He eased sideways and put Jeremy's arm down onto the pillow. Worked like a charm. He found his jeans and T-shirt from yesterday and pulled them on.

Quietly, he slipped down the stairs and out the back door. Spring was finally coming to Starcross. A carpet of wild ginger damp with morning dew tickled his bare feet as he walked the garden looking for whatever had woken him.

The sun rose over the trees. As the long shadows stretched and danced in a breeze, for a moment no longer than the span between two heartbeats, the garden came alive. The unicorn raised her head high and the silver tiger opened its mouth to roar, and the red crow spread her wings, and Queen Skya turned her head and winked at him.

Then it was over. Had he imagined it? Were the remnants of a dream still swirling through his brain?

A single red feather wafted down on the wind and landed at his feet. He picked it up.

"What is it?" Jeremy asked. He stood in the doorway half-dressed and wide awake.

Rafe walked over to him and held up the feather. Jeremy took it from him and then looked up and around.

"Aurora. Did you see her?"

"No," Rafe said. "She just left her calling card. What do you think it means?"

Jeremy didn't answer at first, only stared at the feather in his hand.

"I dreamed we went back to the Crow last night. Emilie was there with a gift for us."

"What gift?"

"I don't know. I woke up before we opened the box."

They looked at each other without speaking. They hadn't been back to the Crow since their return. They'd talked about going to see—just in case—but kept putting it off like a visit to the doctor when you know it'll be bad news.

"Wouldn't hurt to look," Jeremy finally said.

Rafe said, "I'll drive."

When he got behind the wheel and turned the key, the radio came on playing "Landslide" by Stevie Nicks.

"All right, Emilie," Rafe muttered. "We're coming."

The song played on. Jeremy said, "It's not my favorite. Too sentimental."

"You're getting a message from another world, and you're complaining about the song choice?"

"I'm only saying I would have picked 'Edge of Seventeen' or maybe 'Stand Back.' I like her solo work better."

"You're an asshole."

"I have never denied that."

"It's a good thing I love you," Rafe said.

"Or what?"

"Nothing. It's just a good thing I love you."

Jeremy grinned. "It's a very good thing."

Rafe got them to Red Crow in what was probably record time, even for him.

The day was nothing like the day they had left with Emilie. Spring instead of fall. Sun instead of rain. Wildflowers blooming instead of leaves dying. And when Rafe stepped onto the path, he felt—

"Nothing," he said.

"You sure?"

"Last time I felt something pulling me in. Not now. I mean . . . I know the way, but I don't feel that, you know—"

"Magic?"

He nodded.

Jeremy shoved his hands into the pockets of his fleece jacket and shrugged.

"We can still look. Why not, right?" Rafe said.

"Can't hurt to try. Lead the way."

Rafe did remember the way, more or less, though he had to go more slowly and pay attention.

They found the game trail to the Goblin Falls without any trouble, and then a little farther in, they found the hill. Last time they'd scrambled up the steep eastern face of it, but this time they took the long way up the southern slope, as if they both wanted to put off the inevitable.

They reached the top and found the strange tree.

Jeremy went to the hollow and put his hand inside it.

"Nothing," he said.

"Skya warned us."

"I know," Jeremy said, "but then why . . . bring us here?"

Rafe didn't answer. Jeremy answered himself. "Maybe they didn't. Maybe we just wanted to believe." His exhalation turned to mist in the cool morning air. "It was such a good dream, though. Emilie was so happy to see us."

"Come on," Rafe said. "Let's go home."

They took the long way down the hill, following an ancient deer path.

When they reached the bottom, Jeremy pointed ahead. "That's where that nurse and her boyfriend found us. I wonder what ever—"

"Jay?"

"Look." He grabbed Rafe and turned him forward.

A break in the tree cover let sunlight spill onto the forest floor like a window. And in that window of light, Sunny and Freddy drank water from the Goblin Falls.

"Lads!" Jeremy called out. The horses raised their golden and red heads, then galloped toward them, hooves clopping on the stony path.

Rafe and Jeremy stroked the long necks of their horses, ran their fingers through the thick manes. They were real.

"Missed us, did you, lads?" Jeremy asked. "We missed you too, you mangy beasts."

"How?" Rafe said, laughing. Sunny whinnied softly as he demanded more scratches on his head. Already Rafe was plotting logistics. Where to board them until he could build the stables, where to get a horse trailer, what to tell his mother . . .

"Skya did tell us the door's only locked from the inside," Jeremy said. "We can't go back, but they can leave, remember?"

Rafe's fingers felt something tucked under Sunny's saddle. A small square of paper. He unfolded it, read it, passed it to Jeremy, who read it aloud.

"*Dear Rafe and Jeremy, Your lads missed you too much, so I'm sending them to you. By the way, when I said I would see you again, I meant it. The secret the mermaid told me was this . . . A day will come when we will eat Golden Apple Christmas Cake together as snow falls on Halfmoon Hill and on that same night, I will—*"

Jeremy looked up sharply at him.

"*I will dance at your wedding.*" He read the rest of the note quickly. "*She said I wasn't allowed to tell you unless I wrote it to you in a letter and sent it far away. I didn't understand it before but now I do. Until we meet again. Love always, Princess Emilie & the Duke and Duchess of Fritz. P.S. Yes, Fritz finally has a rat friend! I realize this is not particularly important information, especially considering the circumstances, but I wanted to tell you anyway!*"

Emilie's words hung in the air between them. A secret shared from another world. A secret too sweet to keep.

There was a way back. Somehow, somewhere, there was a way. And they would find it together.

Rafe's heart raced. Jeremy folded the note, then opened it, and read it to himself again.

"It took us fifteen years to go back last time," Rafe finally said. "So we shouldn't get—"

"I'm not waiting fifteen years to dance at our wedding."

They stared at each other, daring each other to deny it. Neither said anything. If they could go back . . . if the door opened for them one more time . . .

"Jay, you almost died there."

"You almost died *here*."

It was true. No denying that.

"Don't you want to eat Golden Apple Christmas Cake?" Jeremy asked.

"Never had it," Rafe said.

"Me neither. In Shanandoah, it's only served on Christmas night."

"It sounds good, though," Rafe said.

"I'd like to meet Fritz's girlfriend too."

They laughed, then fell silent again, mute with joy. Sunny put his chin on Rafe's shoulder and whinnied softly again as if to say, *You know you want to go back* . . .

He did. Rafe did want to eat Golden Apple Christmas Cake. He wanted to eat it with everyone he loved. With Jeremy. With Emilie. With Queen Skya. With his mother, who always loved everyone he loved, which was why she loved Jeremy most of all.

If they could go back . . . why not take her with them?

"Rafe?"

"You can still find people," he said. "You still have that gift."

"Gift. Curse. Why?"

"What if I still have mine?"

"You said it was gone."

"I didn't feel anything here, but this door is closed. What if there is another way in?"

He turned a slow circle, as if trying to feel the distant call of magic.

"Anything?"

At first there was nothing, nothing at all but the normal magic of the forest, its beauty and its dangers. But then . . . when he faced due west, he felt the slightest pull toward something far away. Then it was gone.

"I don't know. Maybe."

Freddy began to stamp his foot in impatience.

"Sorry, lads," Rafe said. "Okay, let's focus. You stay with the horses. I'll run over to Mom's and borrow a horse trailer from her neighbor."

Jeremy slipped the note from another world into his wallet next to the torn-apart and taped-up sketch Rafe had made of him so long ago.

"Have you ever driven with a horse trailer?"

"No."

"Well, I have."

Rafe glared but only out of habit. "Okay. Just tell Mom . . . I have no idea. Something."

"I'll tell her they were an impulse purchase. I'll be back as soon as I can."

Jeremy kissed him, then patted both horses one more time.

"Back soon," he promised.

"Don't get lost," Rafe said. "That's an order."

Jeremy bowed. "Yes, Your Highness."

The End

SO HERE WE ARE in Red Crow State Forest, ending where we began, as so many stories do. Maybe you're wondering what happened after Rafe and Jeremy got their horses home, but that's a story for another day.

And I have a kingdom to run.

What? Surely you guessed by now it's me. Remember the fairy-tale recipe? One ingredient in fairy tales is the royal disguised as a nobody. And who's a bigger nobody than a storyteller?

My sister, bless her heart, who wasted her coronation gift on a pencil of all things, better like this story. I did, after all, write it for her.

And in case anyone's wondering how I wrote this book even though I wasn't there for everything?

Well, turns out it *was* a magic pencil. But you don't really need a magic pencil to write a magic book. All books are magic. An object that can take you to another world without even leaving your room? A story written by a stranger and yet it seems they wrote it just for you or to you? Loving and hating people made out of ink and paper, not flesh and blood? Yes, books are magic. Maybe even the strongest magic there is.

Of course, some readers might still be wondering what Shanandoah is and how it came to be. I still don't know. I can only guess, but I think someone saw what was about to happen to me, and they said, "No. Not this time." My sister saved a rat. My prince saved a robin. How many times do we walk past some living creature in need and keep walking? Most days. And then, one day . . . you can't walk away. Maybe someone said, "Not on my watch. Maybe yesterday, but not today. Not this girl."

Or, as they said at my sister's old vet clinic, "You can't save them all, but today we will save one."

Whoever saved me, thank you.

Ah, well, now the story's over, so I'm supposed to say, "And they all lived happily ever after." That's how fairy tales end, and this is a fairy tale.

Except it doesn't feel that happy without Rafe and Jeremy here. There are two empty seats at my table, and my sister spends her few free hours in the library trying to find a way to bring them back. And not a day passes, Aurora tells me, that Rafe and Jeremy don't think of us and long to return to Shanandoah.

And since fairy tales have happy endings, this means one of two things.

Either this isn't a fairy tale . . .

Or it's only the beginning.

THE END?

· ✳ ·

GOLDEN APPLE CHRISTMAS CAKE RECIPE
(modified for this world)

INGREDIENTS

$1^3/_4$ cups all-purpose flour

$1^1/_4$ teaspoons baking soda

$^1/_4$ teaspoon salt

1 teaspoon cinnamon

$^1/_2$ teaspoon nutmeg

$^1/_2$ cup vegetable oil

$^2/_3$ cup brown sugar

1 cup applesauce made from Shanandoah Golden Sun apples (you may substitute applesauce made from Golden Delicious apples from West Virginia)

DIRECTIONS

1. Preheat oven to 350 degrees.
2. Spray a 9-inch round baking pan with nonstick spray or grease it with oil.
3. Mix flour, baking soda, salt, cinnamon, and nutmeg in a bowl.
4. Mix oil, brown sugar, and applesauce in another bowl.
5. Stir the flour mixture into the wet mixture just until incorporated; don't overmix.
6. Pour into the pan and spread evenly.

7. Bake 30 minutes or until a toothpick inserted into the center comes out clean.

8. Cool on a rack for at least 10 minutes, then invert the pan and the cake will release.

9. Cool completely before frosting.

CREAM CHEESE FROSTING

This recipe will make enough to frost a two-layer cake; make multiple batches to frost cakes with more layers. If the cake is being made for a Christmas wedding, make three layers.

INGREDIENTS

2 sticks unsalted butter, at room temperature

8 ounces cream cheese, brick, not tub, at room temperature but not too soft

4 cups soft icing sugar/powdered sugar, sifted (sift after measuring)

1 tablespoon vanilla extract

Pinch of salt

DIRECTIONS

1. Beat butter with whisk attachment in stand mixer for 2 minutes until light and fluffy (scrape bottom of bowl at least once).

2. Add cream cheese, then beat for 30 seconds.

3. Add 2 cups powdered sugar, then gently mix on lowest speed.

4. When mostly incorporated, add another cup, beat on lowest speed, repeat with final cup of sugar. Once it's all mixed in, beat on high for a full 2 minutes.

5. Add vanilla and salt and mix on high 1 additional minute.

6. Frost cake and decorate as you like.

Serve cake on Christmas night.

· ✳ ·

ACKNOWLEDGMENTS

FOR THE RECORD, I am a vegetarian and have been since 2001. I'd be remiss if I didn't acknowledge the cat on my lap right this very moment who is making typing incredibly difficult. I'm leaning hard to the left in order to balance my laptop on the chair arm, but it's worth it. Our two cats, Gizmo (the orange boy on my lap) and MoonPie (our personal living Halloween decoration), are both excellent co-workers in this little book factory that is our home. They don't do much typing or proofreading, but they do keep morale high.

This book exists because of Richard Russo. I realize *The Lost Story* is a far cry from *Straight Man* or *Empire Falls,* but follow me here. I wanted to take a class with Rick at the Key West Literary Seminar (who wouldn't?), and to get into that class, I had to submit a writing sample. I didn't have one. But I had just reread William Golding's *The Lord of the Flies* and couldn't get this idea out of my head that it would be interesting to know what happened to Ralph and Jack twenty years after they got off that island. Obviously, that story isn't in the public domain, so I gave up on the idea and put the book back on my shelf right next to my Chronicles of Narnia set. I looked at the books sitting there side by side and suddenly . . . I knew what to write for my sample pages.

I got into the class. And everybody seemed to like the few pages I'd written about two complicated young men who'd gone to a fantasy world as teenagers and then come home again and had to face the consequences. When Richard Russo tells you he wants to read your book if you finish it, you finish it. Thank you, Rick. And thank you to the rest of that amazing class—Diane Hinton Perry, Allison Alsup, Gerald Goldin, Julie Reiser, Nancy Freund Fraser, Claire Lombardo, Andy Brilliant, Zach Halpern, Mike Hamlin, and Judy Mandel. They are all incredible writers. Look them up. The encouragement I received in that seminar was life-changing. Next time we're all in Key West, the margaritas are on me.

There are so many people to thank. Steven at Fivrr for fact-checking my archery scenes, thank you. Kathleen Quinlan for making sure the horses were well represented, I'm very grateful. My fabulous beta readers Kira Gold, Martin Aguilera, and Bethany Hensel, love you all. And the entire Eagle Creek Writers Group of Lexington, Kentucky, who put up with a lot of bad pages during the first nightmare draft of this book. (If anyone is curious, the version you read is the seventh draft.) And thank you, Karen Stivali, for all your healing support and for creating the fabulous cake recipe. And to all my fellow Bs out there in the LGBTQIA world, this book is especially for you.

With great love and affection, I must thank every single wonderful member of my MFA cohort. Here's to the 2024 class of the Stephens College MFA in TV + Screenwriting—Allie Van Horn, Ashley McLaughlin, Dakota Grace Gibson, Gwen Ogle, Kory Louko, Vanessa Christie, Jane Murphy, Jocelyn Osier, Mercedes Garcia, and Aaron Covalski. Extra-special thanks to early readers Julia Kraemer and Dena Plumer! We miss you, Kathy Nicholas! And many thanks to our fearless leader, Dr. Rosanne Welch, of course!

This book was a nightmare to write until the intervention of one of my Stephens mentors—the brilliant Laura Brennan of Pitching Perfectly. In a few days, she'd broken the story wide open for me. Laura, I would never have figured out this story without you! Thank you times a million.

Thank you to my incredible agent Amy Tannenbaum at the Jane Rotrosen Agency, whose insights were invaluable. Thank you to my amazing editor Shauna Summers at Ballantine. Even when I didn't think

I could pull off this book, you believed in me. Thank you for your brilliant editing notes and encouragement. And thank you to Jennifer Hershey, who reminded me to "let it breathe."

And, of course, I have to acknowledge one of the most beautiful, awe-inspiring places on Earth, West—by God!—Virginia! I'm proud to be your neighbor.

Finally, I want to thank my husband, Andrew Shaffer, who has lived with this book for five years and is going to be very happy that his wife can now move on with her life. Thank you for all your notes. I may not like you very much on the days you give me book notes, but I love you for them when the book is finished and it's so much better because of your help. I couldn't do it without you, and even if I could, I wouldn't want to. But please come and get this cat off my lap so I can eat.

Okay, he's gone now.

ABOUT THE AUTHOR

MEG SHAFFER is a part-time creative writing instructor, a film student, and the author of *The Wishing Game*. She lives in Louisville, Kentucky, with her husband, author Andrew Shaffer, and their two cats. The cats are not writers.

ABOUT THE TYPE

This book was set in Jenson, one of the earliest print typefaces. After hearing of the invention of printing in 1458, Charles VII of France sent coin engraver Nicolas Jenson (c. 1420–80) to study this new art. Not long afterward, Jenson started a new career in Venice in letter-founding and printing. In 1471, Jenson was the first to present the form and proportion of this roman font that bears his name.

More than five centuries later, Robert Slimbach, developing fonts for the Adobe Originals program, created Adobe Jenson based on Nicolas Jenson's Venetian Renaissance typeface. It is a dignified font with graceful and balanced strokes.